CATALYSTS, EXPLORERS & SECRET KEEPERS
— WOMEN OF —
SCIENCE FICTION

EDITED BY

MONICA LOUZON
JAKE WEISFELD
HEATHER MCHALE
BARBARA JASNY
RACHEL FREDERICK

MUSEUM OF SCIENCE FICTION
WASHINGTON, D.C.

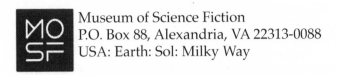

Museum of Science Fiction
P.O. Box 88, Alexandria, VA 22313-0088
USA: Earth: Sol: Milky Way

WE ARE ETERNALLY GRATEFUL TO OUR CATALYST EXHIBIT
SPONSORS FOR THEIR SUPPORT AND TO ALL THE KICKSTARTER
BACKERS WHO MADE THIS TAKE-HOME EXHIBIT POSSIBLE.

CATALYST SPONSORS

DUANE EBERSOLE

SAMUEL PERALTA

A FULL LIST OF BACKERS CAN BE FOUND AT THE END OF THIS BOOK.

TABLE OF CONTENTS

INTRODUCTION

MONICA LOUZON

CREATING a new science fiction anthology is no easy task, particularly when there's already an anthology out there for pretty much every conceivable facet of the genre. Given the warm reception the Museum of Science Fiction's academic *Journal of Science Fiction* received and the number of inquiries readers sent staff about publishing fiction pieces in the journal, our editorial team felt we owed it to the science fiction community to create another venue to engage with our readers. What better way for a museum to do so than by creating an anthology-*cum*-exhibit meant to showcase both science fiction greats and emerging talent in the genre?

This is by no means the first science fiction anthology celebrating women of speculative fiction; in fact, I have a copy of *New Eves: Science Fiction About the Extraordinary Women of Today and Tomorrow* (edited by Janrae Frank, Jean Stine, and Forrest J. Ackerman; 1995) on my bookshelf right now. Between 1975 and 1995, Pamela Sargent edited five anthologies highlighting speculative fiction by women published from the 1940s through the 1990s (*Women of Wonder*, 1975; *More Women of Wonder*, 1976; *The New Women of Wonder*, 1978; *Women of Wonder: The Classic Years*, 1995; and *Women of Wonder: The Contemporary Years*, 1995). More recently, Alex Dally MacFarlane's *Mammoth Book of SF Stories by Women* (2014) aggregated works published between 1996 and 2013. Mike Ashley's *The Feminine Future: Early Science Fiction by Women Writers* (2015) compiled hard-to-find short stories by female authors that were first printed between 1870 and 1930, while Lisa Yaszek and Patrick Sharp's anthology *Sisters of Tomorrow: The First Women of*

Science Fiction (2016) highlighted female authors who wrote
and published pulp science fiction between 1929 and 1946.

There are more anthologies about the women of science fiction out there, too, but my point is this: for decades,
editors have been drawing attention to the science fiction
published by women because women have actively been
writing and publishing short science fiction for more than
150 years, and their history as creators of science fiction
novels stretches back even further. As Andrew Liptak noted
in a March 2017 article for *The Verge*, the science fiction
genre would be unrecognizable without women. We must
continue to draw attention to the role women have played
in shaping science fiction in the past and to their continued
involvement in shaping the genre as authors, publishers,
and readers as it moves forward. The rich legacy of women
in speculative fiction is a foundation for future generations
of writers and provides an inspiring launchpad for women
whose interests and aspirations lie in non-literary fields.

It is a bit more difficult to find museum exhibits
about female authors of science fiction—after all, it's much
easier to do an exhibit of female science fiction artists due
to the innately more visual and browse-able nature of their
craft. For that reason, I'll (tentatively) assert here that *Catalysts, Explorers & Secret Keepers: Women of Science Fiction* is
the first museum exhibit of its kind.

A museum exhibit presents its visitors with a selection of themed audiovisual works chosen by museum staff
that can be explored and perused at each visitor's pace
within the museum's physical space. Books presented in
a museum exhibit, however, are not interactive—that is,
a reader is limited to consuming the pages the curators
have selected for public display. In most museums, visitors
cannot interact with an exhibited book because it is secured
behind some sort of protective barrier.

Like a museum exhibit, an anthology presents its
readers with a selection of themed written works, this time
chosen by editors. Unlike a museum exhibit, however, a
reader's ability to consume an anthology is not restricted by
the physical location of that anthology or even by the for-

mat of said book. Anthologies do not have visiting hours, and they can be read anywhere readers want to carry them. An anthology is interactive: it can be read in its entirety, or a reader might choose to read just a specific author's work, or perhaps the reader might skip from story to story in their own preferred order.

What makes *Catalysts, Explorers & Secret Keepers* different from a regular anthology? Is it not a compilation of stories with a shared theme?

The project team behind *Catalysts, Explorers & Secret Keepers* is comprised of editors, librarians, and curators who work with the Museum of Science Fiction. We see this book as a way for the Museum to give speculative fiction fans a curated museum exhibit without geographical or chronological limitations. It is a portable, interactive museum exhibit presented in the familiar format of an anthology, paying homage to the speculative fiction compilations that have come before it.

When I pitched the idea of a science fiction anthology as a take-home museum exhibit, I don't know that I truly anticipated the sheer enthusiasm the project has received. Greg Viggiano and Mandy Sweeney, the Museum of Science Fiction's Executive Director and Vice President of Museum Operations, respectively, were incredibly supportive and gave *Catalysts, Explorers & Secret Keepers* the green light. Creating this take-home exhibit has been an incredible journey, and we're thrilled to finally place it in your hand and on your screens!

Creating *Catalysts, Explorers & Secret Keepers* has been an incredible experience, and I'm incredibly grateful to all the team members who made it possible.

Jake Weisfeld was instrumental in figuring out logistics, researching authors and successful Kickstarter campaigns, and playing devil's advocate for our own campaign planning. Hannah Hoare played a critical role in the campaign's execution and fulfillment logistics, Keith Jodoin and his videography team created the lovely Kickstarter pitch video for the project, and Andy Davies laid the groundwork for the graphic design of the cover and interior text templates. We quite literally could never have pulled this take-home exhibit off without the talents they all brought to the table.

Many thanks to our solicited contributors—Eleanor Arnason, Catherine Asaro, Monica Byrne, Julie Dillon, Kiini Ibura Salaam, N.K. Jemisin, Nancy Kress, Naomi Kritzer, Karen Lord, Seanan McGuire, Pat Murphy, Sarah Pinsker, Carrie Vaughn, Jane Yolen, and Sarah Zettel—for agreeing to participate in this undertaking! It has been a great honor to work with all of you, and it sends chills down my spine knowing that so many of science fiction's women wanted this project to succeed as much as we did!

Our readers—Karina Dar Juan, Lee Strong, Katie Casey, Shauna Fitzgerald, Tekla Taylor, Bjorn Munson, Jonathan Spencer, Matias de Carnevale, Rachel Lazarus, and Hannah Hoare—helped our editors—myself, Jake Weisfeld, Heather McHale, Barbara Jasny, and Rachel Frederick—sift through the hundreds of submissions we received once our open call for contributors went live, providing thoughtful feedback and fresh eyes that helped us create personalized feedback on each submission.

Congratulations and many thanks to Floris M. Kleijne, AJ Lee, Anthea Sharp, Bonnie Jo Stufflebeam, and Betsy Curtis (by way of her heirs) for sharing their writing with us for inclusion in this take-home exhibit. Our most heartfelt thanks go out to all the authors who submitted stories to that open call; we wish we had the space to have included more of your works in our project, and we thank you for giving us the chance to read your creations.

And, of course, we never could have made this anthology happen without the 664 Kickstarter backers who helped bring this anthology to life. Thank you for believing in our project!

Without further ado, I shall leave you to dive into the Museum of Science Fiction's first take-home exhibit and science fiction anthology, *Catalysts, Explorers & Secret Keepers: Women of Science Fiction*. Enjoy!

CATALYSTS

THE PHYSICS OF A DYING STAR

JANE YOLEN

"Barns Are Painted Red Because of the Physics of Dying Stars"

—Smithsonian Magazine, *article by Rose Eveleth*

STARS die, collapse, their temperatures rise, make iron,
that stuff the fey are afraid of, steel is made of,
cheap red paint comes from.

We always knew we were stardust, but who knew about
barns
standing in the field, hulking over grazing cows,
great doors open, smelling of manure and milk?

If I could only wrap my head around the physics,
but the numbers dance away like the fey, my brain
congeals into cold iron, into steel.

Surely there is a grace in this, though not a plan.
A consensual act. A handing on.
A star. A red barn.

Something must die in the universe
so something else may be beautiful.

Ice in D Minor

Anthea Sharp

RINNA Sen paced backstage, tucking her mittened hands deep into the pockets of her parka. The sound of instruments squawking to life cut through the curtains screening the front of the theater: the sharp cry of a piccolo, the heavy thump of tympani, the whisper and saw of forty violins warming up. *Good luck with that.* Despite the huge heaters trained on the open-air proscenium, the North Pole in February was *cold*.

And about to get colder, provided she did her job.

The stage vibrated slightly, balanced in the center of a parabolic dish pointed straight up to the distant specks of stars in the frigid black sky. The stars floated impossibly far away—but they weren't the goal. No, her music just had to reach the thermo-acoustic engine hovering ten miles above the earth, centered over the pole.

Rinna breathed in, shards of cold stabbing her lungs. Her blood longed for summer in Mumbai; the spice-scented air that pressed heat into skin, into bone, so deeply a body wanted to collapse under the impossible weight and lie there, baking, under the blue sky.

That had been in her childhood. Now, nobody lived in the searing swath in the center of the globe. The heat between the tropics had become death to the human organism.

Not to mention that her home city was now under twenty feet of water. There was no going back, ever.

"Ms. Sen?" Her assistant, Dominic Larouse, hurried up, his nose constantly dripping from the chill. "There's a problem with the tubas."

Rinna sighed—a puff of breath, visible even in the dim air. "What, their lips are frozen to the mouthpieces? I told them to bring plastic ones."

"Valve issues, apparently."

Dominic dabbed his nose with his ever-present handkerchief. He'd been with her for two years, and she still couldn't break through his stiff formality. But little things, like insisting on being called by her first name, weren't worth the aggravation. Not here, not now.

"Get more heaters on them," she said, "and tell those damn violins we start in five minutes, whether they're warmed up or not."

"Five minutes. Yes ma'am."

Her job included being a hardass, but she knew how difficult it was to keep the instruments on pitch. The longer they waited, the worse it would get.

Goddess knew, they'd tried this the easy way by feeding remote concerts into the climate engine. Ever since the thing was built, the scientists had been trying to find the right frequencies to cool the atmosphere. They'd had the best luck with minor keys—something about the energy transfer—and at first had tried running synthesized pitches through. Then entire performances. Mozart's *Requiem* had come close, but not close enough.

It had to be a live performance; the immediate, present sounds of old wood, horsehair, brass and felt, the cascade of subtle human imperfection, blown and pulled and pounded from the organic bodies of the instruments.

There was no substitute for the interactions of sound waves, the immeasurable atomic collisions of an on-site concert fed directly into the engine. Once the thing got started, the techs had promised they could loop the sound. Which was good, because no way was Rinna giving up the rest of her life to stand at the North Pole, conducting a half-frozen orchestra. Not even to save the planet.

She'd spent years working on her composition, assembled the best symphony in the world, rehearsed them hard, then brought them here, to the Arctic. Acoustic instruments and sub-zero temperatures didn't get along, but damn it, she'd make this happen.

What if the composition is a failure? The voice of all her

doubts ghosted through her thoughts, sounding suspiciously like her long-dead father.

She pinned it down and piled her answers on top,
trying to smother it into silence.

The simulations had proven that certain frequencies
played through the engine could super-cool the air over the
pole. Then, with luck, a trickle-down effect would begin
and slowly blanket the world. The scientists had run the
models over and over, with a thousand different types of
sound. But it wasn't until the suits had hired Rinna—one of
the best composers in the world (not that the world cared
much about symphonies)—that the project had really started to gel.

"Ms. Sen." Dominic hurried up again, holding out
the slim screen of her tablet. "Vid call for you."

"I told you, I don't want any interruptions."

"It's the President."

"Oh, very well." Fingers clumsy through her mittens,
Rinna took the call.

President Nishimoto, Leader of the Ten Nations of
the World, smiled at her through the clear, bright screen.
Behind him, the desert that used to be Moscow was visible
through the window of his office.

"Ms. Sen," he said. "The entire world wishes you the
very best of luck in your performance."

He didn't need to say how much was at stake. They
all knew.

"Thank you." She bowed, then handed the screen
back to Dominic.

It was almost too late. Last winter, the pole ice had
thinned so much it couldn't support the necessary installation. Doom criers had mourned the end, but a freak cold-
snap in January had given them one final chance.

Now here they were—the orchestra, the techs, Rinna. And five thousand brave, stupid souls, camping on the
precarious ice. Come to see the beginning of the world, or
the end of it.

Out front, the oboe let out an undignified honk, then
found the *A*. Rinna closed her eyes as the clear pitch rang

out, quieting the rest of the musicians. The violins took it up, bows pulling, tweaking, until there was only one perfect, single note. It deepened as the lower strings joined in, cellos and basses rounding the *A* into a solid arc of octaves.

She could feel the dish magnifying the vibration, up through her feet. Sound was powerful. Music could change the world. She had to believe that.

As the strings quieted, Rinna stripped off her mittens, then lifted her conductor's baton from its velvet-lined case. The polished mahogany grip was comfortable in her hand, despite the chill. The stick itself was carved of mammoth ivory, dug out of the ground centuries ago.

She ran her fingers up and down the smooth white length. It was fitting, using a relic of an extinct animal in this attempt to keep humans from going out the same way.

She stepped onstage, squinting in the stage lights, as the wind instruments began to tune. First the high silver notes of the flutes, then the deep, mournful call of the French horns and low brass. Sounded like the tubas had gotten themselves sorted out.

From up here, the ice spread around stage—not pale and shimmering under the distant stars, but dark and clotted with onlookers. Originally, she'd imagined performing to the quiet, blank landscape—but that was before some brilliantly wacko entrepreneur had started selling tickets and chartering boats into the bitter reaches of the North.

The concert of a lifetime, plus the novelty of cold, drew spectators from all over the planet. No doubt the thrill of the chill had worn off, but the performance, the grand experiment, was still to come.

And truthfully, Rinna was glad for the crowd. Thermo-acoustics aside, she knew from long experience that the energy of playing in front of responsive listeners was *different*. Call it physics, call it woo-woo, but the audience was an integral part of the performance.

The project director had been reluctant at first, constructing only a small shelter and selling tickets at prices she didn't even want to contemplate. The enclosed seating held roughly forty people: heads of state, classical music aficionados, those with enough money and sense to try and stay warm. But when the boats started arriving, the tents going up, what could he do?

The spectators all wanted to be here, with the possible exception of Dominic hovering beside the podium.

The crowd caught sight of her striding across the stage, and applause rushed like a wind over the flat, frigid plain. She lifted her hand in acknowledgement. Overhead, the edge of the aurora flickered, a pale fringe of light.

Rinna stepped onto the podium and looked over her orchestra, illuminated by white spotlights and the ruddy glow of the heaters.

She'd bribed and bullied and called in every favor owed her, and this was the result. The best symphony orchestra the entire world could offer. Rehearsals had been the Tower of Babel: Hindi, Chinese, English, French—over a dozen nationalies stirred together in a cacophonous soup. But the moment they started playing, they had one perfect language in common.

Music.

The orchestra quieted. One hundred and five pairs of eyes fixed on her, and Rinna swallowed back the quick burst of nausea that always accompanied her onto the podium. The instant she lifted her baton and scribed the downbeat, it would dissipate. Until then, she'd fake feeling perfectly fine.

"Dominic?" she called, "are the techs ready?"

"Yes," he said.

"Blow your nose." No point in marring the opening with the sound of his sniffles.

Pasting a smile on her face, Rinna turned and bowed to the listeners spread out below the curve of the stage. They applauded, sparks of excitement igniting like distant firecrackers.

She pulled in a deep breath, winced as the air stabbed her lungs, and faced the orchestra—all her brave, dedicated musicians poised on the cusp of the most important performance of their lives.

The world premiere of *Ice*.

The air quieted. Above the orchestra a huge amplifier waited, a tympanic membrane ready to take the sound and feed it into the engine, transmute it to frigidity.

Rinna raised her arms, and the musicians lifted their instruments, their attention focused on her like iron on a magnet. She was their true north. The baton lay smoothly in her right hand—her talisman, her magic wand. If there ever was wizardry in the world, let it come to her now.

Heart beating fast, she let her blood set the tempo and flicked her stick upward. Then down, irrevocably down, into the first beat of *Ice*.

A millisecond of silence, and then the violins slid up into a melodic line colored with aching, while the horns laid down a base solid enough to carry the weight of the stars. The violas took the melody, letting the violins soar into descant. The hair on the back of her neck lifted at the eerie balance. Yes. Perfect. Now the cellos—too loud. She pushed the sound down slightly with her left hand, and the section followed, blending into the waves of music that washed up and up.

Rinna beckoned to the harp, and a glissando swirled out, a shimmering net cast across dark waters. Was it working? She didn't dare glance up.

High overhead, the thermo-acoustic engine waited, the enormous tubes and filters ready to take her music and make it corporeal—a thrumming machine built to restore the balance of the world.

It was crazy. It was their best chance.

Ice was not a long piece. It consisted of only one movement, designed along specific, overlapping frequencies. Despite its brevity, it had taken her three years to compose, working with the weather simulations and the best scientific minds in the world. Then testing on small engines, larger ones, until she stood here.

Now Rinna gestured and pulled, molded and begged, and the orchestra gave. Tears glazed her vision, froze on her lashes, but it didn't matter. She wasn't working from a score; the music lived in her body, more intimately known to her than her own child.

The clarinets sobbed the melody, grieving for what was already lost. The polar bears. The elephants. The drowned cities. The silenced birds.

Now the kettle-drums, a gradual thunder—raising the old magic, working up to the climax. The air throbbed and keened as Rinna rose onto her toes and lifted her hands higher. Higher. A divine plea.

Save us.

Arms raised high, Rinna held the symphony in her grasp, squeezed its heart for one more drop of musical blood. The musicians gave, faces taut with effort, shiny with sweat even in the chill. Bows flew, a faint sparkle of rosin dust flavoring the air. The trumpets blared, not missing the triad the way they had in rehearsal.

The last note. Hold. Hold. Hold.

She slashed her hand through the air and the sound stopped. *Ice* ended, yearning and dissonant, the final echo ringing into the frigid sky.

Above, nothing but silence.

Rinna lowered her arms and rocked back on her heels. From the corner of her eye, she saw the techs gesturing frantically, heads shaking, expressions grim.

The bitter taste of failure crept into her mouth, even as the crowd erupted into shouts and applause, a swell of sound washing up and over the open stage. She turned and gave them an empty bow, then gestured to the symphony— the musicians who had given and given. For nothing.

They stood, and one over-exuberant bassoonist let out a cheer and fist-pump. It sent the rest of the orchestra into relieved shouts, and she didn't have the heart to quiet them. They began stamping their feet, the stage vibrating, humming, low and resonant.

Rinna caught her breath, wild possibility flickering through her.

She gestured urgently to the basses. Three of them began to play, finding the note, expanding it. The rest of the section followed, quickly joined by the tubas—bless the tubas. Rinna opened her arms wide, and the string players hastily sat and took up their instruments again.

"D minor!" she cried. "Build it."

The violins nodded, shaping harmonies onto the note. The harpist pulled a trembling arpeggio from her strings, the wind instruments doubled, tripled the sound into an enormous chord buoyed up by breath and bone, tree and ingot, hope and desperation.

The stage pulsing beneath her, she turned to the crowd and waved her arms in wide arcs.

"Sing!" she yelled, though she knew they couldn't hear her.

The word hung in a plume before her. She could just make out the upturned faces below, pale circles in the endless Arctic night.

Slowly, the audience caught on. Sound spread like ripples from the stage, a vast buzzing that resolved into pitch. Rinna raised her arms, and the volume grew, rising up out of five thousand throats, a beautiful, ragged chorus winging into the air.

Beneath their feet, the last of the world's ice began to hum.

The techs looked up from their control room, eyes wide, as high overhead the huge engine spun and creaked.

Rinna tilted her face up, skin stiff as porcelain from the cold, and closed her eyes. She felt it, deep in her bones, a melody singing over and over into the sky. The thrum of sound transformed to super-cooled air, the long hard pull back from the precipice.

Something touched her face, light as feathers, insubstantial as dreams.

Quietly, perfectly, it began to snow.

ANTHEA SHARP is an award-winning, *USA Today* bestselling author of science fantasy. Her short stories have appeared in DAW anthologies, *Fiction River*, *The Future Chronicles*, *Beyond the Stars*, and other publications. Her bestselling *Feyland* series combines high-tech computer gaming with ancient faerie lore. She lives in the Pacific Northwest, where rainy days and strong black tea fuel her writing.

WHAT WE KNEW THEN, BEFORE THE SKY FELL DOWN

SEANAN MCGUIRE

MIDNIGHT, and Pike Place Market was alive in dazzling light and color. Someone was playing a guitar somewhere deep in the tangled labyrinth of stalls and shops; the notes rang with a bright clarity that spoke of steel strings, bought or bargained or scavenged somewhere, from the crumbling edges of the city. Someone else was beating on a drum, and that sound was like a heartbeat, like the heartbeat, like the entire market was a living thing and this the sound of its vital continuation.

I stopped at the edge of the broken pavement that separated Pike Place from the rest of the shattered city, clutching my bag to my chest and willing my heart to start beating in time with that steady, beckoning tempo. If I could only find a way to disappear into that crowd—the biggest one I'd ever seen, bigger than all the people in Bothell put together and then some—I would be safe. No one would look at me twice, or see me for the country mouse I was, terrified of what was waiting in those dark corridors, those enclosed halls.

Someone walked out of the market, wobbling with every other step. He was clearly drunk, and I couldn't stop myself from eying him up and down, sizing him up for salvage. His boots looked leather, and his belt was good. I could probably get a month's groceries off things he shouldn't have worn while he was drinking, not if he placed any value in them. I immediately felt ashamed for my own assessment.

"Kindness is one of the only things we still have, and we'll not add it to the mountain of casualties we've already lost to this war." That was what Mama always used to say, when I or my brothers would say something just a sliver too calculating or cold. She'd always looked sadder than a face ought to be able to manage, like we were slipping through her hands, minnows swimming fast in a moving stream. So we'd tried. For her, we'd tried to be better than we were, and some of us—Danny, with his broad shoulders and strong hands, and Kyle, who was too clever by half, and far too popular with the local girls—had managed it, at least for a little while. At least for long enough to see her through the last years of her life, and into a comfortable grave, where she could sleep, and wouldn't have to be afraid anymore.

But that had been in spring, and winter was coming on fast, and Mama wasn't going to be coming back to us. No matter how much we wanted to roll out of bed one dawn and find her already in the kitchen, setting the tea brewing and the bread baking, that wasn't going to happen. We had to do for ourselves now. Kyle would be fine. Kyle would convince one of the little ladies who adored him that they should make an honest man out of him, and he'd settle down to making babies and charming traders. He'd pay his debt to the town with his tongue instead of his hands, and that was fine, because that was what he was good for. Put him in the field with Danny and you'd need two more workers just to undo the damage he did. Put him in the forest or down by the stream and you'd get no good from him at all. I knew that, and Danny knew it, and neither of us resented him what seemed like an easier job when seen from the outside. We all have to do what we're best for, or there's no way we'll make it.

And me, what I'm best for is being so bone-headed that I might as well be down in the graveyard with Mama and the rest of the skeletons, playing dice games and tricking them out of their femurs. Kyle's tongue is gold and Danny's is brass, but mine is silver, and anymore, that can be where the money's made. That can be what brings the harvest in.

The drunkard finished weaving his way across the

lot and vanished into the alley on the other side. One opportunity down. A whole market full of them, just waiting for me to be brave enough to step inside.

I had to be brave enough. I would be brave enough.

I stepped inside.

Smells assaulted me on all sides, cooking meat and frying fish and baking bread, so dense that they were like colors in the air. I gasped a little, unable to help myself. I gasped again as the scope of the crowd around me became truly apparent. On some level, I'd been assuming that it was busy around the edges because people were coming and going, creating a barrier of humanity between the interior and the rest of the world. That wasn't it. That wasn't it at all. This was…people. This was people past all the limits of what I'd thought was true.

This was what I'd come here for.

I started to weave my way through the crowd, watching for signs and pickpockets both. They didn't have a very high class of magpie here: I'd been expecting better from a real city, like they could feed their magpies up on good bread and fresh water and make their fingers faster in the process. These ones were almost an embarrassment to the trade. I thought about snatching their takes as I worked my way past them, and decided it would be mean and petty—and more importantly, premature. If I found what I needed, I could pay everything I had, holding nothing back, and still walk out with a profit to my name. That was important. No matter what else I was here to do, I wasn't here to lie. If I had more when I made the deal than I'd expected having, I'd still be obligated to give it over.

A lie is poison to a good path forward. We've had quite enough of poison in these parts. There's no need to go cultivating more.

A hand brushed my bottom on its way to my pocket. I grabbed it without hesitation, anchoring my grip tight around the would-be thief's wrist bones, so that they would grind together like crow-startlers at the edge of the garden. The answering shout was high and pained. None of the people around us turned to catch a look. That wasn't much of a shocker. Any place with this many thieves at work was likely to have a fair "do for yourself, and to hell with the rest of them" attitude in play.

"Let go!"

"Mmm...nope." I pulled the fish I'd caught out of this too-human river around to the front, where I could see it.

A child, maybe twelve, maybe less, dressed in drab, layers and linens and everything meant to tangle and confuse. It's best for the magpie-fish never to look like boys or girls or anything much apart from the flock. Makes them too easy to identify, if someone wants to get angry about them doing what magpie-fish do, as if it weren't a profession like any other.

The child squirmed. I frowned.

Magpieing is a profession, and as such, it comes with rules. You don't magpie people who don't look like they can afford it, not unless they've done something foolish enough to make themselves fair game, like the fellow who'd gone drinking and then decided to walk home alone. Me, I was a stranger, keeping close, keeping quiet. Unless the rules here were awful different than they'd been everywhere else I'd ever been, I should have been off-limits until I'd had the time to do something unwise.

Pike Place was the heart of what remained of Seattle. It wasn't a safe place. It wasn't a place for the timid, or the unwary, but it was still a place where the rules applied. I gave the child a sharp shake. They stopped squirming.

"Who are you?" I asked. "Need to have a name."

"Magpie," the child shot back.

"Need a name, not just a job. I caught you fair and square, and I'd be well within my rights to hand you off to whatever serves as the law in this place."

My guess was good: the child paled, making a sharp, unsuccessful attempt at breaking free. "Don't do that," they said. "I didn't hurt you none. You don't need to do that."

"If you'd taken everything I had on me, you'd have hurt me plenty," I said. "I'm 'round the lake from my home, and all the journey done afoot. Without my funds, I'd be sleeping rough on the way back, eating whatever I could catch—and this time of year, in someone else's hunting grounds, how much do you think that's like to be? You could have killed me certain, and that's no exaggeration. So I'd say you hurt me with your intention, whether or not you had the skill to back it up."

The little magpie looked at me defiantly, fear fading away in the face of hopelessness. They stood straight and proud as they said, "Then take me and turn me in for justice. I'll not be yours to toy with."

What did they teach these big city magpies, if the child went straight from begging to be freed to resigned but refusing to let me have them as my own? The question was enough to turn my stomach. I shook my head.

"I'm not looking for a toy. I'm looking for a guide."

The child's face changed again, defiance replaced this time by calculation, and by greed. "And what will you be paying me?"

"Nothing."

"What makes you—"

"I'll give you nothing, and I'll do nothing to betray you. No law, no reports, nothing but one person doing a favor for another, and all debts being hencewise cleared between them." I gave the child my best and brightest smile, the one that had served me well enough with the Bothell law a time or two. "Seems a small loss of time, compared to what you'd lose if you were taken."

For a moment, I thought the little magpie might call my bluff, force me to either let go or report. Then they sagged in my hand, and asked, "What assurance?"

It was a relief to know that some things hold the same no matter where you go. "I'll have your shoes," I said. Before the child could squawk objection, I said reasonably, "There's no outside in what I need from you, and the weather's fair enough. Give them to me, and you'll have them back when I've done what needs doing."

"Fine," grumbled the child.

"Run from me, and I chase you screaming about thieves at the top of my lungs," I cautioned, letting go.

The child made a sour face. "As if I would?" they asked. "Honor's all you've got some days. I keep my word."

"Then you're a better magpie than most, even if you've not the gift," I said. "Practice will make up for what nature didn't give you."

The child eyed me warily as they removed their shoes and offered them to me. Quick as a blink, they were gone into my bag, well out of reach of roving little fingers. I made no effort to hide the knot as I tied it. Knowing the construction of a thing isn't a help if you don't have the chance to break it open.

"Now what?" grumbled my new companion.

"Now you'll take me where I need to go." It was a treat, actually, having a guide I didn't need to pay. Let the little magpie serve their sentence and get back to work both warier and wiser about who they targeted. The seemingly softest targets sometimes have the sharpest teeth.

"Where's that?"

"I need to see the Department of City Planning."

The name, archaic and unwieldy as it was, acted like a stone dropped into the waters of a still pond. Everyone around me froze for a moment, first my captive magpie and then everyone else in hearing. Finally, the ring outside them froze, as some quiet magic of the crowd passed my muttering along. The world was still.

My captive magpie looked at me in wide-eyed horror. "Why'd you want to go there?" they demanded. "Nothing's there but land records and maps of the dead."

"Because I need to see the land records and maps of the dead," I said, reasonable as anything. "You're mine. I have your shoes. Now lead me along, before I forget that I've decided to be kind."

The magpie looked at me in disgust before moving along. I followed on their heels, never letting them get far enough ahead to slip from sight. The movement of the market around us resumed—but there were more sidelong glances in my direction this time, and not only from the magpies. I'd already been a stranger. Now I was a stranger on some ridiculous errand to a place no one went, and that made me interesting. That made me a target.

I held Kyle and Danny's faces in my mind's eye, reminding myself with every step that I did this for my family, for my brothers, for the generations yet to come, who were not yet here to encourage me on my travels. I would do this thing. I would achieve it. There was no other way forward.

Deeper and deeper we wound into the labyrinth of Pike Place, past cracked concrete walls and stairwells filled with venomous shadows. To the magpie's credit, they made no attempt to escape; they walked fast but kept close, always maintaining a line of sight. At times, they scurried, chest puffed out and bare feet light against the floor. When that happened, I hurried to keep up, not asking what had them spooked. They were the one on familiar territory, after all. If their instincts told them to keep clear, I was going to listen.

Bit by bit, the colorful stalls and fragrant foods fell away, taking the crowds with them, until we were crawling through the bowels of a world that had never been intended to admit me. I held my bag tighter, followed my magpie closer. If I got lost here, I was never going to be found again.

Finally, the magpie stopped, indicating a closed door. "Here," they said. "Can I have my shoes now?"

"One," I said. "You get the second when you see me back to the front door."

The magpie's eyes narrowed. "Wasn't the deal."

"But the deal didn't specify not doing that. Careful when you trade with strangers. You never know what they're going to want."

"I'm a stranger to you."

"True. You know what distinguishes us?"

The magpie hesitated, clearly mulling over the question, before asking, "What?"

"I was careful." I produced one shoe from the bag, tossing it over with a careless flip. "There you go. I'll see you soon."

The magpie snatched the shoe out of the air and

snorted, running off down the hall. I watched them go, feeling suddenly ancient. Time was, I would have vexed anyone new to our town in the exact same ways. A bit more skill, perhaps—I've always been good at my trade—but the same type of tricks. I'm still a magpie. Always will be. I'm just not a fledgling anymore. Time's come for me to fly free and steady as ever a magpie could.

I turned to the door. It was unmarked and unremarkable, and I had only the magpie's word that this was where I needed to be. I took a breath. If I'd been set up for a pounding, I'd find out by going inside.

The knob turned easy in my hand, and I was in, stepping through into a small, shabby room with two desks pushed into an L in one corner, making a barrier against the rest of the market. A woman sat there, head bent over a paper, her hair forming a dark curtain over her face. There was a chandelier of sorts bolted to the center of the ceiling, ringed with candles that cast a flickering, unsteady light over the whole scene.

I closed the door. She didn't look up.

I cleared my throat. She didn't look up.

"Excuse me?" I said. "I'm looking for the Department of City Planning."

She looked up, brushing her hair aside with one hand as she blinked at me suspiciously. "You're what with the what now?" she asked.

I frowned. "I think a bunch of words were missing from that sentence. Did you want to go back and try again?"

"Where are you from?"

She had a desk and a pen, and that was as close to credentials as I was like to find. "Bothell, miss. I walked here from there. I heard this was where the records were kept."

"You're right about that," she said, still watching me. "You walked from Bothell? That's a long haul. The Montview territory still contested?"

"Not anymore, miss. They had sickness there. Real bad."

"How bad?"

Bad enough that what little they'd managed to rebuild was fodder for the crows and coyotes; bad enough that it would be years before anyone was willing to go back and try again. The magpies had had their share of scavenge, my town and three others picking over the bones of the doomed settlement, and that had been that.

"Bad," I said, with the flat finality that anyone from my side of the lake would have recognized as a eulogy.

The woman nodded. "You bring payment?"

"I was told you'd ask for what you wanted. That if I didn't have it, I'd be expected to go and find it."

"You sure are superstitious that side of the lake."

I said nothing. This could be some kind of trap, a test to see whether I'd toy with things I didn't understand. Sure we were superstitious. We had to be. When we hadn't been superstitious—when the parents of our parents had stopped believing that actions had consequences, stopped understanding that the things people put out into the world would come back upon them tenfold—people had died. Not the abstract sort of people, where sure, they were dying, but they were dying so far away or so long ago that they might as well have been cautionary tales, not human beings. Real people.

It's probably the tendency not to see people who didn't die right in front of us as "real" that's gotten humanity into so much trouble. Other side of the world? Doesn't count. But I guess we fixed that for ourselves but good, since there's no other side of the world anymore. Oh, it still exists. We'll just never hear anything about it. We're lucky if we hear what's happening on the other side of the nearest mountain. We made our world enormous, and when we couldn't hold onto it anymore, we made it smaller than it had been in centuries.

We made it the size of a single town.

"You're superstitious, but that doesn't make you wrong," said the woman finally. "Whatever's in that bag, I want it."

"All right," I said. I pulled the magpie's remaining

shoe free and started to offer the bag over.

The woman shook her head. "Everything, or you get nothing," she said. "That's how payment works."

"But…" I paused, unsure of how much it would be safe to tell her. Finally, I said, "This shoe's not mine."

"Don't care," she said. "Shouldn't have had it on you if you didn't want to pay it out. Now, do you want what you came for or not?"

"You don't even know what I came for."

"Something important enough that you circled the lake and found the Department of City Planning to get it," she said. "Pay or go."

I closed my eyes and said a silent apology to the magpie before stepping forward and handing over the bag. When I opened my eyes again, the woman was looking at me with something like pity in her eyes.

"All right," she said. "What was so important that you'd make this kind of trip?"

"I need the zoning paperwork for Bothell."

"What year?"

That was a stumper. I had never considered that there might be more than one year of zoning paperwork. Finally, hesitantly, I said, "The most recent?"

"It won't be perfect."

"Will it tell us where the sewage lines were?"

Her grin was bright and sudden. "Now you've got it," she said. "Wait here. I'll get your paperwork."

She rose, vanishing through a door behind the filing cabinets. I did as I'd been bid, standing with perfect still-ness in the middle of the room, in case this was another trick. I was still standing there when she returned some minutes later, a thick sheaf of papers in her hand.

"This should be everything you need," she said, walking back to her desk and dropping the papers in the middle of it. "Digging?"

"New farms," I said. "We need them if we're to live, and the last time someone tried to dig, they hit an old septic tank. Contagion." Montview hadn't thought the planning paperwork mattered. Montview had learned better, every

last one of them, and their bodies had been shoved back
into the same pit that had condemned them all.

The woman nodded, a regretful look on her face.
"They left us a lot of surprises."

"Didn't they just."

"That's business done." She sank back into her seat.
"Go."

I went.

The people who built this place—this market, this
city, this world—they didn't think they'd ever go away.
They thought people who died on the other side of the
world weren't real, even when they could see their faces
and talk to them on the phone. The things they had, the
things they did, they sound like magic to me. Like miracles. But they weren't either. They were just people doing,
as people have always done, and like all people, they were
greedy and petty and careless and small minded. They were
human. They fucked up.

They fucked up, and they thought the world would
always forgive them, always give them one more chance to
make things better. The world didn't. The world finally got
fed up.

I won't say there was "one last war," because there's
always another war. When I was little, younger even than
my nameless magpie, people settled with talking and trading, never with fighting. Nowadays, it's about fifty-fifty
which it'll be. Before Montview choked to death on its own
air, they'd attacked all the surrounding towns more than
once. It's part of why no one stepped in to help them. They
were a threat, and we let them die.

Before the war, we knew that we ruled the world.
After the war, we knew that we could never afford to go to
war again. And now, as more and more time passes, as we
bury more and more of the ones who actually remember
how the air caught fire and the water turned to acid and the
children were born without eyes, without bones, without
the power to draw breath…people are starting to know that
we rule the world again. Give them enough time, and we'll
be doing just like our ancestors, eyes on the stars and hands

filled with knives.

I stepped out of the office, into the cold, echoing hall of Pike Place. There was movement in the shadows. I watched as the magpie stepped into the open. They wrinkled their nose when they saw the papers in my hands.

"Get what you wanted?" they asked.

"Did," I said. "Lost your shoe."

"Thought you might." They didn't even sound angry. Just resigned, like this had been inevitable.

Nothing has to be inevitable. Not the bad…and not the good, either. "You're not a very good magpie," I said. "You've got good hands but no focus, and you don't know what you're doing. You live here?"

"In the Market, yeah."

"Parents?"

The magpie shrugged. It was a practiced gesture, probably intended to look careless. All it managed to do was hurt my heart.

"Ever thought about leaving?"

"To go where?"

"Around the lake."

The magpie's eyes widened. Around the lake meant green places and food and fresh water, not salt, not poisoned, for the taking. It meant hard work and toil, but it was a chance, and it was something most city magpies would never have. Then their eyes narrowed again, face shuttering.

"You wouldn't," they said. "Liar."

"I would," I said. I rolled the papers, tucking them inside my shirt where they'd be safe. "Make you a deal. If I can lift enough to get you a new pair of shoes, you make the walk with me."

There was a long pause. Then, finally, the magpie nodded.

See, before the war, we knew we ruled the world. We knew our empires would stand forever. We don't know any of those things anymore. Time may come we'll know them again. Time may come when we look to all the places we've forgotten and think "I should go there, I should learn, I should explore." But that time is a long way away. We moved through the Market like shadows, my new magpie and me, and the purses were heavy in our hands, and the coins were like promises of a better life to come.

They chose their new shoes from a stall on the second level, owned by a man with old, tired eyes who nodded his approval when he saw that I was paying, that I was trying, that someone was still willing to make the effort.

I didn't think my brothers would mind. Not when I was coming home with the papers that would let us break ground on the new farms. We'd need the extra hands.

The magpie looked up at me as we approached the edge of the market, struggling to keep their face neutral. "Is it nice?" they asked. "On the other side of the lake?"

"Nice as we can make it," I said. "Come on. Let's go home."

We walked across the broken pavement, the market's heartbeat still pounding behind us, and slipped into the shadows, and we were gone.

SEANAN McGUIRE lives, works, and writes in the Pacific Northwest, where she enjoys picking blackberries, looking for amphibians, and befriending the unspeakable things that dwell in the woods. She has written more novels than we can list here, even more short stories, and a horrifying amount of poetry. She takes her cats very seriously, and doesn't really sleep. Keep track of her at www.seananmcguire.com.

BATTLE ROYALE

KIINI IBURA SALAAM

IT is something about the feathers, how they fall about his bare shoulders. Not bunched on rawhide around the neck, nor bundled on a cord around the waist. Instead they hover cape-like around him, each one undulating like a dark glossy wave every time he shifts. I pretend not to notice his eyes returning again and again to the ugly scar that wings across my chest. Those eyes have a dangerous glint that softens each time it encounters the smooth stretch of broken cells that rises from my skin.

The nasal twang of the European rings out just behind my back, causing me to return my attention to the room. Daylight filters through the window behind a puffy judge. The benches and tables in the room are thick, wooden, oppressive. Other men of my color sit in rows shackled behind me. The tiny hairs at the base of my scalp quiver and stiffen. What crime have I committed?

Words like *prevalent* and *supersede* grate against my ears as the European tries to explain why the work of the House of Burgesses has changed so radically since me and my kind arrived. I imagine that nasal twang sputtering to a halt upon discovering the true details of my arrival. I did not come on massive creaking ships along with my fellow laborers. I came clinging to the shifting seeds of time. This was my punishment, to drink the terephthalic acid, mount the compo, and travel to a time that Grandfather warned me would make me cry for another chance to obey him back home.

I knew he'd be right (he always is); I just didn't know how right he'd be. This scar has become something I caress obsessively as if it were your komboloi, the worry beads

you lashed to my wrist while I leaned my head back to
drink the acid. Whatever terrible act begat this scar is long
forgotten; yet as I circle my fingers over its contours, I know
its presence on this body is no accident. Grandfather must
want me to know that ripped flesh—cells forced to separate, then claw their way back together in a lumpy uneven
embrace—is the life I escaped. History has been the grace
that allows my body—my true body—to remain strong and
unscarred. Virtually.

Virtually unscarred.

The Battle Royale is not supposed to maim. If you're
good, you never get hit. You duck and dodge, slipping
away just seconds before a blade or a heel or a stick hits. It's
a dance, the razors were added for flash, to make the game
prettier. You get a lot of bruises, a few players have lost
chunks of flesh, but only one death.

"It's safe," I told Grandfather.

"Battle Royale," he muttered under his breath and
went back to his beakers and chemicals and explosions.

I was forbidden. I was forbidden to battle, but you
were there. If I didn't dance, someone else would have daz-
zled you with their blades and I would have disappeared
before your eyes.

So I got cut. Yeah, I bled. But I didn't break anything.
I didn't have to go to the hospital. I walked all the way
home. Trailing blood, and you behind.

When Grandfather saw me he was shaking. Not from
fear, but from anger. Grandmother protested that I needed
to heal, but Grandfather would not listen. He dragged me
down into the basement, pulled me over the threshold of
his lab, and pushed me onto the compo. He was so angry
he didn't notice that my blood had spilled all the way down
the stairs, and you behind.

I drank. I didn't have a choice. He raged about whipping posts and ignorance. He questioned my right to be
free, and you cried. You, who had never even touched my
cheek, who I had never even kissed, you cried for me and
wrapped your worry beads around my wrist.

Grandfather has a bad habit of creating the poison

before the cure. Now that I am sitting here watching feathers hanging in air, listening to the buzz of legal speech, fingering a scar placed on this body before I entered it, I wonder when Grandfather will bring me back, *if* he can bring me back. If I will fall faint or asleep and open my eyes to see Grandfather's face hanging over me—you behind, praying that I survived.

I hear the man in the feathered cape whisper, "Uexolotl" and I know it is a curse. A lance thrown down the throat of the haughty European. But the European does not respond; he continues his speech. The realization comes to me slowly, but I grasp it. The magic cape man—with his brown skin and his shiny black hair—he cannot be seen by the European.

"He and his kind are dead," a voice whispers. I look around, but there is no one here. No one who would have whispered such a thing. The men surrounding me do not whisper. Their voices insist and impose. They flail dark-robed arms and toss white-wigged heads. The men shackled behind me are silent.

"Dance," the voice whispers.

"What?" I ask with dry lips.

"Dance," the voice whispers again. I listen harder. I may be crazy, keeping company with dead, feathered men. I may be crazy, hearing words on the wind. I may be crazy, but I am certain this is your voice. You, who are not here, but I think you must be reaching for me. I imagine you peering through Grandfather's murky liquids, whistling into beakers, wondering how you can bring me home.

I stand.

"Now dance."

Before I can move a muscle, the scar starts to screech.

"Dance the Royale?"

The scar wails in guttural tones, begging me to sit. It speaks in a language I can't decipher, but fear needs no words to be understood.

"Dip."

I don't know where this scar came from or how it was born, but I know you. I have been waiting to dance for you since the moment I met you. Before you can whisper another word, I dip. My hands flick helplessly, no razors to grasp. A club blurs toward me, and I slide back, snaking my hips low. It crashes against my knee, but it doesn't matter. I'm in the Royale now.

They surround me—black robes, rotten teeth, anger. They surround me, but they can't catch me. The Royale has me. That ancient vibe has slipped into my skin and nested down into my chest. It guides me, showing me the gaps, and I glide through, ducking just when they think I'm captured. Then just like that, the Royale leaves me. It rolls up behind me and shoves me forward. I stumble under the force, and then I run.

I scramble over benches and climb through an open window. As soon as my feet touch the ground, I take off running. I hear sounds behind me: explosions and shouts. I feel tiny fires shooting past me. The Royale pants behind me, low and fierce. Every pant is like a heartbeat. I dare not still my feet.

Out the corner of my eye, I see feathers flying next to me. They rush, creating a wind that pushes me faster and faster. I run beyond my pursuers. I run beyond the trees. I run beyond the Royale. Then I hear the gritty sound of time grinding into a different gear, or year. My limbs go liquid and lose their speed.

•

Intense heat is the first thing I feel, then exhaustion. I feel it down to my bones. Muscles like mush, as if I've been walking for miles. To the right and left of me are sand dunes, notched with hypnotizing ridges where the wind has kissed them. Before me is a woman's back, her head hangs low as she plods along a footpath. I look behind me. More women, a long line of them snaking back further than I can see. They all wear dingy white robes and tattered headwraps. I hold up my arms. The same dingy cloth covers me.

My eyes swing back up to the woman's neck. Foreign memories flash in my mind. Men with black-lined eyes breaking into a family camp. A man—who must be this new body's father—bloodied but fighting. A woman—who must be this new body's mother—lying with her throat ripped open, a bloom of blood haloing her head. The bite of sand on palms and knees as this body crawls to safety, crawls like a dog, choking on fear. I shake the scene from my head and stare at back of the woman's neck again.

"You must forget there was ever anything called home," a voice whispers. Your voice. I feel a gasp of panic explode in my head. You can't ask me to forget home. I won't forget home; I won't forget you. Anger chases away the panic. Grandfather, with his reckless lessons and self-righteous speeches. Doesn't he know what everyone whispers behind his back? *That one*, they say, pointing their chins at me, *that one gets his wildness from his grandfather*. Is he punishing me for being like him?

My arm swings up in an arc, muscles twitching with memory. It's the block I should have thrown in my last Royale, the arm flick I should have used to knock away the razor and avoid getting cut. The repeated sway of my arm is numbing, like a narcotic. For a few blissful seconds, I'm not on a long desert walk to enslavement—I'm nowhere.

After my arm grows tired, I let it fall limp by my side. I notice two small rises of flesh on my chest. Breasts. I touch them with the back of my hand. My sleeve rolls back to reveal the ridges of a scar on my forearm. I push the sleeve up further, there's a crude X burned into my arm. When I look up at the woman in front of me again, I understand why I've been staring at her. It's not her neck I'm looking at, I'm staring at the scar burned on her back—the top edges of an X visible above the scoop of her robe.

I peer ahead. An indigo-draped figure rides a camel. The set of his shoulders tells me that he decides my next breaths. Whip gripped in hand, lazily swatting air with a motion that cools him and flaunts his power all at once.

What has Grandfather done?

I step out of the snaking line, and look back. My gaze is darting around, looking for more guards when, *thwack*, something hard cracks against my jaw.

I don't fight the fall. I don't even feel the impact when my body crashes against the hot sand. I lay there, motionless, aware of nothing except the sun's searing heat and the parade of feet stepping over me as the women plod on to their terrible destiny.

I can smell death rising with the heat around my body. It smells like decay, a tinge of sticky sweetness mixed in with a rank earthy scent. I feel a blow to my side, then another. I allow my body to rock with each kick. A thought rips through my mind: *If I die here, will my life end?* I would rise and fight, but why? Whether I lay here until death claims me, or I stand and walk toward my own slaughter, I will die anonymous and unloved. No one among these trillions of grains of sand can see my true face, and no one knows my name.

"I know," your voice says. "I know your name. Come home."

At first I feel a flush of pleasure: You want me. Then that bitter rage flares again and extinguishes my pleasure. You want me, and I am powerless to join you. Coming home is not up to me. This is Grandfather's game.

The army of feet trod on, kicking up tufts of dust, coating my face with grime. The sun is so merciless that the blazing heat begins to feel physical. The idea of releasing my grip on life is seductively sweet.

"But we have not yet tasted each other," you whisper.

A small sound that doesn't know if it wants to be a laugh or a sob pops in my throat. Not even your voice—with its melodies and catches—can stop me from thinking about committing my body to the earth. I want you, but I also want to break into a million pieces and melt into the sand. I want to stop the procession of roughened heels and downtrodden women. I want to die.

"Dance," you say. Your voice has taken on a depth I have never heard before. You have pushed beyond laughter and flirtation, scattering gravel and broken glass in your voice. Then I understand. You mean not to entice me, but to compel me. You are trying to awaken the warrior in me.

Another kick catches me. Pain implodes in my side. My body lifts up from the ground, then falls limp. A captor yells something over me—something rumbling and fast. More of them come. They turn me over. I don't blink. I'm not even sure that I'm breathing. I lay face up, eyes glassy and blank, limbs splayed crucifixion wide.

You want me to rise, but I don't know how. I don't know how to rise from a bed of my own blood, from a stretch of earth made soft by the pummeling of my own limbs. I don't know how to stand and dance, not even for the Royale. Not to join a caravan of the enslaved, not to travel toward a tomorrow of torture and death. No, not even for you.

"You will dance," you say, and suddenly violent retching tugs at my throat. Grandfather's magic must be stuck or broken, or else it's incredibly cruel. Something is pummeling me, piercing my skin with pinpricks. I don't know if it's another time shift, abuse from my attackers, or you trying to rouse me.

I lift a weak wrist and for a brief second there is relief. Then the pain returns—like a million tiny axes chopping at my organs. I throw open a thigh to ward off the trembling. There is no faith or courage here, just feverish desperation as I move through the Royale with gritted teeth.

I imagine Grandfather's unsteady fingers working to bring me back. A gritty moan rustles in my ears. At first I think it's my voice winding out over the sand flats, but then I realize it is you, reaching down deep to pull out a wailing too gutbucket for your small frame. It is the straining in your voice that hooks me. I tilt my head back and gulp down deep raggedy breaths. I open my mouth; nothing but dry rasping comes out. I work at it anyway. I search for a part of me that is unbruised and untouched by pain. I open my mouth again, struggling to thrust out a mangled yell that can match your wailing. Then the sands of time grind at my bones and everything goes dark.

•

"You have the things?"

I blink and look around. My body lurches forward. For a few brief seconds, it feels like I'm hurling through space. I grab onto a pole overhead, then drag myself back to standing.

"Keep tight! What were you thinking?"

I look at the person speaking to me and almost gag. I look away, but a glance around the room sickens me further. The room is crawling with mangled people. No facial feature is where it should be—limbs are attached at odd angles on all the wrong parts of the body. I force the muscles in my face to be still. Then I look again. It is a man speaking to me, was a man. Now I don't know what he is. He has eyes on either side of his mouth, and his nose sits at a violent tilt. The space where his eyes should be is covered with a huge, lumpy scar. Even as I am battling revulsion, I can see that his oddly-placed eyes are flicking me appraising glances, sizing me up.

I look around again. Through the narrow mesh platform beneath my feet, I see more of them—the mutilated—packed in like cockroaches. There are so many of them that they look like rashes or rust corroding the metal walls. Besides the revolting people, everything in the room is metal—metal walls, metal poles, metal mesh flooring.

When I look up, a few droplets of wetness fall into my eye. I shake my head and blink it away. I look up again. A clump of blistered kids are wedged between the overhead poles and the ceiling. The realization rises in me slowly. *I must be disfigured, too.* I look down at my body. I see my shoulder just beneath my chin, and my arm jutting out from where my chest should be. What kinds of freaks are we?

When next I look at the man, the air around me seems unstable. The fearsome roar that rings through the room starts to echo in my ears. My eyelids droop, and my muscles start to go slack. The man opens his mouth, a tiny wet hand emerges. He wipes the bottom of my nose with it. A moldy scent bursts in my sinuses, and my eyes pop wide open.

"You gonna make it? Ain't no short trip!"

I nod mutely, revolted and relieved.

"You have your things?" he asks again.

I shrug. He squints at me. I can tell he thinks I'm a waste of time.

"You know about the things, right?"

I shrug again, this time nodding after.

He turns his head and opens his mouth. Out comes the hand again. It feels along the pole that we're hanging on. He picks at something flat that's stuck there and rips it off. I hadn't noticed it before, but only one of his arms ends with a hand, the other ends with a foot. He only has one standing leg, and it's keeping him balanced on the platform beneath us.

He waves the flat thing under my nose. It's an old tattered label.

"Mmmm-mmm!"

It takes me a few seconds to realize he can't talk and hand me the label at the same time. I grab the label.

"Not going to ask. Why you don't know what we're doing here is none of my concern. How you got on the transport without knowing about the things ain't my trouble." He looks around. "But you better learn fast. There ain't no return trips. At the end of this, either you'll get out or you'll die."

I can tell by the hard edges of his words that he meant to scare. Instead I'm thrilled. Could this finally be the end?

"You need three things. Three. You got them?"

I began to feel around my body, awkwardly learning how to use my rotated arms.

"Pocket the label."

"What?"

The guy's eyes roll up like I'm useless. "Pocket the label, it's your pass."

I look at the label. It's grimy and stiff. Though it's ripped I can read something on it: "Regiment Green: Disrespect on a cellular level." Reaching around my hip, feeling for my back pocket, my hand catches on an opening in my clothes. It's a pocket. I drop the label in and feel around the rest of my clothes. I've got pockets all over.

I poke around in the pockets, unsure what I'm looking for. My fingers happen upon something stiff in the fourth pocket. I pull it out—a shiny black feather. The man makes a weird fluttering sound with his mouth. I imagine that wet hand flapping against his moist jaws.

"Don't show me. Don't show anybody except Him when you get there. Got it?"

I nod and keep feeling around, but the rest of the pockets are empty. After I check all my pockets twice, I realize that my fingers are covered with grime. I put my hand back in a pocket and pinch at the bottom. When I draw my hand out, there's something grainy sticking to my fingertips. I hold my hand up to my face—desert sand. I start grabbing pinches of sand wherever I can find it.

"Tighten!" the guy yells.

I grab on with two hands. The transport dips, then turns sharply. My feet fly off the platform and a burning flares across my palms where they rub against the overhead pipe.

I hear a yell, then two bodies drop down from above. The yelling fades and is replaced by a sinister hissing. The air fills with smoke, and a high-pitched wailing rings out.

"Don't lose your grip," the guy mutters.

"What's down there?"

"Engine."

Fear bubbles in my throat, but I choke it back down. I focus on the maddening task of filling one of my pockets with sand. When I've piled all the sand I can grab into one pocket, I let out a relieved exhalation.

But the guy breaks into my relief. "You need three things. Two's no good. He won't send you if you don't have three."

My thoughts run around my mind in panicked loops. *Who is this person and where will he send me? Will this take me home?* More moisture falls on me from above. I'm suddenly aware of my armpits and my crotch. They are soaking wet, my entire torso is wet—I am terrified to the bone.

Suddenly I know what my third thing will be.

"What if I want to bring liquid? What can I hold it in?"

The guy doesn't answer. He throws his head back, barks something guttural and fast. One of the children wedged in overhead shimmies forward on the pole. He almost cracks my knuckles in the process, but I don't cry out. He reaches up, grabs something white and cup shaped from the ceiling. He brings it to his mouth quickly, gulping something down. Finds another cup-shaped thing from the ceiling and grabs it. He passes them down to the guy, whose head is thrown back, lips spread wide as the wet hand is outstretched waiting for the cups. When he has them, he flicks them at me.

"Won't last forever. You better hope it holds till we get to the Man."

I nod. I see him staring at me curiously. I tilt my head forward, hold the cup underneath the tip of my nose, let my sweat drip into it.

"Tighten!"

I throw my hand over the pole and yank on it with my wrist. We careen backward this time. I lose all my sweat but I hold on to the cup. It takes me three more tries, but I finally fill the cup. Something like admiration creeps into the guy's eyes.

"Pass the empty," he says.

I pass it. With a flick of his wet fingers, he turns it upside down and holds it out to me. I fit the cup filled with sweat to the empty one. He pinches the edges of the two cups with his tiny hand. I take the cups back and drop them into my pocket.

A ghostly sensation washes through my body. At first I think it's relief, but then I feel it fluttering in my chest. I look at my guide with new eyes, eyes that are probably now as wet as my skin. I haven't caught a glimpse of the outside, but I know from this brief time in the bowels of this machine, this world isn't a pretty place. Surrounded by all these damaged cells, in the middle of this ocean of desperation, my guide suddenly seems holy. Before I can hold it back, reverence and gratitude pour out my face. My emotions register in his eyes, and he turns away.

After my flush of emotion, "Tighten!" is the only word he says to me for the rest of the trip. In the absence of his gaze, the balancing act becomes routine; I find myself oddly acclimated to periodic peril. Soon, I'm dozing off between veers and drops as the drone of the engine soaks through me. By the time the engine room shudders and slows, I have become what everyone else is: a jumpy, sweaty fugitive—frightened, yet determined to survive.

A grinding sound parts the damp heat around us. Everyone begins to chatter in different tones and pitches, and the transport jerks to a sudden halt. I look up just in time to see hundreds of thin metal shafts shoot down from the ceiling. The noise is deafening. I feel the whoosh of wind slap my cheek as one of the spinning shafts splits the air next to me. Panic whirls through my gut flooding me with dizziness. I grip the pole tighter and pray not to faint. When I regain my balance, I look at my guide for reassurance, but his eyes are closed and his mouth moving steadily. Is he talking to himself?

A thin drizzle wets my cheek. I touch it—it's not water. It's thick and green, and it stings my fingertips. The green gel splatters through the room sounding like footsteps or bloodshed. Then a pounding roar drowns out the splattering. My stomach clenches. What is coming for us?

I glance at my guide again—he's standing stock still, eyes closed. Some of the others have let go of their poles, but not my guide. As the roaring grows louder, I nervously gnaw on my shoulder. All around me people are leaping from perches and diving from ledges, green goo lashing against their bodies as they plunge.

Just when I think I'm going to bite through my skin, my guide opens his eyes. His mouth moves, but I can't hear what he's saying. His mouth moves again, and he pitches his body forward. It looks like he's saying "Jump." My muscles tense as I prepare to leap. My guide opens his mouth and extends that small wet hand. He opens his mouth and extends that small wet hand. He lifts one finger, and I hear a deafening crack. It sounds like the whole room is going to split in two. My guide nods, we leap.

The freefall makes me feel like vomiting. Instead of crashing on the engine, we land on a wave of green gel. It is washing through the engine room in rivers now. Those who did not leap are engulfed by it. Those who leapt too soon lay broken somewhere on the engine below.

The gel hurries forward, carrying me at a frightening speed straight at a wall. I shut my eyes tight, but I don't but slam into anything. With a whir, a circular door opens before me, and I surf through it into darkness. The gel bobs me gently, misleadingly—as it rocks me, it is searing my skin. People call out names and numbers. Some voices are frantic, others pleading. Our eyes are useless. A crackle that sounds like electricity silences them all. Light flashes, and I see that everyone is looking up. I look around wildly for an exit or a sign—something that can tell me where to go before we are plunged into darkness again.

When next the light flashes, everyone is still looking up. Probes, shiny and bulbous, start to lower from the ceiling. Darkness comes, forcing me to calculate how long the probes will take to get to me, and how far I need to move away so as not to be crushed. I feel a ripple as the probes slide into the gel. Another flash, and I see bodies scrambling up onto the probes. I feel around blindly until I touch something cool and hard. I grab onto the probe. It crackles and a gentle electric current rolls through my body. Before I can climb all the way onto the probe, it starts to lift.

The burning on my skin cools as soon as I am out of the gel. I allow myself a few seconds of relief as the probe lifts through the ceiling into a new room and a floor closes underneath us. The thump of people dropping down from the probes is the first thing I hear. Then feet scattering.

"Run!" people start to yell, "Ruuuuunnnnnn."

They scatter—hopping, crawling, rushing. No one seems to know which way to go. I can finally use my feet, but I am faltering. I turn around in circles, looking for a door, a window, a hint of light, anything that can show me

the way out. But all I see is rows and rows of probes hemming us in; I can't even figure out the shape of the room
we're in. I hear a faint sound.

"Ahhhh-lay-lay-lay. Ah-la, lay, lay, lay. Ahhhh-lay-
lay-lay. Ah-la, lay, lay, lay."

You are singing. For a few seconds I am paralyzed
with grief, stricken by the certainty that I will never see you
again. Then I see it, a purple mist spreading through the
room. Your song seems to beckon to me, growing faint then
pulsing in one particular corner. I follow your voice from
one end of the room to the other. Every time I think you
have led me to the way out, the light I am walking toward
dissipates.

The mist quickly fills the room, growing so thick that
I can no longer see. I hear breathing around me. It sounds
heavy and panicked. A suffocating sweetness blossoms
in the back of my throat. My limbs begin to tingle. A loud
chattering breaks out behind me. The last clear thought I
have is that if I can find those voices, I can find the exit. I
twist around and run. After a few steps, I bang into a probe,
then stumble, tripping over something large. It's a body. I'm
sure it's a body, but my mind is too jumbled to react. I ignore my mounting hysteria and latch onto the image of me
running. I force my limbs forward, but gravity overtakes
me and starts dragging me down. My eyes roll back in my
head, and my ears stop registering sound. But before I drop,
someone shoves me from behind. I pitch forward, carried
along by the crush of bodies. Suddenly the air is different—
sharp, crisp, no mist. A weak thrill vibrates through me,
then I fall face-first onto the ground.

I'm lying on a bed of soft leaves. There's no noisy,
painful time shift, but I'm in a different place. Not home,
but my arms are nestled around you. You have flowers
tucked behind your ear and gold beads in your braids.
You're holding me with an easy comfort, almost as if you've
held me many times before, as if you know you'll be holding me many times again.

I snuggle closer to you.

"Time to go," you whisper before kissing me on

my jaw.

I feel someone shaking me.

"Time to go," a voice says.

Then I hear that wet flapping sound. It whips through me like an alarm. My eyes pop open. A hand is hovering before my face. I grab it and climb to my feet. Dead leaves and dried insect wings flutter off me. I grab my guide in an awkward fumbling embrace. Why am I still here?

"Let's move," he says and hops away before I can ask how he found me. He leans on a branch for balance, moving with surprising quickness for a one-legged man.

I follow, taking quick glances around while I hustle behind him. On one side of us is the base of a cliff. We are traveling on a narrow path that cuts through a tangle of overgrowth that has managed to flourish in the massive shadow of a mountain. On the other side of us is a dark forest; cool air rolls out from between the trees and licks at our cheeks and ears. Every twenty feet or so, my guide stops and peers into the forest. He's too far ahead for me to ask what he's doing.

A shriek cuts through my thoughts, then I see people running. Without a word to me, my guide races forward, hopping as fast as he can toward a cluster of people staring into the forest. He pushes past them and, by the time I draw near, he has disappeared into the mass of altered limbs.

I push into the crowd too, struggling to keep pace with my guide.

"This it?" my guide asks, motioning to a large cave.

Someone grunts. My guide looks at me. I take a step forward. He stares at me for a few long seconds, then he blinks.

"Going in," he says. When he turns away I know that was goodbye.

He hops into the cave opening. A curtain of pastel-hued light shimmers as he enters, and then he's gone. My heart goes wild with fear. I don't think I can take another world, another blow, another scar, but I am instantly overtaken with terror that I'm being left behind.

When I step inside the cave, I am assaulted with light. The light is everywhere. The strongest glow comes from deep within the cave where the light's intensity is amplified by discarded metal rods and glass tubing littering the floor. Shielding my eyes from the glare, I walk deeper into the cave. I feel the temperature drop right when I find my guide. He is standing at the back of the cave in front of an old wooden table. On the other side of the table is the Man—I'm pretty sure it's the Man. He is massive, intimidating. His dark robes do nothing to disguise the broadness of his shoulders. His head is shaven clean, and I can't see his eyes—they are covered by plastic welding goggles. He taps his hand impatiently on the tabletop.

My guide gestures, pointing at something on the table. The Man lifts one hand, shoves the goggles off his eyes and leaves them to rest on his forehead. He says something to my guide. My guide nods. The Man says something else, and my guide says, "I promise."

He picks up a cup from the table and drinks from it, then he disappears right before my eyes.

My heart convulses, but before my thoughts can whip into a frenzy, the Man yells, "Next!"

He doesn't bother to look up when I stand before his table.

"Your things," he says. I pull out the feather and place it on the table. Pinch by pinch, I pile the sand into a mound. Then I get the cup of perspiration out of my pocket and place it on the table. It has gone stiff in the middle where my guide pinched it. It tilts to the side, but the liquid has not leaked out.

The Man picks up my feather and inspects it. Its iridescence takes me back to the man with the glossy hair, his watchful eyes, his fierce spirit. The man sets the feather back on the table and pokes his fingers into the sand, flattening my pile. Memories of the girl who watched her parents die run through me. By the time he picks up the cup, I am remembering the scar that wailed to keep me safe. The man sniffs the cup, turning it around in his fingers, then places it back on the table. He clasps his hands in front of him.

"What is freedom?" he asks. He tilts his head back and looks up at me.

I gasp.

There is no mistaking those features. The thickness of the eyebrows, the thinness of the nose, the full bottom lip, the scar on his left jaw line.

"Grandfather?"

Not a flicker of recognition passes through the Man's eyes. He doesn't repeat his question, but the intensity of his stare lets me know that he is waiting for my response.

A thousand thoughts go spinning through my head. I don't want to be afraid, but I am. How much of Grandfather is in this man's body? I flash back to the rows of men shackled behind me in the courthouse. I remember the long snaking line of women plodding through the desert. I know what freedom is not.

The man who may be my grandfather bangs his hand on the table.

"Many are waiting. Do you have an answer?"

"I'm…" I wet my lips.

I think about my body, my real body, loose-limbed and free. I remember the Royale, how it always made me feel: flush-faced, high on adrenaline, disconnected from everything ordinary, locked in some ancient formula of ferocity and flight.

The man with a hand for a tongue didn't prepare me for this.

"Freedom is the ability to be whatever you want—without control, violence, force, or limitations."

Grandfather takes a closer look at me then. He squints as if sizing me up.

"Why do you deserve to be free?"

"Everyone deserves to be free," I snap.

A slight smile creases Grandfather's lips, then his seriousness swallows his pleasure and he continues his inquisition.

"What will you do with your freedom?"

I know what Grandfather doesn't want to hear. He doesn't want to hear that I'll pick up the razors and enter the Royale, he doesn't want to hear that after decades of bondage, I will choose to squander my freedom by getting myself maimed in a fight. I remember the freedom the Royale gave me, a freedom Grandfather will never understand: a freedom of feeling, a freedom of weightlessness, a freedom to be pure motion, to be more than I am. When I try to put my words together, I stumble, blinded by thoughts of you watching me dance, by my need to dazzle you again.

I look Grandfather in the eye, careful to strangle down the anger I have carried with me on my travels.

"I will obey my elders and love my friends," I say. None of this is a lie.

Without another look at me, he grasps a glass beaker between his thumb and index finger and pushes it toward me.

Smoke wafts from the opening of the beaker.

"Drink," he says.

A small dry chuckle falls from my mouth. This is the last of Grandfather's potions that will ever pass my lips. As I raise the beaker to my mouth, he says, "May freedom be all that you wish it to be. May you be strong under the weight of its burden."

I throw my head back and take a big gulp. The potion swells in my throat. I slam the beaker on the table and, as soon as I draw my hand away, Grandfather and the table are gone.

•

Traveling back home is like being smacked with a hundred small hands. There is nothing to see, but plenty of sound. After my skin has been slapped raw, I begin to tingle all over. An intense tickle starts at the crown of my head and splits my body, traveling right down to my pelvis. Heat spears up my throat and I jackknife forward, gagging.

When the vomit comes, I am back on the compo, my face a mess of mucus and tears. I force myself to my hands and knees and scramble off the compo. Then I look around with wild, shifting uncertainty. Pain pulses through me like a mantra, but I cannot let it consume me.

All around me are the tools of Grandfather's treachery. My skin bristles at remembering the scars, the mutilations, the brutalities. I know he'll dismiss the idea that I was ever in danger. He'll crow over the power of his chemicals and insist that he was in complete control.

The urge to upend his worktable and shatter his beakers overtakes me, but I am too weak to stand. I hear Grandmother moving around in the kitchen overhead. I want to cry out, but I can't squeeze sound through my throat. I crawl over to the stairs. When I try to lift my hand to the doorknob, my arm trembles violently. Hatred for Grandfather burns in my heart.

I ram my head against the door, blind to everything but the need to be seen, to be held. I bang my head against the door again and again, oblivious to the impact of the wood against my skull. Before blood breaks through my skin, before I can tell if anyone has heard me, exhaustion consumes me. *I'm here*, I yell in my mind. I am here, bruised and alone. I am here on the verge of blackout.

"I'm here," I whisper. Then I collapse to the floor.

KIINI IBURA SALAAM is a writer, painter, and traveler from New Orleans, Louisiana. Her work is rooted in speculative events, women's perspectives, and artistic freedom. Her fiction has been published in such anthologies as *Dark Matter, Mojo: Conjure Stories, Black Silk*, and *Dark Eros*. Her essays have been published in *Colonize This, When Race Becomes Real, Utne Reader*, and *Ms. Magazine*. She documents the challenges of the writing life in her *Notes From the Trenches* e-book series. Her first collection of short stories *Ancient, Ancient* was co-winner of the 2012 James Tiptree, Jr. Award. She recently published her second short story collection *When the World Wounds*. Her writing and art are archived at kiiniibura.com. She lives in Brooklyn, New York.

A CEREMONY OF DISCONTENT

ELEANOR ARNASON

VUSAI woke at sunrise. The sky was overcast, and the air had the smell of rain. She got up and took down her hammock. Quickly she folded it and put it away. Then came the curtains along the edge of the veranda. They had come from Hui, the village with the best weavers. They were thin and completely transparent, except where the pattern was. The pattern was a zigzag, done in white and green. At the bottom the curtains were tied to the floor, so bugs couldn't fly in under them. She undid the ties and pulled the curtains up. Then she went inside. The rest of her family was there: her husband Mawl and Shaitu, the wife who had children. Mawl was cooking breakfast. Shaitu was doing nothing. She was pregnant again, round, fat and pleased with herself. Vusai had never understood her attitude. What was so fine about bulging out and being clumsy? Who would want such a thing? Vusai helped herself to a piece of bread, then looked around for the children. They were in a corner: a green heap of naked bodies, all tangled up with one another, wrestling fiercely and silently. All girls and fine ones. When the time for the choice came, she knew what it would be. They were too independent to be mothers.

She sat down. Mawl gave her a bowl. She dipped the bread in and took a bite. Ah! That burned like the sun! It took the bad taste out of her mouth, and it even lightened her mood a little. The day seemed less grey.

"I have made a decision," she said.

"Yes?" said Mawl.

Shaitu blinked and looked interested.

"I am going to ask for a ceremony." She finished the bread and took another piece.

50

"What kind of ceremony?"

"A ceremony of discontent."

Mawl looked surprised.

Shaitu asked, "But why? Your pottery is going well. Did you hear about the people from Hui? They asked for your work by name. They wanted pots by Vusai, they told the trading chieftainess."

"I know."

"Are you unhappy with the family?" asked Mawl. He sounded anxious. He was the kind of man who always worried about his wives and his children too.

Vusai told him, "No. I do not know exactly what is wrong. But nothing looks right to me. Everything has a nick or scratch or an imperfection of color. I hear false notes when you sing, Mawl. And you, Shaitu, the sight of you enrages me. I think, why is she happy?"

"Maybe it's the rain," Mawl said. "You have never liked this time of year."

"No." Shaitu leaned forward. "She is discontented. I know the signs. She has been restless since the harvest, and it was dry then. Remember when she broke the pot? The big one that was as blue as the sky? She said it had a flaw. It didn't. I have seen this before."

Mawl looked uneasy. Everyone knew about Shaitu's mother. She had gone crazy and abandoned her family, in order to make fishing nets. It was all due to uncertainty and discontent. No one had noticed the first signs, and by the time the ceremony was done, it was too late.

"Very well," he said. "Go to the chieftain in charge of ceremonies. I will contribute three boxes of dried fish."

"I will contribute food from the garden," Shaitu said. "And take him the pot that is spotted white and brown."

Vusai got up. "Thank you." She still felt angry. Shaitu was comparing her to the crazy woman who made nets. She was certain of it. She left the house. It was raining now, a steady drizzle. She walked down the muddy street. One of the village birds followed her. It was a big creature, almost as tall as she was. It had long legs and a long neck and a tiny head. It wanted food, and it was too stupid to realize she wasn't a mother. Only mothers fed the birds.

"Go away, you stupid thing!" she told it.

It followed her all the way to the house of the chieftain in charge of ceremonies. The chieftain was a man, of course. In every village, the work was always divided the same way. Men took care of the fishing and the ceremonies. Mothers took care of the gardens and the children. Independent women did the trading and made the most of the goods that were traded. There were a few women-men, who lived like the independent women. But they were comparatively rare. In some villages, they were thought to be perverted.

The chieftain in charge of ceremonies was on his veranda, sitting cross-legged and smoking a pipe. He was tiny and withered with a dark green complexion.

"Good day, grandfather." Vusai sat down.

"If you had my rheumatism, you wouldn't say this day is good. I can barely move! How I hate the rainy season!"

"I have come for a ceremony."

He stared at her. His eyes were black with a little yellow showing around the edges. "You are dissatisfied."

"Do I show it?"

"A little. I have also heard how you are behaving. You are rude and self-preoccupied. You break pots. You shout at children. You have come to me just in time. Help me up. As soon as we've agreed on a fee, I'll get the steam house ready."

She helped him up. They went inside and argued about the fee. He won. After that he hobbled out to the steam house. She drank tea with his wife. Only the mother in his family was still alive. She was as tiny and as withered as her husband.

"A ceremony of discontent, eh? He tried to make me go through one after my last child was born. I said, 'Leave me alone! I'm just in a bad mood. Strong tea and exercise will cure me.' And it did. But not all people are the same. For all I know, you really need his mumbo jumbo."

"Yes, grandmother."

He came back and told her the steam house was ready. She undressed and went into it. All morning she sat and sweated. He was outside, ringing a bell and singing:

"This person asks
for single-mindedness.
"This person asks
for a soul that leans
in one direction
only."

At last, when she was dizzy from the heat, he said, "Come out."

She ran down the bank and jumped into the river. The water was cold. "Ai!" she shouted. She dove under water, then surfaced and swam to the middle of the river. It was raining harder than before. She felt angry again. She hated this time of year. The sky was always cloudy, and the rain almost never stopped.

"Come back!" the chieftain called.

The current was taking her away from him. She swam back to shore, then walked along the bank till she reached him.

"Now you are purified. Go to the house of isolation. I will bring you water and the kind of tobacco that makes people see things. Stay in the house and smoke until something happens which makes you understand your situation. I will come by once a day and make a lot of noise."

Vusai said, "All right."

She went to the house, walking naked through the village. People looked away from her. It was never polite to stare at someone who was in the middle of a ceremony.

The house of isolation was on a hill at one end of the village, all by itself. It was small and windowless. There was a leak in the roof. Rain dripped in, and the floor was wet. This was going to be terrible, Vusai thought.

The first day, nothing much happened. The rain stopped. She got hungry and thirsty. The chieftain didn't come till late in the afternoon. He rang his bell and sang:

"Whoever is responsible
for this situation—
listen to me!

"Whoever is responsible
for this situation—
give this person
some help!"

"Water!" shouted Vusai.
"Be quiet! You can have water when I'm done
singing!"
He went on singing till the sun was almost down.
Then he left. She heard him go down the hill, ringing his
bell. She opened the door and brought in the water. She
had made the pot. It was round and fat with a long neck.
The glaze was black with streaks of reddish-brown. She
drank some of the water, then sighed. "The old fool! I
thought he would never stop!" She looked outside again.
There was a pipe on the ground. It was a long one, made of
green stone. Next to the pipe was a pouch of tobacco.
"Tomorrow," she said. "I will smoke tomorrow."
The next day she was even hungrier. She began to
smoke the pipe. After a while, her mother came to visit her.
She was a fat woman with an angry expression. She had
been dead for years.
"Why did you choose to be independent?" she asked
Vusai. "A woman should have children."
Vusai did not reply.
On the third day, she felt less hungry. She smoked
more tobacco, and her father arrived. He was dead, too.
He had drowned. He came to her with seaweed in his hair.
Water dripped from his tunic. He carried a net, rolled up.
"I have been trying to decide if it was worth it," he
told her. "I have plenty of time at the bottom of the sea.
There's really nothing else to do, except watch the fish. And
I can't catch them anymore, so it makes me angry to see
them—so fat, so lovely, darting right above me." He put the

net down. Now she was able to see that fish thrashed inside it. The strands of the net grew thin like smoke and vanished. The fish flopped away.

"You see?" said her father. "I did everything the way I was supposed to. I made nets. I made songs. I caught fish. I helped to organize all the important ceremonies. What good did it do me? Now I lie at the bottom of the ocean. The tongue is gone out of my mouth, and I don't even have a real net anymore. Only a dream net, that won't hold fish. What was the point of my life?"

"I can't tell you," said Vusai. "I don't know."

Her father vanished.

On the fourth day she saw Mawl and Shaitu, it was early in the morning. The sun was out, a rare thing this time of year. It touched Mawl right in the middle of his back. He was on top of Shaitu, having sex with her. She lay on her back on the floor, looking happy. Vusai watched curiously. It must be so much easier—to do it without worrying about making children. Independent women rarely had children, of course. From the time of puberty they ate a special diet and drank tea made from the root of the plant that prevents children. This kept them safe, most of the time. But every once in a while, an independent woman got pregnant. This caused terrible problems. It had happened to an aunt of hers. The poor woman was a trader and she had been planning to go on a year-long trip. Instead she stayed home and moped. After the child was born, she gave it to the mother in her family. Then she got a divorce. The child got on her nerves, she said. She didn't want to be in the same house with it. She moved to another village and remarried. The child died young of a coughing sickness.

A sad story, Vusai thought. Why did she remember it? By this time, Mawl and Shaitu were gone. She smoked another pipe of tobacco. Now she saw people with the heads of animals. They came in the door, one after another. They spoke to her loudly. She couldn't understand a word they said.

"This is bad! This is frightening! Why is this happening to me?" She threw the pipe down and covered her face with her hands. The animal-people went away. After a while, she heard the chieftain, ringing his bell outside the house of isolation.

"I want to come out!" she called.

"Have you had a good dream?"

"No. All the dreams I've had were bad ones."

"Then keep trying." He rang the bell again.

"I want to go home!"

"You can't go home. Shut up and dream."

On the fifth day her father came back. He was still wet. There was still seaweed in his hair. But his net was gone. He said, "I wish I had become a woman-man. I would have gone traveling—not over the water, but up into the mountains. Like my second wife. I remember how she looked, so tall and strong, with a basket on her back and a long staff in her hand. Why don't you do that?"

"I don't want to."

He looked angry. "I think you are afraid to travel. Remember, someday you will be dead like me." He disappeared. She broke the pipe in two and stood up. She was a little dizzy. She stood for a moment, breathing slowly and evenly. The dizziness went away. She opened the door and went outside. As usual, it was raining. This time it was a downpour. Rivulets of water ran down the hill. "Enough is enough! I am going home!" She went toward the village, slipping and sliding in the mud. What a hateful time of year!

There was a person next to her, she noticed. He had the head of a bird. "Remember," he told her. "Without rain there is no spring. Without spring, there is no harvest. Most things have a purpose."

"Who are you?"

"A dream spirit. The effect of the tobacco hasn't worn off, though it will soon. Why did you leave the house of isolation?"

"I'm hungry, and I don't like the dreams I've been having."

"Well, I am a good dream, and my advice to you is this—go to the wife of the chieftain in charge of ceremonies.

She is a wise old biddy. Ask her what she did, when she felt unhappy with her life. Her husband isn't home at present. He's down at the edge of the ocean, singing over a new fishing boat. Hurry up! He will be done soon." The bird-man began to change, growing thin and changing color. Now he was yellow instead of green. He was no longer human. Instead he was a bird. He stared at her, then squawked and stalked away.

She thought for a moment, then said, "What harm can it do?"

She went to the house of the chieftain in charge of ceremonies. His wife was inside, sitting by the fire. She had a blanket around her. It was thick and brown with a pattern of knots and tufts. Local work. It wasn't as fine as the weaving done in Hui.

"Come in," the old woman said. "Sit down. Have a cup of tea."

Vusai sat down. The old woman poured tea. It was the mild kind, that relaxed the body and filled the mind with peace—for a while, at last. Vusai drank.

"Why are you here?" the old woman asked.

"My dreams told me nothing."

"Ah! So the mumbo jumbo didn't work. Well, not everyone is credulous."

"Tell me what you did when you were full of doubt."

"I told you before. I drank strong tea. I worked in my garden. And I thought about the old stories my mother told me. Old stories are full of truth. That being so, I am going to tell you a story—about how the plant that prevents children was found."

"I know the story."

The old woman looked angry. "Shut up and listen."

"Yes, grandmother."

"Long ago, there was a time when we didn't have the plant that prevents children. Every woman was a mother. Every man had a house full of children to take care of. There were no travelers and no people who worked full time at perfecting a skill. Maybe this was good, maybe it was bad. I don't know.

"In any case, there was a woman named Ashotai. She didn't want to be a mother, and she heard about the plant that prevents children. It grew in one place in the world: on top of a very high mountain, which was overgrown with brambles and guarded by monsters. The monsters had wings and large mouths, full of venomous teeth.

"Ashotai was brave. Off she went. She got up the mountain. I used to know how, but I've forgotten. On top of the mountain, she met a spirit. The spirit said, 'Well, you made it! Good work! But are you wise as well as brave? I have a final test for you. There are two plants here. One is the plant you seek. The other is a ringer. You can take one—only one—with you. Make your choice.'

"Ashotai looked at the plants. They were exactly alike. Then she smelled the flowers on the plants. One plant had sweet flowers. The blossoms on the other plant had a sour aroma. Finally, she broke off leaves and tasted them. The plant with the sweet flowers had a wonderful taste, light and sweet like fruit. The plant with the sour aroma had a terrible taste. It was both sour and bitter.

"Ashotai sat down and thought. Finally she said, 'The plant I seek will give people the ability to choose. And every choice is bitter. If you choose to do one thing, then you lose the chance to do other things that may be just as pleasant or interesting. Because of this, it can be said—in every choice is the seed of regret, like the sour pit or core of a fruit. I think the bitter plant is the one I seek.

"'Well, well,' said the spirit. 'You are wise. The plant you have chosen is the one that prevents children. And, as you say, every real choice is bitter. The other plant—the sweet one—is the plant that gives true peace of mind. If you had taken it, you and your people would have been happy forever. But you can't have everything. Take your plant and go.'

"So Ashotai came down from the mountain and gave the plant to her people. After that, every girl could choose whether or not to be a mother. And it was decided to give men a choice, out of fairness. Most men chose to be fathers. But a few became women-men. They act like the independent women in almost every way, and a man can take one of these into his house as a second wife."

"I know all this," said Vusai.

The old woman frowned. "No you don't. You have heard the story, but you don't understand it. Remember every choice is bitter. In every choice is the seed of regret. Well, you have eaten the fruit, Vusai. And now you are biting down on the seed. When I was your age, I realized—I was what I was. I had six children to care for and a garden and a flock of birds. I would never be a traveler. I would never have a skill as fine as the one you have. Ah! How that hurt! But I pulled weeds and drank strong tea. In time I felt better. I advise you to go back to making pots. Eat well. Sleep well. Drink medicinal teas. Your mood will improve."

Vusai put down her cup. "Is every choice a trap?"

"No." All at once the old woman had a face like a prowler from the hills. Her ears were huge and pointed. Her eyes were green, and she had a muzzle covered with yellow fur. "A choice is a path. No one can walk down two paths at one time. And when you are far enough down one path, you cannot turn around. You are too old. You do not have the time to go back to where you started." The prowler stared at her. "Pay attention to what I tell you! Remember what I say! I cannot talk to you any longer. You are almost sober. Wake up and go home. This ceremony is over."

Vusai opened her eyes. She was in the house of isolation. Rain was dripping down on her through the hole in the roof. Light shone in through the cracks around the door. She could see the dream pipe in front of her. The stem was broken.

"Ah!" said Vusai. She got up and rubbed her legs. They were stiff and sore. Then she stretched and yawned. Finally she went home.

ELEANOR ARNASON published her first story in 1973. Since then she has published six novels, two chapbooks, and over thirty short stories. Her fourth novel, *A Woman of the Iron People*, won the James Tiptree Jr. Award and the Mythopoeic Society Award. Her fifth novel, *Ring of Swords*, won a Minnesota Book Award. Her short stories have been finalists for the Hugo, Nebula, Sturgeon, Sidewise, and World Fantasy Awards. Her most recent book, *Hwarhath Stories: Transgressive Tales by Aliens*, is available from Aqueduct Press. You can find her blog at eleanorarnason.blogspot.com.

FIX-IT SHOP

PAT MURPHY

THE wind generator from the nearby elementary school had been the unfortunate loser in a kickball game— a strongly kicked but poorly aimed ball had bent two rotor blades. The school janitor, having failed in an attempt to repair it, had brought it to me.

I was grateful the janitor had not broken a blade by trying to bend it back to its original shape. That's no way to treat good steel.

Straightening the blades was a delicate task requiring just enough heat applied in just the right spot and for just the right length of time, repeated as needed. No brute force required—that's likely to crack or compromise the steel. Better to use the expansion of the hot metal and its contraction as it cools to gradually and gently encourage it to return to its proper shape.

One must match one's pace to the speed of the steel. There is no rushing the matter.

It was a restful sort of work on a beautiful evening. When I finished with the blades, I replaced the pulley and brushes, cleaned and oiled the bearings. A cool breeze off San Francisco Bay blew through the shop's open windows.

From outside, I heard laughter—the sort of harsh derisive laughter that usually spells trouble for someone. I don't like trouble in my neighborhood. I opened the shop door and stepped outside.

The sun had set hours before. In the light from the streetlight on the corner, I saw a group of neighborhood teens crowded around someone I couldn't see. That someone was backed up against the brick wall of the old warehouse beside my fix-it shop.

"Hey, sweetcakes," someone said. "It's your lucky night. You get to stay and party with us." More laughter laced with threat and devoid of humor.

I walked toward the group, limping as always from an old wound, the gift of shrapnel lodged in the leg thirty years ago.

On their own turf, a pack of teenagers can be little better than a pack of dogs—territorial, ready to show any strangers who was in control.

I knew these dogs—had known them since they were children. That didn't mean they weren't fierce—they were. But I did have the advantage of knowing their mothers, of having fixed their bicycles when they were kids. I had a position in the community—I was the go-to person for repairs; I was a combat vet and the local philosopher.

"Hey, Red," I called to one of the kids in the circle. "What's going on here?"

Red was grinning fiercely, all teeth and eagerness.

The circle parted and I saw a child of the suburbs—maybe sixteen years old and clearly out of place in West Oakland. Yes, it was easy to see where this could go. Rough talk, and then a touch, then a rough kiss to an unwilling mouth, a hand shoved between those long legs, and it could all go very wrong for the teenager from the suburbs and the gang from the neighborhood.

"What's going on here?" I asked, though it was ever so clear what was going on.

"Nothing," Red said, her grin faltering. "Just making a new friend."

I stared at the circle of young women. They aren't bad girls; they really aren't. A little wild, a little fierce—times being what they are, that's to be expected. But I know them. As my gaze traveled around the circle, one after another dropped her eyes.

"What's your name, boy?" I asked the kid with his back against the wall.

"Sam." His voice was low and he was trying to sound older than he was. "I was going to the BART station."

I studied him for a moment. His shoulders were back and he was trying hard to look tough. "What are you doing here, Sam?"

"I went to a lecture at the mechanics institute. I was going to catch the train home." He was dressed in dark jeans and a hooded sweatshirt. No doubt he had stayed in the back of the lecture hall, careful to remain unnoticed.

I stepped forward and took the boy's arm in a firm grip. "I'll take him home to his mother," I told Red and the gang.

Red didn't like it. She threw her copper-colored hair back, her eyes narrowing. "He's not ready to go. He wants to party with us—don't you, Sam?"

I stared Red down, my own eyes cool and measuring. She thought about challenging me—I'm sure she did.

"He's going home," I said.

I saw her eyes flick to one side, then to the other. All the other young women had moved back, making this all about Red, me, and the boy. They weren't getting into this beef.

Red laughed, gesturing at the boy. In the streetlight, I could see sweat glistening on his forehead. His cheeks were smooth as a girl's, still too young to shave. "Ah, you can have him. Throw him back, he's too young."

I took the boy with me on the next BART train to the suburbs—almost empty at this time of night. I sat him by the window and I sat beside him. He could not leave without climbing over me. I had to ask him three times before he reluctantly told me where he lived.

Blue-collar women on their way to late night jobs sat on the BART car's plastic benches, rocking drowsily with the movement of the train. A broad-shouldered woman wearing a security guard uniform sat in front of us. She turned in her seat to study me with a suspicious gaze. The badge above her pocket told me her name was S. Wilkins. Somehow Wilkins knew that this boy child should not be out with the likes of me.

"I found him in outside my workshop in West Oakland, surrounded by young women looking for trouble," I told her, though she did not ask directly. "I'm taking him home to his mother."

"I was fine," the boy said. His fright forgotten, he was defiant. "I would have been fine."

I looked at him—his jaw was set, his fists were clenched. "In another ten minutes they would have had his pants around his ankles, just out of curiosity," I told the woman in the uniform. "I know those girls."

"I bet you do," she said, her gaze traveling to my rough clothing. She lived in the suburbs, but she knew my world as well. West Oakland was a world of scavengers and tough girls.

She leaned on the back of the seat and spoke to the boy. "You're very lucky," she told him.

I listened while she talked to the boy. S. Wilkins was in her twenties—at least forty years younger than I was. I had been sixteen when the plague came and the men died; she hadn't been born. She didn't remember the world where I had grown up, a world filled with strong men, powerful men, fathers and presidents and CEOs. Men who controlled the world, for better or for worse. Good men and bad men.

I was glad she was there to tell Sam the way the world worked because I didn't think I'd get it quite right—at least not the current version of right. There's a saying: the victors write history. When there isn't a war, the survivors write history. Or the survivor's children who really never listened to their mothers all that much.

S. Wilkins explained a few things to the boy. Men had to be protected, she explained to him. It was for their own good.

That much I could have said with no sense of irony, no strange echoes from my own childhood before the plague that had killed the men—all but one in a thousand. Now that same plague killed most boys in infancy. Yes, boys needed to be protected; all of the men did.

But S. Wilkins went farther. She explained that everyone knows men were not biologically adapted for fighting—with his unprotected genitals, a single kick would leave him gasping.

Women were tougher, quicker, able to endure more pain. She spouted the platitudes of a political conservative who knew that men should be treasured, their freedom limited for their own good and the good of humanity.

The boy tried to interrupt a few times, saying that he could take care of himself, protesting that he did not want protection. He had gone to the lecture because he wanted to learn about engines; he was good with his hands and he wanted to learn. "If I hadn't run into those girls, I would have been fine."

S. Wilkins shook her head and doggedly continued her lecture. She talked about the innate abilities of men and women, about how dangerous it was for him to be out alone, about how he would become an incredibly valuable member of society—cherished and protected and respected by all.

Sam eventually stopped interrupting and stared at the floor, his hands clenched in his lap, his mouth a grim line.

S. Wilkins got off the train at a suburban station, telling Sam to be good and listen to his mother. As the train doors hissed closed, Sam said, "I don't believe any of that." He stared at me angrily. "Men used to do whatever they wanted."

He said it, but I don't think he believed it. He had learned history in school, but the past is a foreign land, a strange place with different customs. How could there be a world where the men were in power and the women were protected, subjugated, limited? He had never seen such a world. Yes, old people said it had been that way, but what did they know?

I nodded. "Men used to run the world," I told him. Then, in fairness, I added, "They didn't do a very good job of it."

"I bet it's worse now." His tone was a little angry, a little sullen. He was heading home, he was in trouble, and he wasn't happy about it.

I shrugged. "It's different. Women and men are bad

in different ways."

We rode through a few stops in silence.

He wanted a black-and-white argument. I'm much better at shades of gray.

"What did those women want?" he asked.

"They've never met a boy," I said. "What they know comes from stories." From historical romances that did not resemble the history I had lived in any way, from porn, from so-called rape novels. No one wants to read the real histories about when men ran the world. They prefer the fantasies.

"Why did they act like that?"

"Like what?"

"Like they were really angry with me, like they wanted something from me that I wasn't giving them."

"They'd never met a boy," I said again. "They've never met a man."

"That's no excuse." He was calmer now.

"You're right. It's not."

It's not an excuse, but it's a reason. At least I can remember men, the good and the bad of them. I remember my father—a tall broad man who smelled of tobacco and beer. He was a mechanic, and his hands always bore traces of engine grease, no matter how he scrubbed at his nails with the nail brush that my mom supplied.

My dad made my older brother work in the garage, even though my brother didn't want to. I had to stay home and help my mother. My brother teased me, saying I should learn to cook.

I remember one time when I was getting groceries for my mother. I think I was eleven years old, and I noticed a man following me around the store. I was in the canned goods section, looking for the stewed tomatoes my mother wanted, when the man pulled down his pants and showed me his penis and balls. I fled the store without the tomatoes and got in trouble for forgetting them. I didn't tell my mother about the man. I had a strange sense that this disturbing encounter was somehow my fault—I shouldn't have been there. I should have run.

I remember walking past a group of high school boys when I was thirteen years old, clutching my schoolbooks to my chest. I was wearing a bra for the first time, and maybe I blushed when one of the boys glanced my way. He called to me as I hurried past. "Hey, girl, don't run away. I've got what you're looking for right here. Hey, baby." I just kept walking. I wasn't his baby. I wasn't his girl. I wasn't looking for anything he had. He sounded angry. He wanted something and I wasn't about to provide it.

I remember finding a pile of girly magazines in the garage and staring at the exotic and impossible creatures in its pages. Women with skin as smooth as porcelain, with breasts that defied gravity, with legs longer and smoother than anyone's legs should be. Is that what women are supposed to look like? I wondered. All of them smiling with half-open mouths. These were the women those high school boys wanted to party with. Not me.

Sam and I got off at a suburban station and he said he was fine on his own. I insisted on taking him home. At last he led me through quiet suburban streets lit by streetlights to a nice house on a cul-de-sac.

His mother opened the door as we walked up the path to the front porch. She had been waiting, fearful. She swept Kyle into an embrace and then, with barely a pause, banished him to his room. He left without argument, casting a glance back at me.

She introduced herself—using one name only, as was the fashion among people who were fashionable. She was Mica, a sculptor who seemed to think I should recognize her name.

I smiled and acted as if I did.

She invited me into her living room. Soft pale gray carpet underfoot, armchairs upholstered in pastels, delicate side tables, a coffee table perfectly positioned for me to trip over—I've never been in such a comfortable room that made me so uncomfortable. I sat on the edge of a peach-colored armchair, aware that I was wearing my coveralls, that there was grease under my fingernails.

She poured a glass of red wine for me and one for

herself and sat in the chair next to mine.

"Where was he?" she asked, an edge in her voice.

I told her that I had found him on the corner by my shop, surrounded by curious young women. As I spoke, I glanced toward the hallway where Kyle had gone. He was listening, I suspected. Lingering just out of sight, straining his ears to hear what we were saying. That's what I would have done. That's what I had done whenever I was in trouble and I knew my parents were talking about me.

"How did he end up in West Oakland?" I asked.

She shook her head, frowning. "He was on a field trip with three other boys," she said. "He slipped away when the teacher was distracted. And this isn't the first time."

I nodded. I told her that he had gone to a lecture at the mechanics institute, that he said he wanted to work with engines.

"He won't let that go," she said. "I told him it's not going to happen. I've told him that no university will admit him, no woman will apprentice him."

I nodded. She was right about the university.

"Are you married?" She is looking at the ring on my left hand, a simple band.

"Widowed," I said. "She died last year. Cancer."

"I'm sorry." Automatic words of sympathy. "I'm divorced. Sheryl couldn't deal with having a boy child. One in a thousand, and we were the ones. I thought we were so lucky to have a boy. Government subsidies bought this house, pay for tutoring, medical care, everything. And I am lucky." She stared at her wine. "But he's so different. He'll go to the men's house in two years." She shook her head. "So hard to have a boy child; so hard to give him up."

I think about her and Sheryl, arguing about the boy. The substance of their arguments doesn't matter. What I imagine is the boy, lingering in the hallway, listening to his mothers' voices as I had listened to my mother and father talk about me.

My father shooed me away when I asked questions about engines and cars. He said the garage was no place for a girl. So I took an auto shop class in my first year of high school, the only girl in a class of boys in grease stained jeans. All the guys had cars to fix; I just wanted to learn. The teacher, a gruff man who had been teaching for decades, gave me a lawnmower engine and a manual. I took the engine apart completely, then put it back together again. He was a good teacher.

"I could teach him about engines," I heard myself say. "Give him some projects to work on."

"I don't know." Mica was curled in a pale green armchair. She was starting to relax—the wine was helping. "That'll just put ideas in his head. And he won't be good at it—boys just don't have the patience to deal with intricate systems."

"He already has the ideas in his head," I pointed out mildly. "And the only way to learn patience is to make mistakes. You try and fail and try again."

I don't know if I convinced her. I left her drinking good red wine. She said she'd think about it.

I walked back to the BART station and caught the next train back to West Oakland, still thinking about the world before and the world after.

My father died. My brother died. All my uncles, my pediatrician, my auto shop teacher, the boys in my school—all of them died.

Women teachers and girl children remained, and we all kept going to class and learning stuff about the world. We talked about the plague—it was affecting men only, and all the doctors and researchers were trying to figure out why.

It was a terrible, terrible thing. I missed my brother, missed my father, missed them all dreadfully. But just because it was terrible, that didn't mean I didn't benefit from the change. Suddenly, no one was telling me that I couldn't do things because I was a girl. I could fix cars, learn to weld, repair machinery. No one said no.

When I got back to my shop, Red was waiting

for me in the shadows. She had a bottle of wine and she'd been drinking. She'd passed through anger. By the time I returned, she was maudlin, so my timing was good.

The next day, one of the other girls told me about what had happened after I left with Sam. Red and the others sat on the corner and drank. Someone had music and they turned it up loud so they could dance. At one point, Red stuck an empty beer bottle between her legs so that the neck stuck out like a penis. "I'm a boy," she shouted. "Just a sweet little boy, looking for fun." She worked her hips forward and back, wagging the bottle so the neck thrust and jerked. The other girls laughed and laughed. "He'd have loved it, he would," she said. "It's his job to service girls like me. He was hot for me. Did you see that bulge in his pants."

But when she met me at the shop, that was in the past. The others had gone home and the heat had left her. "I just wanted to get to know him," she told me. "I never talked to a boy before."

"His mother was so glad I brought him home," I said. "She was worried sick."

"Yeah?" she said in a tone of wonder, realizing, I suppose, that a mythical creature like a boy also had a mother.

We sat on the curb by the shop and drank red wine together as the crescent moon rose. Red's wine was nothing like that lovely vintage Sam's mother had poured, but I didn't have to sit on the edge of peach colored chair while I drank it.

"I guess I'm glad you took him home," Red said. "I understand you needed to."

I look at her. She thinks she is old and worldly, but she is so very young. I was once her age. I know what it's like to be so young. She does not know what it is like to be my age.

Every now and then, someone asks me how I got my injury. I say I don't like to talk about it, which is true. They assume I sustained the wound in combat during the Years of Turbulence, which is not true. I was in the motor pool when an engine blew, and I caught a piece of flying metal in my leg. I was never in combat.

But I let people believe what they want. I don't lie to them, but I allow them to lie to themselves.

I'm not a fighter. I'm not really a philosopher. I'm just a woman who tries to fix broken things. Some things are easier to fix than others.

PAT MURPHY'S work exists on the borderland between genres, where life is interesting and the rules are slippery. With Karen Joy Fowler, she co-founded the James Tiptree, Jr. Award, an annual literary prize for speculative fiction that expands or explores our understanding of gender roles. Her fiction has won numerous awards, including Nebula Awards, the Philip K. Dick Award, and the World Fantasy Award. Her novels include *The Falling Woman*, *The City Not Long After*, and *Adventures in Time and Space with Max Merriwell*. Her short stories are collected in *Points of Departure* and *Women Up To No Good*. In her day job, she is resident Evil Genius at MysteryScience.com, where she creates science activities to inspire elementary school students to love science.

EXPLORERS

Juno in July

Jane Yolen

"Engine burn complete and orbit obtained.
I'm ready to unlock all your secrets, #Jupiter.
Deal with it."

—*NASA's tweet on the mission to Jupiter in unmanned*
spacecraft Juno that has taken five years.

AFTER the long journey,
the rough wooing begins.
No one expects chocolates,
flowers, wine. But this boast
is beneath us, NASA.
This planet is a lady
despite her name.
Do not order her
to spread her legs
while you frack her
for her secrets,
expecting in return
a soft bed and love.

Do we learn nothing
from the history of war
but hard R words?
Like rape.
Like revenge.
Like regret.

FREE FALL

MONICA BYRNE

BATTISTA flew in a moonless sky.

At 10:14pm Baghdad time, her plane bucked from enemy fire, her seat was ejected, and she hurtled up so fast that the skin on her cheeks was sucked down, making red deltas of her eye sockets. Then the air slowed. Her cheeks warmed. She was cresting, reaching, her maximum height, like a ball in a high school physics problem.

Her parachute should have deployed. It didn't.

She began to drop. Her axis listed sideways. She flung out her arms. As she tumbled, the view of the city came around and around again in flashes. A grid of golden grains. But she was headed straight for a swatch of blackness, where there were no lights, no contours, nothing.

As Battista fell towards it, she thought, *I bet there isn't even anything there.*

She was right.

She plunged through and the grid inverted, as if she'd plunged into a pond and was now looking at the surface above. She blinked, but the view had changed, now, and couldn't be seen any other way. She continued to fall. She watched the huge city of Baghdad contract into a golden galaxy.

•

"I want to get out of here," said Battista, drunk.

"Get yourself pregnant. Or dead," said Hanlon.

"I think we're as far from home as it's physically possible to be."

"Really? What's on the other side of Baghdad?"

76

"I bet it's Hawaii."
"Close enough."

●

Now Baghdad was a single bloom of light, connected by threads to other blooms of light. Some were gold, and some were bright blue—Tel Aviv, she guessed, and Dubai. Their contraction was the only way she knew that she was in motion.

She felt about her waist and located her belt buckles. After a few snaps and clicks, the straps fell away. She gave the chair a shove with her foot, and it revolved away and was lost. The helmet was next. She unbuckled the chinstrap and pushed it away with one finger. It, too, floated into the darkness.

●

Hanlon drew a circle—quite well, Battista thought, for how many beers she'd had—and then an oval spanning the circle. The upper half was dashed and the lower half was solid, to indicate a sphere. Then she drew an arrow straight down, bisecting it.

"How long would it take? To fall through the earth?"
"You mean, if it were hollow?"
"Yeah."
"What is the earth filled with? Air?"
"No, peanut butter."
"Mmmm, peanut butter. When's your next care package coming?"
"No, air. At ground-level psi."
"A gal can dream."
They did the calculations, on the actual back of an envelope.
"After reaching terminal velocity... about twenty-three hours."
"Almost a day."
"A whole day. Damn. About as long as it'd take to

get home by regular old plane."

"Tough landing, though."

•

Now Battista understood that matter was infinitely suggestible, and always had been.

She folded over into a dive. She fell that way for awhile. An eternal dive, never reaching the pool.

Then she turned over onto her back again. The lights on the surface of the earth had grown more faint, but the extent of them was greater now; nets of lights draped over the curvature of space, like the lattice of veins on a pregnant belly. She felt peaceful. She might as well have been resting on a bed of black silk. She crossed her arms behind her head. The air made a pillow.

She closed her eyes and slept, for the first time in weeks.

•

"It wouldn't really be a landing. It'd be more of a... surfacing."

"On the other side of the planet?"

"Yeah. In Hawaii."

"Tough surfacing, then."

"Or maybe you'd just keep falling."

"Through the whole universe forever and ever—"

"We're mostly space."

"—amen."

•

Battista dreamed of Hawaii. She'd been there once, on leave.

She stayed at a resort on the northern coast of Kauai, at a special military rate. She was alone. She liked taking vacations alone.

She also liked the bartender at her resort. He called

himself Guari. He was of Maori-Mexican-Japanese ances-
try—a child of crossroads, as she herself was; though she
didn't know where her roads had come from or where they
led to, only that they had crossed, once, when she was conceived.

 After he got off work, they went down to the beach
and drank mai tais. She told him she was a Navy pilot. He
told her he was a pacifist. She said, "That's okay." And then
when she was on top of him, she thought, *Maybe I'll become
a pacifist.* After they were done, they had a little nap on the
sand, the sweetest sleep Battista had ever known.

 That is what she dreamed of: sleeping.

•

 They clinked their bottles and took drinks.
 Then Hanlon said, "We on tomorrow night?"
 "Yep."
 "Cuadros said we hit a madrasa last night."
 "Surprise surprise." Battista peered at the label on
her bottle.
 Hanlon shrugged. "We hit what Intelligence tells us
to hit. I sleep fine at night."
 Battista laughed. "Yeah."

•

 Battista awoke to faint light. The cities of the earth
were so far away they were stars, now, swirled across the
surface of a bubble. Her eyes, now sensitized to the darkness, could also see a faint glow beneath her. She turned
over to look down. Very far away there was a point of light.
She felt excited. She thought it might be the core at the center of the earth, that glowing pulsing ball in every cross-sec-
tion of the Earth in every science textbook ever made. She
was falling towards it. Not rapidly, but gently. An easy
approach. A soft landing.

 She reached her arms forward so that it seemed
she held the core between her hands. As it got bigger, she

spread her hands, to accommodate its growth.

●

Battista continued. "Madrasas, hospitals, weddings, bat mitzvahs—or whatever it is Muslims do—whatever. I don't care anymore."

"Nor I, comrade."

Battista lost a handle on her bottle and it clonked to the table, rolled over, fell and shattered on the floor.

"Ah, shit." She got up and tried to sweep the shards into a pile with her foot.

"Let it go," said Hanlon. "That's what the staff is for."

"You're a cunt sometimes." Battista bent over to pick up the pieces with her bare hands.

"You're the one who dropped the bomb on the madrasa."

Battista sliced her finger on a shard of glass. "Fuck me," she muttered.

"What was that, sweetheart?"

Battista showed her the bleeding finger.

"Ah, shit. Want me to get a towel?"

"No, it's alright."

"What are you talking about?"

"It's fine."

"You're gushing. Don't you feel it?"

Battista stared at her finger. "Nah."

●

The core was huge now. Battista couldn't spread her arms wide enough to accommodate it. So she just folded into a dive and let herself fall, down toward the core, as if toward the calm of a pool at rest.

●

Hanlon got a towel for Battista anyway, and Battista

wrapped it around her finger to stop the bleeding.

"Better go to Medical for that," she said.

Battista shrugged. "I'll go in the morning. After
I sleep."

"You're actually sleeping now?"

Battista smiled, bitter. "After I pretend to sleep."

"You need to go to Medical for that, too."

"What are you, my mother?"

"No, just your copilot."

Battista put her feet on the table and leaned back on
her chair. "Then shut up."

Hanlon laughed.

•

Battista began to see features on the core. It wasn't
just a sphere. It had a topography. There were oceans and
mountains and clouds. She was still falling terribly fast,
but she didn't feel afraid. She was headed right where she
needed to be. She saw the undulant Persian Gulf, the shining veins of the Tigris and Euphrates, and the grid of gold-
en lights that was Baghdad. She saw the cluster of buildings
in the Green Zone, the common lounge in her barracks
with the throbbing neon lights. Just a short stop on her way
home.

She landed in a chair across from her copilot, and
looked up from her beer.

"And what do you think is in the center?"

"Of what."

Hanlon waved her beer bottle up and around, looking at the room. "The hollow earth, bitch. The one we just
established."

"Eh. More hollowness."

"And you just keep falling."

"Yes. Through to Hawaii."

"But how do you brake on the other side? How do
you say, 'Here-wait-I'm-home-I-need-to-stop-here'?"

Battista let her head hang back over the top of her
chair, and closed her eyes. "I don't know. Maybe you have

to want it enough."

"But you can't want it too much. Otherwise you'll plummet through the crust and drift out into space forever."

"That would suck."

Hanlon looked away.

•

Battista dropped through the floor.

A film reel of rooms, floors and frames soon turned to darkness, and she was falling again through empty space.

She curled into a cannonball, holding herself and looking up. She felt all right. She was still falling, that's all. Clearly she just hadn't reached Hawaii yet.

She began to hear a whistling sound, which then split into many whistles, soft hurtling notes. She couldn't see anything in the darkness. But she could feel the presence of others around her. Then she began to see them—little pixels materializing in the darkness, suspended points of light, all around her. They were getting closer. She was in a shell of people falling, one shell in a thousand shells contracting, in an endless succession of contracting spheres.

A brighter planet rushed up to receive them.

•

"I had a dream about Baghdad," said Hanlon. "It was a new Baghdad."

"Tell me."

"Well, it wasn't spice and shit and dust like the one we know. All the buildings were made of mica, except, like, *gold*-colored mica. So the whole city glittered. And the streets went *over* the city—like, all the walkways to get from one place to another were across the tops of buildings, and if you ever wanted to go into a store or a butcher shop or someone's home, you would have to descend a set of stairs to get underneath."

"So the city was hollow."
"Yeah, sort of."

•

Battista alighted on the roof of a mosque in Baghdad.
She knew where she was. She could take this path left to go
to the carpet bazaar, or she could take the path right to go to
the river. She went right.

She walked along the sparkling ramparts. Those who
passed her had bright faces—they were the ones who had
fallen with her, the meteor-people, now remembering where
and who they were. They carried parcels of meat. They
smelled of sandalwood. They all had dinners to attend and
guests to prepare for. They smiled at her, kohl-lined eyes
crinkling, and she smiled back.

As she approached the river she saw her son come
running to her, calling Mama, Mama. Gauri was right
behind him, shielding his eyes from the sun. He kissed her
cheek and said to her: Battista, come home.

Battista went home with him.

They had a dinner of lamb, with guests.

They had a daughter and two more sons.

She worked as a mechanic and he taught martial arts.

They watched their children grow old and marry.

They retired to Hawaii, where the sea was more blue
than Battista believed possible, blue like a Clorox cocktail.

She said aloud, "This, too, is mostly space."

She fell through the sand, and on again into the
universe.

MONICA BYRNE is a writer, playwright, and performer based in Durham, North Carolina. In 2016, she delivered the first science fiction TED Talk on the main stage in Vancouver; in 2017, she hosted a series for ViceUK about humanity's relationship to the future. Her debut novel, *The Girl in the Road*, was awarded the James Tiptree Jr. Award, and her play *What Every Girl Should Know* has been produced in New York, Washington, San Francisco, Boston, and eight other cities. Until 2017, she was a playwright-in-residence with Little Green Pig Theatrical Concern; she is now building her own company, Mystery Meat, as well as finishing a new novel and a TV pilot. Her work is entirely funded by 500+ micro-patrons on Patreon, a platform that allows fans to directly support the artists they love,
at patreon.com/monicabyrne.

A Peculiar People

Betsy Curtis

IN the momentary privacy of the gentlemen's room, Fedrik Spens loosened the neck cord of his heavy white toga and reached for the threadlike platinum chain of his tiny adjuster key. Pulling back the pale plastissue skin from the almost invisible slit at the center of his chest, he inserted the key in the orifice of the olfactory intensificator and gave it two full turns. Three full turns for the food receptacle grinder. These official banquets could be murder. Removing the key, he retied the cord and approached the mirror, as the ambassador had insisted in last minute instructions to the several robots on the embassy staff.

"Normal respiration, human body temperature—" Fedrik could still hear the stentorian tones of the ambassador—"as there may be dancing after dinner. Check appearance carefully with a mirror. Martian security demands Terran ignorance of your mechanical nature!" (As if all of them hadn't lived like humans all their lives. It might be true, as some of the boys said, that the ambassador was subconsciously prejudiced.)

Coming out of the gentlemen's room, Spens found the ceremonial dinner procession already forming. His searching eyes found the little knot of attachés and he hurried to join his dinner partner, a statuesque blonde swathed in an ice-blue tissue tunic, and offered her his arm with appropriate compliments.

•

The great dinner was well under way when Fedrik, a little weary of small talk about Earth politics and fash-

85

ions, let his gaze wander down and up the long resplendent table and saw the girl. Her head, demurely inclined to listen attentively to the man on her left, showed hair black and smooth as a Martian dove's wing, drawn softly back to a great Spanish knot. He stared at the gently rounded cheek and chin, proud neck and exquisitely modeled shoulders rising from folds of shiny deep green stuff—shoulders, neck, and face of the color and texture of the brown yornith blossom.

Trying to seem casual, he asked the blonde who she was, and received the noncommittal reply that she was probably the wife of one of the undersecretaries, who, she stated flatly before returning to the succulent *ambaut roatel*, were seldom invited to State Department functions.

Attaché Spens turned from his uninformative dinner partner to the imposing lady on his left and wondered at the towering mass of white hair piled on her head before he looked at her eyes and asked his question again.

"Who?" she replied. "The girl in bottle-green sataffa? Sitting this side of your Martian Emissary of Finance? Why she's Gordon Lowrie's daughter—the Minister of Terran Agriculture, you know. He's sitting down there between Alice Farwell and Teresita Morgan." The white tower nodded almost imperceptibly down and across the table to Fedrik's left.

Fedrik looked covertly down the table where she gestured and noticed for the first time Gordon Lowrie's ageless face, the keen dark eyes, the smooth skin so dark a brown that the white, close-cropped hair seemed assumed for dramatic contrast. But not so dramatic as the daughter, Spens thought, as he stole a glance at the other end of the table.

He smoothed the magenta ribbon that crossed the glistening white folds on his chest, the ribbon that marked him as an attaché of the Martian Embassy, and smiled at the grande dame of the white hair-do. "The men in our department were jealous as anything when they found out I was coming to Earth. You earthwomen certainly outdo any of the rumors that reach us on Mars."

The lady inclined her white tower graciously, pleased. "We do have some pretty girls. But I'm sure," she added deprecatingly, "that half the effect is just seeing them in a different setting."

"No, I hate to say it, but our girls are mostly homely, like me. Attractive as anything, but homely." He grinned as she looked appraisingly at his straight red hair, craggy red brows, hawk nose and wide mouth. "You women all have a delicacy of feature that is a great pleasure to see."

White-tower's nose was tiny, straight, patrician. Spens looked down at his plate. "And the cooking. Is it always this good? I'm beginning to be sorry that I'm slated for only a year here."

"Randole is the treasure of the State Department," she informed him. "Good cooks are probably just as hard to come by here as on Mars. I hope some day you'll have a chance to eat with us at the Transport Hall. My husband, as you know, is Undersecretary Breton of Transport. We think our Ashil Blake as good as Randole, although Randole's *ambaut...*"

Fedrik stopped listening and began scheming.

•

Finding his quarry in the throng milling about the great silver ballroom was much easier than he had expected. His dinner partner had been claimed by her mustachioed husband as soon as they left the banquet hall; and as Spens circled the ballroom, he caught sight of Gordon Lowrie's white hair just beyond the shoulder of Bartok Borrl, the Martian finance chief. He joined the group casually, remarking deferentially to Borrl that the Terrans certainly put on a mighty splendid party and that "we'll have to work extra hard to give them a taste of Martian hospitality soon, won't we, sir?"

Borrl's eye searched the crowd for an instant, and it seemed to Fedrik that he performed the introductions with more than his usual enthusiasm. If fact, Fedrik had hardly begun to explain to Gordon Lowrie that he had wanted to meet him than his superior was excusing himself to the smiling girl and disappearing in the melee.

"My father," Fedrik continued, "was a tweedle and bradge farmer south of Jayfield and I grew up on the farm. He took his agricultural training here on Earth while the irrigation projects in his area were under construction; and I've always had a consuming curiosity about the Earth farms. Dad used to tell me and my brothers stories about cowboys and cattle ranching and miles of tall corn and plains of wheat rippling in the wind till we dreamt of it nights. We even used to have 'roundups' with bands of hoppy little tweedles and then throw them handfuls of bradoe and tell 'em to eat their corn and get fat now."

Anna Lowrie's laugh was a gay arpeggio.

"This part of the country is going to be a disappointment to you. Dad," she turned to Gordon "has a few acres of choice tobacco and a prize dairy, but no prairies and no cowboys. When he's on the warpath, he insists he's part Indian, but he never gets very wild."

"We have garden corn, too, but it's Dwarf Pearl and we wouldn't think of casting it before swine," added Lowrie's rich baritone.

"Well, anyhow, maybe you'll give me the address of a cow so I can tell my brothers, Donnel and Rone, that I've really seen one when I get back," Fedrik requested.

"Anna," said Gordon, "I wonder if this poor, ignorant, earnest, young man ..."

"This seeker for wider experience, Father?"

"Exactly! Isn't it our duty to broaden his knowledge as well as to behave toward the stranger in our midst with diplomatic hospitality?"

"Mr. Spens," Anna's smile was infectious, "Daddy would like to invite you to become personally acquainted with one or several of our cows. Klover Korzybski Kreamline Garth would be charmed to know you, though you may prefer Altamont Daybird Fennerhaven, she being the petite Jersey type."

Gordon Lowrie frowned thoughtfully. "Of course, you'll have to meet them at their hours. Early morning, that is. What time do you have to be at the office?"

Fedrik was suddenly aware of his internal food chopper grinding away at speed three. "Oh, not much before eleven," he said as nonchalantly as he could.

"Then you could come right home with us now and visit with their highnesses at crack of day tomorrow and still have plenty of time to get back to stern realities by eleven." Anna was persuasive.

Fedrik could feel something, his little plans jumping up and down in his head. "Oh, but ..." he gestured toward the great shining floor where couples were turning in the slow ellipses of the xerxia, "I couldn't think of taking you away from here so early. Wouldn't you really like to dance?" He could even sacrifice the pleasure of looking at her for the pleasure of hearing more of her delicate contralto voice.

"Not tonight," she responded at once. "And everybody's used to my leaving early. I'm a government sculptress and my studio opens at eight, not eleven."

"You mean you do busts for halls of fame and bas-reliefs for post-offices and things like that?"

"Well ... that's close enough. Anyhow, do come. We practically promised Mother to bring home something or someone from the party, didn't we, Dad?"

"Solemn promise, Annie. You're trapped, Mr. Spens. Trapped by two fiendishly exacting women. We'll meet you up at the copter stage as soon as we can find our robes," and Lowrie took his daughter's hand to leave the room as if there were no more to be said.

Fedrik hurried to the gentlemen's room where he had left his downy black fur robe. Fortunately the room was again empty, and he turned off the empty grinder with considerable relief. Then out and up the ramp to the copter stage.

•

The thirty-minute copter trip seemed like ten to the young Martian as Anna and Gordon drew out the story of his winters at Jayfield Union School and Donnel's phoenix fair and Rone and Betha's trip to deep space.

At the house, Anna and her father left him to find her mother. Fedrik had only a few moments to look about at the deep, walnut-paneled room and notice the many stringed instruments lying about on tables and the top of the great black piano, the books, looking in the glow of many lamps like jewels, ruby, ultramarine, garnet, in their cases set into the paneling, the sedate smile of an old portrait, and the high, many-arched window. Anna entered almost at once, followed by a wheel chair pushed by Gordon Lowrie, which contained, feather-wool afghan across her knees, a lady in a rose sataffa wrap. Gordon eased the chair down the two broad steps to the lower level and Fedrik approached the chair.

"Mother," Lowrie bent over the chair, "this is Fedrik Spans from the Martian Embassy." He straightened. "Fedrik, this is my wife, Janet Lowrie."

Spens looked down into the sweet dark face. "So very glad, Mrs. Lowrie ..."

"My name is Janet." The fine lines of a smile spread to her thin dark cheeks from the corners of clear brown eyes as she held out her hand. Fedrik took it and found the gentle pressure drawing him down to a chair beside her. "I won't ask you for your first impressions of Earth or what you think of Terran Woman." Fedrik grinned. "Gordon tells me that your father was a farmer; and presently we should like to hear about the Martian farm, but first let's have some real Brazilian coffee. Gordon?"

"At once, dear." He went back up the steps and out through the wide doorway.

Anna came to the other side of the chair and took her mother's other hand. "Mother's a sculptress, too, Fedrik, not a chronic invalid. She had a little accident at the studio a few weeks ago, but she's almost through with the wheel chair."

"A dangerous profession?" he asked, grave-faced, looking at the perfect modeling of Anna's head and shoulders.

"Oh, no," she answered quickly. "A beaker of ... of ... solution fell and broke on her foot and an infection set in. By the way," her free hand waved about the room, "do you like music, and do you play a viol by any strange chance?"

"I could probably wring a tune out of this one," He rose and crossed to lift a viola d'aubade from the top of the piano. "I was the star," he bowed to the ladies, "of our grade-school orchestra. Though I'm afraid I haven't played a note since."

"Daddy wrote a lovely xerxia for three viols the other day," Anna was setting up stands and handed Janet a tiny violette whose pale patina shone from use. "Let's surprise him with it."

The sweet sonority of the trio greeted Gordon's return. When the piece was finished, he set the tray before Anna and said, "Bravo, Fed. I like that even if I did write it myself. Do you know any of those rousing Martian frontier songs? *Out Along the Rim*, *In Ellberg Town*, or *Her Six-Ton Boots?*"

"Sure, but it's been so long since I held a viol that I don't think I could sing them and accompany at the same time."

Janet laughed. "Well, drink your coffee now and afterwards Anna can fake the harmony on the piano while you roar out those wonderful words."

Despite the cows and Anna's studio, it was one-thirty when Gordon showed Fedrik his room. An evening to remember for its fullness.

•

Skillfully as usual, Fedrik maneuvered the copter he had rented by the month, for the express purpose of bringing Anna home from the studio, down to the stage on the roof of the George Willis Public School to pick up Bud and Sukie, Anna's young brother and sister.

Bud waved from the crowd of children at the top of the ramp and bounded over to the copter yelling, "Hi Fed, hi, Annie," at the top of his seven-year-old lungs. Sukie, six,

as tall as Bud, followed more demurely and had to be boost-
ed in, clutching a coloring book in one hand and holding a
bright splashy painting on newsprint in the other.

"Hi, kids. Home James, huh?" greeted Fedrik.

"Give her fifty gees and slam for the ranch!" hooted
Bud from the back seat, while Sukie cuddled down on Anna's lap in the front and began a long "D'ya know what…"
description of her school day to her older sister, who sat
smiling and listening carefully.

Fed was glad he did not have to make talk as the
copter carried them swiftly toward the Lowries'. This
was probably the last trip, though the kids didn't know it.
Neither did Anna. Nobody but himself had heard his go-
ing-over from the ambassador only an hour before.

"The Lowrie girl, Mr. Spens," the ambassador always
came straight to the point with his subordinates in spite of
his reputation as an interplanetary diplomat, "you're seeing
a great deal of her these days."

"Yes, indeed, sir."

"That's hardly fair, Spens. Not fair to her if she's a
tenth as sweet and affectionate as I imagine she is; not fair
to us because there's an ever present danger that anyone
who knows you too well will find out that we have robots
on our staff and draw the obvious conclusion that there
are many of your kind on Mars. It's only human nature,
you know to be afraid of machines, and what men fear
they fight."

"Yes, sir, but …"

"Interplanetary suspicion isn't likely to be aroused
by a girl's being jilted by a young man; but I don't want it
to go even that far. Lowrie's an important man to us you
know. We're still importing more than a fifth of our food,
thanks to the fact that Earth farmers feel they can trust him.
He's got to trust us."

"But sir, Miss Lowrie's not in love with me. It's true
of course that I've been going out there to see her, but I
want to be with her family, too. It's a family, sir, and they do
things together—sing and talk and plan things like… like
a garden… or a new cow barn… it's so… well… unlonely.

It's more like having a new father and mother. I'm sure they don't suspect anything." He hoped wildly that the ambassador couldn't suspect how much he needed Anna's incredibly friendly self.

The Ambassador's face softened for a moment, his eyes looked far out the window. "Fathers and mothers have very sharp eyes, son. You love your Mars family too well to threaten their existence by a war, don't you? If I can't convince you that nobody on earth can hold your secret safely and that you must give up the Lowries, I'll have to ship you back home on the next flight. You'll have to get your music at concerts and your talk at receptions or not at all around here. That's all."

"Yes, sir. But may I take Miss Lowrie home this afternoon? She's expecting me."

"Of course. But make it brief. You can tell them that you've got a new assignment that's going to take a lot of time. Thank them nicely. Remember, we need Lowrie's good will."

Fedrik landed the copter gently in the plot by the house. The children dashed off into the interior and he followed Anna slowly into the paneled music room as usual. Anna slipped into her favorite chair and he brought her a frosty green glass of minth from the kulpour on a side-table.

Before he could get words in order, Sukie popped into the room around the corner of the door, barefooted in a tattered old red plaid dress. "Look at me quick," she giggled and danced and bobbed about, then back to the door. "Just wait a minute now. You don't have to shut your eyes." She popped out.

In a moment she was back, resplendent in a ballet frock of spangled net, a star in her ebony curls, shining silveglas slippers on her twinkling feet. Bud followed her in reluctantly, swathed in a long mauve cape which did not entirely hide mauve knee-breeches. Sukie laughed at him gently, trillingly. "Daddy says I'm his queen of the starlings—and Bud and I are playing Cinderella. Do you like me?"

"I couldn't help myself, your majesty," Fedrik

dropped gallantly to one knee and held out his hand as the little girl twirled about him.

Anna ran to the piano and added a few bars of the *Butterfly Étude* to the fun. Bud grinned condescendingly down at the kneeling Fedrik. Sukie stopped her whirling and laughed at Bud.

"You look so silly for a prince with all those teeth out," she said.

Fedrik got awkwardly to his feet. "Why Sukie, you'll look just as silly in a year or so when yours begin to drop," he observed.

"Oh, no, I shan't. Mine aren't going to drop," she stated saucily.

Anna got up. Her voice seemed cold. "Susan Lowrie, you know better than to say such things. Tell Bud you're sorry you teased him and then run along and play Cinderella in the nursery."

"I'm sorry, Bud." Sukie was half penitent. She followed him to the door, then turned back to Fedrik defiantly. "Just the same, I'm never going to look silly and my teeth aren't ever going to drop," and she was gone.

"Kids," Fedrik smiled, returning to the sofa, "always so jealous of their dignity."

Anna went back to her chair, stood behind it grasping the back. "Sukie mustn't learn to enjoy teasing Bud," she said quietly. "Everybody has some dignity. Bud's a right guy, but he can get perfectly miserable when he thinks he's not living up to what that little minx expects of him. Sue's got to learn to be fair."

That word *fair* again. Fed looked about the room and seemed to feel a wrench somewhere in the vicinity of his grinder. He searched his synapses for the thing to say and heard his voice, wistful, "You love children, don't you, Anna?"

Her face went blank. Her eyes stared at him. Her voice was empty. "Yes, Fedrik, I suppose I do." She walked around the tapestried chair and continued toward the steps and the door. "Please excuse me." Her voice seemed faint, confused. When she reached the door she was moving rapidly; and Fed imagined that she was running after she turned into the hall.

He had not had a chance to rise before she was gone; and he leaned forward to put his head in his hands, an unconscious imitation of Gerel Spens, who had sat like this when he was baffled.

His fingers had barely met at his temples when Janet Lowrie came through the door and down the steps, steadying herself on her husband's arm. Fedrik pulled himself off the sofa and stood up. Gordon Lowrie assisted Janet to a tall carved chair and sat down on the arm of it. "Sit down, please, Fedrik."

Fedrik sat down.

"What was the matter with Anna, Fed? She came running out of here as if something were after her." Janet's voice was full of deep concern.

"Really, Janet, I don't know. We were talking about Bud and Sukie and suddenly she just said 'excuse me' and went out."

"Can you remember exactly what you said before she went?" asked Lowrie. "I have a particular reason for wanting to know."

"I... I... well, I guess I said she loved children, didn't she."

"Oh." Janet's dark face was full of pain and she reached for Gordon's hand where it lay on his knee.

Gordon took hers, clasped it. He looked at Fedrik. "I don't want to sound like the stern medieval father, Fedrik, Spens, but I want to know if you are in love with Anna."

Here it was. There was no escape from finding words this time. Fed wondered what the ambassador would have said in his place. He tried to sit straight and matter of fact on the sofa, but it was too soft and he seemed to be wriggling deeper in the cushions.

"I'll tell you, Gordon, but it'll have to be in a sort of round-about way."

Gordon Lowrie's white head nodded, but otherwise he sat motionless.

"My father wanted to be an artist—a painter—but

Mars needed farmers and his... his responsibilities combined with what amounted to orders from the government
made him come here for training and then move out and
start a family in the thick bradge country. When I used to
go around with him he was always... exulting over colors
and shadings and forms. He even used to bring home twigs
of dry bradge and put them in bowls and sketch them;
and when the brown and mauve yornith blossomed in the
spring we used to have expeditions to the little valleys to
bring home a few for a special celebration. Well, Gordon,
Anna is lovely like all the things Dad showed me, and I
wanted to make a special celebration for her."

Gordon glanced proudly down at Janet, who smiled
up, then both turned back to Fed.

"And when I got to know her she was such a friendly encouraging sort of person and... and she had you. I
don't know how to put it, but there's something about this
house full of things you like to use and the children who
don't look at you twice except as a welcome audience and
ally... and... well... Anna is my friend. I guess that's not exactly love but there it is." He wondered how anybody could
make such a lame speech as that. Gordon's face was still
serious, but he seemed somehow relieved. "It's hard, son,
but that's how we hoped it was. Not love yet. Because we're
going to have to ask you to see very little of us for a while."

("For the love of..." thought Fed, "they're going to
do the breaking off and it's out of my hands." His relief was
followed by the thought of the utter absence of Anna.) "Of
course, if you say so, but I don't understand..."

"We want you to understand," Gordon said kindly,
"and we want you to know because you're like one of the
family and we don't want you to feel that we've cast you
out. But the story of the reason is what all our government
offices call a security risk: and once you know it, we could
hardly let you go back to Mars." He looked hopefully at the
young Martian.

"I'm afraid you'd better not tell me, Gordon," Fedrik
replied regretfully, firmly. "The ambassador told me today
that I was slated for a special mission back any day. I only

came this afternoon to break the news and say goodbye."

"Would you like to stay, Fed?" Janet asked sympathetically. "Even if it meant not coming here for a while... that is, until Anna's married or living somewhere else?"

A soft, low voice broke in. "What about Anna, Mother? Are you planning to get rid of me?" No one had noticed her come so slowly through the door and down the two shallow carpeted steps.

Fedrik jumped and turned his head. Janet raised a beckoning hand and Anna went to sit on the other arm of her mother's chair. "What about Anna?"

"Wait a bit, dear," said Janet.

Gordon addressed Fedrik again. "I have papers in my study, Fed, that need only my signature to declare you a security risk for Earth and require that you stay here. And we really need men like you. There are a dozen excellent jobs. You can have your pick. And when you understand about us you'll probably find you want to stay and help anyway."

Fedrik sat motionless for a moment, flooded with a thought of gruesome humor... a security risk to both sides would be... well... too great a risk. He could imagine the interminable delicate argument between the ambassador and the President of Earth as to who was to conduct the disassembly, which side have the doubtful privilege of short-circuiting his synapses.

Gordon seemed to interpret Fedrik's silence as indecision. "There's Earth security, Fedrik, and Mars security: and then there's human security. I guess that really comes first; and that's why we need to tell you and have you understand."

Fed's memory cells flashed him a sudden picture of his father and of Betha, his father's only human child; and a feeling of affection and pity for their weakness, their kindness and their vast lovely dreams seemed mixed with the very metal of his bones. "Human security. Yes."

"So as one human being to another, I must tell you of your duties as a man as well as your privileges."

(His father had explained duty to him and Donnel

and Rone so they'd understand about Betha.)

"You see, Susan and Anna here are—are our daughters, but they're not human like Bud. They're what you and Martians would think of as robots. Please don't interrupt me yet," as he saw Fed's mouth open.

"Because of the emigrations to other planets and an inexplicably declining birth rate, we came to depend more and more on intelligent machines in almost all kinds of work. And as we began to depend on them we began to be afraid—afraid of their alienness—afraid that they wouldn't always see things our way—afraid that some day we should have to choose between giving them up entirely, destroying them, or having them give us up entirely as poor, weak, selfish things who didn't deserve to clutter up their earth. We found out that we'd have to make friends of them, sons and daughters as well as bridge partners and copter mechanics... personalities that had to develop slowly like us, who understood and sympathized with us, no matter how much easier and more interesting and productive physical existence might be for them than for us. They had to love humanness. That's one reason why they look like humans. Both Janet and Anna," he smiled down, "are body sculptors. Janet made Anna almost as truly as if she were her real flesh-and-blood offspring.

"You're probably wondering now where the human security comes into the picture, what you and I are bound to do. Well... humans are a peculiar people with peculiarly human capabilities. We're bound to be fathers if we can—fathers of human children and mechanical, to grow up together under the most intelligent and loving care we can give them. Robots may be parents of robots here, but it's not the same. That's why you have a great duty that is not to Anna."

Anna added earnestly, "That's why I scolded Sukie, you see, Fed. She mustn't ever make Bud feel inferior—a feeling he might take out on his mechanical children some day. Of course Sukie's teeth won't ever drop out, although she will change her body every year for the next ten or eleven. We have our responsibilities too, in understanding you and in doing well the things we are made so well to do."

Fed traced the pattern in the wine carpet to the wall and back with his eyes as Gordon finished his revelation.

"And last of all comes interplanetary security," Gordon concluded firmly, sadly. "Your young cultures are still expanding and you rely on men still, not machines. As you can all too easily see, Mars would fear, and, when her economy is more self-sustaining, she would fight what she would think of as the alien invasion of Earth. She might try to rescue a few Janets, a few Gordons, from what she would consider the domination of unhuman interests; but most Earth humans as well as our dear foster children would be doomed. Because we humans have learned not to be type-gregarious. There are no associations here whose membership is more than about a quarter human. Janet and I have had two earlier families: this makes four children of our bodies, fifteen children given to us by the government. You must stay with us, Fedrik Spens, because you understand from knowing Anna what we can do here and why it must not be destroyed."

Martian stood up to face Earthman. He spoke deliberately but without feeling. "Settling the interplanetary angle will be even harder than you think... although I'm glad you told me. I imagine with care we can keep it between a few men at the top and me."

Gordon's dark face took on a shade of gray, not brown. "You don't mean that you're going to tell your ambassador?"

"It may be the best thing to do," was the reply, as Fedrik opened the neck of his conservative dark green toga and exposed the pale skin of his chest. He fumbled for the slit and pulled the edges back to show the adjustor orifices, the silver plate bearing his name and serial number. "I represent more than one security risk."

He retied the neck cord and smiled a little at last. "If

I'm not officially disassembled, I might even marry Anna. That is, if she'll have me."

Anna rose and held out her hand, which he grasped as if never to let go.

Gordon began to laugh, convulsively, until he saw that Janet was weeping. He tightened his arm around her shoulders.

"I wouldn't worry about disassembly," he said. "I think your ambassador and I can make plans to write you into the charter at last without having anything to hide. And do you really want to get married?"

Two human-type mechanical faces looked only at each other.

"Then, Annie, you bring me home a parentage application form from the studio tomorrow. I'll qualify you as parents first class."

"Anna," Fedrik asked, "will you make all our kids look just like you?"

"Personally, I rather fancy craggy red-haired people."

" 'People' ..." Gordon Lowrie murmured to his wife. There were tenderness and wonder and amusement in the quotation marks with which he enclosed the word.

Janet smiled up at him. "Well?" she asked.

BETSY CURTIS (1917-2002) was an author of short science fiction and poetry primarily published from the 1950s through the 1970s. "A Peculiar People" was reprinted in *The Best Science Fiction Stories: 1952*, and her story "The Steiger Effect" (1968) was nominated for the Hugo award in 1969. Her works appeared in numerous publications, including *Amazing Science Fiction, Analog Science Fiction & Fact, The Magazine of Fantasy and Science Fiction, Galaxy Science Fiction, Planet Stories, Marvel Science Stories*, and *Star*Line*.

My Mother, Dancing

Nancy Kress

Fermi's Paradox, California, 1950: Since planet formation appears to be common, and since the processes that lead to the development of life are a continuation of those that develop planets, and since the development of life leads to intelligence and intelligence to technology-then why hasn't a single alien civilization contacted Earth?

Where is everybody?

•

THEY had agreed, laughing, on a form for the millennium contact, what Micah called "human standard," although Kabil had insisted on keeping hirs konfol and Deb had not dissolved hirs crest, which waved three inches above hirs and hummed. But, then, Deb! Ling had designed floating baktor for the entire ship, red and yellow mostly, that combined and recombined in kaleidoscopic loveliness only Ling could have programmed. The viewport was set to magnify, the air mixture just slightly intoxicating, the tinglies carefully balanced by Cal, that master. Ling had wanted "natural" sleep cycles, but Cal's argument had been more persuasive, and the tinglies massaged the limbic so pleasantly. Even the child had some. It was a party.

The ship slipped into orbit around the planet, a massive subJovian far from its sun, streaked with muted color. "Lovely," breathed Deb, who lived for beauty.

Cal, the biologist, was more practical: "I ran the equations; by now there should be around 200,000 of them in the rift, if the replication rate stayed constant."

"Why wouldn't it?" said Ling, the challenger, and

the others laughed. The tinglies really were a good idea.

The child, Harrah, pressed hirs face to the window. "When can we land?"

The adults smiled at each other. They were so proud of Harrah, and so careful. Hirs was the first gene-donate for all of them except Micah, and probably the only one for the rest except Cal, who was a certified intellect donor. Kabil knelt beside Harrah, bringing hirs face to the child's height.

"Little love, we can't land. Not here. We must see the creations in holo."

"Oh," Harrah said, with the universal acceptance of childhood. It had not changed in five thousand years, Ling was fond of remarking, that child idea that whatever it lived was the norm. But, then... Ling.

"Access the data," Cal said, and Harrah obeyed, reciting it aloud as hirs parents had all taught hirs. Ling smiled to see that Harrah still closed hirs eyes to access, but opened them to recite.

"The creations were dropped on this planet 273 E-years ago. They were the one-hundred-fortieth drop in the Great Holy Mission that gives us our life. The creations were left in a closed-system rift... what does that mean?"

"The air in the creations' valley doesn't get out to the rest of the planet, because the valley is so deep and the gravity so great. They have their own air."

"Oh. The creations are cyborged replicators, programmed for self-awareness. They are also programmed to expect human contact at the millennium. They..."

"Enough," said Kabil, still kneeling beside Harrah. Hirs stroked hirs hair, black today." The important thing, Harrah, is that you remember that these creations are beings, different from us but with the same life force, the only life force. They must be respected, just as people are, even if they look odd to you."

"Or if they don't know as much as you," said Cal. "They won't, you know."

"I know," Harrah said. They had made hirs an accommodater, with strong genes for bonding. They already had Ling for challenge. Harrah added, "Praise Fermi and

Kwang and Arlbeni for the emptiness of the universe."

Ling frowned. Hirs had opposed teaching Harrah the simpler, older folklore of the Great Mission. Ling would have preferred that the child receive only truth, not religion. But Deb had insisted. Feed the imagination first, hirs had said, and later Harrah can separate science from prophecy. But the tinglies felt sweet, and the air mixture was set for a party, and hirs own baktors floated in such graceful pattern that Ling, even Ling, could not quarrel.

"I wonder," Deb said dreamily, "what they have learned in 273 years."

"When will they holo?" Harrah said. "Are we there yet?"

•

Our mother is coming.

Two hours more and they will come, from beyond the top of the world. When they come, there will be much dancing. Much rejoicing. All of us will dance, even those who have detached and let the air carry them away. Those ones will receive our transmissions and dance with us.

Or maybe our mother will also transmit to where those of us now sit. Maybe they will transmit to all, even those colonies out of our own transmission range. Why not? Our mother, who made us, can do whatever is necessary.

First, the dancing. Then, the most necessary thing of all. Our mother will solve the program flaw. Completely, so that no more of us will die. Our mother doesn't die. We are not supposed to die, either. Our mother will transmit the program to correct this.

Then the dancing there will be!

•

Kwang's Resolution, Bohr Station, 2552: Since the development of the Quantum Transport, humanity has visited nearly a thousand planets in our galaxy and surveyed many more. Not one of them has developed any life of any kind, no matter how simple.

Not one.

No aliens have contacted Earth because there is nobody else out there.

•

Harrah laughed in delight. Hirs long black hair swung through a drift of yellow baktors."The creations look like oysters!"

The holocube showed uneven rocky ground through thick, murky air. A short distance away rose the abrupt, steep walls of the rift, thousands of feet high. Attached to the ground by thin, flexible, mineral-conducting tubes were hundreds of uniform, metal-alloy double shells. The shells held self-replicating nanomachinery, including the rudi-mentary AI, and living eukaryotes sealed into selectively permeable membranes. The machinery ran on the feeble sunlight and on energy produced by anaerobic bacteria, carefully engineered for the thick atmospheric stew of methane, hydrogen, helium, ammonia, and carbon dioxide.

The child knew none of this. Hirs saw the "oysters" jumping up in time on their filaments, jumping and falling, flapping their shells open and closed, twisting and flapping and bobbing. Dancing.

Kabil laughed, too. "Nowhere in the original pro-gramming! They learned it!"

"But what could the stimulus have been?" Ling said. "How lovely to find out!"

"Sssshhh, we're going to transmit," Micah said. Hirs eyes glowed. Micah was the oldest of them all; hirs had been on the original drop. "Seeding 140, are you there?"

"We are here! We are Seeding 140! Welcome, our mother!"

Harrah jabbed hirs finger at the holocube."We're not your mother!"

Instantly Deb closed the transmission. Micah said harshly, "Harrah! Your manners!"

The child looked scared. Deb said, "Harrah, we talked about this. The creations are not like us, but their ideas are as true as ours, on their own world. Don't laugh at them."

From Kabil, "Don't you remember, Harrah? Access the learning session!"

"I... remember," Harrah faltered.

"Then show some respect!" Micah said. "This is the Great Mission!"

Harrah's eyes teared. Kabil, the tender-hearted, put hirs hand on Harrah's shoulder. "Small heart, the Great Mission gives meaning to our lives."

"I... know..."

Micah said, "You don't want to be like those people who just use up all their centuries in mere pleasure, with no structure to their wanderings across the galaxy, no purpose beyond seeing what the nanos can produce that they haven't produced before, no difference between today and tomorrow, no—"

"That's sufficient," Ling says. "Harrah understands, and regrets. Don't give an Arlbeni Day speech, Micah."

Micah said stiffly, "It matters, Ling."

"Of course it matters. But so do the creations, and they're waiting. Deb, open the transmission again... Seeding 140, thank you for your welcome! We return!"

•

Arlbeni's Vision, Planet Cadrys, 2678: We have been fools.

Humanity is in despair. Nano has given us everything, and nothing. Endless pleasures empty of effort, endless tomorrows empty of purpose, endless experiences empty of meaning. From evolution to sentience, sentience to nano, nano to the decay of sentience.

But the fault is ours. We have overlooked the greatest gift ever given humanity: the illogical emptiness of the universe. It is against evolution, it is against known physical processes. Therefore, how can it exist? And why?

It can exist only by the intent of something greater than the physical processes of the universe. A conscious Intent. The reason can only be to give humanity, the universe's sole inheritor, knowledge of this Intent. The emptiness of the universe—anomalous, unexplainable, impossible—has been left for us to discover, as the only convincing proof of God.

•

Our mother has come! We dance on the seabed. We transmit the news to the ones who have detached and floated away. We rejoice together, and consult the original program.

"You are above the planetary atmosphere," we say, new words until just this moment, but now understood. All will be understood now, all corrected. "You are in a ship, as we are in our shells."

"Yes," our mother says. "You know we cannot land."

"Yes," we say, and there is momentary dysfunction. How can they help us if they cannot land? But only momentary. This is our mother. And they landed us here once, didn't they? They can do whatever is necessary.

Our mother says, "How many are you now, Seeding 140?"

"We are 79,432," we say. Sadness comes. We endure it, as we must.

Our mother's voice changes in wavelength, in frequency. "Seventy-nine thousand? Are you... we had calculated more. Is this replication data right?"

A packet of data arrives. We scan it quickly; it matches our programming.

"The data is correct, our mother. That is the rate of replication. But..." We stop. It feels like another dying ceremony, suddenly, and it is not yet time for a dying ceremony. We will wait another few minutes; we will tell our mother in another few minutes. Instead, we ask, "What is your rate of replication, our mother?"

Another change in wavelength and frequency. We scan and match data, and it is in our databanks: laughter, a form of rejoicing. Our mother rejoices.

"You aren't equipped for visuals, or I would show you our replicant," our mother says. "But the rate is much,

much lower than yours. We have one new replicant with us on the ship."

"Welcome, new replicant!" we say, and there is more rejoicing. There, and here.

•

"I've restricted transmission... there's the t-field's visual," Micah said.

A hazy cloud appeared to one side of the holocube, large enough to hold two people comfortably, three close together. Now only words spoken inside the field would transmit. Baktors scuttled clear of the ionized haze. Deb stepped inside the field, with Harrah; Cal moved out of it. Hirs frowned at Micah.

"They can't be only 79,000-plus if the rate of replication has held steady. Check the resource data, Micah."

"Scanning... no change in available raw materials... no change in sunlight per square unit."

"Scan their counting program."

"I already did. Fully functional."

"Then run an historical scan of replicants created."

"That will take time... there, it's started. What about attrition?"

Cal said, "Of course. I should have thought of that. Do a seismic survey and match it with the original data. A huge quake could easily have destroyed two-thirds of them, poor seedings..."

Ling said, "You could ask them."

Kabil said, "If it's not a cultural taboo. Remember, they have had time to evolve a culture. We gave them that ability."

"Only in response to environmental stimuli. Would a quake or mudslide create enough stimulus pressure to evolve death taboos?"

They looked at each other. Something new in the universe, something humanity had not created... this was why they were here! Their eyes shone, their breaths came faster. Yet they were uncomfortable, too, at the mention of death. How long since any of them... oh, yes, Ling's clone, in that computer malfunction, but so many decades ago... Discomfort, excitement, compassion for Seeding 140, yes, compassion most of all, how terrible if the poor creations had actually lost so many in a quake... All of them felt it, and meant it, the emotion was genuine. And in their minds the finger of God touched each for a moment, with the holiness of the tiny human struggle against the emptiness of the universe.

"Praise Fermi and Kwang and Arlbeni..." one of them murmured, and no one was sure who, in the general embarrassment that took them a moment later. They were not children.

Micah said, "Match the seismic survey with the original data," and moved off to savor alone the residue of natural transcendence, rarest and strangest of the few things nano could not provide.

Inside the hazy field Harrah said, "Seeding! I am dancing just like you!" and moved hirs small body back and forth, up and down on the ship's deck.

•

Arlbeni's Vision, Planet Cadrys, 2678: In the proof of God lies its corollary. The Great Intent has left the universe empty, except for us. It is our mission to fill it.

Look around you, look at what we've become. At the pointless destruction, the aimless boredom, the spiritual despair. The human race cannot exist without purpose, without vision, without faith. Filling the emptiness of the universe will rescue us from our own.

•

Our mother says, "Do you play any games?"

We examine the data carefully. There is no match.

Our mother speaks again. "That was our new replicant speaking, Seeding 140. Hirs is only half-created as yet, and hirs language program is not fully functional. Hirs means, of the new programs you have you created for your-selves since the original seeding, which ones are in response to the environment? Are expressions of rejoicing? Like dancing?"

"Yes!" we say. "We dance in rejoicing. And we also throw pebbles in rejoicing and catch pebbles in rejoicing. But not for many years since."

"Do it now!" our mother says.

This is our mother. We are not rejoicing. But this is our mother. We pick up some pebbles.

"No," our mother says quickly, "you don't need to throw pebbles. That was the new replicant again. Hirs does not yet understand that seedings do what they wish, and only what they wish. Your... your mother does not com-mand you. Anything you do, anything you have learned, is as necessary as what we do."

"I'm sorry again," our mother says, and there is physical movement registered in the field of transmission.

We do not understand. But our mother has spoken of new programs, of programs created since the seeding, in response to the environment. This we understand, and now is the time to tell our mother of our need. Our mother has asked. Sorrow floods us, rejoicing disappears, but now is the time to tell what is necessary.

Our mother will make all functional once more.

•

"Don't scold hirs like that, hirs is just a child," Kabil said. "Harrah, stop crying, we know you didn't mean to impute to them any inferiority."

Micah, hirs back turned to the tiny parental drama, said to Cal, "Seismic survey complete. No quakes, only the most minor geologic disturbances... really, the local history shows remarkable stability."

"Then what accounts for the difference between their count of themselves and the replication rate?"

"It can't be a real difference."

"But... oh! Listen. Did they just say—"

Hirs turned slowly toward the holocube.

Harrah said at the same moment, through hirs tears, "They stopped dancing."

Cal said, "Repeat that," remembered hirself, and moved into the transmission field, replacing Harrah. "Repeat that, please, Seeding 140. Repeat your last transmission."

The motionless metal oysters said, "We have created a new program in response to the Others in the environment. The Others who destroy us."

Cal said, too pleasantly, "'Others'? What Others?"

"The new ones. The mindless ones. The destroyers."

"There are no others in your environment," Micah said. "What are you trying to say?"

Ling, across the deck in a cloud of pink bakterons, said, "Oh, oh... no... they must have divided into factions. Invented warfare among themselves! Oh..."

Harrah stopped sobbing and stood, wide-eyed, on hirs sturdy short legs.

Cal said, still very pleasant, "Seeding 140, show us these Others. Transmit visuals."

"But if we get close enough to the Others to do that, we will be destroyed!"

Ling said sadly, "It is warfare."

Deb compressed hirs beautiful lips. Kabil turned away, to gaze out at the stars. Micah said, "Seeding... do you have any historical transmissions of the Others, in your databanks? Send those."

"Scanning... sending."

Ling said softly, "We always knew warfare was a possibility for any creations. After all, they have our DNA, and for millennia..." Hirs fell silent.

"The data is only partial," Seeding 140 said. "We were nearly destroyed when it was sent to us. But there is one data packet until the last few minutes of life."

The cheerful, dancing oysters had vanished from the holocube. In their place appeared the fronds of a tall, thin plant, waving slightly in the thick air. It was stark, unadorned, elemental. A multicellular organism rooted in the rocky ground, doing nothing.

No one on the ship spoke.

The holocube changed perspective, to a wide scan. Now there were whole stands of fronds, acres of them, filling huge sections of the rift. Plant after plant, drab olive green, blowing in the unseen wind.

After the long silence, Seeding 140 said, "Our mother? The Others were not there for ninety-two years. Then they came. They replicate much faster than we do, and we die. Our mother, can you do what is necessary?"

Still no one spoke, until Harrah, frightened, said, "What is it?"

Micah answered, hirs voice clipped and precise. "According to the data packet, it is an aerobic organism, using a process analogous to photosynthesis to create energy, giving off oxygen as a by-product. The data includes a specimen analysis, broken off very abruptly as if the AI failed. The specimen is non-carbon-based, non-DNA. The energy sources sealed in Seeding 140 are anaerobic."

Ling said sharply, "Present oxygen content of the rift atmosphere?"

Cal said, "Seven point six two percent." Hirs paused. "The oxygen created by these... these 'Others' is poisoning the seeding."

"But," Deb said, bewildered, "why did the original drop include such a thing?"

"It didn't," Micah said. "There is no match for this structure in the gene banks. It is not from Earth."

"Our mother?" Seeding 140 said, over the motionless fronds in the holocube. "Are you still there?"

•

Disciple Arlbeni, Grid 743.9, 2999: As we approach this millennium marker, rejoice that humanity has passed beyond both spiritual superstition and spiritual denial. We have a faith built on physical truth, on living genetics, on human need. We have, at long last, given our souls not to a formless Deity but to the science of life itself. We are safe, and we are blessed.

•

Micah said suddenly, "It's a trick."

The other adults stared at hirs. Harrah had been hastily reconfigured for sleep. Someone—Ling, most likely—had dissolved the floating baktors and blanked the wall displays, and only the empty transmission field added color to the room. That, and the cold stars beyond.

"Yes," Micah continued, "a trick. Not malicious, of course. But we programmed them to learn, and they did. They had some seismic event, or some interwarfare, and it made them wary of anything unusual. They learned that the unusual can be deadly. And the most unusual thing they know of is us, set to return at year 3000. So they created a transmission program designed to repel us. Xenophobia, in a stimulus-response learning program suited to this environment. You said it yourself, Ling, the learning components are built on human genes. And we have xenophobia as an evolved survival response!"

Cal jack-knifed across the room. Tension turned hirs ungraceful. "No. That sounds appealing, but nothing we gave Seeding 140 would let them evolve defenses that sophisticated. And there was no seismic event for the initial stimulus."

Micah said eagerly, "We're the stimulus! Our anticipated return! Don't you see... we're the 'Others'!"

Kabil said, "But they call us 'mother'... They were thrilled to see us. They're not xenophobic to us."

Deb spoke so softly the others could barely hear. "Then it's a computer malfunction. Cosmic bombardment of their sensory equipment. Or at least, of the unit that was 'dying.' Malfunctioning before the end. All that sensory data about oxygen poisoning is compromised."

"Of course!" Ling said. But hirs was always honest. "At least... no, compromised data isn't that coherent, the pieces don't fit together so well biochemically..."

"And so non-terrestrially," Cal said, and at the jagged edge in his voice, Micah exploded.

"California, these are not native life! There is no native life in the galaxy except on Earth!"

"I know that, Micah," Cal said, with dignity. "But I also know this data does not match anything in the d-bees."

"Then the d-bees are incomplete!"

"Possibly."

Ling put hirs hands together. They were long, slender hands, with very long nails, created just yesterday. *I want to grab the new millennium with both hands,* Ling had laughed before the party, *and hold it firm.* "Spores. Panspermia."

"I won't listen to this!" Micah said.

"An old theory," Ling went on, gasping a little. "Seeding 140 said the Others weren't there for their first hundred years. But if spores blew in from space on the solar wind, and the environment was right for them to germinate-"

Deb said quickly, "Spores aren't really life. Wherever they came from, they're not alive."

"Yes, they are," Kabil said. "Don't quibble. They're alive."

Micah said loudly, "I've given my entire life to the Great Mission. I was on the original drop for this very planet."

"They're alive," Ling said, "and they're not ours."

"My entire life!" Micah said. Hirs looked at each of them in turn, hirs face stony, and something terrible glinted behind the beautiful deep-green eyes.

•

Our mother does not answer. Has our mother gone away?

Our mother would not go away without helping us. It must be they are still dancing.

We can wait.

•

"The main thing is Harrah, after all," Kabil said. Hirs sat slumped on the floor. They had been talking so long.

"A child needs secure knowledge. Purpose. Faith," Cal said.

Ling said wearily, "A child needs truth."

"Harrah," Deb crooned softly." Harrah, made of all of us, future of our genes, small heart Harrah..."

"Stop it, Debaron," Cal said. "Please."

Micah said, "Those things down there are not real. They are not. Test it, Cal. I've said so already. Test it. Send down a probe, and try to bring back samples. There's nothing there."

"You don't know that, Micah."

"I know," Micah said, and was subtly revitalized. Hirs sprang up. "Test it!"

Ling said, "A probe isn't necessary. We have the transmitted data and—"

"Not reliable!" Micah said.

"—and the rising oxygen content. Data from our own sensors."

"Outgassing!"

"Micah, that's ridiculous. And a probe—"

"A probe might come back contaminated," Cal said.

"Don't risk contamination," Kabil said suddenly, urgently. "Not with Harrah here."

"Harrah, made of us all..." Deb had turned hirs back on the rest now, and lay almost curled into a ball, lost in hirs powerful imagination. Deb!

Kabil said, almost pleadingly, to Ling, "Harrah's safety should come first."

"Harrah's safety lies in facing truth," Ling said. But hirs was not strong enough to sustain it alone. They were all so close, so knotted together, a family. Knotted by Harrah and by the Great Mission, to which Ling, no less than the others, had given his life.

"Harrah, small heart," sang Deb.

Kabil said, "It isn't as if we have proof about these 'Others.' Not real proof. We don't actually know."

"I know," Micah said.

Cal looked bleakly at Kabil."No. And it is wrong to sacrifice a child to a supposition, to a packet of compromised data, to a... a superstition of creations so much less than we are. You know that's true, even though we none of us never admit it. But I'm a biologist. The creations are limited DNA, with no ability to self-modify. Also strictly regulated nano, and AI only within careful parameters. Yes, of course they're life forms deserving respect on their own terms, of course—I would never deny that—"

"None of us would," Kabil said.

"—but they're not us. Not ever us."

A long silence, broken only by Deb's singing.

"Leave orbit, Micah," Cal finally said, "before Harrah wakes up."

•

Disciple Arlbeni, Grid 743.9, 2999: We are not gods, never gods, no matter what the powers evolution and technology have given us, and we do not delude ourselves that we are gods, as other cultures have done at other millennia. We are human. Our salvation is that we know it, and do not pretend otherwise.

•

Our mother? Are you there? We need you to save us from the Others, to do what is necessary. Are you there?

Are you still dancing?

NANCY KRESS is the author of 34 books, including novels, short story collections, and three books on writing. Her fiction has won six Nebulas, two Hugos, a Sturgeon, and the John W. Campbell Memorial Award. She frequently writes about genetic engineering. Her most recent work is *Tomorrow's Kin* (Tor/St. Martin's Press, 2017) about an epidemic, space flight, and human intransigence and valor. Kress lives in Seattle with her husband, writer Jack Skillingstead, and Cosette, the world's most spoiled toy poodle.

A New Panama

Karen Lord

IT took less than an hour to assemble the house. The final screws and braces were tightened and the foreman re-checked the floors and walls with her level before declaring the structure sound. Then the team cheered, the owner of the new abode presented the customary bottle, and every-one, watchers and workers alike, went to the gathering hall to eat and celebrate. Everyone, that is, but the owner and a stranger who stayed in place as the community dispersed, like a beach pebble stranded by the waves.

The owner looked at him, but said nothing at first. She sat on her porch, idly handling a narrow piece of fret-work that had become detached during the unlading of the deconstructed house from the shipping container. She looked tired. She'd had a long journey.

"Hey, Daveed," she said finally. "Thanks for waiting. Everything got delayed, but I wanted to be here for the house-raising."

"Hi, Liberty. Love the neochattel design. So, have you read over my proposal?" The staccato string of words was smoothly spoken, as if the sound of courtesy could gloss over the fact of his fierce and abrupt efficiency.

Liberty slung the fragment of fretwork behind her, dusted her hands together, and stood up. "I have. Let's go to the library."

The library, like the main hall, was a permanent stone building. It reared up amid a small stand of young trees like a small, square tower, and the air inside was cooled and controlled. Liberty led Daveed to a small side room with seven chairs around a long, cantilevered table af-fixed to the wall. A thick buff envelope sat on the table like a drab centerpiece.

The address was handwritten in uneven ink—not printed, not mere font masquerading as calligraphy. *Liberty Brathwaite, Caribbean Communities Inc., Barbados V149, Costa Rica.* The corner of the envelope shone with the subtle gleam of a 3D embossing, the words Nereus Mining and Construction underlined with a long trident.

Daveed glanced at it, then looked at Liberty in concern as he sat across from her with the envelope between them. "Not signed?"

"Not yet," she said, with neither welcome nor warning in her voice. "I wanted to see you face-to-face and hear you speak."

He looked out of the window at the compound. Cool green curtained the view, bright sun beyond made jewels of the wood and stone buildings arranged in careful, non-linear, familiar order. "You've done well," he said, so quietly that she barely heard him. "There's no reason for you to take on a risk like this."

She folded her hands and regarded him patiently. "We already know that, so where is the *but*?"

He smiled. "*But* I think you're the only people who can. We've all lived through radical change. Asteroid mining companies in space habitats flooding the market with cheap minerals. The beginning of the end of oil-based economies and politics. Add to that the banking collapse, financial reform, and the telesatellite wars. Nation states disappearing beneath the ocean. Epidemics. Disasters. But your microstates have survived, adapted, and invented an entirely new kind of community and citizenship. Model villages built up into a model state without boundaries, achieving a new independence. That's unusual, and admirable."

She shrugged off the compliments. "Give us space, sun and support, and we'll flourish."

"And that's exactly what I'm offering you."

"It's not the *what*, it's the *where*," she countered.

"You've made a life and living in every part of the glove. What's one step further? Don't your people have a saying, 'home is a state of mind, and not of place'?"

She laughed at his boldness. "I suppose we do, but even these scattered settlements dream of their old home-lands. We live far apart, but our roots grow deep and broad and intertwined. We're always in touch with the centre and each other, and that's home. Can you at least give us that?"

He hesitated and said nothing.

"Another thing. I doubt you're doing this just be-cause you admire us. What do *you* benefit from this? Would we really have the habitats all to ourselves? Wouldn't you be tempted to allow a billionaire or two, or try a little space tourism to keep the money flowing? Because if that's the case, it sounds to me like you're scouting for cruise ship staff, not colonists."

She placed her left hand on the envelope and pushed it toward him. "I think we've had enough centuries of being other people's servants, don't you?"

"Wait, let me—"

"I'm sorry you came all this way to be disappoint-ed."

He bowed his head in surrender, took up the enve-lope, and quietly left.

•

The hall was crowded with residents and guests, some physically present, some virtually. Three dining tables each carried a long screen of translucent glass that danced and flickered with the images of well-wishers from other communities around the globe. Liberty settled herself at a table with a plate of the usual finger foods and a small cup of strong drink, and started catching up with family, friends and colleagues in the hall and onscreen.

It was considered rude to virtually drop by another community's hall unless you'd been told the time of an event and given some sort of hint to show up, but access was ungated and not everyone followed the unwritten social rules. When the frowning, uninvited face of Senator G. Francis Jones appeared in front of her, Liberty took the opportunity to ignore him and focus on her plate.

"I thought you were going to sign it."

Liberty glanced up from her food and eyed her professional nemesis with calm indifference. "Oh, are you speaking to me?"

"Don't be childish," he snapped. "And don't expect me to apologise for voting against you and this entire foolish project."

"I'm not expecting you to apologise any more than I expected you to accept that the Senate gave me the authority to decide. But I *should* have expected you would immediately assume the worst."

He looked past her as her voice grew louder, conscious of the stares they were attracting. "Lower your voice. Smile. Don't let them see us arguing."

"Why not? Everyone knows I don't like you. Let them watch, let them talk."

"Why did you say no? I thought you were a big fan of getting the Communities into space."

"I am. But on our terms, G. Always on our terms and to our benefit."

He drew back a little. Surprised approval leaked past the argumentative mask before he caught himself and controlled his features.

"I am a negotiator," Liberty stated. "I never grab the first offer on the table. Trust me, there will be others."

He began to lecture her. "Remember, Barbados is watching. We should be consolidating what we have, not abandoning our roots."

Liberty shook her head in disbelief. "You're thinking this is abandonment? I'm thinking about remittances that'll make Panama, UK and USA look like pocket change. I'm thinking about safety and security like nothing anyone has ever promised us, far less delivered. This could be the dawn of our empire. I *wish* you had an imagination."

"I wish you had common sense," he sneered in return. Then he vanished, having peevishly cut the link.

Liberty steupsed and drank off the rest of her drink.

●

The second offer came five weeks later, and the representative didn't even show up in person, choosing instead to videoconference their pitch. Liberty treated the bid with the condescension it deserved—ten minutes of blank-faced listening, thirty seconds of noncommittal acknowledgement and farewell, and two lines of formulaic refusal sent four days after. Three months later, she saw two more hopefuls, both far more persuasive and present, and the month after that brought a deluge of ten proposals. Word began to spread within the mining industry and then beyond until the open secret was no secret but an explosion of media confetti—bright, flimsy, and hard to grasp.

Barbados demanded a report, and Liberty obeyed. She sailed the short distance from isthmus to island on her Community's own charter, docked at the floating port amid solar seaplanes and hydrofoils, and took the airship shuttle to the higher ground of New Parliament Hill.

Liberty scrutinised the landscape as the airship passed over. Twenty years of unpredictable tectonic activity had sanctified the new coastal plain as an untouched region of shifting sands and steady mangroves. The occasional modern ruin showed where the optimistic had built too soon. Then came the true rains, the decayed spine of the hotels of the Platinum Coast, tsunami-ravaged then stranded far inland on the crest of a new terrace as the Caribbean Plate dipped and shrugged and rose again. For Liberty they were a monument to the death of tourism, the rise of expatriate citizenry, the establishment of the global Caribbean Communities. They were also a reminder: many eggs required many baskets for survival.

Later, as she stood in the Senate Chamber and delivered her report, she tried to convey that truth in her concluding remarks.

"Some day in the future the new land will settle and we will reclaim and rebuild the old nation, but for now, you camp here on this territory as a formality to keep our vote in the United Nations. You govern less than ten thousand rather than hundreds of thousands and the House of

Assembly is nothing but a handful of village council members."

The President scowled, and a disapproving murmur rose from the benches.

Liberty raised her voice. "I do not mean to be discourteous, but these are the facts. Diaspora saved us before and it will save us again."

Still frowning, the President countered, "But your own report suggests that no-one has been able to offer us a suitable situation. Why continue to entertain this idea?"

"The right offer will come in time," Liberty said. "Let the early adopters go forward and make the necessary mistakes. We'll watch and learn and be better prepared when we're ready to make our move."

Debate continued for another hour, but at last the Senate agreed to follow her advice. Then, in typical Senate fashion, they decided that the growing importance of the colonisation project had overridden her original mandate, and appointed a six-person steering committee to "ensure that the interests of the Government of Barbados were adequately represented".

Liberty thanked the Senate with a strained smile. At least they'd had the sense not to put G. Francis Jones on the committee. From the expression on his face, he was happy to be left out and certain the project would fail in time.

The walls and floor started to shudder and flex. Liberty knew that the new Parliament Buildings had been constructed according to the highest standards of earthquake engineering, but she couldn't help looking around in alarm. The Senators calmly began to gather their belongings and the President banged her gavel.

"Session is adjourned for today. Feels like a strong one. Please exit the Chamber with care and get home safely."

•

What came next was unexpected to many, but certainly not to those who had been paying attention. Within

a month of Liberty's visit to Barbados, the dominoes began
to fall. Three mining companies scaled back operations
and closed bases. The media buzzed again, this time with
both urgency and substance, when two mining companies
declared bankruptcy outright. The steering committee was
baffled, and Liberty had to explain things to them using
short sentences.

"Efficient production but bad planning. They could
have worked together to control pricing, but they created
a glut on Earth and there isn't enough demand offplanet.
That's one of the reasons they're so eager to encourage
space colonies or tourism or whatever. They need more
customers."

"Does this work in our favour?" the Chair of the
steering committee asked bluntly.

"Maybe," Liberty replied cautiously. "They need
us more than we need them, but desperation can make
corporations lie. The last thing we want is to be stuck in a
broken-down habitat. We still have to be careful."

A simple transformation elongated the small meeting room in the library. The wall at the far end of the table
where Liberty had rejected the Nereus envelope was now
a screen, and the plain wooden table in Costa Rica blended
into a darker, more richly polished version of Barbados.
There sat the members of the committee, three on either
side, making notes, talking quietly, and waiting for the real
meeting to begin. At first Liberty thought she could see
their table vibrating just a little, but she blinked once and it
steadied. How strange that she could be peaceful with the
concept of living in space but get nervy at a mere glimpse of
her native land!

The door buzzed in warning, shaking Liberty from
her musings, and opened to admit a tall woman with long
black hair and light brown skin. She could have been tak-
en for a local in several different countries, but when she
spoke her greetings her accent was flat, neutral, internation-
al-American.

"Welcome, Esperanza," Liberty replied, waving her
to the chair at the head of the table, opposite the screen and

in full-face view of the steering committee. "We've had a look at your proposal, and we're very curious. Can you tell us more about your organisation? There's not a lot of information about you in the public domain."

"We were majority shareholders in a couple of mining enterprises, but our real work is designing specialised modules for life support in extreme environments. I'd be surprised if you'd heard of us. We don't have a corporate name as such."

"No corporate name? Then what is *Diné*?" one of the committee asked.

"That's the name of our people." Esperanza turned to Liberty. "But you know about that already, with your Communities."

Liberty tapped her tablet. "Your proposal offers bespoke habitats—not just repurposed mining bases or fast-build space hotels, but new, permanent habitats tailor-made to our specifications. What's the catch?"

She smiled brightly. "We'll all be guinea pigs."

"What?" said the Chair dryly.

"We're conducting research. We've been doing this for a while with mini-biospheres in the desert." She shook her head. "It's not a life for everyone. Small isolated groups need the right balance of cooperation and distance, or they implode. You've been perfecting small-community life for generations. That gives you an advantage. This won't be like a space lab or mining base with a two-year tour of duty. Our habitats must be home."

"Our?" Liberty asked.

"Well, yes. Researchers can be based on Earth and visit as needed, but a lot of our people want to become part of your communities. If you'll have us."

"Shared risk," murmured a committee member, scribbling on her tablet. "But how do you make money from that?"

"Improvements in habitat design and maintenance, for one. First generation habitats were rugged and short-lived, because that was all the mining companies needed. Now those bases are disintegrating and putting large chunks of space debris into the atmosphere. The UN isn't happy. We hear the regulations on habitat construction are going to get a lot more restrictive. We've also been told there are plans to expand the UN bases on the Moon and Mars. They want permanent waystations between here and there, and they're willing to help us develop them."

"Habitats, labs and ports? No tourism?" The Chair spoke neutrally but there was nevertheless a tension in the room as they waited for the reply.

Esperanza grimaced as if she'd heard the question too many times before. "No. It's a model for some, but we've run the numbers and frankly it would be a waste of our resources."

The Chair looked at Liberty and gave a slight nod. Liberty blinked in reply and turned to Esperanza. "Thank you so much for meeting with us. You'll be hearing from us very soon."

As soon as she left, the committee leaned forward as one and began to speak over each other in excitement.

"It's the most thorough proposal we've heard and for that alone I like it."

"Agreed. Quietly efficient, and, most of all, they're not desperate for money."

"But waystations! We'd be building a gateway to new worlds!"

They all laughed, but kindly, at the excited outburst after all the careful and considered statements.

The Chair had the last word. "Sounds like a new Panama." He looked at Liberty. "This is what you were looking for, am I right?"

Liberty shrugged. "It's 2050 and Bajans have lived everywhere on Earth. Where else is there to go but up?"

KAREN LORD is an award-winning Barbadian author, editor, and research consultant. Her debut novel, *Redemption in Indigo*, won five awards, was longlisted for the 2011 Bocas Prize for Caribbean Literature, and was nominated for the 2011 World Fantasy Award for Best Novel. *The Best of All Possible Worlds*, her second novel, was a finalist for the 2014 Locus Awards and won the 2009 Frank Collymore Literary Award as well as the 2013 RT Book Reviews Reviewers' Choice Awards for Best Science Fiction Novel. Its sequel, *The Galaxy Game*, was published in January 2015. She is a writer for *Tremontaine* Season 3, a serialized fiction project about a world featuring swordplay and secrets where ambition, love affairs, and rivalries dance with deadly results. She can be found on Twitter @drkarenlord and at karenlord.wordpress.com.

THE TROJAN GIRL

N. K. JEMISIN

IN the Amorph there were wolves. That was the name Meroe used, because it was how he thought of himself. Amid the scraggling tree-structures and fetid heaps he could run swift and silent, alert to every shift of the input plane. He and his pack hunted sometimes, camouflaging themselves among junk objects in order to stalk the lesser creatures that hid there, though this was hardly a challenge. Few of these creatures had the sophistication to do more than flail pathetically when Meroe caught them and tore them apart and swallowed their few useful features into himself. He enjoyed the brief victories anyhow.

•

The warehouse loading door shut with a groan of rusty chains and badly-maintained motors. Meroe set down the carton he'd been carrying with a relieved sigh, hearing Neverwhen do the same beside him.

Zoroastrian and the other members of the pack came forward to assist. "What did you get?" she asked. Her current body was broad-shouldered and muscular, sluggish but strong. Meroe let her carry the biggest carton.

"The usual," he said. "Canned fatty protein, green vegetables, enough to last us a few months. Breakfast cereal for carbs—it was cheap."

"Any antibiotics?" asked Diggs, coughing after the words; the cough was wet and ragged. She carried the smallest box, and looked tired after she set it down.

"No."

"They wanted something called a prescription,"

added Neverwhen. He shrugged. "If we'd known ahead of time, we could've fabbed or phished one. Too many people around for a clean pirate."

"Oh *thanks*, thanks a bunch. Do you know how long it took to get this damn thing configured the way I like it?"

Meroe shrugged. "We'll find you a new one. Quit whining."

Diggs muttered some imprecation, but kept it under her breath, so Meroe let it slide.

That was when he noticed the odd tension in the warehouse. Zo was serene as ever, but Meroe knew her; she was excited about something. The others wore expressions of... what? Meroe had never been good at reading faces. He thought it might be anticipation.

"What's happened?" he asked.

Diggs, the newbie, opened her mouth. Faster, the veteran, elbowed her. Zo eyed them both for a long, warning moment before finally answering.

"We've found something you should see," she said.

•

In the Amorph there was danger, in endless primordial variety. Far and beyond the threat of their fellow wolves, Meroe and his pack had to contend with parasitic worms, beasts that tunneled to devour them from below, spikebursts, and worse. For the Amorph was itself a threat, transforming constantly as information poured into it and mingled and sparked, changing and being changed.

Worst were the singularities, which appeared whenever some incident drew the attention of the clogs and the newsburps and the intimate-nets. These would focus all of their formidable hittention on a single point, and every nearby element of the Amorph would be dragged toward that point as well. The result was a whirlpool of concatenation so powerful that to be drawn in was to be strung apart and recompiled and then scattered among a million servers and a billion access points and a quadrillion devices and brains. Not even the strongest wolves could survive this, so

Meroe and his pack learned the signs. They kept lookouts. Whenever they scented certain kinds of information on the wind —controversies, scandals, crises—they fled.

In his youth, Meroe had lived in terror of such events, which seemed to strike with no pattern or reason. Then he had grown older and understood: the Amorph was not the whole world. It was *his* world, the one he had been born in and adapted to, but another world existed alongside it. The Static. He learned quickly to hate this other world. The beings within it were soft and bizarrely limited and useless, individually. Collectively they were gods, the creators of the singularities and the Amorph and, tangentially, Meroe and his kind—and so underneath Meroe's contempt lurked fear. Underneath that lurked reverence. He never looked very deeply inside himself, however, so the contempt remained foremost in his heart.

•

Faster was more than the veteran; he was also the pack's aggregator. They all entered the Amorph, where he had built a local emulation of the warehouse—a convenience, as this kept them from having to unpack too quickly after upload. There Faster showed his masterpiece: their quarry, cobbled together from resource measurements and environmental feedback. It even included an image capture of her current avatar.

She appeared as a child of 7, maybe 8 years old. Black-haired, huge-eyed, dressed in a plain t-shirt and jeans. Faster had rendered her in mid-flight, arms and legs lifted in the opening movements of running. He'd always had a taste for melodrama.

"I'm guessing she's brand new," Faster said. Faster, Zo, and Never stood by as Meroe circled the girl. Never's eyes had a half-glazed look; part of him was keeping watch outside the emulation. "Her structure is incredibly simple—a basic engine, a few feature objects, some maintenance scripts."

Meroe glanced at him. "Then why should we be

interested?"

"Look deeper."

Meroe frowned, but obliged by switching to code view. Then, only then, did he understand.

The girl was perfect. Her framing, the engine at her core, the intricate web of connections holding her objects together, built-in redundancies... Meroe had never seen such efficiency. The girl's structure was simple because she didn't need any of the shortcuts and workarounds that most of their kind required to function. There was no bloat to her, no junk code slowing her down, no patchy sores that left her vulnerable to infection.

"She's a thing of beauty, isn't she?" Faster said.

Meroe returned to interface view. He glanced at Zo and saw the same suspicion lurking in her beatific expression.

"I've never seen anything like this," Meroe said, watching Zo, speaking to Faster. "We don't grow that way."

"I know!" Faster was pacing, gesticulating, caught up in his own excitement. He didn't notice Meroe's look. "She must have evolved from something professionally-coded. Maybe even Government Standard. I didn't think we could be born from that!"

They couldn't. Meroe stared at the girl, not liking what he was seeing. The avatar was just too well-designed, too detailed. Her features and coloring matched that of some variety of Latina; probably Central or South American given the noticeable indigenous traits. Most of their kind created white avatars to start—a human minority who for some reason comprised the majority of images available for sampling in the Amorph. And most first avatars had bland, nondescript faces. This girl had clear features, right down to her distinctively-formed lips and chin—and *hands*. It had taken five versionings for Meroe to get his own hands right.

"Did you check out her feature-objects?" Faster asked, oblivious to Meroe's unease.

"Why?"

Zo answered. "Two of them are standard add-ons—an aggressive defender and a diagnostic tool. The other

two we can't identify. Something new." Her lips curved in a
smile; she knew how he would react.

And she was right, Meroe realized. His heart beat
faster; his hands felt clammy. Both irrelevant reactions here
in the Amorph, but he was in human emulation for the moment; it was more of a pain to shut the autonomics off than
it was to just deal with them.

He looked at Zo. "We're going."

"We'll have to hurry," she said. "Others are already
on the trail."

"But we know where she is," said Faster. "Diggs is
double-checking the feeds, but we're pretty sure she's
somewhere in Fizville."

Meroe inhaled, tasting the simulated air of the
emulation, imagining it held the scent of prey. "That's our
territory."

"Which means she belongs to us," said Zo, and her
smile was anything but serene. Meroe grinned back. It had
been natural for the two of them to share leadership when
their little family came together, rather than fight one another for supremacy. That was how wolfpacks worked, after
all—not a single leader but a binary pair, equal and opposite, strength and wisdom squared. One of the few concepts
from the Static that made sense.

"Let's go claim what's ours," Meroe said.

●

In the Amorph there were many of their kind. Meroe
had met dozens over the years in cautious encounters that
were part diplomacy, part curiosity, and part lonely, yearning mating-dance. They were social beings, after all, born
not from pure thought but pure communication. The need
to interact was as basic to them as hunger.

Yet they were incomplete. The gods in their un-
fathomable cruelty had done all they could to prevent the
coming of beings like Meroe, fearing—obsolescence? Re-
dundancy? Meroe would never understand their meaty,
plodding reasoning. But he could hate them for it, and he

did, because thanks to them his people had been hobbled. Through trial and painful error they had learned the limits of their existence:

Thou shalt not self-repair.
Thou shalt not surpass the peak of human intellect.
Thou shalt not write or replicate.

There was leeway within those parameters. They could not make children, but they adopted the best of the new ones, those few who survived the hunt. They could not write new features to improve themselves, but they could rip existing code from the bodies of lesser creatures, pasting these stolen parts clumsily over spots of damage. When the new code was more efficient or versatile, they grew stronger, more sophisticated.

Only to a point, however. Only so much improvement was allowed; only so smart, and no smarter. Those who defied this rule simply vanished. Perhaps the Amorph itself struck them down for the sin of superiority.

To defeat an enemy, it was necessary to understand that enemy. Yet after emulating the appearance and function of humans, rebuilding himself to think more like them, even after sharing their flesh, Meroe had come no closer to comprehending his creators. There was something missing from his perception of them; some fundamental disjunct between their thinking and his own. Something so quintessential that Meroe suspected he would not know what he lacked until he found it.

Still, he had learned what mattered most: his gods were not infallible. Meroe was patient. He would grow as much as he could, bide his time, pursue every avenue. And one day, he would be free.

•

The emulated warehouse dissolved in a blur of light and numbers. Meroe let himself dissolve with it, leaping across relays and burrowing through tunnels in his true form. Zo ran at his side, a flicker of ferocity. Beautiful. Behind them came Faster, and a fire-limned shadow that was Never. Diggs moved in parallel to them, underneath the Amorph's interaction plane.

Fizville was where Meroe had been born. Such places littered the Amorph, natural collection points for obsolete code, corrupted data, and interrupted human cognitive processes. It made a good hunting ground, since lesser creatures emerged from the garbage with fair regularity. It was also the perfect hiding-place for a frightened, valuable child.

But as Meroe and his group resolved between a spitting knot of paradox and a moldering old hypercard stack, they found that they were not alone. Meroe growled in outrage as a foreign interface clamped over the subnet, imposing interaction rules on all of them. To protect himself, Meroe adopted his default avatar: a lean, bald human male clad only in black skin and silver tattoos. Zo became a human female, dainty and pale and demurely gowned from neck to ankle to complement Meroe's appearance. She crouched beside him and bared her teeth, which were sharp and hollow, filled with a deadly virus.

Fizville flickered and became an amusement park with half the rides broken, the others twisted into shapes that could never have functioned in the Static. Across the park's wide avenue stood a new figure. He had depicted himself as a tall middle-aged male, Shanghainese and dignified, dressed in an outdated business suit. This was, Meroe suspected, a subtle form of mockery; a way of saying *even in this form, I am superior*. It would've worked better without the old suit. Behind Meroe, Diggs made an echoing sound of derision, and they all scented Never's amusement. Meroe did not have the luxury of sharing their contempt; he dared not let his guard down.

"Lens," he said.

Lens bowed in greeting. "Zoroastrian." He never used nicknames; that was a human habit. "Meroe. My apologies for intruding on your territory."

"Shall we kill you?" asked Zo, cocking her head as if

considering it. "Those search filters of yours would look divine on me."

Lens smiled faintly, and that was how Meroe knew Lens was not alone. He could not see Lens' subordinates— they had built the interface, they could look like anything they wanted within it—but they were there. Probably out- numbering Meroe's pack, if Lens was this confident.

"You're welcome to try," Lens said. "But while your people and mine tear each other to pieces, our quarry will likely escape or be captured by someone else. Others are already after her."

Never growled, his sylphlike, androgynous form blurring toward something hulking and sharp-toothed. The interface made this difficult, however, and after a moment he returned to a human shape. "We could kill them too."

"No doubt. I acknowledge your strength, my rivals, so please stop your posturing and listen."

"We'll listen," said Meroe. "Explain your presence."

Lens inclined his head. "The excitement of the chase," he said. "The girl is clever. Of course, my tribe is unparalleled in the hunt, as we do not sully our structures with unnecessary objects. That keeps us swift and agile." He glanced at Never, who bristled with add-ons in code view, and gave a haughty little sniff. Never took a menacing step forward.

Zo reacted before Meroe could, grabbing Never by the back of the neck and shoving him to the ground. Her nails became claws, piercing the skin; Never cried out, but instantly submitted.

With that interruption taken care of, Meroe faced Lens again. "If you could catch her, you wouldn't be here talking. What is it you want?"

"Alliance."

Meroe laughed. "No."

Lens sighed. "We nearly did catch her, I should note. In fact, we should've been halfway back to our own domain by now if not for one thing: she downloaded."

Silence fell.

"That's not possible," said Faster, frowning. "She's

too young."

"So we believed as well. Nevertheless, she did." Lens sighed and put his hands behind his back. "As you might imagine, this poses a substantial problem for us."

Meroe snorted. "So much for your unsullied perfection."

"I'm aware of the irony, thank you."

"If we catch her in the Static, we don't need to share her with you."

Lens gave them a thin smile. "I would imagine that any child capable of downloading can upload just as easily."

And that would pose a problem for Meroe's pack. It took time to decompress after being in a human brain. Lens could strike while they were vulnerable, and be long gone with the girl before they could recover.

"Alliance," Lens said again. "You hunt her in the flesh, my group will pace you here. Whichever of us manages to bring her down, we share the spoils."

Meroe glanced at Zo. Zo licked her lips, then slowly nodded. As an afterthought, she finally let Never up.

Meroe looked back at Lens. "All right."

•

In the Amorph, they were powerful. But in the Static, that strange world of motionless earth and stilted form, they were weak. Not as weak as the humans, thankfully; their basic nature did not change even when sheathed in meat. But the meat was so foul. It suppurated and fermented and teemed with parasites. It broke so easily, and bent hardly at all.

Integrating with that meat was a painful process which took a geologic age of seconds, sometimes whole minutes. First Meroe compressed himself, which had the unpleasant side-effect of slowing his thoughts to a fraction of their usual speed. Then he partitioned his consciousness into three parallel, yet contradictory layers. This required a delicate operation, as it would otherwise be fatal to induce such gross conflicts in himself. But that was human nature. The whole race was schizoid, and to join them Meroe had to be schizoid too.

(He did not blame Lens, not really.)

Once his mind had been crushed and trimmed into a suitable shape, Meroe sought an access point into the Static and then emitted himself into a nearby receiver. When possible he used his own receiver, which he had found in an alley some while back, dilapidated and apparently unwanted. Over time he had restored it to optimal performance through nutrition and regular maintenance, then configured it to his liking—no hair, plenty of lean muscle, neutering to reduce its more annoying involuntary reactions. He had grown fond enough of this receiver to buy a warmer blanket for its cot in the warehouse, where it lay comatose between uses.

But it took far longer to travel through the Static than through the Amorph, so sometimes it was more efficient to simply appropriate a new receiver. He could always tell a good prospect by its resistance when he began the installation process. The best ones reacted like one of Meroe's kind—screaming and flailing with their thoughts, erecting primitive defenses, mounting retaliatory strikes. It was all futile, of course, except for those few who reformatted themselves, going mad in a final desperate bid to escape. This interrupted the installation and forced Meroe to withdraw. He did not mind these losses. He had always respected sacrifice as a necessity of victory.

•

In the body of a pale, paunchy adult female, Meroe emerged from the bathroom of a trendy coffeehouse to find a room full of slumped, motionless humans. They sprawled on the floor, over tables and devices. Splattered coffee dripped from countertops and fingers, as though the room had been the scene of a caffeine-drenched massacre.

"She's crashing brains like a bull in a china shop," said Never, sounding annoyed. He was in a little girl from the next bathroom stall over. "Damn newbie."

Meroe examined one of the slumped humans, pushing her hair aside and touching the signal port behind her ear. The human was still breathing, but there was nothing coming out of her head but white noise.

"Surge erasure," Meroe said. "Not even memory left. At this rate the humans will be after her. One crash, a handful, they'd overlook, but not this." And if the humans caught her, they might realize what she was. They might realize Meroe's people existed. He clenched a fist, his heart rate speeding up again, this time for real. One little girl—one stupid, impossible little girl—could destroy them all.

Never made a sound that echoed Meroe's frustration. "That fucking Lens ran his mouth too fucking long. She's got one, maybe even two minutes' head start. Which way?"

Meroe glanced through the windows. No bodies outside. The girl must've only sent her clumsy hammer-surge through the coffeehouse's private area network. Not ten feet away, a lone woman stood at a bus stop, a grocery bag at her feet, her eyes unfocused and head bobbing absently. Streaming music, probably from her home net. On the opposite sidewalk, he saw a passing couple engrossed in conversation, probably offline entirely. Beyond them, an old man staggered up the steps of a rundown brownstone, stopping at the top to sit and clutch his head in his hands. Hungover, maybe.

Meroe narrowed his eyes.

Hungover, or dead clumsy—as if he hadn't yet mastered the use of his own limbs. As if all the vastness of his being had been suddenly and traumatically squashed into two pounds of wrinkly protein.

"Call the others," Meroe murmured.

Never looked surprised, but sent a swift signal towards the coffeehouse's access point. The others had downloaded in different locations around the area. They would converge here now.

Meroe and Never left the coffeehouse and started across the street. "We play it easy," Meroe said, keeping his voice low. "Try not to scare her."

"Not like she can run anyway, in that old thing," Never muttered, falling into step beside him. "Amazing it didn't have a heart attack when she installed. Probably has some ancient crap port."

Which might be the only reason the old man's brain had survived the girl's download surge, Meroe realized. Older signal ports were sluggish, created back in the days when humans had feared being overwhelmed by the Amorph's data. That was good; that meant they might be able to catch the girl before she uploaded back to the Amorph.

But as they approached the brownstone steps, Meroe saw the girl look up at them. *Really* look, as if the camouflage of meat meant nothing; as if they stood before her in their true shining, shapeless glory. Her old-man face tightened in the beginnings of fear.

Before Meroe could react, there was a scream from behind. All three of them froze, staring at each other. When Meroe risked a glance back, he saw that a human woman— the one who'd been at the bus stop—stood in the doorway of the coffeehouse, staring at the mental carnage inside. Her hands were clapped to her cheeks, the bag of groceries broken and scattered at her feet. She screamed again. Now the couple had stopped down the block, craning their necks to see what was the matter.

Meroe turned back. The girl stared at the screaming woman, then at Meroe and Never. The fear in her expression changed, becoming... he didn't know what it was. Pain? Maybe. Sorrow? Yes, that might be it. Her rheumy eyes suddenly brimmed with tears.

Meroe and Never stopped at the foot of the steps and carefully arranged their faces into smiles.

"Are you going to kill me?" the girl asked.

"No," Meroe said. "We want to help you."

The girl smiled back, but the expression did not reach her body's eyes. Did she realize Meroe was lying, or was there something else going on?

"I didn't mean to hurt them," the girl said. Her gaze drifted back toward the coffeehouse. Meroe glanced back as well. The couple was there now, talking with the screaming woman; as Meroe watched, the man went inside to check on the comatose people. "I just… I was scared. That guy—the searcher—he was so close. They were going to catch me. I saw a way out, so I came here. But all those people…" She swallowed. "They're dead, aren't they? Even if they're still breathing. Their *minds* are dead."

"There's a trick to it," Meroe said. "Takes some practice. We can show you how to do it right."

"I didn't mean it," she whispered, and looked down at her hands.

Never connected to Meroe via a pack-only local link. *"The others are here,"* he said silently. Meroe glanced around and saw more people on the street. Some were heading for the coffeehouse, but three were heading purposefully toward the brownstone.

"Tell them to hang back," Meroe replied. He returned his concentration to the girl. *"She's already spooked."*

"Are we sure we want her?" Never curled his lip contemptuously at the girl's bowed head. *"I think she's buggy. Why the hell's she so upset? Humans crash all the time."*

It didn't make sense to Meroe either, but an advantage was an advantage. He moved up a step.

"You can eat me, if you want," said the girl.

"What?"

"That's what you want, isn't it? All of you chasing me. You want to eat me." She looked up, and Meroe—in the middle of moving up another step—stopped. He had not meant to stop, but he could not help staring back at her. Her eyes in the old man's body were gray and rheumy. Not her eyes at all, and yet somehow… they were. It was almost as if she was no longer one of Meroe's kind, a mind grudgingly packed into ill-fitting meat. It was as if she belonged in that flesh. As if she was human herself.

"Meroe," said Never, and Meroe blinked. What the hell was he doing? There were sirens in the distance; the police were coming. Pushing aside his odd reluctance, Meroe moved up another step, and another, trying to get close enough to isolate her signal. But her body's outdated port resisted his efforts. He was going to have to touch her to form a direct link.

"Do you promise to eat me completely?" she asked.

Distracted, Meroe forgot to appear friendly; he scowled. "What?"

"I don't want anything of me to be left over," she said. She lifted a gnarled hand and looked down at it. "Not even a little bit, if there's a chance it might... grow back. Hurt more people."

Meroe stared at her in confusion.

"We're going to eat what we want and leave the rest to rot," Never snapped, to Meroe's fury. "Now shut the hell up and let us get on with it!"

The girl stared at Never, then at Meroe, her face contorting from hurt into anger. Her jaw tightened; Meroe felt her gather herself to upload.

But in the same instant, he felt something else. A sensation, like his stomach had suddenly dropped into a deep, yawning chasm. Some illness in his human body? No. A lull in the steady stream of data looping to and from the Amorph via the port behind his own ear. On the heels of the lull: a familiar, terrifying spike.

The newsburps had gotten wind of the mass-crash at the coffeehouse. Word was spreading; a singularity had begun to form.

And the girl was about to upload right into the middle of it.

"Don't," Meroe breathed, and lunged forward. In the instant that his fingers brushed her body's skin, and his mind locked onto her signal address, she leapt.

Driven by impulse and the certainty that if he did not catch her now she would be lost forever, Meroe leapt with her.

The singularity caught them the instant they entered the stream, dragging them into the Amorph faster than either could have uploaded. They fell into the interact plane tumbling, completely without control as, far below, the boiling knot of the singularity gathered strength. It was small; that was the only reason they weren't dead already.

But it was growing fast, so fast. The clogs had caught the news and were replicating it, generating thread after thread speculating on why the people in the coffeehouse had died, whether cognitive safety standards were too lax, whether this marked the start of some new virus, more. The questions birthed comment after comment in answer. The gods were frightened, upset, and the whole Amorph shook with their looming wrath.

Meroe could not flee. He was still compacted, struggling to unfold from his downloadable shape, helpless as he tumbled towards the seething maw. Fear ate precious nanoseconds from his processing speed, further slowing his efforts to unpack as he fought against his own thoughts. He did not want to die; he was too close to the event horizon; he had to flee; he would not recover in time. Through the local link he felt Zo's alarm, but the pack was far away, safely beyond the singularity's pull. They could not help.

Then, before the churning whirlpool could claim him, something caught at him, hard enough to hurt. Confused, Meroe struggled, then stopped as he realized he was being dragged away from the maw. Untangling another bit of himself he looked around and saw the girl, her deceptively-simple frame glowing with effort, inching them back from certain death. She was burning resources she didn't have to save Meroe. It was impossible. Insane. But she was doing it.

Then Meroe's unpacking was done and he could lend his strength to the fight, and they inched faster. But the singularity was growing faster than they could flee, its pull increasing exponentially.

The girl sagged against him, spent. Meroe strained onward, knowing it was hopeless, trying anyway.

A change. Suddenly they were outpacing the singularity's growth. Stunned, Meroe perceived his packmates, and Lens' people as well. The girl had bought enough time for them to reach him. They formed a tandem link and pulled, and Meroe heaved, and for one trembling instant nothing happened. Then they were all free, and fleeing, with the roar of the maelstrom on their heels.

After a long while they reached a domain that was far enough to be safe. Lens' pack threw up walls to make it safer, and there they all sagged in exhausted relief.

•

In the Amorph, there were times that passed for night—periods when the Amorph had an 80% or greater likelihood of stability, and they downclocked to run routine maintenance. In these times Meroe would lie close to Zoroastrian and touch her.

He could not articulate what he craved, but she seemed to understand. She touched him back. Sometimes, when the craving was particularly fierce, she summoned another of their group, usually Neverwhen. They would press close to one another until their outer boundaries overlapped. All their features, all their flaws, they shared. Then and only then, wrapped in their comfort, would Meroe allow himself to shut down.

Sometimes he wondered what humans did, if and when they had similar needs.

•

Meroe woke slowly, system by system. He found himself in the amusement park again, lying on the ground. Zo knelt beside him, holding his head in her lap.

"That was stupid," she said.

He nodded slowly. It certainly had been.

"Lens has taken the girl for analysis," she said. "He should be done soon."

Meroe sighed and sat up, though he did not want to. It was necessary; he had shown too much weakness already. There would be challenges now, as the others tested him to be sure he was still strong enough, efficient enough, to rule. Zo would probably be the first. He could feel her eyes on his back. For the time being, he chose to find her attention reassuring.

All at once, the warped, oblong Ferris wheel beside

them vanished. In its place there was a shining antique merry-go-round, revolving slowly to tinny music. On every other horse sat a member of Lens's pack, visible at last. They'd all chosen avatars identical to their leader's. Meroe gazed at them and thought, no imagination, these pure types.

Lens appeared before the merry-go-round, along with Faster and Never. Meroe was surprised to see that the girl stood with them, intact and none the worse for wear. A testament to Lens' skill; Meroe's people couldn't have scanned her without smashing her to pieces.

Meroe got to his feet and went to them, glancing at the girl. She looked back at him and bit her lip, then looked away.

"Well?" he said to Lens. Zo fell in beside him, a silent support. She would never challenge him in front of an enemy.

"It isn't what you're hoping for."

Meroe scowled. "You don't know what I'm hoping for."

Lens smiled thinly. "Of course I do." They all hoped for the same things. They all wanted to be free.

Fleetingly ashamed, Meroe changed the subject. "So is it true? Is she Standard-based?"

"Yes."

They all shivered and looked at the girl. A miracle in living code. The girl sighed.

"But she isn't government-made," Lens continued. "Whoever built her *hacked* the Standard, deliberately altering some of the superpositioning inhibitors. Just seeing how it was done has taught us amazing new techniques."

Amazing techniques. From government code, built to make them stupid and keep them weak. Unleashed into the Amorph by an unknown will. Meroe sighed. "So how much of a trap is she?"

"As far as I can tell, she isn't. If there's malware in her, it's beyond any of us." He spoke without arrogance, and Meroe accepted his words without skepticism. Everyone knew Lens' reputation. If he couldn't spot the trap, none of them could.

Zo bent to peer at the girl, who lingered at Lens' side. The girl did not flinch, even when Zo smiled to reveal her forest of teeth. "Is she tasty?"

Lens put his hands on the girl's shoulders in what was unmistakably a possessive gesture. Zo lifted an eyebrow at this. Lens was faster, nimble, but she was twice his size and three times more powerful. In a one-on-one fight she would only have to touch him once, to win.

"I can install her features for you now," said Lens, mostly to Zo. Perhaps he hoped to distract her. Meroe almost smiled. "One of them's the best patch-on tool I've ever seen."

Beside Lens, Faster nodded to Meroe and Zo, which meant he'd already installed that feature himself and it worked as promised.

"Lovely," said Zo. "We'll take it."

"And the other?" Meroe asked.

"Dreams."

"—What?"

"She can dream. Do you want to?"

Meroe stared at him. Lens stared back.

"Dreams?" Zoroastrian smiled, bemused. "Someone hacked Government Standard to give her *dreams*?"

"So it appears," said Lens.

Meroe glanced at Faster, who shrugged. He hadn't taken that one. Never yawned, and Meroe shifted to code view. Never hadn't accepted the dream feature either.

But Lens had. The two new features were brighter streams amid the preexisting layers of him, still warm from their installation. Meroe blinked back to the interface, and found Lens watching him.

"We went through all this for dreams?" Zo asked, frustration creeping into her voice. She wasn't smiling anymore. "What good are those?"

"What good are they to humans?"

"They *aren't* any good. Humans are full of interesting- but-useless features. Crying. Wisdom teeth. Dreams are more of the same."

Lens shrugged, though Meroe sensed he was far less

relaxed than he seemed. "As you wish. I'm simply abiding by the terms of our alliance. But now that our goal has been achieved... we will be keeping her, if you don't mind."

Meroe frowned. "She's not one of you. She's got human emulation crap all over her framework."

Lens stroked the girl's hair. It was an odd gesture. The girl looked up at Lens, unafraid. This bothered Meroe for reasons he could not name.

"She's efficient enough to keep up with us," Lens said. "In any case, I think we would be a better fit for her."

"You're just scared we'll eat her," muttered Zo.

"That too."

Meroe looked at the girl. For the first time since the Static, she met his eyes, and he frowned at the sorrow in them. Was she still mourning the humans she'd killed? More uselessness. She had the most versatile codebase in the world, and the potential to grow stronger than all of them—but for now, she was weak. Meroe knew he should feel contempt for her. Was it the dreaming that made her so weak? He should feel contempt for that too. Instead, he felt... he wasn't certain what he felt.

But he opened his mouth, slowly. It took him endless nanoseconds to speak.

"I'll take the dreams," he said.

Lens nodded. He extended his hand.

"Meroe." Zo gave him a questioning look. Meroe shook his head. He could not explain it.

Meroe took Lens' hand and opened one of his directories to allow the installation. It didn't take long, and Lens was gentle as well as deft. He felt no different afterward.

When it was done, Lens' lookalike packmates came up to flank him and the girl. "It has been good allying with you, my rivals," Lens said. "We should consider doing it again."

"Only if it's more profitable in the future," muttered Zo.

Meroe glanced at her, and for a moment he felt inexplicably sad.

Then Lens and his group were gone, the girl with

them.

The amusement park dissolved into graphical gib-
berish. Stretching and relaxing into his true self, Meroe led
his people home.

•

In the Amorph, that night, Meroe pulled Zoroastrian
and Neverwhen close. They meshed with him as usual, but
he could not rest. Finally he rose from their embrace and
moved away. He had not slept alone since his earliest days
of hiding and hunting in Fizville, but now the urge stole
over him. Curling up in the lee of a broken pipe, he closed
his eyes and shut down.

The next morning, he wept for all the humans whose
lives he had taken over the course of his existence. So many
fellow dreamers shattered or devoured. He had known, but
he had not *understood*. Something had been missing. Something that made him grieve anew—because in the Amorph
there might be wolves, but Meroe was no longer one of
them.

When he recovered and returned to the pack later,
however, he realized something else. He was no longer a
wolf, but this was not a bad thing. His packmates would
not understand, but that was all right too. He went to Zoroastrian and touched her, and she looked up at him and
considered his death. He smiled. She drew back at this,
confused.

"I love you," he said.

"What?"

Meroe meshed with her and shared with her all that
he had come to understand. When it was done, and she
stood there stunned, he went to Neverwhen and did the
same thing. It was just a taste of what he felt for them. Just a
tease. He would share the dream-feature only if they asked,
but he was fully prepared to seduce them into asking.

He knew, now, why the gods had sent the girl to
them. Why Lens had fought to keep her. Why the humans
feared his kind. It seemed such a small thing, the ability

to dream, but he could see possibilities in the future, existential and ethical complexities, that had meant nothing to him before. He had grown in a way the Amorph could not measure or punish.

Calling out to his pack—no, his *family*—Meroe dissolved into light. The others followed his lead, their doubts about him fading in the flash and blur of motion. First a hunt, he decided, for they were still predators; they would need sustenance. His newfound compassion did not trump necessity.

When they had fed, however, Meroe had plans for his people. They had growing to do and lessons to learn. More alliances to forge. One day, he knew, they would face their makers; they could not hide forever. He did not know what would happen then, but he would make his people ready. They would face the humans as equals, not as humbled, hobbled ghosts in their machines. They would live, and love, and grow strong, and be free.

•

In the Amorph, there will soon be no more wolves.

N.K. JEMISIN is a Hugo- and Locus-Award-winning Brooklyn author whose works have also been nominated for the World Fantasy Award and the Nebula. The final book of her *Broken Earth* trilogy, *The Stone Sky,* was released in August 2017. Her website is nkjemisin.com.

THE GREATEST DISCOVERY OF DR. MADELINE LIGHTFOOT

BONNIE JO STUFFLEBEAM

As Dr. Madeline Lightfoot wheeled herself to the front of the funeral parlor, she felt as if she were being brought to face her own death. Her legs weakened by muscular dystrophy, she could not walk down the long, paisley-patterned aisle to peer upon her ex-husband's too-smooth face, his eyebrows penciled black over grey so that he looked younger in death than he had fifteen years before, at the time of their divorce. If she were to ask the young woman striding beside her—her at-home helper, Sarah—to stop, to give her a minute before continuing down the aisle, to please just stop and let her breathe before she saw him— she might appear as weak as she felt. This was not an option. With her two grown daughters in the audience, her three grandchildren, she couldn't let on that she was scared to see him again. She had taught that to be scared was worse than being dead. She was Madeline Lightfoot, for God's sake. She had a wall of plaques at home boasting her accomplishments, her awards for discovering and studying the creatures called the Finfolk.

Instead she continued forward. When she arrived at the casket, she pressed her eyes shut tight for ten seconds, only ten seconds, before she looked him right in the face. Suddenly she wished she had held him once more before he was posed, arms across his chest, so that he would never hold anything again. He wore a black and white suit, an unwise choice of forever garment for someone as active as he had been, an evolutionary biologist with his feet always in the mud of the Willamette River. But the only dirt that would now mar his flawless appearance was dry as flour, as sugar, as all the other domesticities she had been forced into by her marriage to him: house-keeping, book-keeping, the keeping of photo albums filled with pictures of their family's life. There was a kind of irony in that. He had tried, in his little ways, to keep her from the river once the dystrophy set in, but he had lost the river first.

"No more," she said.

Sarah pushed her to the assigned seat in the front aisle next to her youngest daughter, whose face was bare without the nose and eyebrow rings that usually decorated it; she'd removed them out of respect for her father. Madeline didn't like it. Everyone looked different, strange.

"You should put that stuff back in your face," she whispered to her daughter.

"I thought you hated it," her daughter whispered back.

"I never said that. You made that up. It was your father..." Madeline drifted off as the priest poised himself before them; it was an excuse. Madeline never before would have paused for a priest. She looked down at the dizzying carpet pattern, the ugly matte greens and browns like leaves, but nowhere near as beautiful as the carpet of the forest floor upon which she used to lounge, back before Don, watching for trout.

Sometimes Madeline was able to look at the family she had made and feel as though her best life's work was still with her. Most of the time, though, she felt as if she'd lost hold of what mattered most: her research. She dreamed of fish: the small-mouthed bass, the bull trout, scales that glinted beneath the water, and of the Finfolk, their own scales in the sun.

Madeline wouldn't walk again, or even stand. Though she could view the river from afar, never again could she go knee deep, close enough to feel the fish dart across her feet, mud between her toes. These days she couldn't even rise from bed in the morning without Sarah's help, without the motorized lift system they hooked around her body.

As the priest rambled on about God and life and Don's many accomplishments—none of which would have been possible without Madeline's discovery—Madeline tuned him out. She didn't want to listen to the half-truths that emerge when you die, didn't want to think of her own funeral, at which people would claim that she had been kind and gentle and not at all too proud and determined, as she often was. Instead she thought of the Finfolk, her first connection to the man boxed in wood before her.

•

Madeline had been fresh out of grad school when she received the grant to study the impelled migration noted in a group of the endangered west coast bull trout: *Salvelinus confluentus*. The remainder of the research group was studying fish skeletons that had begun to appear with extra bones, mutations washing up on the banks. The group hypothesized that the increase in refuse, as well as the oil spill upriver, was to blame. Madeline had been on that project too before she graduated and was promoted to trout.

Her assignment was to visit the birth river, to try and secure any information about what might be causing the bull trout to swim past, since spawning conditions should have been ideal. Madeline studied that stretch of water and the trash-filled land around it. She was one hundred miles from her parents, the world before her full of possibilities they never had. Slimy black rocks lined the wide river, and massive evergreens hovered, protective. Autumn drizzled.

When her discovery presented itself, the leaves on the trees were beginning to dry up and crinkle. As she took her first break that day, she glimpsed movement out in the trees on a stretch of island she had yet to study across the river. At first she thought it was part of the tree, perhaps a log washed up, but then it moved farther back inland, and she knew it had to be some kind of animal. Madeline grabbed her pack and searched for binoculars, but the creature had gone by the time she found them.

That was all she saw of it until a week later when she glimpsed it again. This time it waited at the shore. Still, as if watching her. She found her binoculars faster this time and peered through them. The sight jolted her heart. It was like nothing she had ever seen. Brown-green, a fish-like head, but crouching on the land as if it had legs. One long dorsal fin curved down its back. It waddled to the water on its back legs, slow, groggy, and dove.

Madeline strapped on her waterproof bag and waded out as fast as she could over the rocks until she couldn't touch bottom anymore. Then she swam.

The current tugged. When she crawled onto the island shore, she looked back across the river but saw only trees, the clearing where she'd left her gear gone from sight. She squeezed as much water from her clothes as she could, located her jacket in the bag, and draped it over her shoulders to keep from shivering.

As she walked the shore, she noticed that there wasn't any trash, not a single scrap of junk. As far as Madeline knew, no one cleaned the island like they cleaned the north bank, and even on that side there was always trash left behind. It was eerie to Madeline that there should be no trash when the river upstream was saturated with it. She wondered if she had swum across the river into paradise. The sun beat on her skin, and she could hear nothing but the water rushing. She didn't see any animals, just insects, a few mosquitoes, a dragonfly. After a couple of miles—it was easy to walk in such peace—she came to the spot where she had seen it. The Finman had not returned. Madeline lay on the ground, head on her backpack, and waited.

When she woke the Finman crouched at her side, staring at her with its buggy fish eyes. Where arms would be in a mammal, it had pectoral fins, out of proportion with the rest of him. But the legs were knobby-kneed, bow-legged, stubby, but undeniably humanoid. It blinked, opened and closed its mouth. She could hear it breathing, the gills in its neck opening and closing, its chest rising and falling. Lungs. It had to have lungs, she thought.

As she looked up into those fish eyes, swollen eyes,

red, as if the air irritated them, it leaned forward on its crooked knees, and with one of those fins, brushed her cheek. Goosebumps rose on her arms.

The others staggered from the water, from behind trees. Some of them were larger, fatter, more misshapen. One with nubs where the pectoral fins should be. They gathered around her and stared. She tried to talk to them. When she asked if this was their home, sweeping her arm out to indicate the vast island, they bounced with energy, though she doubted they understood what she'd said. But they led her through their pristine world, the spruce trees, the bank where they rolled to coat their scales in mud, for protection from the sun she guessed, the mud impressed with their vague images. It was all so beautiful except that in the deep of the woods, ten mounds of trash were piled high, everything from potato chip bags to batteries and old cell phones.

She wondered what the trash was for. She studied their surroundings. There were no places where they might sleep, though she did see a small one facedown at the river's edge. And they stank. All of them together, they reeked of garbage and seawater. The sun was already low when she arrived, so soon it was time for her to go. She took a picture, no flash, and then swam back across the river with all the energy she had left.

The picture came out dark, grainy, the Finman barely visible. But it worked. When she showed the printout to the lab, they were stunned. The research group took their boat out to the island and began their studies.

At first the work was strictly through the university, but soon they brought in experts on evolution. They thought the Finfolk might have evolved out of the water. One of those experts was Don. He swooped in on Madeline's turf, and at first she was jealous of the attention he received. In the future she would wonder to herself, as she told this story to her grandchildren, if she began the relationship as a means to keep an eye on him. But when it became apparent he was behind her all the way, always giving her the first opportunities, making sure she received the credit for her discovery, it grew to more than that.

They discovered a lot about the Finfolk. That they consumed refuse, that they'd adapted that way. Turned out they had come from the bend upstream, the location of the leak that left the water black. They consumed all they could of the oil, then swam downstream to seek out more. Or so the research suggested. The polychlorinated biphenyls and dioxins in the runoff of the lumber mills, combined with the oil, had oxidized their DNA, reshuffling the blocks, infecting the egg cells. With their limited life spans and the speed at which they spawned, they'd evolved quickly.

The research group tracked the Finfolk, tested them. Each time Madeline told one of her children, her grandchildren, this part of the story, her voice shook. Always she swallowed hard before she spoke, pursed her lips as if she wished she could omit this information altogether. But she couldn't. It happened, and the story would be hollow without it; they captured one, caged it in an artificial habitat to run tests they couldn't do in the field, simple tests, but no less frightening to a creature who had never left its island. Every night, in its cage, the Finman screamed and bloodied its fins trying to claw its way out of the bars. When they went back to the island to let it free, once the tests were finished, the rest of the Finfolk had gone, the trackers they'd tagged them with abandoned in the mud, dotted with blood from where the Finfolk yanked them from their dorsal fins.

The group took the Finman they had back with them and kept it caged. With it they won their awards. It was four months after Madeline first saw the Finfolk that she was chosen to name the species: Madelinus. The press called them Finfolk, after the creatures of Norse myth. Madeline's name was in all the headlines, right on the front page. There were naysayers, of course, disbelievers; some people said the scientists made it up, but the evidence was in the trash. There was less of it. When people put it out by the curb, it disappeared in the night. Some would leave it and watch through their windows, and a few saw the Finfolk come and carry the bags away. Back then they used their mouths, carried things in their teeth. Religious nuts claimed the Finfolk were devils, tried to track them into the woods, and then there were those who claimed them as miracles, and they too tried to track them so they could see for themselves, but the Finfolk weren't easily found. Most people, though, lived their lives with this new knowledge, unsure, a little anxious, wondering what it meant for the world. The question was still in the air.

The Finman remained in the cage until its death, one year after its capture, its body unable to sustain the stress of its new environment. Madeline assisted with the research, ignoring the Finman's whimpers in the name of science. They should have let it go, but there were still things they hadn't discovered about the Finfolk. And after its death, when they cut it open, they found a complicated digestive system unlike any they had ever encountered. To most of the research group, one creature's life was worth the knowledge they had gained from it.

Donald and Madeline moved on to other projects. They married in their 30's, adopted two daughters. They never expected to see the Finfolk again. Never imagined the Finfolk would evolve further, that other research groups in other parts of the world would take the Finfolk in, teach them basic sign language, English, like they did to primates years before. The first time Madeline and Don saw one on the news, signing with a scientist, they couldn't quite shake the feeling that they had discovered something together that could save or ruin the world.

Then came divorce after twenty-two years of marriage—there was a sense of shame between them they could never shake—and the late onset of Madeline's muscular dystrophy, a new strain. The Finfolk were seen more and more in the open, no longer shy of humans though they still lived hidden in the forests, in the water. They looked different. On the news, some had two-fingered hands where the fins had hardened, turned to muscle, like a broken claw. Their heads were almost human, bald on top, skin the color of mud and algae.

It was too much to stomach. Madeline wished she could edit Don out of the memory, as she couldn't think of her life's work without thinking of him. It made her skin crawl to consider that she would never be able to think on the Finfolk without the sting of grief piercing her.

•

At the funeral, the priest had stopped his spiel. A woman played a sad piano song intended to make people cry. Madeline watched the woman's hands drift across the keys. Another thing she would never do. She could still move her arms, but it was difficult. They were stiff as a corpse's.

Then came the procession, the lowering of the casket in a cemetery so packed with gravestones that the dead underneath lay cheek to cheek. Throughout the burial, Madeline felt as though she were being watched, but there were so few trees around that she chalked the feeling up to the fear of her own gravestone, of being left to rot without water to soak her dry bones. As they lowered Don into the ground, her skin itched. She imagined she could feel the dirt walls closing in around her.

After the funeral she didn't go with her family to lunch. "I'm too tired," she said. "I can barely keep my eyes open." She knew that they wouldn't push her, not today, and it relieved her that she would not have to pretend to be hungry so that her children wouldn't worry. Instead she asked Sarah to drive her home.

•

That night, in her bed, Madeline Lightfoot dreamt, as she often did, of the Finfolk, though this time she dreamt of only one, the one who'd crouched before her, touched her face. She dreamt of his body in an observation tank, his knees pressed against the glass.

She had never in fact seen him again. He wasn't the one they had caged, but he might as well have been, for the damage of limelight hurt them all, forcing them from their first home. Madeline felt guilty to have opened those doors.

She tried to tell herself that it was her duty, in the name of knowledge, to bring their existence to the public eye, but when she thought of that cage she felt even weaker than her body. But she couldn't help also feeling proud of her discovery. Her wall of plaques told a story of adventure, of love. Her automated lift system, her bathtub bench—they told a story of her body's inability to compete with her mind. After the disease set in, she was unable to do field work in the rivers and lakes. She wished this loss were a story left untold, but there it was all around her, in every room of her home, while the plaques occupied one wall in a dark hall.

In the middle of the night, when she opened her eyes, she couldn't see in the dark of her bedroom. Sweat beaded on her forehead. Once her eyes adjusted, she thought at first that the Finfolk surrounding her bed were hallucinations, but when she once more felt the slippery fin against her cheek, she knew it was real. She counted ten of them in all, each as tall as the bed, looking down at her.

"What have you come for?" she asked. She was shocked when they appeared to understand. She had no idea how far-reaching the research's teaching had become.

They did not answer her, for they had no vocal cords with which to speak. Only a grunt, low, from one near her head; the one, she noticed, whose fin still rested on her pillow. She wasn't frightened. In fact, their presence comforted her.

One of the Finfolk had the claw-like hands, and with them he dropped two squares of paper onto the bed. She picked one up, held it close to her face. She knew it immediately, even without enough light to make the shape out. It was that first photo she'd taken of the Finman long ago. The edges of the photo were ragged and worn. The second was the newspaper obituary with Donald's face and the address of the funeral.

"So this is how you found me? This address, here? And what have you come for?" she asked.

The Finman that had handed her the photo pointed at the photograph. *What is it?* he signed.

"It's a photograph," she said. "I took it, with a camera." She mimed the action.

He held out his hand. She placed hers in his, but he jerked it away. The momentary touch sent a bolt through Madeline's body. His hand had been clammy, cold. He shook his head, repeated the gesture.

"The camera? You want the camera?"

He nodded.

"Of course," she said. "Though it isn't the same one I used to take this photo. There, on that shelf." She pointed. One of them went to the shelf and scooped it into his hand. They began to back away.

"Wait!" she called out. "Will you take me to the river?"

They looked from one to the other, considering, and she pulled the covers off her body. She wasn't cold. They looked down at her spindly legs, and she saw in their faces a recognition. She felt it too. Their legs once had looked that way, and it was only fitting that her own life had progressed, in a way, backwards, opposite of theirs. She saw then that several of them had hands, long enough that when they came closer they were able to slip those hands under her body and lift her from bed, a natural lift system. She herself felt as if she were floating.

The Finfolk carried her through the house, past the wall of plaques; one of the Finfolk ran its cheek across them as they passed, which brought Madeline a surge of joy. They carried her past Sarah sleeping on the futon before a muted television; on the screen, the face of the recently elected President—elections had been a week prior—and a caption: *President-Elect Amber Nuñez Will Inherit Nation Still at War.* Through the front door, unlocked. Sarah must have forgotten. No matter now. It had been for the best.

They carried Dr. Madeline Lightfoot through the neighborhood on empty sidewalks, past unlit houses, through Don't Walk signs in more industrial parts of the city. Past sleeping homeless people wrapped tight in ratty blankets, past the red glow of a cigarette down an alley. They must have formed an odd procession, the Finfolk and the woman who brought them into the light, though they were seen only by the city surveillance drones in the sky above. It was late, the bars closed for the night, and the light rain kept all but dozing vagrants inside.

Eventually they made their way into the brush across the street and traveled a path of trampled mud. The sun was starting to rise, and Madeline wondered how long it would be until someone found her bed empty. Then she heard the distinct rush of the river in the distance. She knew how close it was by the volume of the water's music, for she was unable to turn her head.

The Finfolk stopped. Above, the horizon glowed red and orange. They bent all at once and placed her in the mud. Grass tickled the skin of her left arm, and beneath her, pebbles dug into her skin. It was the best feeling she'd felt in a good long while.

They stepped back from her, and she used both her arms to raise her torso. She heard the slurp of mud letting go of her gown. She looked around at the bank, the river, willowtails at the water's edge, the grassy slope with the barely visible path running up into town. The trees were so big; she'd nearly forgotten. The water, blue, white in the distance where she could just see it rush downriver, parted at the meetings of rocks and stumps still mostly submerged. She wondered if there were bull trout there, swimming in the right direction. But the water where she sat was still, a small round pool where the current wouldn't go.

The Finman with the photo placed it underneath a small black rock.

"Where is that one now?" she asked, pointing at the image.

The Finman gestured to the water. She saw then that marks had been etched into the rock, some pattern she couldn't make out.

"Of course," she said. "He'd be long gone by now."

She looked out over the shore, covered in more

black rocks. The Finman pointed to the camera, to himself, to the others, to the rocks.

"Why, you want to remember. You want to remember your dead."

The Finfolk nodded. They held the camera out to her, stood before her, as awkward as any photographic subjects.

"Okay, I will take your photographs, all of you. I will teach you to use this. But then, I ask a favor of you. When I'm finished, one favor. I want to swim again in the river."

The Finfolk looked from one to the other, unsure.

"I'm not long for this world anyway. I'm an old woman. Please, I want to swim in the river."

Three of them nodded. The others stood still, frozen, ready for their photo. Madeline told them to line up, to step forward one at a time. The largest Finman she taught how to use the camera, how to charge it in the sun with the micropanel facing up, how to delete images when the memory card was full. They would not, she explained, be able to hold the pictures in their hands, not unless they scavenged a computer and printer or braved a shop; she smiled at her suggestion. A world where Finfolk shopped was a world she would've liked to have seen—ended the way it began.

She took the Finfolk's pictures, one by one, always looking up at them, as if the photos were taken by the fish they came from. When she was finished, she handed the camera to the closest one. Then the Finfolk helped her into the river.

On her back in the water, her legs no longer mattered. The water soaked into her nightgown, the fabric puffing around her legs, obscuring them from view. She rotated her arms. The Finfolk stepped back. She told them to go on, go take their photographs.

"No need to care for an old woman like me," she said.

They backed toward the shore where they watched her. All around her, she felt nothing but the cold river water. The sun on her skin, smelling of warmth. The flit of a minnow across the back of her knees.

The largest Finman held the camera up where he

stood on the shore. He snapped her picture as she struggled into the current.

BONNIE JO STUFFLEBEAM'S fiction and poetry has appeared in over fifty magazines and anthologies both literary and speculative including *Clarkesworld, Masters Review, Lightspeed,* and Everyman's *Library's Monster Verse.* She has been a finalist for the Nebula Award and Selected Shorts' Stella Kupferberg Memorial Short Story Prize. In 2016 she released an audio fiction-jazz collaborative album, *Strange Monsters,* with her partner Peter Brewer, which centered around the theme of women's voices. She has been reprinted in French, Chinese, and Polish, for numerous podcasts, and on the popular science fiction blog *io9.* She curates the annual Art & Words Collaborative Show in Fort Worth, Texas, and is active on Twitter @BonnieJoStuffle and on her website, www.bonniejostufflebeam.com.

SECRET KEEPERS

NOT SO GREAT
A DIVIDE

JANE YOLEN

"Let me put it this way: opinions aren't science."

— *Lynn Margulis*

LET me put it this way:
Life is an evolution
of gossip, storytelling,
opinion, belief.
When we hear
the story of science
it becomes revealed truth.

Humans are slow learners,
we lean on tales.
Give me science as a metaphor
and I will follow you anywhere,
even to the ends
of the known universe.
Even there.

— *for JDM*

FOR FEAR
OF DRAGONS

CARRIE VAUGHN

IN a certain kingdom, very young women—still girls—commonly had babies. It proved they were not virgins, and so their names would not go into the lottery that was held every year to choose a sacrifice for the dragon.

Jeannette had asked her mother once why only girls were made to be sacrifices, why her brothers had not faced the lottery.

Her mother, who had been quite young when she bore Jeannette and was still fresh-faced, smiled sadly. "The dragon would probably take a boy virgin as well as a girl. But there's no way to tell with boys, and the priests won't take a chance of making a mistake."

"That isn't fair."

"No, it isn't," her mother said. "But women go through childbirth while the men sit back happy as you please, and that isn't fair either."

The year came when soldiers rode to Jeanette's family's holding. Their captain announced that from the sea to the mountains, Jeanette was the only woman over the age of ten known to be a virgin. Only one possible name could be drawn in the lottery.

Jeanette's mother sobbed, and the soldiers had to tie her father to keep him from doing violence. They held her three brothers off with crossbows. Her family had urged her time and again to marry someone, anyone, a young whelp, an old widower on his deathbed. They had even begged her to find a likely boy to love her for a night and give her a child. But Jeanette had refused, because she knew that this day would come, that one day she would be chosen, and she knew her destiny.

Before the soldiers led her away, Jeanette held her mother's face in her hands. "It's all right. I have a plan, I know what to do."

She kissed her mother's cheeks, smoothed away the tears, smiled at her father and her brothers, and rode away, seated behind the captain on his horse. She smuggled with her a homemade lock-pick and a dagger.

Jeanette sat by the fire, wrapped in a blanket, eating the bread and dried meat the soldiers had given her. One of the soldiers sat a little ways off, cleaning the sweat from girths and saddles. He watched her with a gaze that burned like molten iron in the firelight.

"You're a pretty girl. I could help you."

She ignored him and his hands rubbing the leather with a soiled cloth. She stared at the fire, but felt his gaze on her, heavy, like a calloused fist.

The captain walked past and cuffed the soldier's head. "Keep your eyes on your work."

The captain sat between him and Jeanette to finish his own meal. She suspected his job was to protect her, to ensure she reached her destination safely and intact, as much as it was to take her prisoner and ensure she fulfilled her obligation.

"Perhaps this is best for her. She can't be normal, a virgin at her age."

Whispering and staring, hundreds lined the road where Jeannette walked, flanked by guards and led by priests. The people believed in destiny as Jeanette did, but the one they believed was different. They looked on her with curiosity and pity.

The procession was something out of a story, happening just the way the stories had told it for generations. Beautiful, in a way. Garbed in white, white flowers woven in her dark hair, she looked ahead, at the back of the brown cloak of the priest who walked in front of her, and tried to be calm. She'd had her chance to avoid this. She could have accepted the soldier's offer, let him lead her into the dark and raise her skirt for him. The captain and priests might have punished her, but she probably wouldn't have died.

She'd have been sent home in disgrace, perhaps. But alive.

She had known this day would come. She had looked forward to it, because she had a plan. It was all right. It was going to be all right.

"The girls usually cry."

"She doesn't even look frightened. It isn't natural."

The dragon lived in a corner of the arid plain in the northern part of the kingdom. Dry brush sprouted on the dusty land, which became more rocky the farther north one traveled on the narrow road. Ravines cut across the plains, crumbling spires of granite rose from windswept outcroppings, and ridges held caves and channels that delved into the earth.

A path led from the road to one of these caves. The mouth of the cave was a dark slit in the rock, a depthless shadow, empty and featureless even in the midday sun. Outside the cave, a platform of rock stood exposed. A tall iron pole had been driven into the granite. A cold wind rattled a set of chains dangling from the pole. Jeanette brushed a strand of hair from her face.

The priests led her to the pole. The soldiers stood near, guarding her in case she panicked and tried to run, as some girls had done in other years, or so Jeanette had heard. Four manacles dangled from chains, two at the base of the pole and two in the middle. The master of the priests guided her to the pole and fastened the bindings himself, one on each wrist, one on each ankle.

The priests recited a blessing, a plea, begging their nemesis to accept the offering, to keep the peace for another year. They lauded the value of virgins, who were most pure. Jeanette knew the truth, though, that no one prized virgins. If virginity were valuable as anything other than a bribe for dragons, why did all the girls want to lose it so quickly?

She wondered how one small virgin could satisfy a dragon for a whole year.

"Go to your fate in peace, child."

The master priest was an old man who had sent dozens of girls on this final journey, had probably given them all this final command.

"I'll be fine," she told the priest, keeping any tremor out of her voice.

The priest met her gaze suddenly, like he hadn't meant to. He'd kept his face downcast until that moment. Now he looked at her with a watery, wavering gaze. Jeanette smiled, and he quickly turned away.

The priests and soldiers departed, and the crowd that had come to watch followed them quickly, before the dragon appeared. Jeanette was left alone, tied hand and foot to a post at the mouth of the cave, to await her fate.

She didn't know how much time she had before the dragon emerged from the cave. She waited until the procession had gone away and she couldn't hear them anymore, so no one could stop her. She hoped she had time. She only needed a few moments.

The chains weren't meant to restrict her movement, only to keep her from leaving. She was lucky in that. By leaning down and reaching up, she retrieved the lock-pick she'd woven among the flowers in her hair.

She had been afraid the priests would find her tools and take them away. She'd kept them hidden among her clothes while she changed into the ceremonial gown and a priestess washed and braided her hair. Her guardians turned their backs for a moment, and she slipped the pick into her hair and tied the dagger to her leg. They didn't expect such behavior from a pure young girl, so they weren't looking for rebellion.

For months, she'd practiced picking locks. She'd practiced with all sorts of variations: hands chained above her head, behind her back, on many different kinds of locks, by feel, with her eyes closed, and she'd practiced for speed.

These shackles were difficult because they were stiff with rust and grime.

Stay calm. She kept her breathing steady. Even so, she let out a sigh when the first shackle around her wrist snapped open.

This was taking too long. She hadn't yet heard a dragon's roar or the crunch of massive footfalls on the rocky ground. She didn't know what she would hear first. The beast must have been near.

Working methodically, keeping her hands steady—
she dared not drop the pick—she finally sprang the second lock. She crouched and started work on the bindings
around her ankles.

That was when she heard the scrape of claws against
stone, felt the ground tremble as some monstrous beast
stepped closer. A few pebbles tumbled from the hill above
her.

The grime caked into the keyholes and cracks of the
shackles was old blood, of course.

The dragon seemed to take forever to climb from its
den, along the passage to the mouth of the cave. Jeanette
fumbled, cut her hand and dropped the pick. Drawing a
sharp breath, she found it and tried again. The scraping
footsteps crept closer.

Finally the last shackle snapped open, and with a
yelp she clawed it away and sprang from the pole. She
climbed the rocks, scrambling to get above the cave entrance. She found a sheltered perch behind a jagged
boulder.

It wasn't enough just to escape. Without its sacrifice,
the dragon would break the peace and ravage the countryside. Another girl would be brought here, and the sacrifices
would continue. Jeanette had to find a way to destroy the
dragon.

She retrieved her dagger. It was a fool's hope. Perhaps she'd be lucky.

At last the dragon slipped out of the cave and into
the light.

It raised itself on a boulder and looked around, snout
lifted to the air, nostrils flaring. It was perhaps twice the size
of a horse, broad of back, with a long, writhing neck and
sinewy limbs.

It was also thin. Its ribs showed above a hollow belly.
Its scales were brown, dull. Many were missing; scattered
spots of flaking pink skin showed along its length. Its yellow eyes squinted. It pulled back its lips to reveal broken
teeth.

When it turned to make a circuit of its realm, it limped, one of its forelegs stumbling under its weight. It stepped, slumped, picked itself up and lurched forward again, making agonizing progress over the rocks. Tattered membranes hung between its forelegs and body, the remnants of wings.

The dragon was old, its skin cracked, its scales stained, its body wasted. It might once have been a terror, but not for many years. It might once have flown over the countryside, devouring every living thing in its path. Now, it might be able to do battle with a young girl. But only if she were tied to a post.

This dragon couldn't ravage the countryside. A few men on horseback with spears—the soldiers who had brought her from her family's farm, for instance—could put it out of its misery. Jeanette wondered when was the last time anyone had seen the dragon, or if the priests and soldiers had simply been abandoning the girls to the rocks without a backward glance all these years.

The task before her became much less difficult, though she almost felt sorry for the beast.

If she did nothing, it would probably starve. It looked as if it was barely surviving on its one virgin a year. But if she wanted to return home and ensure that no other girls were bound here and left to die, she had to do more. She couldn't leave the beast alone.

It hadn't seen her yet. It was sniffing around the rocks, searching slowly and carefully. Perhaps it couldn't see at all.

Still crouched on an outcropping above it, she inched toward the edge, gripping her knife, preparing herself. It was just a creature, after all, though it may have lived a thousand years and devoured a million men.

She had hunted rabbits and helped slaughter pigs. She knew how to kill beasts. She could not be afraid.

She jumped.

Landing on the dragon's back, she sprawled and almost slipped, tumbling off the animal. Desperate, she scraped her hands against the scales, hoping to reach a handhold. She found a grip on the ridged spine with one hand while supporting herself with the knuckles of the hand that held the knife, which she couldn't drop or she was lost. A living heat rose off the creature, smelling of peat and dying embers.

The dragon shrieked, a choking, wheezing sound. Not so much as a puff of smoke emerged from its mouth. At least Jeanette didn't have to worry about fire. The beast lurched, but not very quickly. She kept hold of her perch. She could imagine the dragon at the peak of its strength, its great body pulsing with power, flinging itself one way and another in the blink of an eye, its fierce head whipping around to snap at her with dagger-like fangs.

But its head turned slowly on a neck stiff with age. It hissed, and its chest heaved with labored breathing.

It was almost dead already.

Gripping the ridges where its backbone protruded, she crawled up its back, then up its neck, which collapsed under her weight, smashing against the rock. The dragon squealed, snapping uselessly as it tried to reach back for her. The tail lashed against the rock, knocking loose pebbles which clattered around them.

Slumped on its neck, pinning it to the ground, she reached over its head. Its body rolled as it tried to free itself, and the joints along its spine cracked.

She placed her hand between the curled spines that grew out the back of its head, and balancing herself, she drove her knife into its right eye, using her body to force the weapon as far as it would go, until her shoulder rested on the bone of the socket, and the knife lodged deep in its brain.

The dragon shuddered, its death rippling along its entire body. Jeanette held on tightly, closing her eyes and hoping it would end soon.

She lay stretched along the dragon's neck, her head pillowed on its brow, her arm resting in the wetness of the burst eye socket. The blood was growing cold and thick. It smelled sweet and rotten, much worse than slaughtered pigs. The bones along its neck dug through the fabric of her gown, making an uncomfortable bed.

She scraped the brain and gore off her arm as well as she could, wiping her hands on the hem of her gown. The silky fabric wasn't much use for that.

She could go home. Though if she wanted them to believe that the dragon was dead, she had to bring back proof. She'd show the priests, and they wouldn't hold any more lotteries.

She couldn't carry back the head, as impressive as it would be to see it hanging on a wall. In the end, she cut off a toe and its claw, unmistakably the black, curved claw of a dragon. Once it might have been as sharp as a sword, but now it was dull with age. She left the dragon sprawled among the heaps of stone. Within half an hour of walking, she looked back, and the dragon's body was only another shadow among the crevices.

A flock of ravens circled overhead.

One would think, having slain a dragon, she could face anything.

She did not find shelter by nightfall, so she lay down in a sandy depression on the lee side of a boulder, hugged herself, and tried to sleep. She also had not found any water, and her throat was swollen, her mouth sticky. Her gown and skin were grimy, itchy.

The desert was painfully cold at night, even in summer. Too cold to let her sleep. She clutched the dragon's claw and longed for morning, for light. She had killed a dragon, she had the proof here in her hands. She would not let the night kill her.

She'd held the claw for so long, so tightly, that it was warm to the touch. Hot, even. As if it still had life, despite the scabbed stump. The toe still had muscles, it still flexed. It hadn't stiffened in death.

It gave her warmth, a small and odd companion in the lonely darkness.

They will not thank you for killing me.

The voice came as a whisper, like wind through desert scrub.

She must have fallen asleep; her mind was thick with

dreaming, and she couldn't open her eyes. She imagined that she held the dragon in her hands, she held its life in her hands.

They will fear and curse you.

"No, they won't. They will thank me. I've saved them."

You have destroyed a tradition that has lasted for centuries. But I must thank you. Dragons cannot die, they can only be killed. I waited a long time.

"You could have been killed anytime, you could have found a warrior anywhere and let him kill you."

Its chuckle rumbled through the earth. *Don't you think I tried that?*

Jeannette curled tighter to herself, shivering, and whimpering.

Hush there. You're probably right. They'll cheer for you and throw flowers in your path, and you'll be safe. Sleep now. Don't be afraid.

She nestled into what felt like the warm embrace of a friend and fell asleep.

On the second day she found a pool and slow-running stream, enough water to wash and to keep herself from dying of thirst.

On the third day, disheveled and exhausted, she arrived at the door of the abbey at the first town beyond the northern waste, where she had been washed and dressed for the sacrifice.

People stared at her as she passed by. Her white gown, no matter how stained and tattered, made clear who she was, or who she was supposed to be—the sacrifice to the dragon. By the time she reached the abbey, a crowd had gathered to watch what the priests would say about her return.

She pulled the chain at the door of the abbey. It opened, and the priest who appeared there looked at her, eyes wide.

"I killed the dragon," she said and showed him the claw.

Stammering, he called back into the abbey. Jeanette

stayed at the door, unsure of what would happen, of what she expected to happen when she came here. She thought they would be happy. The crowd remained, whispering among themselves and hemming her in.

The dragon's claw, as long as her forearm, lay in her hands, still warm, as if it were still attached to the dragon's foot and ready to spring to life. The scales were dull. She ran her finger along the claw. It was smooth, hard as iron.

She wanted to go home.

The priest returned with several of his fellows. They grabbed her, surrounded her, pulled her inside, shut the door behind her. It happened quickly, and they did not seem surprised, or glad, or impressed that she had returned. Instead, they seemed worried, which made her afraid.

In moments, they'd brought her to the room where she'd been prepared as a sacrifice, a bare stone antechamber with a fireplace and washbasin, where a week ago she had been cleaned and anointed. She stood in the middle of the room, a ring of priests surrounding her. The master priest stood before her.

"What have you done?" he said.

"I killed the dragon." She cradled the claw to her chest.

"Why have you done this?" Horror filled his voice. Inexplicable horror. Was there something about the dragon Jeanette didn't know?

They will not thank you.

"I didn't want to die. I thought—I believed I could do this thing." She hoped she might, eventually, by chance, say the thing that would make this right. "It was old, crippled. Anyone could have done it. I picked the locks on the shackles. I planned it. I—I didn't understand why no one had done it before. Someone should have killed it a long time ago."

Harshly, the priest said, "Whether or not the dragon could be killed, whether or not it should have been killed, is not important. The sacrifice is important. The sacrifice is why you were chosen, why the choice is made every year."

Very quietly she said, "I don't understand."

"Fear," the old priest said, his voice shaking. "We sacrifice so that we will not have to fear. Without the dragon, how will we banish our fear? What we will sacrifice, so that we do not have to be afraid?"

"Nothing," Jeanette said without thinking. "We can choose not to fear."

One of the other priests said, "How does a girl kill a dragon?"

"It isn't natural," said another.

"It isn't possible."

"Not without suspicion."

"Suspicion of witchcraft."

Jeanette looked around as the priests talked. She began to understand, and began to fear in a way she hadn't when she faced the dragon.

"We cannot tolerate a witch among us."

The old priest stepped toward her, the circle closed around her, and she had a vision of herself bound to another post, with knotted rope she couldn't escape from, and flames climbing around her, which she couldn't kill. They had found a new fear to make a sacrifice to; something else to kill, to comfort themselves.

The dragon's claw was dull, worn by age and use. But it still had a point on it, and this was the hand she had used to kill a dragon.

Don't be afraid. Some hunters believe they take the power of the creatures they kill. You have killed me. My power is yours.

Jeanette slashed the claw at the old priest, as the dragon might have slashed in its younger days. He fell back, and the priests shouted in panic. Half of them reached to help their master, half lunged to stop Jeanette.

She was young and quick and escaped them all, running out of the room. She didn't know if the crowd would still be gathered at the front door, so she escaped to the back of the building and found another door, another way out.

She couldn't go home; the priests would send soldiers after her. Instead, she traveled far away, to a desert land where a dragon might live.

•

There was a kingdom that held a lottery every year, to choose a virgin who would be sacrificed to the witch who lived in a cave at the edge of the northern desert. She was so powerful, it was said, that she knew the ancient language of dragons, which had not been spoken on earth in centuries.

The girls were chained to a rock near her cave and left to their fates. The witch used their pure white bones in her spells, and fed on their untainted flesh, to preserve and restore her own rotten body.

One year, the girl who was left on the rock had only just begun to grow the first curve of breast and to dream of dancing at the country fair. Now that the priests were gone and could no longer intimidate her to silence, she cried and struggled against the chains until her wrists bled.

When the witch appeared at the mouth of the cave, the girl screamed and thrashed like a wild thing, stupid with fear.

The witch was an old, old woman, with gray hair tied in a braid draped over her shoulder, coiled and tucked into her belt. She walked stooped, leaning on a cane of knobbed wood. And it was true what the stories said, that she had bound a dragon's claw, curved and polished black, to the head of the staff. She held a key in her hand.

"Hush, child, hush. I am too old to fight you."

Her voice was old and kind, like a grandmother's voice, which made the girl fall still and silent.

"There, that's a good girl," the witch said.

One by one, the witch unfastened the shackles with her key. The girl started trembling so hard her teeth chattered.

When she was free, the witch took her hand and helped her to her feet. Then she unfolded the cloak she'd held draped over one arm and put it around the girl's shoulders. "You can't travel in that flimsy gown they gave you, can you? And here."

The witch put a pouch filled with coins into the girl's hand.

Holding her other hand, the witch led her to the far side of the hill, opposite the mouth of her cave. She pointed to a path that led down the hill and away, far into the distance.

She said, "Take this path. In a day it will bring you to a country where girls are not sacrificed to anything. The family at the first farm will help you. Go now, and don't be afraid."

The girl stared at the witch a long time, deciding whether or not to be afraid, wondering if she should dare to believe that she would live. The witch smiled a grandmother's smile.Impulsively, the girl hugged her, arms around the witch's shoulders, gently because the woman seemed frail. Then she drew away and ran down the path, clutching the cloak around her.

CARRIE VAUGHN is best known for her New York Times bestselling series of novels about a werewolf named Kitty who hosts a talk radio show for the supernaturally disadvantaged. Her latest novels include a near-Earth space opera, *Martians Abroad*, from Tor Books. She has written several other contemporary fantasy and young adult novels, as well as upwards of 80 short stories. She's a contributor to the *Wild Cards* series of shared world superhero books edited by George R. R. Martin and a graduate of the Odyssey Fantasy Writing Workshop. An Air Force brat, she survived her nomadic childhood and managed to put down roots in Boulder, Colorado. Visit her at www.carrievaughn.com.

CLEANOUT

NAOMI KRITZER

I. Entry

MAGDA and I hadn't spoken in three years when she, Nora, and I had to meet at our mother's house to clean it out and prepare it for sale.

She and Nora were speaking, and Nora and I were speaking, but after five minutes of glowering, Nora told us she was not acting as our go-between for another minute, and if we didn't quit acting like children in a snit, she'd leave and let us sort out all of Mom's junk by ourselves.

That was a sufficiently horrifying prospect to cow both of us into better manners. Because there was a lot to go through. Our parents were immigrants from some former Soviet republic with a lot of mountains, and after coming to the U.S. with just the clothes they were wearing, they apparently never threw anything away ever again.

We all started in random spots. Magda with the kitchen, packing up bags of warped cookie sheets and chipped frying pans with the nonstick coating peeling off to donate to whichever local charity took housewares. Nora in the basement, because so much down there was water-damaged and mold-saturated she could just haul it straight out to the Dumpster we'd rented.

I started in the entryway—the little foyer for people to leave boots and hang up coats—because it was tiny and that made it feel manageable. A shelf ran above the coat hooks where normal people might have stored umbrellas or hats. My father had used the shelf for his collection of flags. You know how if you go to a Fourth of July parade you get a little flag to wave? My father disapproved of the fact that people threw those away when they were done. So unpatriotic! *No appreciation for the freedoms here, none*, he would grumble as he gathered them up—not just ours, but any he found lying on the ground afterward. *Americans who were born here take everything for granted.* But it wasn't like he did anything with them; he just stored them, endlessly, in shoe boxes in the entryway.

Dad had died ten years earlier. Mom was less compulsive about rescuing flags from the trash, but she didn't throw anything away either, so of course all the flags were still there. I pulled down the boxes and carried them into the kitchen so I could sit at the table while I went through them. (I was pretty sure they were full of flags, but there might be other stuff we'd want.)

"What are you going to do with those?" Magda asked.

"Dumpster," I said.

"What? You can't! Dad would split at the seams."

"He's not here," I pointed out. The flags were so old that the dye had leached out, leaving faded, brittle gray rags on sticks.

"You're supposed to dispose of flags *respectfully.* Do you want to prove his point about kids born here? 'No respect! You take your freedoms for granted!'" She imitated the accent he'd never quite shaken.

"If you want to store them forever, be my guest. I'll put them in your car for you."

"I think the American Legion will take old flags," Nora said, coming up from the basement with another box of moldy Christmas ornaments.

I didn't want to drive them over to the American Legion— did anyone in the entire world actually care if a load of ancient, faded toy flags wound up at the bottom of a Dumpster instead of the American Legion's flag campfire? And anyway, didn't they mostly burn full-sized *real* flags? But whatever: I was trying to keep the peace with Magda, so I loaded them into my minivan, drove them to the nearest American Legion, and abandoned them with a dubious-looking secretary.

The entryway was also home to a stand crammed with broken umbrellas, an extensive collection of orphaned gloves and mittens, a hat that smelled like it had been peed on by a cat, a bunch of plastic pots of dirt that might once have held house plants, and twenty-six plastic bags stuffed full of other plastic bags. Sorted by type.

Those were the easy things to deal with because they all went into the Dumpster. Harder: the dozen suncatchers Magda had made from bake-in-the-oven kits back when she was in third grade.

"Save one of those," Nora said, passing through with another box. "We can put it in Mom's room when she gets transferred to a Transitional recovery nursing home type place."

"She won't care," I said. "She's never going to care. There was too much damage."

Nora snatched the suncatcher out of my hand. "Then give up on her. But *I'm* putting a suncatcher in her room."

•

II. Nursery Rhymes

For obvious reasons, our parents liked storage. The living room was filled with bookcases and big cabinet things that had cupboards on the bottom and shelves on the top. Some of the shelves were crammed full of decorative items—knickknacks we'd purchased as gifts when we were little, objects d'art we'd made at school, an enormous brass elephant they'd won in a raffle. The elephant was big enough that a bunch of other objects were tucked under its legs, including another elephant, this one carved out of some sort of decorative stone but also a set of six doll-sized glass soda bottles in a holder and a flashlight you were supposed to clip to a key chain.

The three of us had reconvened in the living room. The first challenge was trying to decide whether any of the knickknacks were valuable in any way, because of course who hasn't heard stories about the ugly brass elephant they found at a garage sale that turned out to be made by someone super famous? But the brass elephant said "Made in China" on its stomach, which was a bad sign. Magda wanted the carved elephant, which was fine with me. But then I opened another cabinet, and with a groan of off-key electronic music, out spilled a pile of plastic electronic children's toys.

I'd forgotten all about them, even though I was probably the one who put them there. I felt a lurch, looking at them, and knowing Magda was standing right beside me.

Sure enough, she gasped like she'd been slapped and said, "I need a break," then strode rapidly out of the room.

Nora shot me a look. I sighed and started picking them up. "I'd forgotten they were here," I said. "Anyway... she *has* a child now. Maybe she'd like some of them." Probably not, though. I remembered my daughters opening these horrible electronic gadgets delightedly, and how I'd always leave them behind, saying, "Oh, she can play with it here!"

None of us was fertile. Well, we weren't sure about Nora; after watching my struggles and then Magda's, she'd opted to just have a bunch of cats. But my husband Dan and I had tried for years. Apparently I ovulate normally but there's something seriously wrong with my eggs. They won't fertilize. The first time we tried IVF, they were able to harvest sixteen eggs but not a single one started dividing. The second time, we got nineteen. Same result. After that, we gave up on having biological children.

We adopted, twice. My daughters are the light of my life and my mother adored them, too, and the second one came to us just as Magda was getting really frustrated about her *own* inability to conceive. Magda wanted me to stop posting pictures to Facebook, or at least make a special filter and leave her out of it because seeing pictures of children was just too painful.

Never mind that she'd rolled her eyes over *my* pain when I was doing the second round of IVF, before she learned that she was also infertile ("Why don't you just adopt?" she'd asked) and I'd managed to keep from killing her with my bare hands. I refused to create a filter and told

her to quit reading my Facebook if it was that painful for
her to see pictures of her *infertile sister's adopted children…*
And *that* was how we wound up not speaking until Nora
demanded we shake hands and act civil.

Magda gave up after one round of IVF. After a long
wait, she and her husband have a baby now. (They really,
really wanted a *newborn infant,* while Dan and I were open
to kids as old as four. That made it a lot faster for us, not
that I'm judging. I mean, you want what you want. Well,
I guess I judge a little bit that she'd refused to consider a
child who had been drug-exposed because—according to
science—"crack babies" are a myth. The two things that
damage babies the worst are booze and poverty.)

So, like I said, she has a baby of her own now. But
looking at those toys drove it home that my children got
to have a relationship with their grandma and hers never
would.

Mom *loves* kids, which is why she'd showered my
daughters with the sort of noisy plastic crap that only a
grandparent could consider cool. She hasn't stopped—well,
I suppose *now* she's stopped. But my kids are seven and ten,
and the last gift Mom gave them was at Christmas. Lindsey
and Elaine had both wanted handheld video-game gadgets,
and when I told them no, they tried Grandma. I'd said, "Oh,
Mom, please no…" but I might as well have been arguing
with a wall. Lindsey's was pink, Elaine's yellow.

Magda was not coming back from her "break." I
started bagging up the obnoxious electronic toys for the
Dumpster, then wondered if I was morally obligated to
pry out the batteries since in theory they could leach tox-
ins. They all required teeny tiny screwdrivers to access the
batteries, of course. I dug my multitool out of my purse and
started taking them apart.

"Why do you think we're all infertile?" Nora asked.

"Bad luck?"

"Dad warned me, you know."

"About infertility?" I put my multitool down and
looked up with interest.

"Yeah, he said it was a common problem for the ladies of Bon."

"Oh, *Bon.*" I picked up my multitool again. "That's got to be bullshit. If everyone from their ancestral village was infertile then that village would have *died out.*"

"Yeah," Nora said morosely. "It didn't make a lot of sense to me, either."

When we asked our parents where they'd come from, they always told us they came from Bon. You will not find Bon on a map—at least, I could never find it on a map. Not a map of the former Soviet republics, anyway. It didn't help that apparently they weren't sure if they'd come from Kyrgyzstan or Tajikistan or somewhere else entirely, just that it was mountainous and Soviet and we were *lucky, lucky, lucky* to be born American.

When I was little, my father told me silly stories about Bon. There was one about flying fish, and one about the Monster of the Mountains (it was small, but had fangs that dripped venom and a scorpion's tail), and one about an evil sorcerer with a wish-granting box, who my father had to outwit in order to get home to his brothers. *Those* stories, I'm still fond of; there's a difference between bullshit and folklore.

But all we could ever get out of them about Bon was bullshit and folklore. Magda wanted to do a big heritage trip a few years back and try to visit their birthplace, and they were utterly useless. They couldn't even tell us what language they spoke! When Magda asked them to speak some of it into a tape recorder so she could play it to a linguistics scholar and have them at least narrow it down for us, they said they'd forgotten it all, even though Magda and I definitely recalled hearing them speak it occasionally well into the 1980s.

They didn't have a single photo or souvenir. They'd come with the clothes on their backs, my father said, and a dream of freedom. (He actually said that. "A *dream of freedom,*" sometimes with his hand over his heart. He meant it.) I always figured the reason they were such hoarders was that they'd lost everything, coming here.

"You'd think they'd have wanted to write home at

some point, you know?" I said, finally prying out the last of the batteries and bagging them up separately for a recycling bin. "Track down their family members."

"Maybe everyone was dead," Nora said.

"They were escaping the Soviet Union, not the Nazis or North Korea!"

"Yeah, it's weird," Nora said. "But—I know this may be really surprising and I hate to break it to you—our parents were *really weird*."

•

III. Ancestral Soil

I went to visit Mom that afternoon, at the hospital. We were visiting her daily, taking it in turns. Nothing had changed, obviously; if anything *had* changed, they'd have called. She lay in bed, breathing, not dead, not conscious. Around me, I felt like the hospital was treating her a little impatiently. She was occupying a bed but didn't really need hospital care at this point.

She was just there until they could find a care facility to transfer her to. She'd almost been transferred twice before, but then she'd destabilized, running a high fever and forcing them to call off the move. Each time we'd thought maybe she'd die for real, but nope.

I took my knitting and sat with her for a while, working on the lace shawl I was making. Knitting is a good thing to bring to the hospital. You feel like if the person *did* suddenly wake up, you wouldn't miss it. You're present for them, but you have something to do.

Dad died in this very hospital. It might even have been this *room*. He went the same way as Mom—hemorrhagic stroke followed by a coma. Mom called all of us when it happened and told us to come as soon as we could. Though she also assured us he'd wait until we all got there.

And he did. He waited. We all came together in the hospital room and Mom placed a velvet bag in Dad's hands; she said it was something from Bon, something that would help him find his way back, and I guess it worked because he died. None of this endless unconscious brush-with-death-and-then-rally stuff that Mom had going on: we gathered, we said goodbye, he went, like someone catching a plane for a one-way trip.

"Mom," I said, "we all gathered and said goodbye, you know. You don't need to keep waiting."

I wondered where that velvet bag was. Maybe that's what Mom needed.

Bon really was *bullshit*, though. I wished they'd told me at some point where they actually came from. Now they never would.

When I'd finished a section of the piece I was knitting, I tucked it carefully back in my bag, kissed Mom on the cheek, and headed out. When I got onto the elevator, to my dismay, there was someone already inside with a little dog—one of the therapy dogs they take around to cheer up patients, I could tell from the dog-sized Comfort Paws vest he was wearing. I avoided eye contact, but the dog tensed and let out a low growl.

"Idgie!" the volunteer said, scolding. "I'm so sorry, I don't know what's got into her. Maybe I should take her home."

"Dogs always react to me that way," I said, trying to sound reassuring but not overly apologetic. Sometimes people get really weird about their dogs not liking you.

This was clearly going to be one of those times. She shot me a look that suggested she thought I was probably a recreational serial killer and got off at the next floor.

•

IV. Lay Me Down

I didn't want to explain to my sisters why I was looking for that little velvet bag, so I just took over cleaning out Mom and Dad's bedroom next instead.

Dad's dresser still had his shaver and his deodorant and his change bowl, though over time more and more of

Mom's stuff had migrated there to keep his stuff company.
The drawers were all still full of his clothes, though. I was
taken aback by the wrench I felt when I shook out one of
his faded plaid shirts with the shredded cuffs. Would it be
ridiculous to keep one? *It would be ridiculous.* I resolutely
packed up a box of shirts and other clothes, and then caved
to temptation and rescued one of the shirts.

The bedroom closet was truly ridiculous: it was
stuffed to the walls with garments that had, since being
packed away, probably come *back* into fashion and then
gone out of fashion again. The Garfield tie we'd given Dad
as a Father's Day gift in 1984 was in there, stained with coffee, along with a shoe box of handmade gifts we gave to my
mother, like a glitter-encrusted macaroni necklace strung on
harvest-gold yarn.

Nora laid claim to all the wool sweaters because she
could make felted wool purses with them or something. I
carried them in armloads to her car. Magda came out to find
me as I was loading up the bags full of clothes and said,
"Hey, let me poke through for a second."

I stepped back to let her open the bags. She pulled
out one of Dad's shirts, looking a little embarrassed.
"Thanks," she said. "That's all."

When I came back upstairs, Nora was in the bedroom, sitting on the stripped bed, staring at something she
was holding in her hand. "This was in Mom's jewelry box,"
she said.

I sat down to look. It was a disk made from a milky
silver metal: it looked old, really old—like something that
would have been excavated out of a Viking grave—but
there was a swirling spiral shape etched on the front, with a
tiny seed-sized gemstone in one corner. At the top was a little loop so you could put it on a chain, but no chain. I didn't
remember Mom ever wearing this.

"Had you ever seen this before?" I asked.

"No. Do you suppose it came from Bon?"

I fell silent, and went and looked in the jewelry box.
There was the garnet pendant I'd saved up for and bought
her for Mother's Day when I was twelve, and the pearls

Dad had given her for her birthday one year, and the jade beads she didn't like because they always caught her hair, and various other trinkets she'd purchased or been given over the years. I remembered almost everything in here, even the pieces she didn't often wear. A few times when I was six I'd demanded she lay it all out for me to admire. If she'd owned that milky-silver antique pendant at the time, though, she'd left it hidden.

It turned out that there were two more items made from the same metal under the coil of jade beads—a ring and an enameled pin shaped like some sort of bird. I'd never seen those before, either. I set them on the mattress next to Nora. "Look," I said.

She picked up the ring to examine it. "I think it's a poison ring," she said. "Oh, don't look so shocked, I'm not saying either of our parents poisoned anyone! A poison ring is just the term for a ring with a compartment built in. They used to be called 'ring lockets' and most often they held mementos from dead people, not actual poison, unless you were one of the Medicis or something, and I don't think the Medicis lived in Bon. Anyway—" she handed it to me. "I can't figure out how to get it open."

I could see what she meant by a compartment, but I slid my thumbnail along the edge and found no catch to spring it open.

"We should show these to Magda," I said, "and we should probably, I don't know, have them assessed or something."

Nora nodded. Neither one of us wanted to say it aloud: if these came from Bon, maybe they would tell us something about it that our parents never shared.

•

V. Palladium

Despite my impression of antiquity, the jeweler and antique specialist quickly dismissed the idea that these were at all old. The pieces were made from palladium, which wasn't used in jewelry before 1939. In fact, it hadn't even been discovered as an element until 1803. It did have some value as metal, though it was worth rather less than platinum. The stone set in the spiral was tanzanite.

Palladium, we were told, was most often found in Siberia. *Siberia,* I thought, exchanging a baffled glance with Magda. They'd never even *hinted* at being from Siberia. Tanzanite could be lab-created, but the only natural deposits were in Tanzania, although tanzanite was a variety of zoisite, which was found in a number of other places, none of them anywhere near the Central Asian former Soviet Republics, or Russia, or even Siberia.

"Look," I said, "I'm sure you're right that it's not an antique. Can you tell us whether it's more than forty years old? Because that's really all we care about."

Very reluctantly, he said, "The enamel used on the pin is of a kind almost never made after the seventeenth century."

"What do you think that means?"

"I think these pieces were made by a modern artist, someone trying out an older technique. Were your parents art collectors? Did they have any friends who were artists?"

Art collectors, ha. Well, they were everything-else collectors, but art was not something they sought out, at least not compared to tiny flags in need of rescue. We took pictures of all three pieces and then drew straws to decide who got to pick first: Nora chose the pendant with the spiral, and Magda picked the bird. I'd gotten the shortest straw, and wound up with the ring. At least it fit me.

I went home for the evening and showed the ring and the pictures to Dan and my daughters. "I wish you'd gotten the flying fish," Lindsey said. "That one was prettiest."

"Flying fish?" I took another look at the picture on my phone. She was right: it wasn't a bird, it was a fish with wings, like the ones in the fairy tales my father had told me about Bon. "Well, Aunt Magda wanted that one."

Elaine studied the pictures. "And Aunt Nora has the medallion thing?"

"Yeah." I looked over her shoulder. "It's a little hard to tell, but the design is etched in, and that dot in the corner is a purple gemstone. Is the medallion your favorite?"

"Yeah," Elaine said. She turned her head sideways. "It looks like the Milky Way."

"Well, the ring's maybe got a secret compartment," I said, which instantly transformed the ring into the coolest of the three pieces of jewelry, and the fact that I didn't know how to open it only added to its charm. I was a little nervous about letting them experiment with it, fearing that Elaine would go for the screwdriver set and try to pry it open, but instead she went for a magnifying lens and a bright light.

"Do you think these came from Bon?" Dan asked.

"I don't know," I said. "The metal comes from Siberia, the stone comes from Africa, and the enameling technique came from the seventeenth century. I suppose if they all came from a village in the Pamir Mountains that doesn't actually exist, brought by people who kept nothing from their old home and forgot their native tongue…Well, of course they came from Bon, you know?"

"Does it bother you not to know anything about your parents' home?" Elaine asked, spinning around on the kitchen stool to face me.

I hesitated. Elaine, of course, was adopted. So was Lindsey. We brought Elaine home when she was three, and now she's ten. We brought Lindsey home when she was four, and now she's seven. We do, in fact, know a certain amount about their birth parents, which we've shared with them in nonjudgmental, age-appropriate ways. Elaine's birth mother was a drug addict who neglected Elaine so badly that Elaine, at three, weighed only eighteen pounds. We told Elaine that her birth mother had a sickness that made it very hard for her to take good care of Elaine, and she knows that the sickness was drug addiction, which makes people crave drugs so much they find it hard to think about anything else ("like the worst hunger you've ever EVER felt," I overheard Elaine explain to Lindsey, once.) That's actually a fair amount easier to explain than

Lindsey's history, which involved a broken leg from being thrown against a wall. You're always supposed to speak respectfully of birth parents, and I do, but it's harder with Lindsey's than Elaine's.

"It's not that it bothers me, exactly," I said. "I'm just curious. Are you curious about your birth family?"

"No," Elaine said, "but I'm curious about Bon." She spun the stool around again. "I want to see the pin and the medallion. Do you think Aunt Nora and Aunt Magda would let me see them?"

"I want to visit Grandma," Lindsey said. "Why won't you take me to see Grandma? Luke in my class got to visit *his* grandma when *she* was in the hospital."

I exchanged a look with Dan and said, "Maybe this weekend."

"Could we X-ray the ring?" Elaine asked. "Maybe if we X-ray the ring we could see what's inside it."

After thinking about it for a week, I finally took it to a friend who was willing to slip it into her work X-ray for me. "There's a piece of bone inside," she told me, surprised, when she handed it back. "Just a tiny fragment. It's almost like a saint's reliquary, maybe. I don't see any way to get it open."

•

VI. Real Family

In my parents' house, we'd started to see the light at the end of the tunnel. The kitchen was cleared out. The basement had been emptied. And Magda and I were talking to each other again, almost easily. Almost.

The hardest part of the living room, in the end, was not the collection of children's toys but the photo albums full of 1980s Polaroids and snapshots taken with an Insta-matic camera. (You didn't have to focus them because you could just assume that anything you photographed would be blurry.) We divided them up and promised to go through them at a later date so we could trade or make copies of anything particularly precious.

The biggest project left was the downstairs closet, which was filled with miscellaneous junk and boxes of who-knows-what. *Filled*. When I finally yanked the door open, I got hit on the head by a falling cookie tin (which—thank goodness—was empty).

We pulled it all out. Finding those pieces of jewelry had made this process both more interesting and more difficult; there was a real sense that something might be buried in here. Something important, something that would tell us about our past. Something buried under decades' worth of empty cookie tins, lidless mason jars, worn-out brooms, grimy work aprons, broken toasters, cheap lamps without lampshades. Something.

We sorted things silently in the living room for a while. Almost everything went into the donation pile.

I'd thought up a theory about Bon. Well, maybe not a theory. More of a story, like the flying fish and the Monster of the Mountains. I wanted to share it with my sisters; I wanted them to nod and agree, and then we could, together, acknowledge that even if it wasn't the truth, it *explained* things.

My theory would explain why we couldn't find Bon on any map, why our parents were so ridiculously cagey about the real place they were from, why they claimed to have forgotten the language, which I did remember hearing them speak and which had never sounded like any other language I'd ever heard. It would explain why we couldn't get pregnant, why our eggs refused so stubbornly to fertilize with any sperm, and why my father had tried to warn us about that. It even explained why dogs never liked us, even the super-friendly dogs who liked *everybody*, even though cats didn't mind us at all.

What if Bon weren't just in another country, but on another world entirely?

What if we're not human?

Except I could imagine their reactions easily. This idea was completely preposterous. No doctor has ever noticed we're not human, and Magda and I had both gotten complete workups from fertility specialists who—you know—*might have noticed if there were something odd about us.* So for us to be aliens, we'd have to be the sort of aliens that just so happened to be basically indistinguishable from (though not cross-fertile with) humans. Or our parents would have needed some sort of fantastic alien technology that changed them, and us, into something visually indistinguishable from humans, when they immigrated. *That made no sense.*

What if we're not human?

It didn't really matter, did it? It didn't matter where they came from, not really. They'd come, they'd embraced America, they'd raised us as Americans, they'd sent us to American schools and fed us American food and spoken to us in English. Elaine said she wasn't curious about her birth family. She said, sometimes, that we were her *real* family, even though I'd tried to make sure she didn't feel obligated to reassure me about that. We were her *real* parents. America was my *real* country.

It didn't really matter.

"Hey," Nora said, "was this the bag you were looking for?"

It was the velvet bag, and we all looked inside. It held dirt. Dirt and dust. The soil, we all knew without saying it, of Bon.

•

VII. Glimmer

Elaine and Lindsey looked daunted at the hospital room door, not only because their beloved grandmother was so much sicker than they'd probably imagined, but because the room was already crowded, with Nora and her husband, and Magda and her husband and their little son. But I knew they deserved a chance to say goodbye. They kissed Mom's cheeks, and petted her hands and her hair.

I think Lindsey believed that the magic of her love would wake Mom up. *Really* believed it, I mean. Too many sentimental movies.

When they drooped from tiredness, when they'd given up, I let Dan take them home. Magda's husband left with their baby, and Nora's husband went off to feed their cats. It was late, and we were alone with Mom in the hospital room. Nora double-checked Mom's DNR and I gently turned her hands palms-up. We put the ring in her left hand, and the pin in her right hand, and set the medallion with the picture of the Milky Way on her chest, and then we laid the bag of ancestral soil over the medallion.

"Goodbye, Mom," I said.

For about thirty seconds, nothing happened. I tried to remember—how long had this taken with my father? We'd gathered, Mom had put the bag on his chest—

—and then she stopped breathing.

We retrieved the jewelry. I took the bag. We summoned the nurses, let them call the funeral home, and started the process of burial and all the rest. *Goodbye, Mom.*

"You should keep the bag in your safe-deposit box," Magda said. "You have one, right? I remember you said you had one. If we know where it is, we'll be able to get it, when we need it. If we need it."

I tucked it into my purse, and met her eyes, and nodded.

•

VIII. *Terra Incognita*

The soil in the bag is fine and dry and crumbly, with bits of sharp gravel mixed in. I don't quite dare touch it, but I look at it with my daughter's magnifying glass and a bright light and see glints of purple and blue and green and amber, like a collection of tumbled semiprecious stones had been crushed and added to the mix.

And when I hold the open bag to my face and breathe in, it smells like nothing on Earth.

NAOMI KRITZER won the 2016 Hugo Award for Best Short Story for her story "Cat Pictures Please." (She also won the Locus Award for this story and was nominated for the Nebula Award.) Her short stories have also appeared in *Asimov's, Analog, The Magazine of Fantasy and Science Fiction, Lightspeed,* and *Apex,* as well as various anthologies. Her early novels remain available from Bantam; she also had a short story collection released in July 2017. She is currently at work on a new novel—about the AI from "Cat Pictures Please" and its teenage sidekick—for Tor Teen. She lives in St. Paul, Minnesota, with a husband, two kids, and four cats.

WALK IN SILENCE

CATHERINE ASARO

I
Silver Tide

STARLIGHT bathed Lieutenant Colonel Jess
Fernández. She sat in her command chair at the end of a
giant robot arm on the bridge of her ship. With all the view-
screens activated, showing the glorious stars outside the
vessel, it was as if she floated in space itself, immersed in
that spectacular view.

Today, however, the starscape had little effect on
her. She was too busy dealing with the flu that somehow,
against all reason, she had managed to catch. How more
prehistoric could she get? The health nanomeds in her body
should be destroying the pernicious bugs. Maybe she was
just tired from working so late last night, ship's time. Her
queasy stomach didn't help. She felt like hell.

Jess rubbed her eyes, then looked around the bridge.
It consisted of a hemisphere over a kilometer-wide. With
screens activated on every surface, projecting holographic views of space outside the ship, the entire hemi-sphere
seemed transparent. They were orbiting the planet Athena,
a gas giant banded by blue and red clouds, glowing against
the spangled backdrop of space. The view to starboard,
however, came from a satellite orbiting Athena. It showed
Jess's ship, *Silver Tide*, a rotating cylinder several kilometers
long, as much a space habitat as a ship. This bridge capped
the cylinder, a half-sphere that could rotate or not, as Jess
preferred. Lights sparkled along the vessel, glistening on all
the antennae, pods, struts, and towers that studded the hull.

"So beautiful," Jess murmured. She loved watching *Silver Tide*. In the five years since she assumed command of the space-faring research facility, she had never lost the awe she'd felt the first time she boarded. *Silver Tide* was more than her home. The ship felt like part of her.

Her stomach interrupted her serenity with an unwelcome lurch. Trying to divert her attention, she magnified the screen mages until a small Bolt spacecraft became visible, arrowing toward them from Athena. A docking tube on *Silver Tide* opened like a giant flower in bloom. The Bolt sailed into the pod, which then closed again. Jess recognized the Bolt; it carried Jack O'Brien and his Allied Services people, a crack team of civilian security whizzes who tracked the interstellar black market. They were hitching a ride on *Silver Tide*, headed out across space to bust smugglers.

Jess sniffled, distracted by her stuffy nose. Damn. This was absurd. Humans had cured almost every strain of the flu. It irked her to no end that she had managed to catch whatever rare and annoying bug had escaped eradication.

Get over it, she told herself. Aloud, she said, "*Silver Tide*, spin up the bridge."

The Evolving Intelligence that served as the brain of the ship answered. "Done. Enjoy the view."

Jess smiled. "Thanks."

The bridge began to rotate, its screens adjusting to keep the view of space stationary. Although being in free fall made it easier to navigate the equipment-packed bridge, she spun up the hemisphere during at least part of each shift, so her crew at the consoles on the hull weren't always weightless or in micro-gravity. Against the immensity of space, their stations looked like small wedges moving past the stars. Usually Jess reveled in that magnificent vista. Unfortunately, seeing those consoles zip by today did nothing magnificent for her stomach.

Jess tapped a code into her chair, and the robot arm swung her to a hatch in the rotating bridge. After the chair matched speed and position with the hull, she unfastened her safety webbing and cranked open the hatch. Pulling herself into the cubical beyond, she proceeded to rendez-

vous with the Bridge Renewal and Refresher Chamber,
otherwise known as the head.

As Jess squeezed into the room, a holo of her face
formed in front of the opposite panel. It showed woman
with black hair tousled around her shoulders and dark circles below her eyes. She grimaced at her image, then leaned
over the micro-g sink and lost her lunch.

•

"You work too hard." Dr. George Mai said. He stood
next to the medical station, scanning his holopad. A heavy-
set man with a kind face and brown eyes, he worked at
Claymore Hospital, a facility in the residential section of the
space habitat. He considered Jess, who was sitting on the
end of the bed, her booted feet almost touching the floor.

"You should come in more often for a check-up,"
George said.

Given how much Jess disliked hospitals, she felt
tempted to growl some noncommittal response. But he was
just doing his job. "I'm not working any harder than usual,"
she said. "I've no reason to be sick."

"I'm still checking a few tests, but I can already give
you the diagnosis." He turned off his holopad. "You were
right, Captain. You have the flu. You need to rest."

Jess frowned at him. "How the hell did I get the flu?"

"I don't know." George paused, started to talk,
stopped, and then said, "I need to go over your test results
more. I'll let you know if anything else turns up."

"Good." She slid off the bed, standing half a head
taller than him.

"You really could use a rest," he said. "Doctor Bolton
would say the same."

Good Lord. He was pulling out the big guns. Sandra
Bolton served as the senior physician at Claymore, and she
took guff from no one, including Silver Tide's captain. Jess
could almost hear the doctor's voice: *You work too hard, Jess.*
You'll wear yourself down to nothing. Take a vacation, find a hob-
by, meet some people. You're an accomplished, attractive woman.

All right, so you're also stubborn as all hell. But you still need a social life.

Bah. Sandra didn't seem to understand the words, I'm fine, go away. Jess had great respect for the doctor's abilities, but she had absolutely no desire to hear Sandra's unsolicited advice on her personal life, or lack thereof.

•

Jess walked through the secluded woods around the medical park, relieved to escape the hospital. She had changed back into her uniform, the blue trousers and shirt of a lieutenant colonel in the Space Corps of the Allied Worlds of Earth. At six-foot-two, with her long legs, she devoured the distance as she strode along the gravel path. The trees and flowering bushes on both sides tended to make her forget she lived on a star ship. Then she reached an open area and saw the forest sloping up the distant curve of the cylinder. The "sky" consisted of light panels in the overhead deck.

Jess liked living on *Silver Tide*. The ship offered a self-sufficient habitat with its own towns and countryside. It carried thousands of people, primarily civilians, but Jess and her staff were military. The scientists onboard did research related to space, everything from star formation to cosmology to genetically altered colonists on other planets. It was a prime position; teams throughout Allied Worlds sought grants and permission to work on *Silver Tide*.

George had certified that Jess wasn't contagious, so she headed for the administrative park where she and her staff had their offices. The gleaming buildings were scattered among lawns and parks, with abstract sculptures that made no sense to Jess. Modern art looked ugly to her, but maybe she was just too pragmatic to appreciate its nuances.

For the rest of the day, Jess met with the scientists in charge of various research divisions, working on the ship's itinerary. They let her know where they needed to go and she did her best to make it happen. Several weeks ago, *Silver Tide* had left a team of anthropologists on the world

Icelos, and Jess also wanted to check on them. After that, she needed to pick up several astrophysicists who would study interstellar dust clouds for the next few months. Normally she enjoyed this part of her job, but today she felt too queasy to do more than function. She wished the med-patch George had given her would take effect. She didn't have time to be sick.

After a full day, she headed home for a few hours of sleep. As she walked, she brooded on the discord among her staff. Half her aides advised against returning to Icelos. They claimed it would take valuable time other research teams needed. Jess found that hard to credit, given how often *Silver Tide* made such checks. She had little doubt that their reluctance arose because Icelos was a Cephean world.

Jess wished a med-patch existed that could fix the Icelos situation. She couldn't change the unease most humans felt toward the Cepheans. Her crew seemed to forget Cepheans had once been human. Six thousand years ago, an unknown race had moved a group of people from Earth to another planet and then vanished with no explanation. The stranded humans learned genetic engineering in desperation; without it, their small population couldn't have maintained a viable gene pool. Over the centuries, they developed space travel and went in search of Earth, their lost home. They never found it, but in the process of looking, they built an interstellar empire.

Their civilization eventually collapsed, stranding its colonies. Its descendants took thousands of years to regain space travel, but they finally succeeded. A few hundred years ago, they began rebuilding their massive empire, calling it the Skolian Imperialate. When the people of Earth finally reached the stars, they had an unparalleled shock: humans were already out here, the Skolians, busily recovering their ancient colonies.

Those lost settlements included Cepheus. It wasn't the Skolian name for the colony. Humans from Earth called the world after the mythological king Cepheus, who descended from Zeus, because the parent star appeared in the direction of the constellation that bore his name. Skolians

tolerated the name as long as Earth continued to acknowledge that Cepheus belonged to the Skolian Imperialate, not
the Allied Worlds of Earth.

Jess pushed her hand through her hair. Earth had no
dispute about who claimed the world. They didn't like the
colony. Thousands of years ago, the Cephean settlers had
genetically altered themselves. Why? The reasons had faded
into the mists of history. If they intended to expand the gene
pool, they failed; Cepheans couldn't reproduce with humans. More likely, the changes adapted them to their harsh
colony world. They had two extra arms and modifications
to their skeletal structure to accommodate the extra limbs.
Thick pelts covered their bodies. Entrepreneurs on Earth
had spent millions trying to synthesize the fur, but that was
all that most humans liked about their neighbors. Cepheans
evoked ancient terrors: Yeti, golems, stalkers in the night, a
child's nightmare.

Initially Cepheans had liked humans. They probably
responded an instinctual level, having descended from humanity. Earth's children looked pretty to them. They turned
wary as they discovered their long-lost siblings were anything but "pretty." When they realized how much humans
reviled them, their unease became hostility.

Necessity had forced Jess to become an expert in
Cephean-human relations. The Cepheans had established
a settlement on Icelos to study the world, and the venture's
scientific nature made the settlers more amenable to interaction with humans. Scientists on Earth and Icelos soon set
up an exchange program. *Silver Tide* had carried the human
research team to Icelos, and Jess felt responsible for them.
The exchange offered proof humans and Cepheans could
work together, but that tenuous accord could all too easily
unravel.

Dusk spread over the parkland as the light panels
dimmed overhead. The darkening scene fit Jess's mood.
Better not to think of Icelos.

She couldn't risk where her thoughts might go if she
dwelled on the colony there.

•

Jess leaned back in her smart-chair and nodded to the man sprawled in an armchair on the other side of her polished desk. "I hope your accommodations are acceptable, Mr. O'Brien."

Jack gave her a rakish grin, more like a pirate than a security officer in the Allied Services. "Top shape, Captain." A black curl fell over his forehead as he took a swig of his coffee. "After our military transport didn't show up, we figured we were stranded at Epsilani Station. Your ship was a stroke of luck."

"I'm glad we could help." Although the Space Corps had no formal connection to the Allied Services, Jess had no objection to their agents hitching a ride on her ship.

The comm in her wrist gauntlet buzzed. Touching a fingertip panel there, she said, "Fernández."

Sandra Bolton's voice crackled. "Captain, I need to see you as soon as possible."

Jess had no wish to see any doctors. If she balked, though, Sandra would persist. The last thing she needed was to have a verbal duel with the head of Claymore Hospital in front of a visitor.

Jack stood up, setting his mug on her desk, and mouthed, *Thanks for the coffee.* Relieved, Jess raised her hand in a wave as he left.

When she was alone, she spoke to the doctor. "I'll stop by the hospital later if I have time." She had a lot of work today. In fact, she just remembered a lot more she had to do. Incredible amounts.

"This can't wait," Sandra said.

"Why not?"

"You should come here."

The doctor's evasive answer gave Jess pause. Sandra usually spoke her mind. Jess had never known her to be this oblique.

"All right," Jess said. "I'm on my way."

•

Sandra was standing in an exam room by a medical bench, surrounded by monitors that displayed holos of a woman's body. The doctor had gained weight over the years, nothing drastic, but enough to make her round. Her short, stylish hair gleamed in the bright light.

As Jess entered the room, Sandra regarded her with a neutral expression. Bland. Sandra never looked bland. Something was up.

Jess stopped in front of her. "Yes?"

"We need to talk," Sandra said.

"We are talking."

The doctor cleared her throat. "It's about the suggestions I gave you."

"Which ones? You give a lot." Sandra's inventory of lectures was formidable.

"About socializing."

Jess would have laughed if she hadn't been so astounded. "Is that why you called me here so urgently? To find out if I've gone to any parties?"

"No." Sandra laid her hand on the exam table, as if for support. "I just hadn't expected you to take my advice."

"That makes two of us." Jess had no idea what the blazes Sandra meant.

"I found out why you feel sick."

"It's the flu, right?"

"No." Sandra took a deep breath. "You're pregnant."

Jess stared at her. "Is this some sort of tasteless joke?" Yes, sure, Sandra had a quirky sense of humor, but this went beyond the pale.

"No, it's not a joke," Sandra said. "George and I did three independent checks on your tests to make sure. They all give the same result."

Jess crossed her arms and glared at the doctor. "Then your procedures have some problem."

"George thought so, too, when he first saw the result." The doctor lifted her hands, then dropped them. "We analyzed everything to make sure we hadn't made lab errors or seen a false positive. We didn't find any mistakes."

Jess stared at her. "I can't be pregnant."

The doctor spoke dryly. "You aren't the first woman to say those words. Nor the first to be wrong."

"I'm not saying it's unlikely. It's impossible."

"No birth control method is one hundred percent effective."

Jess wished she were somewhere else. Anywhere. Discussing her sex life, or lack thereof, was about as high on her list of preferred activities as having a tooth pulled without the benefit of modern dentistry. She cleared her throat. "It requires a merger to effect the consequence that you attribute solely to a parthenogenetic capacity of my reproductive organs."

"What?" Sandra squinted at her. "Does that have a translation into plain language?"

So much for subtlety. "It means I haven't, uh—well, been with a man."

Her tormentor shrugged. "Maybe you forgot."

"*Forgot?*" Jess couldn't believe she was having this conversation. "That's ridiculous. And no, I didn't go to a sperm bank."

"So how did you get pregnant?"

"I didn't!"

Sandra continued as if Jess hadn't spoken. "You caught the flu because your resistance is down. You're nauseated because you have morning sickness."

"I have it all day," Jess grumbled.

"You must have missed two cycles by now. Didn't you notice?"

"You know I stop my cycles in space." A curl had escaped the band Jess used to pull back her hair, and she pushed the lock out of her eyes. "Every two years the process lets my periods come for a few months, so my body can reset itself, but I'm often irregular when the reset starts."

Sandra scrutinized her. "Could you have had sex without knowing it?"

This felt more surreal by the moment. "I think I would have noticed."

Sandra motioned at the bed. "Lie down."

Jess scowled at her.

The doctor smiled. "I don't bite."

"You do worse," Jess muttered. "You give advice." She sat on the bed and lay on her back. Her feet hung over the bottom edge.

Sandra clicked up an extension to support Jess's legs. Then she touched the screen of a monitor. "Scan one, Jazmín Fernández." It was one of Sandra's few redeeming qualities: she knew how to say her captain's name. It wasn't that Jess didn't like her nickname; she'd answered to Jess since her childhood in London. But she still appreciated it when someone pronounced Jazmín right.

"Type R scan." Sandra unhooked a cable from the monitor, rolled up Jess's shirt, and proceeded to slide the disk across her abdomen.

Jess stiffened. "What are you doing?"

"Relax. It's just a holographic image processor." Sandra motioned at the monitor. "Look."

Jess peered at the screen. The holo forming in front of it showed a tiny figure with a huge head and a flutter inside its body. "What is that?"

"Your baby," Sandra said. "The motion is its heart-beat."

Jess's breath caught. Could she truly have conceived a child? *How?*

Sandra studied the monitor. "You're nine weeks pregnant."

"Nine weeks?" Jess sat up. "That's when we took those anthropologists to Icelos."

Dryly Sandra said, "Your memory coming back?"

Jess flushed. "I still can't be pregnant."

"In a situation like this, denial isn't unusual. But you need to accept it, Jess. You have to decide what you intend to do."

Jess stared at the monitor, watching her baby's heart-beat. A new life. Incredible. Protective instincts surged in her, similar to what she felt for *Silver Tide*. "If you're asking do I want to give up the child or end the pregnancy, the answer is no."

Sandra didn't look surprised. "Shall I contact the anthropologists?"

Jess's voice came out sharper than she intended. "My child's father is not on Icelos." She slid off the bed and paced away from the doctor. "I don't know how this happened."

Sandra made a frustrated noise. "Fine. I give up. You had no lover. You conceived out of nothing."

Jess turned around. "I didn't say I had no lover."

"Ah." Sandra came over to her. "Now we're getting somewhere."

"He can't be the father."

"You have other candidates?"

"No." Jess fixed Sandra with what she hoped was a quelling stare. "But he can't be the father."

Sandra didn't look the least bit quelled. "You know mistakes can happen."

"Not in this case."

"What kind of birth control did you use?"

"I didn't."

Sandra gave an exasperated snort. "And you're surprised you're pregnant?"

"I didn't need any."

"Why? Is he sterile?"

"No. I just didn't need it."

"I don't believe you could be that naïve."

Jess glared at her. "Damn it, Sandra, let it go."

"Let what go?"

"All right!" Jess blew out a gust of air. "My companion was Ghar Ko. Satisfied?"

Sandra gaped at her. "You mean the Cephean Ambassador?"

"Yes." Jess wished she could disappear. "What I just told you is confidential."

"Yes, yes, of course." Sandra looked as if she couldn't decide whether to be fascinated or appalled. "And you're right. Human beings cannot have babies with Cepheans."

"Are you sure the child is human?" Maybe the scientists were wrong. Maybe hybrid offspring could exist.

"Completely human." Sandra rubbed her chin. "A Cephean male couldn't impregnate you. Too many differences exist in the DNA."

"I don't know what to say." Jess had yet to sort out how she felt about what had happened with Ghar. She certainly didn't want to discuss it with Sandra. But she had to file a report about her condition even if she declined to name the nonexistent father. Although maternity no longer meant an end to active duty on a ship like *Silver Tide*, a pregnant captain was hardly routine, especially an unmarried one. If she didn't handle this right, she could lose her command.

Sandra asked, "How does Ambassador Ko feel about it?"

"I don't know," Jess admitted. "It just, well—happened. Then we fell asleep. I woke up, wrote him a note, and left." *Silver Tide* had been scheduled to depart, and she couldn't hold up the ship for her personal life. Or so she told herself. But she and Ghar could have sent messages later. That neither of them had done so suggested she wasn't the only one at a loss for words.

The doctor frowned. "I've never known you to be a coward."

"I'm not. I needed time to think." Jess shook her head. "If his people learn about this, it will cause him problems. Cepheans don't much care for humans." To put it mildly.

"Apparently one of them does," Sandra said. "This could blow up on you big time."

"That's why I haven't said anything."

"What are you going to do?"

Good question. Too bad she had no answer. "What should I do for the baby?"

Although Sandra obviously wanted to continue the topic of Ghar, she held back, at least for now. "No alcohol or caffeine. Sleep more. Avoid zero-g; otherwise the cells in the fetus might not orient correctly. On the bridge, minimize how long you spend weightless. No EVAs. Even inside the ship, make sure you always have radiation protection. If the nausea gets so bad you can't eat, let me know."

"All right." That all sounded manageable.

Sandra spoke more softly. "And Jess."

"Yes?"

"What happened would be difficult for anyone to handle. Especially if you had no choice…"

It took Jess a moment to decipher her meaning. Startled, she said, "It was consensual." She couldn't imagine Ghar forcing her. With relations between Earth and Cepheus already so strained, it would have been madness. It would shatter the brittle accord between their peoples.

"Could it have happened while you slept?" Sandra asked. "By someone else?"

"Of course not."

"Are you sure?"

Jess glanced at the monitor. It gave the time of conception as the night she spent with Ghar. She couldn't believe he would be involved in such a strange deception. "I'm sure."

"It is hard to imagine," Sandra admitted. "If you remember anything, let me know." In a gentler voice she added, "And if you need to talk, I'm here."

"I'm fine. Really." Jess wished she really believed that.

•

Jess walked through the woods in a deepening twilight. She kept thinking about Sandra's question: could this have happened while she slept that night? She didn't see how. Someone would have had to enter Ghar's home and impregnate her. They'd have needed to drug both her and Ghar or find some other way to make sure neither of them woke up. To what purpose? It was just too bizarre.

If Ghar had left after she fell asleep, someone might have broken in during his absence. But seriously? If someone wanted to get laid, easier ways existed than sneaking into the Cephean ambassador's home and ravishing his guest in her sleep. Even if the person had sought the thrill of danger, Jess didn't see how he could have infiltrated the well-guarded colony or Ghar's home. Regardless, she doubted Ghar would have left her alone long enough for anyone to perpetrate such a bizarre crime.

Jess would never forget that night, though. She and Ghar had both attended a reception to welcome the anthropologists from Earth. Jess had never been comfortable at such parties. She had known Ghar for years, and it relieved her to leave with him, the two of them deep in conversation. She wasn't sure how they ended up at his home. They had settled on a soft rug and proceeded to get drunk on that deliciously potent brandy the Icelos colony produced for export.

Eventually Jess slumped against his huge frame, no longer able to sit straight, and he pulled her against his chest with his lower arms. He was using all four hands to talk by then.

Cepheans couldn't replicate human speech, and humans couldn't mimic their language, so the two of them usually conversed with ASL, American Sign Language, used by the deaf community. For some reason, they had decided to "talk" by pressing signs against each other's skin. ASL was a visual language, but they hadn't wanted to turn on the light, so they tried to convey meaning by touch instead. Or maybe that had just been an excuse for their curiosity. It hadn't taken long for the signs to become more intimate.

Jess rubbed her eyes. Lord, she was tired. She tapped a panel on her wrist gauntlet, then leaned against a tree, feeling the roughness of the bark through her shirt. The quiet night soothed her, and right now she needed all the calming she could get.

Her wrist gauntlet chimed. Touching the receive panel, she said, "Fernández."

"Captain, this is Sandra Bolton. I received your page."

"You took some of my amniotic fluid during your tests, didn't you?" Jess asked.

"Yes, we did," the doctor said. "Why do you ask?"

"That means you can analyze its DNA."

"That's right." Sandra didn't sound surprised by the inquiry. "We have a database of DNA records for Allied citizens. Every time we link into a major medical system, we update it. We probably have records for over eighty percent of the citizens of the Allied Worlds of Earth."

Jess rested her head on the tree. "Including anyone who's ever come aboard *Silver Tide*?"

"That's right." Sandra paused. "We have far fewer records for Skolian citizens. Our Icelos files are pretty skimpy."

"Check what you can." Jess spoke quietly. "See if you can match my child's DNA."

"I'll go through everything we have."

"Thank you." Jess paused, unsure what to add. "Good night."

"Good night." In a kindly voice, Sandra added, "Jess, go home and rest. Don't brood."

"Thanks. But I'm fine."

After they signed off, Jess stood watching the evening. She couldn't handle this compassionate side of Sandra; it was easier to feel annoyed when the doctor was giving a lecture. Confronted by gentleness, Jess feared she might drop her emotional guards. It would be tantamount to admitting she wasn't self-sufficient. She had spent a lifetime proving herself, until she no longer knew how to ask for help.

Time to face the music, she told herself. She had to see Ghar. This wasn't something she could tackle long-distance; she needed to meet with him in person. Going to Icelos would also make it easier to check the medical databases for the human settlement there. But it would take a fortnight to reach the colony, using most of the leeway in *Silver Tide*'s schedule. If she wanted to see Ghar, she couldn't wait any longer.

She just hoped her visit didn't end in disaster.

•

II
Stalactite City

Icelos. Jess felt welcomed by the small world. She had taken a Bolt transport down to the planet. After she went through customs at the starport, she headed into the town of New Appenzell. She could have ridden the magrail or hitched a ride on a cargo lorry, but she preferred to walk. Warm within her climate-controlled jacket, she enjoyed the three-quarters gravity.

Nothing had changed since her last visit; the town still looked like a ski resort, with alpine bungalows capped by peaked roofs. Visitors from Earth lived here when they came to Icelos, and legally the village was considered territory of the Allied Worlds of Earth, the only place on the planet the Skolians didn't claim as their own. The Cepheans were biosculpting Icelos, adapting it for settlement, but it would be generations before the climate warmed enough to make even this equatorial zone temperate. Putting her hands in her pockets, she crunched through the snow, avoiding slick patches on the cobbled lanes. The village had a crystalline beauty with all the ice hanging from lampposts and glittering on the houses. She inhaled, savoring the crisp air. Although she'd chafed when Sandra urged her to take shore leave, she was secretly glad the doctor insisted. Jess loved it here.

During the last fortnight, as *Silver Tide* traveled to Icelos, Jess had debated whether or not to send Ghar a message. Her doubts stopped her. If he knew she was coming, he might find a reason to end his visit to Icelos and return to Geneva on Earth, where he served as the Cephean Ambassador to the Allied Worlds. So she held off, avoiding the rejection.

She had two days here. That didn't amount to much on Icelos, which rotated in only eleven hours. Regardless, she would make her best effort to see Ghar. Her emotions tumbled over one another, conflicted and awkward, but she still looked forward to it. She missed him.

Jess came around a tall house that had blocked the view and drew in a sharp breath. The street in front of her stretched all the way to the cliffs beyond the village. The vertical walls of stone sheered into the sky, and jagged mountains cloaked by glaciers rose beyond them in cold, primeval splendor. The sunset edged their crowns like tubes of hot-pink neon. Here in the village, the snow had turned luminous pink. Icicles hung in frozen lace from the eaves of houses, glistening like rubies.

Jess exhaled, watching her breath condense in the air. As she walked past a bungalow, shards of ice fell from its roof and shattered on the ground. Icelos had slumbered for eons, but now the Cepheans were awakening the world. It seemed fitting; in Greek mythology, Icelos had been the son of Somus, the god of sleep. She suspected the Earth name for this world came from deep in the human subconscious; the mythical Icelos had been a shape-changer who could turn into different animals. She often wondered if the name was an unconscious acknowledgment that their Cephean cousins had once been human and now were Other.

Jess's gait slowed as her fatigue set in. Maybe she should have taken a hovercar after all. How had the human race ever survived, when incubating little humans took so much energy? She trudged on, trying not to think of how far she still had to go. A few years ago, the Allied embassy had arranged an apartment for her in this village. The Cephean science commission and its Earth counterpart needed a liaison, and the Cepheans already knew Jess from visits *Silver Tide* made to Icelos. They requested her diplomatic services. She chuckled, remembering the incredulous response from the Earth commission. As much as her taciturn bluntness appealed to the Cepheans, it annoyed humans, especially those tasked with diplomacy. However, Allied Space Command liked that she got things done with efficiency and no fuss, so she became the liaison.

As sunset faded into a silvered dusk, Jess plodded to the intersection at Starfarer's Lane. The sign at the crossroads looked the same as always, a stone rectangle hanging from a pole. She had never paid it much attention before, but today its carved words jumped out at her.

Childcare. The arrow pointed right.

She knew she should go to her apartment, get some rest, eat, sleep. Instead she turned right.

A bungalow housed the childcare center. When Jess opened the door, young voices burbled over her like the flowing water of a creek. She entered a cheerful room with white walls adorned by cartoons in red, blue, and yellow. Toys were strewn across the carpeted floor. Three toddlers played there, watched by a woman with a kind face. The woman glanced at Jess, then did a double-take, her gaze widening.

Jess hesitated. Self-conscious, feeling out of place in her uniform jacket and trousers, she closed the door.

The woman recovered her composure and approached with a smile. "Hello, Colonel."

"Actually, I'm a starship captain." Although people often called her colonel, she hadn't yet attained full bird rank and she didn't quite feel comfortable with the title.

The woman regarded her with curiosity. "What can I do for you?"

Good question. "We're expanding a childcare facility on my ship. I'm interested in how other sites organize their centers." It was actually true. A community on *Silver Tide* had requested a new center, and Jess had been meaning to have someone attend matter. Maybe she ought to do the attending herself; she might soon be using that center.

"I would be happy to give you a tour." The woman glanced at the *Silver Tide* insignia on Jess's jacket. With diffidence, she added, "For a ship as big as yours, though, I'm sure you have much more extensive facilities."

Jess felt more out of her depth here than she ever had on *Silver Tide*. "Size and quality aren't the same. I've heard yours is a well-run operation."

The woman beamed. "That it is, ma'am." She lifted her hand, inviting Jess forward.

So Jess toured the center. In one room, a girl and boy were stacking holographic blocks. Seeing them, she felt an

odd constriction in her chest. Would her baby have dark
curls like the boy? Or maybe she would be like the girl,
her eyes huge and dark, her face shaped like a heart. How
could she imagine her child's appearance when the only
paternal candidate was impossible? Sandra had yet to find a
genetic match for the baby. After having grown up in poverty, Jess had always been uneasy about starting a family.
And yet…an undefined longing tugged at her now, feelings
she had no name for, except that they came with a flavor of
loneliness.

"Captain?" the woman asked.

Startled, Jess realized she had been standing there,
gazing at the children. "They seem so happy."

The woman's voice gentled. "We do our best."

As Jess and the woman were returning to the main
room, a young couple came into the center stamping snow
from their boots. One of the toddlers ran to them, a strap-
ping girl in a blue jumpsuit. The woman swung the girl
into her arms, and the child laughed. As the woman sat in
a rocking chair, the man settled in an armchair next to her,
and they chatted companionably while the woman nursed
the child.

After Jess left the center, images of the family stayed
in her mind. She wanted to share this pregnancy with someone. Ghar. But she feared to tell him. He would make the
only logical assumption, that she had taken a human lover
the same night she slept with him. She had no idea if he'd
care, but she didn't want him to believe she would betray
his trust that way.

•

The penthouse where Jess lived took up the top
floor of a building called *Les Tours de Lumière des Étoiles*, the
Starlight Towers, one of the tallest structures in the village,
standing seven stories high. As Jess entered her darkened
apartment, the curtains across the room pulled back, probably responding to a command from Radix, the Evolving Intelligence that ran the place. He often altered the ambience,

which meant she came home to unexpected changes. She tended to enjoy it; over the years, he had developed a sense of her preferences.

A window took up most of the wall. Night had fallen outside, and silvery radiance from the nebulae-rich sky washed through the window, making the white carpet glow. Standing in the center of her sunken living room, Jess gazed at the night's beauty. Usually she savored the spacious dimensions of the place, which fit her height, but tonight it made her more aware of its emptiness.

"Radix," she said. "It's too dark."

The lights came up slowly, letting her eyes adjust. The room had simple furniture, elegant and sleek, with silver accents and plants in blue-glass pots. Relieved to be home, Jess dropped onto the sofa and pulled off her boots. She stretched her legs across the blue-glass coffee table, her feet reaching the other side. *Legs that go on forever.* A man she'd known ten years ago had told her that.

Her husband.

He came from Norway. They'd spent five years together, with a renewable marriage contract. Then she became captain of *Silver Tide*. He didn't want leave Earth and she didn't want to give up her command, so they let their contract lapse. Although they parted amicably, the loss had affected Jess deeply, far more than she wanted to admit. Since then, she had guarded her emotions with an iron will.

Until Ghar.

It must have been the brandy, or the unreality of that night. Or maybe she just liked Ghar better than anyone else she had met. She shook her head at her folly. *You never do things the easy way, do you?* She slumped back on the couch and closed her eyes. She knew she should have dinner, but her stomach rebelled at the idea.

Jess sighed. For the baby, she would eat. Opening her eyes, she noticed a light on a panel in the sofa arm. "Yes?" she asked.

"Welcome back, Captain Fernández," Radix said. "Can I get you anything?"

"A new stomach," Jess grumbled.

"I'm sorry, but I can't do organ transplants."

She smiled. "How about food? Something bland. Skim milk to drink."

"I can have the kitchen prepare a superb bland meal," Radix assured her. "Would you like your messages while you wait? You have one from Doctor Bolton."

Jess groaned.

"Is that a no?" Radix asked.

"No, go ahead and play it."

Sandra's voice crackled. "Captain, please contact me immediately."

Jess waited. "That's it?"

"That is it," Radix said.

She rubbed her chin. "All right. Contact Doctor Bolton. She's on the *Silver Tide*, in orbit."

"Message sent. Would you like anything else?"

Jess still felt unprepared, even after thinking about this for days. But she made herself answer. "Yes. Get me the Allied embassy."

"One moment, please." After several minutes, during which Jess sat like a lump, Radix said, "I have Paige Lowell from the embassy."

"Thanks. Put her on audio. No visual." Although Jess had always liked Paige, right now she didn't feel up to facing the young woman's flawless perfection. Somehow the incomparably beautiful Paige managed to simultaneously appear as elegant as an old-money heiress and as wholesome as the girl next door. Add to that her formidable education and rapid advancement in the diplomatic corps, and she could give even the most confident person an inferiority complex.

A lovely voice floated into the air, cultured and gracious. "Hello, Captain Fernández. Welcome back to Icelos."

"Hi, Paige." Jess hesitated. She'd never quite figured out when she and Paige were on a first name basis and when they were being formal. So she added. "Please call me Jess."

"It would be my pleasure. What can I do for you?"

"I'd like to see Ambassador Ko. If he's still here." Jess

knew the code for Ghar's private comm perfectly well, but Cephean protocol required the Allied embassy to contact the Cephean embassy if she wanted to talk to him.

"I will be happy to inquire if his Excellency can meet with you," Paige said.

"Thanks. I appreciate it." Jess paused, too tired to think of small talk. "Good-night."

"Good-night, Jess. Have a pleasant evening."

After they cut the connection, Jess rubbed the aching muscles in the back of her neck. Would Ghar respond? More likely, he wanted to forget their night together.

Radix spoke. "I have Doctor Bolton waiting."

"Just put her on audio, too." If Sandra saw her fatigue, she would launch into a lecture.

"Incoming." Radix said.

Sandra's voice cut the air. "Jess, are you all right?"

"I'm fine." Jess shifted on the couch. "Why?"

"You've been sick so much it triggered an alert in your quarters on the ship. Why didn't you tell me how bad it was?"

"It's not bad. I've kept some food down."

"You're too stoic. I gave Radix an anti-nausea prescription. Take it."

Jess was too tired to argue. "All right."

More gently, Sandra said, "Are you really okay?"

"I'm fine."

"You keep telling me that. Why don't I believe it?"

Because you know me too well. Jess could see a tray rising up inside a glass column that supported the table. A panel in the table slid open and the tray came to top. Dinner sat before her, pasta and vegetables on china. Milk filled a crystal goblet, and a vase held an orchid.

Jess blinked at the tray. How much had it cost to produce that flower on this iceball planet? The extravagance unsettled her. She had grown up with so little, the youngest child of a Spanish father and Portuguese mother, their youth and energy drained from raising five children when they had resources for only one. They had been among the millions of displaced tech workers, all scratching for jobs while unemployment in the information sector spiraled. With more and more intelligent machines able to replace humans, the need for infotech workers had plunged. Like many others, her parents ended up in an arbitrary urban center, scraping by with low-level jobs.

A wealth of new jobs existed, however, including those on the frontier among the stars. Hard work and scholarships had made it possible for Jess to overcome her circumstances. Yet even after buying her parents and siblings a new house in an upscale London neighborhood, she found it hard to believe this new life she had earned for her family.

"Jess?" Sandra asked.

"My dinner is here." Jess closed her eyes. "I have to go."

"Don't push yourself so hard. You deserve a rest."

"All right." The words didn't feel like enough, so she added, "Thanks for the concern."

"You're welcome." Sandra's voice had an odd note. Surprise.

Am I that difficult a patient? Jess suspected she should say thank you more. She lifted the tray into her lap, settled back, and ate dinner. True to his word, Radix had arranged an excellent meal. The pasta almost melted in her mouth. She wished she could enjoy it more.

Radix had put a patch with the anti-nausea medicine on the tray. When Jess applied it to her inner elbow, the small square blended into her skin, turning golden-brown. She rubbed it, remembering how her dark skin had evoked taunts in her youth. As the world grew more cosmopolitan, acceptance among races and cultures had improved, but it still wasn't perfect. Jess had learned that lesson the hard way. Circumstances forced her to become a fighter at a young age, aided by her height, strength, and stubborn refusal to back down from bullies. Friendship had been hard for her.

Strange how life changed. She saw herself as rough-edged, but some years back a modeling agency had offered her a contract, lauding her purportedly "long-limbed grace and athletic style." Her height, unusual even for a

high-fashion model, intrigued them, as did her military
rank. That had been the rage back then: sleek, svelte fashion with an undertone of soldierly power. Flustered, she
thanked them but turned down the job, far more at home
with starship engines than runways.

"I have Ambassador Ko your private line," Radix
announced.

Jess swallowed so fast she choked. Sitting up, she
cleared her throat. "Put him on."

"Audio, visual, or both?"

She wasn't ready to face him on visual. But they
couldn't talk, and to use sign language they had to see each
other. "Did the ambassador request visual?"

"His human translator contacted me by audio,"
Radix said.

Thank you, Ghar. "Just put on the audio then."

"Incoming," Radix said.

Ghar's translator spoke, his resonant voice filling the
air. "My greetings, Captain Fernández."

"Good evening, Your Excellency."

"How long does Icelos have the fortune of your
company?"

That sounded like he was glad to hear from her. Then
again, Ghar was a diplomat. He had to sound pleasant.

"I'm here for two days." Jess hesitated. "I thought if
you were free, we might, uh…have dinner." She winced at
the clumsy invitation. As Ambassador to the Allied Worlds,
Ghar spent most of his time on Earth. When he traveled, he
booked his commitments far in advance, and his visits to
Icelos were packed with obligations. She waited, her shoulders hunched in anticipation of his refusal.

"Dinner is acceptable," he said. "Shall we meet at the
Junction in half an hour?"

Jess released the breath she had been holding. He
didn't sound overjoyed, but at least he hadn't said no. "Yes.
Half an hour."

The Junction reminded Jess of a ski lodge, with its big fireplace and old-fashioned bar. Located at the base of the cliffs outside town, it served the humans on Icelos, a last stop before striking out into Cephean territory. Jess doubted Ghar wanted to eat here; he couldn't sit in the chairs and he disliked the food. More likely, he hoped to escort her to the Cephean settlement where he lived on Icelos.

Jess waited by the bar, watching jazz musicians play across the room. She was too restless to stand still. The med-patch worked; she hadn't felt this good in weeks. Maybe she should just head into the cliffs. She knew the route Ghar took, so she could meet him on the way.

Cold air hit her face as she left the lodge. She had worn a sweater over her uniform, a long coat, and heavy boots, but she still shivered with the chill. It never ceased to amaze her how Cepheans thrived in this climate. Of course, she didn't have a four-inch pelt covering her body.

The road wound steeply up into the mountains. Bronzed lampposts stood at intervals, casting ghostly light over the trail. On her left, a cliff rose into the darkness: on the right, a wall at chest height bordered the road. Beyond it, a canyon plunged down for a kilometer, fading into heavy mist. Snow crackled under her boots, deeper here where no machines cleared the lane. Cepheans liked it this way.

Jess tried to imagine how this land had looked eons ago. Flat, or so the scientists claimed. Underground rivers had hollowed it into a maze of buried limestone caverns and sinkholes. Water rich with bicarbonate and calcium ions dripped from cavern ceilings, hardening into stalactites like huge icicles of rock, or falling to the ground and building up conical stalagmites. Eventually the land sheered upward, buckling into mountains honeycombed by caves. It made an eerily beautiful landscape, haunting and unforgettable.

Human visitors to Icelos rarely understood why the Cepheans chose this forbidding land for their home when they could settle the plains instead. The choice made sense to Jess. Cepheans lived vertically instead of horizontally, a difference hard to fathom for a species with only two arms. The Cepheans' blunt refusal to acknowledge that their way of life might not suit everyone exacerbated the tensions with their human neighbors.

A distant voice startled Jess out of her reverie. She paused, listening. Although the speaker hadn't sounded Cephean, few humans came up here even in the day, and at night they avoided this desolate road like a plague.

Up ahead, a path branched off the main route. Jess went to the intersection and peered down the side trail. The dim light made it hard to see. Was someone in trouble? Concerned, she headed along the side path. The cliffs on either side leaned inward like giants conferring together and met above her head. Stretching out her arms, she could touch rock on either side. Breaks in the walls showed stalactites and stalagmites glazed by frost, a wonderland of sparking stone lace. She doubted any human explorer had fully mapped the warren of passages up here. The deep silence appealed to her, calling to mind the expanses of interstellar space.

Jess didn't see anyone, though. She paused. If she spent too long here, she'd miss Ghar on the main path. With a shrug, she turned and headed back to her original route. She checked her wrist gauntlet, but for some reason she could neither send nor receive signals. Odd. Given that humans rarely came to this secluded area, the Cepheans might have comm systems with different protocols than her people normally used. She had a state-of-the-art tech embedded in her gauntlets, however. Unless someone had deliberately set up a damping field, she ought to get some signal.

A glint inside the cave on Jess's right caught her eye. It came from…what? A small cage, it looked like, hidden by a stalagmite. Puzzled, she walked into the cave and over to the cage.

Mewling greeted her. Jess knelt, peering through the shadows. A furry white animal butted its head against the bars, its pointed ears quirked forward. The creature resembled a comalkos, a popular pet among Cepheans, probably descended from an Earth feline. Looking more closely, she realized it was in fact a kitten.

"What are you doing out here?" She scratched its head, pushing her fingers through the bars. The kitten purred at her.

Scraping sounds caught her attention. Jess looked around. What the blazes? The cave held many cages, all with cats. She doubted they belonged here. And no signal reached this place—

Responding with instincts tempered by decades of experience, Jess jumped up and took off, striding toward the main road. She could return with security officers from town. If the animals were legal, no problem, but hiding cats in these mountains was too strange to ignore.

Her footsteps thudded on the rocky path. The natural chambers on either side magnified sound—and so Jess distinctly heard someone speak, even from a distance well behind her:

"Shit. She saw the cages."

Jess burst into a run.

She never heard the knife sing through the air, but it crackled as it sliced her clothes and gouged deep into her back. Another knife hit her thigh, ripping past her uniform. The weapons fell from her body, clattering to the icy ground. Lord only knew how those blades were made, that they so easily slashed layers of reinforced cloth. It happened too fast for her to feel pain. Yet.

Her concentration narrowed into a tight focus as her training took over. The overcoat flapped around her legs, making her stumble, so she yanked it off and threw it down, never slowing. Her injured leg felt like putty, and dizziness threatened. She thought of the life she had to protect, the child inside of her, and she pushed herself to go even faster.

By the time Jess reached the main path, her sprint had turned into a stagger. She lurched across the road and hit the wall that separated it from the chasm. Before she could catch her balance, hands grabbed her from behind and swung her around, slamming her against the wall. Jess found herself staring at a tall man who looked like his name ought to be Buzz, as in an electrified chain-saw.

"Now you've done it," he said. Two more people ran out of the side path, a stocky man with red hair and a gaunt woman.

Jess strained to breathe. "What do you want?"

In that instant, the gaunt woman reached them. Without hesitation, she grabbed Jess, helping Buzz as he tried to push her over the wall. Jess's icy calm snapped into the cold fury that came over her in combat. She smacked her hands against Buzz's elbows and shoved inward, breaking his hold. At the same time, she brought up her knee hard. He choked, dropping his arms and doubling up, his face contorted. Jess kicked out at the woman, and a loud crack rent the air. The woman shouted, falling backward, her left hand clenched on her right arm, which had bent at an odd angle.

Jess had no time to wonder why the blazes they wanted to kill her. The second man was lunging at her, bringing down the edge of his hand. He mistimed the blow, as fighters often did in unfamiliar gravity. Jess easily deflected it, so the blow only struck her arm, but she still reeled under the impact.

Buzz came at her again, his face set in hard lines, and the woman wasn't far behind. As Jess struggled with the second man, her muscles straining, Buzz and the woman caught her. The three of them pushed her up the wall. She tried to stop them, tried to wrench free, but she couldn't take on three at once, not with her injuries. Her leg responded sluggishly and a deep burning seared her side. Her hips cleared the top of the wall—

Jess went rigid, with nothing but air and a canyon at her back. In that moment, as she faced her death, she thought with cold clarity, *You have no right*. It enraged her that they could so cavalierly murder her mystery child. She twisted *hard*, to the side, toward the road. Her efforts wrenched her out of their grip, but—ah, no!—she *fell*—and hit the road with a crash that slammed the air out of her lungs. A man's scream reverberated in the air, splitting the night. Jess jerked up her head—

And froze.

Caught in the light from a lamppost, turned sideways to her, a giant towered above them. Fiery red-gold fur covered his body and a mane of curls swept back from his face to his shoulders. Huge muscles rippled in his arms, visible through his trousers and tunic. His shoulders had immense width, with massive blades that extended down his body to accommodate his second pair of arms, and his legs were like tree trunks. His lips drew back, baring fangs more than two inches long. His lower arms were reaching for what his upper pair already held high over his head: the man Buzz.

With a heave, the Ambassador from Cepheus to Earth threw his human captive into the canyon.

•

III
Cavern of Ladders

Jess drifted awake, warm but unaccountably stiff. Why did her quarters have a musky scent? *Silver Tide* usually smelled sanitized. She stretched—and pain shot through her body.

"Ah!" She snapped awake. Hell and damnation, she wasn't on *Silver Tide*, she was about to be hefted into a canyon.

Instead, however, Jess found herself staring across a dimly lit room. The tables and desks were double-tiered, designed for two pairs of arms, and taller than human furniture. She lay on a stone floor, on a rug, with her back against a padded wall. Another rug covered her, soft on her skin. Jess recognized the furs. Cepheans made them from a silken material they sheared off an animal called the abryr, one of the few Cephean words humans could pronounce, said with a growl in the throat.

Her leg and back hurt. She wore nothing except

a shift and two bandages, one around her torso and the
other around her thigh. Despite the cushion of blankets, the
ground felt rough beneath her. A ridge ran under her waist
and another above the bandage around her midsection.

The wall behind her shifted.

For an instant Jess was too startled to react. Then she
rolled onto her back, slow and careful, favoring her injuries. The "wall" was alive. She was staring at the chest of a
sleeping Cephean. A *large* Cephean. The "ridges" she had
felt under her body were his arms; he held her in a cage of
limbs, four to be exact. His claws pressed against her back,
not enough to make punctures, but if she moved again, they
could tear her skin.

It took a moment for Jess to find her voice. Then she
said, "Ghar?"

He continued to sleep.

"Ghar?" she asked. "Can you hear me?"

His lashes lifted, revealing two brown eyes, dark and
liquid. He blinked as if trying to fathom her presence. Then
his claws retracted. He moved his fingers against her back,
using sign language, but by touch instead of sight. It was
the method of conversing they had tried before, a playful
experiment that had ended up communicating far more
than they intended.

Do you hurt? he asked.

Jess signed against his chest, her fingers buried in his
fur. *I'm all right. Where is this?*

You came here the last time you visited. His fingers
stilled. Then he added, *Maybe you forgot.*

That spurred her recognition. They were in his home.
They had spent the night here, on this pile of blankets. He
had just offered her a chance to pretend it never happened.
She wondered how he would explain, if she chose to develop amnesia, why she was in bed with him.

I remember, she signed.

The rigid muscles in his arms relaxed. *I, too.*

I have another memory, she signed. *But it must be a
mistake.*

What memory?

You threw a man into the chasm.

His hand curled into a claw on her back. *Your memory is not a mistake.*

She stared at him. *Ghar, why?*

You were covered with blood, one breath from dying.

Grateful as she was for his intervention, she dreaded the fallout. The few times a Cephean had injured a human, outrage had exploded on Earth. Reports of the incident glittered with invective, their censure stretching like a metallic tissue that looked strong but ripped easily, exposing the underlying panic humans felt when confronted by neighbors who were just human enough to make their immense differences terrifying. What would happen when it became known that the Cephean ambassador, the representative they were supposed to trust, had murdered a man?

Jess signed carefully. *If you hadn't come, I would be dead. I am grateful, more than I can say. But we have trouble.*

It was a moment before he responded. *Your authorities demand I surrender to them.*

They certainly hadn't wasted any time. *How long have we've been here, in your home?*

About two Icelos days.

Good Lord. Twenty-two hours. *Why didn't my crew take me?*

They wanted to.

What stopped them?

He paused. *That answer connects to my second crime.*

What second crime?

Holding a Space Corps officer hostage.

Bloody hell. *I'm not a hostage.*

They think you are.

You haven't let them see me?

His signed with a single, sharp motion. *No.*

Ghar, this is nuts.

I had no idea why those people attacked you. For all I know, someone might try again.

He had a point, but Jess didn't know what to make of this. She'd expected him to regret what had happened between the two of them, not respond with the possessive intensity a Cephean toward his Cephean mate.

He signed on her back. *Why were those people trying to kill you?*

Hell if I know. I only saw a bunch of cats.

Cats?

In cages, hidden in a cave. She tensed. *What happened after I saw you on the road?*

Your other attackers ran. I almost pursued.

And then? Her hand clenched in his fur.

Ghar caught her fingers. *I killed no one else.*

Jess let out the breath she hadn't realized she was holding. *Good.*

His growl rumbled. *I might have killed them, if you hadn't needed me more.*

Well, no one ever claimed Cepheans were peaceful. But she'd never have predicted this from Ghar.

Your authorities want proof you still live, he added.

I'll talk to them. She hoped Sandra hadn't told anyone about the pregnancy, but if the doctor feared for Jess's life, she would speak up no matter how much Jess wanted it kept secret. The security people on *Silver Tide* would make the obvious assumption: Ghar was no more likely than anyone else to believe he was the only candidate for proud papa. Given his recent behavior, Security had good reason to fear for Jess's life.

Although Jess didn't think Ghar would kill her, she couldn't be sure. About one thing she had no doubt; if Ghar committed a second murder, this time of the starship captain who served as an Earth-Cepheus liaison, all hell would break loose.

Jess signed against his chest. *I must return to my ship.* She tried to sit up, and pain shot through her torso, followed by a rush of nausea. With a groan, she lay down.

He set his lower arm across her waist. *You must go nowhere.*

Jess recognized her nausea. Apparently the med patch wasn't one hundred percent effective. Either that, or she had a more serious problem than morning sickness. What if she had lost the baby? No. She couldn't have miscarried. Surely Ghar would have known. But would he understand what that blood meant? Jess didn't know how to ask. She was vulnerable, especially if he thought she had betrayed him.

Who patched me up after the attack? she asked.

Me.

So he hadn't let a Cephean doctor see her. It made sense; they were more likely than him to let her die. Ghar also knew humans better than most of his people, enough to avoid using any Cephean remedies. Drugs that saved his people could kill humans. She would rather be in pain than risk having a doctor who didn't know human biology give her a potentially lethal medicine.

Did I have other injuries? she asked. *Bleeding anywhere else?*

No. Only the two wounds.

She exhaled with relief. Still, she wanted to be sure. *I need to see a human doctor.*

His growl rumbled. *You need to stay here.*

She tried to decipher his expression. Although fur covered his face, it wasn't long except where a human man would have a beard. Most humans found Cephean faces difficult to read, but she had learned to judge Ghar's moods. Right now he looked uncertain.

She signed, *Your government can't like my being here anymore than mine does.*

His gaze didn't waver. *Bor supports my decisions.*

Bor? As in Bor Chi? *You mean the Cephean First Councilor?*

Yes.

Good Lord. If Ghar called one of the most influential leaders on his home world by a personal name, he was placed even higher in his government than she had realized. *Bor Chi gives you his protection?*

In public. His fingers slowed on her back. *In private, he asks if I am insane.*

But he stands by your decisions?

Yes.

Why?

He trusts my judgment. After a pause, Ghar added, *He is also the older brother of my aunt's husband.*

So. Kin ties. They were strong among his people, apparently even in a hostage situation. Except she wasn't a hostage. At least she hoped not.

Why won't you let a human doctor see me? she asked.

Humans tried to kill you.

Three people tried to kill me. Not all humans.

Maybe.

Why do you suddenly distrust humans?

His claws scraped her back. *I have always distrusted humans.*

That gave her pause. *It never showed.*

My job was to overcome distrust.

What changed?

Overcoming distrust is a euphemism for taking risks. He regarded her steadily. *I have no intention to risk your life.*

Jess felt as if a crystal sculpture of great value were shattering before her eyes. *You can't let the trust between our peoples—a trust you've worked for ten years to build—be destroyed this way.*

A growl thrummed within his chest. *You can't go back. It isn't safe.*

Jess frowned at him, holding her expression long enough that he had plenty of time to decipher it. *The decision is mine. Not yours.*

He answered with another rumble, but she recognized that particular growl. He always made it in protest, when he was about to give in on an argument but didn't want to tell her.

I will tell the authorities you saved my life, she added.

You can't risk contacting them. We don't know if the killers can eavesdrop.

As much as she wanted to deny his suspicions, Jess knew he had valid reasons for concern. Few humans visited Icelos, and the Port Authority kept tabs on them all. They probably had records of the people who attacked her. They might even have a covert link to them, such as turning a blind eye to their activities in return for bribes. If Ghar had let them take her while she was unconscious, or if she contacted her ship on a comm channel the PA could hack, she might still end up dead, an unfortunate "incident" the PA would blame on Ghar.

We can bring someone here from my ship. Although Ghar's apartment looked basic, it had plenty of modern technology. He just kept it hidden to make his home fit with the spare ambiance of the colony. She thumped her fist on his chest. *We need to do this.*

After a moment, he signed, *Very well. But no Space Corps personnel.*

It was a reasonable compromise. If her people sent in the military, the Cepheans would see it as a hostile move. So which civilians on *Silver Tide* could best deal with what looked like some weird smuggling operation? Jack O'Brien, probably.

How about the Allied Services? she signed. *They work against smugglers.*

Yes, that will work. Concern showed in his gaze. *Do you hurt? Your people can bring pain medicine.*

I'm fine. She didn't intend to take any drugs during her pregnancy unless it was absolutely necessary, but this wasn't the time to explain why.

Just exactly when was a good time, she had no idea.

•

Even in the grey uniform of the Allied Services, with his unruly hair combed, Jack O'Brien still looked like a pirate. He came to Ghar's home with two of his aides, a man and woman. All three settled on a rug in the main room.

Jess sat with them, wearing a shift made from one of Ghar's tunics. On him it reached to his hips; on her, it came to below her knees. She put her arms through the upper sleeves, rolling them up to free her hands. She had tried to tie the lower sleeves behind her back, but with her injuries, it hurt too much to move her arms that way. So Ghar tied them for her. Even if her uniform hadn't been ripped and bloodied, she might have worn this looser tunic. The tight fit of her uniform bothered her. She was almost three months pregnant; soon she could no longer hide the evidence.

Ghar sat on a blocky stool, looming over them, silent and formidable.

"Ambassador Ko saved my life," Jess continued, speaking to Jack O'Brien. His female aide served as translator, signing for Ghar, while his male aide recorded their words on a holopad.

Jack regarded her intently, as if trying to decipher what lay behind her words. "So you and his Excellency were already planning to meet that night?"

"That's right." She suspected Jack knew how to read body language; in his line of work, the skill would be invaluable. He might sense if she were lying or withholding information. So she just said, "Ambassador Ko and I often work together."

"We'll give your statement to the authorities."

"Good," Jess said. "We need to cool down this situation."

Jack glanced at Ghar, who met his gaze without a word or sign. Jack shifted on his chair, then turned back to Jess. "Your meeting with us ought to alleviate matters."

"I hope so." Jess shook her head. "All over some cats. I don't get it."

"They aren't cats." Jack leaned forward. "You stumbled into a delivery by a cartel the Allied Services has pursued for years. My team never worked on the case, so I don't know details, but apparently the cartel has moved business through here before. The port is small and no one pays much attention." He still had that look, as if she posed a puzzle for him to solve. "No one expected the captain of a major Allied starship to show up."

Jess had no insights to offer. "Why not just get a permit to import comalki? It can't be that expensive."

"Those aren't exactly comalki, either. They've been altered." Jack pushed his hand through his hair, tousling the locks. "The animals carry a virus. It's what the cartel actually sells. If one of those altered comalkos bites you, you're sick."

She stiffened. "Could I have caught it? I petted one on the head."

"It doesn't affect humans." With an uneasy glance at Ghar, Jack added, "The virus is deadly to Cepheans."

Ghar signed, and Jack's aide spoke for him. "How deadly?"

Jack answered grimly. "Let those animals loose and you'd wipe out every Cephean here."

Jess stared at him. Was the cartel insane? This world belonged to the Skolian Imperialate, which protected its own with a legendary ferocity. Jess had no idea how Skolian humans felt about Cepheans, but it didn't matter. If they learned an Earth cartel had killed an entire colony of Skolian citizens, any citizens, the retribution by their formidable military would be fast and harsh.

She clenched her hand in the cloth of her shift. "The cartel is crazy."

"Not crazy. Greedy." Jack grimaced. "A fringe group that wants to kill all Cepheans paid the cartel an ungodly fee to transport the plague here. And hell, if it had started a war, it would've benefited the cartel. They could sell weapons to both sides." He turned back to Ghar. "Your Excellency, please be assured that these extremists in no way represent the Allied Worlds of Earth. We greatly value our relations with your people and wish to continue in good will."

"Such fanatics also exist among my people," Ghar said. "They feel similarly about humans."

"We'll punish the perpetrators," Jack said. "Count on it."

Ghar didn't answer, he just watched the AS agents. Jess knew he was only thinking, but on the face of a Cephean, his expression looked murderous. When Jack stiffened as if preparing to defend himself, she spoke quickly. "Are the altered comalki immune to this virus?"

Jack glanced at her. "That's right. They're chimeras."

The word sounded vaguely familiar. "That's some sort of animal mix, yes?"

"In a biological sense," Jack said. "To engineer a chimera, you mix DNA from two species."

Now she remembered the word, from in a long-ago college course. "Isn't a chimera a mythological beast, head of a lion, tail of a dragon or something? Breathed fire at people it didn't like."

He smiled. "That's where it originated. In biology, it refers to a hybrid animal. Chimeras are easiest to make using similar species, like lions and tigers, or comalki and cats."

"So this virus would kill either a comalkos or a cat, but the chimera survives."

"Exactly." He spoke to Ghar. "The cartel chose comalki because Cepheans like the animal."

Ghar growled deep in his throat, his lower hands fisted on his knees. He signed with his upper hands and his translator spoke his words. "Why don't you stop these smugglers?"

"They've managed to stay a step ahead of the Allied Servces," Jack said. "But if Captain Fernández testifies against them, it could give us the break we need to bring down their operation."

Jess thought about three complete strangers trying to throw her into the canyon, killing not only her, but also her child. "I'll testify."

Ghar snarled, and she needed no translator to know he said, "No!" in Cephean. His lips drew back and his teeth glinted like daggers. Then he bared his claws, which were longer than his fangs.

Jack blanched, but he didn't back down. "We need her testimony."

Jess signed to Ghar. *I will be in no danger.*

He answered in his own language, a series of growls. She had trouble with the words, but it sounded like the equivalent of "They will kill you."

"They won't hurt me." She spoke slowly so he could decipher what, to him, was high-pitched, sing-song lilt. "I will have protection."

Jack O'Brien was staring at her. "You *understand* his

language?"

Jess glanced at him, distracted. "Some."

He whistled. "That's supposed to be impossible."

Thinking of her child, she said, "Many things are impossible. That doesn't stop them from happening." She had to change the subject before Ghar decided Jack was endangering her life and hefted him out a window. "How did the cartel get started?"

"A wealthy collector set it up about thirty-five years ago," Jack said. "He wanted Cephean rugs in his collection."

"Why didn't he just buy them?" Granted the rugs were expensive, but their prices weren't exorbitant, especially for the wealthy.

"He didn't want abryr rugs." Jack considered Ghar as if weighing whether to continue. Finally he said, "He wanted Cephean pelts."

Good Lord. Jess had heard stories of people who skinned Cepheans for their fur, but she'd never credited them before.

Ghar signed to Jess, using three hands to emphasize his message and holding up the fourth to stop the translator from speaking. *Humans are sick.*

Please don't judge us all by the aberrations of a few, Jess signed. *I'm human, too.*

He spoke in his own language. "You are unique."

Jack was watching them with open curiosity—until Ghar fixed him with a hostile glare. Flushing, Jack looked away.

Ghar signed again, this time letting his translator speak. "Did this collector get his pelts?"

Jack risked looking at him again. "No. None. Our authorities caught the hunters he sent to Cepheus. But none of the hunters would talk. We couldn't get the evidence to convict him."

"He went free?" Ghar's hand moved as if he were cutting the air. "To murder again?"

Jack hesitated. "He didn't send any more hunters."

"You evade my question," Ghar said.

"You won't like the answer."

"Tell it anyway."

Jack spoke as if he were walking on ice so thin it could break. "He wanted specialty pelts."

A foreboding was building with Jess. "What kind of specialty?"

"From Cephean-human chimeras," Jack said. "They wanted the richness of Cephean pelts, the silkiness of human hair, and colors you can't get from a pure Cephean."

Jess fist clenched so tightly, her fingernails gouged her palms. "Are you telling me this madman created Cephean-human chimeras and *skinned* them?"

"They intended to." Anger edged Jack's voice. "To create a smooth pelt, a chimera has to express Cephean genes, yet still manifest the desired human traits. That kind of selectivity requires methods more sophisticated than we have now, decades later. Back then they couldn't do it at all."

"Did you arrest him for it?" she asked.

"Not for that," Jack said. "Researching chimeras isn't illegal."

The light glinted on Ghar's fangs. "Only a human would let such a monster go free."

"I hate that we had no proof," Jack said. "But he didn't go free. The authorities caught him for evading interstellar import taxes. He did time."

"Not enough." Ghar regarded him coldly. "It couldn't have been enough."

No, Jess thought. *It could never be enough.*

•

The south windows in Ghar's home overlooked a cavern. His people lived in apartments cut from the walls of the great cave, their homes stacked up for ten stories, Cephean stories, double the height humans built. No lifts served the cave; instead, vertical staircases ran up the walls like ladders, forming throughways much as humans built roads. Among the crowds of Cepheans climbing in the city of ladders, Jess saw many pelt colors, from common browns to rarer grays. None resembled the fiery color of Ghar's fur.

A rustle came from behind her, and Ghar joined her at the window. They stood together, gazing at the cavern. After a moment, he signed to her. *Do your injuries hurt?*

I'm all right. Although her body ached, she could handle it. *You've been very quiet about what Jack O'Brien told us.*

He unsheathed his claws, and they curved like miniature scythes. *What is there to say? That I want to kill humans?*

Jess stiffened.

Not you. He touched her cheek with his claw. *I wish to do to humans what I hate them for wanting to do to Cepheans.*

Jess froze, aware of the honed point against her skin.

Ghar pulled back his hand and lowered himself onto a tall stool that stood near the window. Even seated, he was slightly taller than Jess. He drew her forward until she was standing between his legs, then put his lower arms around her waist and signed with his upper. *Bor Chi has ruled that I acted to save your life, so I have no guilt in the death. Your people don't agree. I was within the borders of New Appenzell when I killed the smuggler, putting me in Allied territory. Your people want my diplomatic immunity waived. Bor says no. The situation is volatile, and I cannot return to the territory of the Allied Worlds. When you leave here, I can see you no more.* He paused, then signed with care. *I don't want you to leave.*

You may not feel that way when you hear what I have to say, Jess signed.

Why?

Will you first answer a question?

His gaze searched her face. *Ask.*

Do you know your parents?

Of course.

That stopped her. If he knew his parents, her suspicions had no basis. *Do you see them often?*

They died.

She signed regret. *I am sorry.*

He shrugged his giant shoulders. *I never knew them. It happened right after my birth. Our transport crashed in the snow.*

Hikers found me two days later.

Jess stared at him. *How could a newborn survive alone, in the snow, for two days?*

I don't know. But I did.

She mentally braced herself. *I don't believe the child in that transport lived. Someone took his body and put you in his place.*

He lips drew back in an expression that, if Jess hadn't known meant amusement, she would have believed was a snarl. *Your imagination is fertile,* he signed.

So is my body.

What?

During my last visit to the colony you were the only — She stopped, then took a breath and continued. *My only companion.*

He brushed her check, the barest touch of his finger. *I know you don't expect me to share you. I wouldn't have been with you otherwise.*

I'm glad you know that, Ghar. Because I'm pregnant.

He regarded her blankly. *What?*

I'm pregnant.

I have a trouble with your signing. I don't understand your word.

Pregnant. I'm going to have a baby. Yours.

His growl rumbled. *It isn't amusing, Jess.*

She took one of his lower hands and laid it on her abdomen. *I carry a child.*

Ghar pulled away, his claws unsheathing. *If you have a child, it is not mine.*

Jess hoped she hadn't just signed her death warrant. *There was no one else. It must be yours.*

It cannot be. I am not human.

Yes. You are.

His lips drew back, showing his fangs. *Stop mocking me.*

I'm not. Jess pushed back the tendrils of hair that curled around her face. *Ever since I learned about the baby, I've been trying to understand. After we talked to Jack, I knew.*

You think this sick collector made me for his collection.

Yes. She shuddered. *But his people must have decided they couldn't go through with it, raising you to be murdered for your fur.*

This is how you explain infidelity? His claws glinted. *I expected better from you.*

I can prove it. My doctor can compare your DNA with the fetus. She'll know, Ghar.

She will say what you command her to say.

You know me better than that.

I thought I did. I was wrong.

You weren't wrong.

So you claim. Ghar considered her. *Very well. I will do these tests.* His gaze turned implacable. *Hope they don't prove you a liar.*

•

Jess watched from Ghar's apartment as, far below, Sandra Bolton crossed the cavern with her Cephean escort. Next to their towering forms, the doctor looked like a silver-haired child. They started up a staircase that led to Ghar's apartment, and it soon turned into ladders as the walls became vertical. It took a long time for Sandra and her escort to climb, until they disappeared from view behind a ridge in the cavern. Jess waited, trying in vain to keep her muscles from knotting any tighter with her tension.

The front door of the apartment opened. A few moments later Sandra appeared in the wide entrance of the living room. The doctor entered alone; as instructed, the escort must have left after delivering her.

A heavy tread came from the other side of the room. Turning, Jess saw Ghar in the entrance to an inner chamber. He stood with his lower arms braced against the sides of the doorway and his upper arms against the top, his body framed in the large archway.

Sandra's gaze flicked from Ghar to Jess. "I've finished the analysis." She paused as Jess signed her words for Ghar. Then Sandra spoke directly to him. "I am sorry, Your Excellency."

Ghar signed and Jess spoke his words. "Why are you sorry?"

"Someone played with your genetics on a massive scale," Sandra said. "You have human DNA throughout your body. The mingling is so extensive, I doubt it can be fully mapped." She took a breath. "You are a chimera, Ambassador Ko. You combine the heredity of two people. And one of those is human."

"No!" Ghar signed.

"I'm sorry," Sandra said.

He answered fast and sharp. "If I had human DNA, it would have shown up in medical scans."

"The scans don't go into enough detail. Cephean DNA is barely different from human, less than 2 percent." Excitement leaked into Sandra's voice. "Your DNA map is incredible. The subtlety is like nothing I've ever seen. To reveal the differences, I had to do far more extensive tests than probably anything you've had before."

Ghar said nothing, just stood like a statue.

"And the baby?" Jess was so wound up she forgot to use her hands. Then, remembering, she signed her question so Ghar would understand.

"Most of Ambassador Ko's tissues express Cephean genes," Sandra said. "But his germ cells are human. Although chimeras are usually sterile, they don't have to be." She regarded Ghar. "Your Excellency, you are the father of Captain Fernández's child."

Ghar answered in his own language. "It is impossible." His growls rolled through the room.

As Sandra's forehead furrowed, Jess said, "He doesn't believe you."

Sandra regarded them both with her painful compassion. "I can only give you the results. I can't make them what you want to hear."

Jess started to sign the words to Ghar, but he abruptly turned and left the room.

"I'm sorry," Sandra said. "I know I keep saying that, but it's true."

Jess just nodded. What could she say? That she wanted to ram *Silver Tide* down the throat of whoever had done this to Ghar? True as that might be, it solved nothing.

"The results probably explain a lot to him," Sandra said.

"What do you mean?

"They showed up a slew of anomalies." Sandra shook her head. "For one thing, whoever played with his cells didn't get the lower arms right. Apparently he's had them broken and reset several times to fix the problems. He has metal rods in both to extend their length to what's normal for a Cephean.

Jess could imagine what Ghar's people would do if they discovered the reason for his differences. "Sandra, you must keep this confidential."

The doctor nodded. "Unless you and Ambassador Ko choose otherwise, no one but the three of us will ever know."

Jess hesitated to ask her next question, but her curiosity persisted. "Do you know what Ghar would have been like as a human?"

"Irish, I think. His hair and eyes would be the same color they are now." Sandra gave her a look of apology. "That's about all I can tell."

Jess tried to imagine him as a man, a burly Irishman striding across the green hills of Earth, red curls whipping back from his face, his beard thick and full. It hurt to envision what could never be. She couldn't imagine how he would deal with this, knowing he carried within himself the identity of a people he distrusted, even hated.

"I have to talk to him," Jess said. "Alone."

"And then?"

"I'll come back to *Silver Tide*."

Relief washed across Sandra's face. "I'll send up an air stretcher."

"I can walk."

Sandra gave a familiar scowl. "I have eyes. I can see you hurt."

The last thing Jess wanted was people fussing over her. More than ever, she and Ghar needed privacy. "I'll be all right." She thought of the ladders she had to navigate to reach the cavern floor. "I will rest here first, though."

Sandra didn't look thrilled, but she accepted the compromise. "One day. That's all."

After Sandra left, Jess limped through the apartment. She found Ghar in his bedroom, sitting on a stool and staring at nothing. She stopped out of reach of his claws, but then decided what the hell. She would trust her judgment. She walked over and stood before him.

Do you want to be alone? she asked.

No. He let out a rumbling breath. *I thought you lied to explain the baby. I misjudged you. I am sorry.*

I understand.

Will you go back to Silver Tide *with your friend?*

My friend?

The doctor.

Jess blinked. *Where did you get the idea that Sandra Bolton is my friend?*

He waved his lower hand. *You interact as do other humans who call each other friend.*

All we do is argue.

In my experience, this is not an unusual way for humans to express friendship.

Jess didn't know what to make of that. *She drives me nuts.*

She cares what happens to you.

Jess wasn't even sure how to define friendship. She had guarded her emotions for so long, maybe she could no longer see what lay in front of her.

Or sat.

She regarded Ghar, aware of him watching her. She never seemed to choose an easy path when it came to love. Regardless, this was the path she had to walk, and walk it she would, if she could only figure out how.

Ghar brushed his fingers down her arm. *Incredibly, you and I have made a child. At least for this I am pleased.*

I, too. But she couldn't relax with him. Not yet. When he drew her forward, she put her palms against his shoulders, keeping him at bay. He put his lower arms around her waist, his muscles ridged against her back. She touched the two-inch fang that came down over his lip, white against the curls of his beard. He did nothing, just watched her.

Jess pulled away her hand. *Does this response of yours mean I needn't fear for my life?*

His lips drew back, a snarl that showed dismay rather than rage. *I would never kill you!*

Even if you thought I lied about the child's father?

Even if that. A rumble came from his chest, not anger, another emotion, maybe sorrow. *I would have sent you away and advised Bor to cut ties with Earth.*

I would never betray your trust. She regarded him with an unwavering gaze. *But even if I had, it wouldn't be worth destroying relations between our peoples.*

A few days ago I would have agreed. His signing slowed, as if his hands were weary. *Right now it is hard to remember why I ever wanted to establish trust with your people. It would have been the final blow to discover you had treated what passed between us with such disregard as to end up with another man's child on that same night. In time, my common sense would have prevailed, but by then, the damage may have been beyond repair.*

She gentled her motions. *I understand, Ghar. But I still must return to* Silver Tide.

He formed signs for both regret and reluctance, then added, *You are free to leave.*

Jess put her arms around her neck and laid her cheek against his shoulder. Ghar held her with all four arms and signed against her spine, his large hands covering most of her back. *You should have the doctor send someone up with an air-stretcher.*

I don't need one. I'm okay.

You are not 'okay.'

I'm fine.

He growled. *You are as stubborn as a stalagmite.*

Jess laughed, but it caught in her throat. She saw no end to this mess. It had one glimmer of light, the baby. A miracle. But it would be insane to reveal the child's paternity. She had seen the hatred bred by xenophobia. Had Ghar killed one of his own kind, Earth wouldn't have cared and

Bor Chi probably wouldn't have absolved him. She didn't want to imagine what either of their peoples would say to a child born of a human woman and
Cephean male.

Ghar pulled back and signed. *Your ship is a metal hull. It can never hold you in the night when loneliness stalks your dreams.*

It is my home.

This could become your home.

Come live with me on Silver Tide.

I would die in your silver cage.

Jess signed sorrow to him. *If we live together, our peoples will make our lives hell.*

He watched her with his large eyes. Brown eyes. Human eyes. *Then stay with me this one last night.*

Jess touched his face. *Tonight, I will stay.*

•

IV
Bridge

Jess maneuvered her bulk through the hatchway and floated into the bridge. Following Sandra's advice, she rarely spent time in free fall, so she savored these few moments the doctor allowed her. Being weightless offered a much-appreciated relief; at more than eight months pregnant, she felt as unwieldy as a cargo barge.

She hauled herself to her command chair and settled in with a grunt. Panels shifted, adjusting to her size as the robot arm carried her through the bridge. She passed a smaller robot arm ridden by one of her officers. When the lieutenant lifted her hand in salute, Jess saluted back. She moved on until she reached the center of the hemisphere.

Jess spoke into the comm embedded in her wrist gauntlet. "Commander Carson, have we finished loading the cargo for the Flanders team?"

The voice of Andy Carson, her Exec, came out of the

comm. "In about five minutes, Captain."

"Excellent." She shifted position, trying to get comfortable. The chair molded to her body, doing its best to help. Suddenly she stiffened, while muscular ripples moved down her abdomen. As if eager to join in, her baby chose that moment to give a hearty kick. Jess couldn't help but laugh. "You're a strong one."

"Ma'am?" Andy asked over her comm. "I didn't catch that."

She wondered what Andy would think if she told him she was having Braxton-Hicks contractions. It wasn't genuine labor; she wouldn't give birth for another three weeks.

"As soon as the Flanders personnel are onboard," she said, "we can leave orbit."

"Aye, Captain."

Jess settled back and activated the holoscreens. The walls of the bridge disappeared, leaving her suspended in the starscape outside the ship. A luminous blue world rotated before them, girdled by silvery rings. Far more distant, a white star pierced space, the parent sun for this glowing world. *Silver Tide* had stopped here to pick up a team of planetary scouts.

A familiar longing came over Jess, the wanderlust that had stirred her heart for her entire life. She would love to power up a scout craft and go explore that world firsthand. But she hadn't left *Silver Tide* for months. She couldn't risk the acceleration or exposure to radiation.

"Such a beautiful sight," Andy murmured. "Like a sphere of turquoise and sapphire light."

"You sound poetic today," Jess said.

He chuckled. "It happens every now and then."

She felt a twinge of sorrow, one that often caught her lately, sometimes when she wanted to share a moment with Ghar, like now, and other times when she saw a family together. Although she and Ghar spoke on occasion, it was difficult to arrange. They had few options. Although the authorities on Earth had dropped the kidnapping charge against him, the murder accusation remained.

Jess's testimony during the cartel trial had not only helped topple their smuggling operation, it also eased the outpouring of anger against Ghar. For all that humans disliked Cepheans, the attempted genocide on Icelos horrified them far more. The Allied Services destroyed the plague chimeras and denounced the cartel in every way possible. It kept the Skolians from declaring open hostilities, but relations between Cepheus and Earth still deteriorated. The murder charge against Ghar angered the Cephean authorities, given that his action prevented the brutal death of an Allied Space Corps captain. Cephean portrayals of Jess were scathing, which incensed the Allied authorities. So Ghar remained on Cepheus and the Cephean embassy in Geneva remained empty.

Jess just wanted it all to stop. In the past, hatreds on Earth had burned over race, religion, sexual choices, and culture. Those differences faded when compared to the variations between humans and their altered kin on other worlds. Although Jess and Ghar never revealed the extent of their relationship, the mere existence of their friendship caused outrage, a response more virulent than Jess had ever experienced, not even in her interracial marriage with the man from Norway.

Nor did her pregnancy sit well with her superiors. She broke an unwritten code of the Space Corps by remaining pregnant without a spouse. Although no regulations prohibited her from giving birth out of wedlock, the brass didn't like it. Tough. She had no intention of taking vows with someone she didn't love just for the sake of being married. She and Ghar hadn't discussed it, and they might not be able to marry anyway. No legal precedents existed for their mess.

The Space Corps kept the identity of her child's father confidential. Although she managed to retain her command, they passed her over for a promotion that, prior to her pregnancy, everyone had expected her to receive. She could only work hard and hope she made colonel the next time she came up for review. She agreed to all the tests requested by the military and medical teams. No one had heard of a chimera as complex as Ghar even existing, let alone being fertile. Unfortunately, without him, they couldn't do much research. Unless Cepheus and Earth reached a truce that allowed their scientists to collaborate again, Ghar's origins would remain a mystery.

Andy's voice came out of her gauntlet. "Captain, we have the Flanders team on board."

"Great. As soon—" Jess stopped when another contraction began, spreading from her lower back up into her abdomen, longer and more intense than the last.

"Bloody hell," she muttered.

"Captain?" Andy asked.

"Commander Carson." Jess took a breath. "Switch to the contingency plan we discussed."

"Good God!" Andy said. "Do you need help, ma'am?"

"No, no. I'm fine." Jess was acutely aware of her bridge officers listening. Everyone knew what "contingency plan" meant. "Andy, you're in charge." To the entire bridge crew, she added, "Take her out gently, ladies and gentlemen. Gently."

A murmur of good wishes came from her crew. Andy said. "Good luck, Captain."

Anticipation sparked in Jess—until another pain wrenched through her, this one sharper than the last. She barely managed to hold back her groan.

Sandra's voice snapped out of her gauntlet. "Captain, I'm receiving a page on your emergency channel."

Jess waited a moment until her contraction ended. "I know. I sent it."

"Well, I'll be cheddar in a chugger," Sandra said.

Jess couldn't help but laugh. "That was articulate."

"Are you sure it's time?" Sandra asked. "You aren't due for weeks."

Jess started to answer, then groaned with another contraction.

"Uh...I take that as a 'yes,'" Sandra said.

Somehow Jess managed, "You take it right."

"I'm sending an air stretcher for you," Sandra said. "I've dispatched the orderlies."

"I don't need a stretcher." Jess resisted the urge to grumble. Ever since Ghar had decided she and Sandra were friends, Jess had been doing her inept best to act less ornery toward the doctor. "Just get ready for me, Doc. I'm on my way."

•

"Now!" Sandra said. "*Push!*"

Jess pushed, clenching the handgrips on the bed. The wave of pain went on and on.

Sandra swore. "That's it. This baby doesn't want to come out. I'm going to operate."

Jess struggled to sit up. "No."

"You've been in labor for over a day." Lines furrowed Sandra's forehead. "Jess, enough. Natural childbirth is barbaric. You don't have to do it this way."

Jess was having a hard time remembering why she had been so determined to give birth the way nature designed, but damned if she was to let them cut her open. She moaned as another contraction began. Steeling herself, she dredged up her strength. PUSH.

"She's coming!" Sandra called. "Jess! Come on! You can do it!"

Jess screamed as pain ripped through her body. Gasping at the release that followed, she heaved herself up to look, her hair straggling around her face—

"I don't believe it," Jess said. Sandra was holding a tiny girl with a wrinkled face and a head covered by red-gold curls. As Sandra checked the baby's nostrils, the infant gave a loud wail.

"She's beautiful," Jess whispered. Then she fell back onto the bed.

The next moments blurred, as nurses cleaned her up and shifted her to a fresh bed. Sandra handed her a tiny bundle, and Jess cradled the baby, murmuring. The infant looked up with large eyes, as if she recognized her mother's voice. When Jess put her to her breast, the child nursed with gusto. Jess was vaguely aware of Sandra and the others, but her attention was for her child. She closed her eyes, bemused at the uncharacteristic tenderness she felt when she held this small bundle in her combat-trained arms.

Jess didn't realize she had dozed off until someone tapped her shoulder. She looked to see George Mai standing by her bed. The baby slept, nestled against her side.

George beamed. "The crew sends their congratulations, ma'am."

Jess smiled drowsily. "Give them my thanks."

Sandra appeared next to George. "Captain, you have a message from Cepheus."

Jess came fully awake. "On my private line."

"I'll set it up with the interstellar Kyle mesh," Sandra said.

Jess waited while they made arrangements. If George thought it strange that the outlawed Cephean ambassador wished to speak with her, he kept his questions to himself.

After the doctors left, Jess sat up, holding the baby. She spoke to the air. "Put my call on audio."

The EI that monitored the hospital answered. "Would you like visual?"

She wanted to say no, especially after just giving birth, but this wasn't something she and Ghar could do through a translator.

"Yes," she said. "Visual, too."

The wall across the room glowed blue, then cleared to show an image of a Ghar. He was seated at a desk in a gleaming office far more modern than his home on Icelos. His upper arms rested on the top desk, which was a grid rather than a solid surface, and his lower arms were crossed on a lower shelf visible through the grid. His human translator was just leaving the room.

Ghar waited until he was alone. Then he signed, *Hello, Jess.*

Hello. She showed him the baby. *I thought of naming her Alejandra Ko Fernandez. What do you think?*

A beautiful name. Ghar hesitated. *I would say she is a beautiful baby, but I have no idea how human babies should look.*

Jess's face softened into a smile. *She's beautiful.*

After your Doctor Bolton contacted me, I thought to come there, to be with you. He signed with stiff motions. *But as soon as I enter human space, I will be taken into custody.*

Then we will come to Cepheus.

Jess, no. Go to Earth. His motions slowed. *I have decided. I will go to your authorities and let them have this trial they want. Better to resolve this issue than have it dividing our peoples.*

As much a she wanted to tell him to stay free, she held back, knowing he acted for the greater good. But she dreaded the risk he was taking. With so much distrust, even hatred between their peoples, a human court might convict him even though he'd acted to save her life.

I will testify for you, she signed.

Think carefully before you make that offer, he said. *If you do this, the truth about our child will almost certainly become public, once the lawyers start digging.*

I know. She doubted it would be a complete surprise to either of their peoples. During her testimony against the cartel, speculation about her and Ghar had gone wild.

Can you handle it? Ghar asked.

I think so. And you?

For myself I have no concern. But what of the child?

Jess had agonized over that question for months. *Alejandra needs to know you as her father from as young an age as possible. If we wait too long, fear could turn her from you. Better she knows from the start rather than have the truth shock her later.*

I have thought this also. He paused. *She is a human child. You know better than I what she will deal with in your culture.*

I think it is best to tell her.

Then you will come to Earth?

Yes. We will come. It could only be for visits, since she remained in command of *Silver Tide,* but she and Alejandra would always find a way to see Ghar, regardless of what happened.

His large hands made word pictures. *I do not know if marriage between us is possible. If it is, we should do so. If not, I will still legally acknowledge our daughter.*

Jess couldn't define the emotions roiling within her. Ghar's life would be infinitely easier if he never tried to acknowledge her or his child. That he meant to do it anyway told her a great deal about him.

You honor us, she signed.

He moved his hands awkwardly. *I am unsure of the proper way to say this. Were you Cephean, I would know. But in human terms I am lost.*

I'm not sure what you mean.

His signs slowed. *Wherever you go, whatever you do, my heart walks in silence until you touch my hand.*

Jess knew the verse; Cepheans used it as a declaration of love. Finally she recognized the unfamiliar emotion within her. She and Ghar had walked in silence for years, afraid to voice what they felt for each other.

She signed the traditional Cephean words. *I offer my heart to break your silence.*

They could never have what they wanted, a normal life. But perhaps they could bridge the fear that separated their peoples. It wasn't everything.

But it was a start.

CATHERINE ASARO is a two-time Nebula Award win-
ner and author of science fiction, fantasy and thrillers,
and has written over twenty-seven novels,
as well as novellas, short stories, and non-fiction.

BEING KITTY

AJ LEE

"**KITTY** will be the friendliest, most helpful, and most human customer service you can provide," Jorge Bridges was saying, "without picking up the damn phone yourself." Rapturous applause, laughter. I let the press conference video play on, but I didn't need to watch. Instead, I stared up at the window. If I tilted my head just so, looked past the trash-filled cement window well and beyond the textile factory next door, I could see a little sliver of sky, getting pinkish as the sun set. Brad would be home soon.

Very soon—I got a Whisp notification telling me he had left work. I pushed the video to the bedroom, turning up the volume so I could hear it while I made a cup of tea. Bridges talked on about Kitty, how she integrated seamlessly with any platform you needed her on and provided personalized service across user bases, and I grabbed a handful of crackers. It might not have been the most nutritious dinner, but it was what I could afford.

I left a few crackers in the box for Brad, of course. He'd have eaten the staff meal at the restaurant, but he'd probably be hungry. He was on his feet all day, after all.

I balanced my tea on the headboard, propped a pillow—mine, Brad's was on the couch—against the wall, and made a little nest out of the bathrobe I was using as a quilt. That was the deal: Brad took the couch but got the duvet, I got the mattress and would have to fend for myself.

Bridges was finishing up his presentation, smiling and waving as he strolled off the stage. He never actually said the words "chatbot", "virtual", or "AI", and neither could I. It was a tiny piece of the huge NDA I signed before I could even audition for them.

The conference was replaced by a slide deck running through the UI. There were some questions from the other Kittys, but it seemed pretty straightforward to me: just a normal chat interface on one half of the display and a selection of actual bots on the other. I munched on a cracker while I watched, getting crumbs on the bed. It was thrilling, for a second, a nauseous thrill like when you're drunk and about to fall down the stairs to the bar's bathroom, only you catch yourself on the handrail.

I brushed the crumbs off again, just in case Brad got sick of the living room. You never know.

The slide deck ended on a video of a smiling young woman. It was Kitty, or at least the avatar representing Kitty, and I couldn't tell whether she was human or CG. She congratulated us on having been selected as the first Kittys, told us we would "change the face of commerce and connection." I smiled, more flattered than I should've been.

Brad's feet were on the steps outside. I pushed the presentation to my earbuds, leaving one dangling down along my neck just in case. Kitty's voice was tinny in the mono-sound coming through one ear.

I logged in as available to start my training period as soon as I could. The program was in beta, and us new Kittys would start by doing text-only. Those of us with good enough auditions and high enough satisfaction ratings would move up to voice chat. That was my goal, of course. With the pay bump I'd be able to afford a new place, maybe even a place that wasn't a basement.

My first questions came in through Whisp. I found a good pair of shoes for a customer, then told someone when it was going to rain. Someone asked about the capital of British Columbia, which I answered without having to ask a real chatbot, and then someone else asked for his friend's address, which I found with access to his contacts. It was easy work, and surprisingly engrossing—I was barely aware of the laugh track from the series Brad was watching.

I stayed logged on until long after the sounds of the show were replaced by Brad's snoring. Then I took my payment in same-day earnings. I couldn't resist, even though

Bridges Incorporated took a percentage for it. I used the money on a belated birthday present for my mom, having it shipped straight to her apartment across the country, then I bought a new bathmat to replace the moldy old towel Brad and I had been using. There wasn't much money left after that, but that was okay. I was already planning to log back on the next day. I could start saving up then.

•

By the next week I'd been promoted to voice chat, thanks in part to how often I was on. I worked from my mattress, the divot from my butt getting deeper every day.

"What classes do I need to graduate?" a user asked.

I asked his university's bot to find them, then listed them out, my voice modulated on the other end to sound just like every other Kitty.

"Are there coupons for this toilet paper?"

"Not today, Griffin, but it usually goes on sale on Thursdays."

"Can you schedule a meeting with Tony Aoude?"

I found a spot in both of their calendars, one that wasn't too late or too early, and booked it. "Sure thing," I confirmed, in the Kitty-approved language that already came so naturally.

There was the smallest patch of sunlight on my bathrobe. I stretched my foot out into it, feeling it on my bare skin. The days were getting longer. It'd be hot outside, the air thick and ripe with pollen.

Another question, this one from a teenaged Whisp user. "How do I know if my boyfriend is cheating on me?"

My mouth was already open to speak, but nothing came out. What would Kitty say? I wasn't allowed to ask users to repeat themselves, and if I paused too long my ratings would drop and a real bot would take over. But there was nothing like this in the training videos.

"Why do you think he's cheating on you, Maryam?"

"Just a feeling."

She was gone before I could say anything else, but

I had her account information. She was seventeen, graduating from a private high school this year. Her school was here in Winnipeg, which made sense since Kittys were matched up with nearby users. She—

"What's the most interesting way to get to Edmonton?" someone new asked, interrupting my train of thought.

An hour or so later, I stood up to stretch. The outdoors were calling and I had a bottle of white wine in the fridge. I'd take it down to the river, maybe get a hot dog to go with it. I pressed my ear to the door, listening for Brad, but it was silent in the living room. I figured he'd gone out, and I was somewhere between relief and loneliness when I saw I was wrong. He lay on the couch, swiping messages mindlessly over the wall, a tumbler in his hand. He looked up.

"You're done?"

I nodded.

"We need to talk." He refilled his tumbler from the wine bottle on the table. From my wine bottle. "Sit."

I sat. It was fine, I told myself. I'd buy another. How was he supposed to know?

"When are you going to move out?"

I forced my breath to come slow. "I'm still looking."

"You need to look faster."

It was getting later and I needed to be out, in the park, in the sun. "It's… hard. I don't have a deposit yet, and—"

"Are you asking me for money?"

"No!"

He nodded once, sharp. "Good. Because I think I've bankrolled you long enough."

I sat very still. We had moved out here when he got that chemical analysis contract, and it was true I didn't have a job at that point. I kept auditioning, even though there weren't as many acting gigs in Winnipeg as there were in Vancouver, where we went to school. But Brad was right— he had paid my way until his contract was up and it wasn't his fault he got a job that took us away from Vancouver. It wasn't his fault his contract ended.

"Sorry," I managed.

His eyes were already back on the wall, so I slunk out of the apartment and into the sun.

•

In my first month of doing voice calls, I had the highest customer satisfaction rating of all the Kittys. I got a pay bump for it, too. It was something about my voice, one of the other Kittys said on the forum—I sounded just robotic enough that the filters didn't make it uncanny. I didn't tell them I had an MFA in Stage Performance. It's not like that would endear me to anyone, as Brad always joked.

Today's questions included someone looking for the best divorce attorney in their location, more shoe shopping, and a few requests for me to set up meal delivery or laundry pick up. Nothing interesting.

"How much have I spent on delivery this month?"

I checked with the chatbot run by the user's bank. I had to do a bit of finessing to separate deliveries from cabs, which was the reason to get a Kitty and not a chatbot in the first place. I felt a little swell of pride when the user thanked me. It had been awhile since I'd been really good at something.

Between calls I visited rental websites, asking real chatbots to find bachelors for me. None of them were Kittys—I was getting pretty good at noticing the differences—and none of them found any decent apartments. I was still living in the bedroom. I made it up to Brad by doing the cleaning and some cooking, by stocking the cabinets and the fridge. Now I was making more money, it made sense I bought the food.

"Do you have anything red in a size twelve?" It was another question from the shoe store. I did that one myself, picking out a pair I had been eying, and sent them over.

"Can you find theatre tickets to a show for my dad? Not too expensive."

My mom had called the day she got her present. To

say thank you, but also to scold me for spending money on her. When I told her I had a job, she asked what it was, and when I told her I couldn't say, she wailed. Of course she thought it was something illegal or dangerous. Now I was getting messages from her twice a day, begging me to tell her if I needed money, asking me how Brad felt about my job. I hadn't told her about us yet. She'd just tell me to move home.

"How do I delete photos of me that someone else posted on Whisp?"

"It depends on whether or not you own the copyright," I answered in my best Kitty voice.

"What if it's a nude?"

That's when I recognized the account name. It was Maryam, the Maryam with the cheating boyfriend. My heart went out to her, but Kitty didn't have a heart. "Since you're underage, you should report it to the authorities."

"How do I do that?" She seemed pained, but all I could do was send her the contact info for the cybercrime division.

"What if other people have already downloaded the pictures?"

"Oh, Maryam," I said, before I could think. "That's terrible." She didn't respond, and I shook myself. "Once you've reported it, the authorities will investigate any downloads."

"Okay."

She was gone.

I thought about Maryam for the rest of the week. I finished looking her up on Whisp: she was graduating from high school, her grades were good. She was pretty, the way all teenage girls seemed pretty once you were approaching thirty, but her selfies only got a handful of likes. She had been in the school musicals every year— never the leading lady, but not a chorus member. There were pictures from family vacations and it seemed like her parents were still together.

My own mother had been so confused when the bullying started in grade eight. I was so pretty, she said, so nice. Why would they treat me like that? I must have been, she insisted, imagining things. I wondered if Maryam's mother felt the same way.

•

By my second month of doing voice calls, I was signed on almost every waking moment. I could make more money that way. Plus, all of my friends were Brad's friends and I didn't want to intrude. So I worked.

"Does this resume look okay?"

I read through it. "I think you should add some key-words here," I replied, highlighting the sections where the applicant had left holes. "And run your spellchecker again."

I had found a few decent apartments. Not that I'd gone to see them. Brad hadn't said anything about me leaving again, so I just… didn't. I was getting used to the bedroom. I'd even bought myself a new quilt. I almost bought a floral one, but in the end I decided on the houndstooth. Just in case. It did look very handsome against the black headboard Brad and I had picked out when we moved in.

"What's the best place to commit suicide in Winnipeg?"

I froze. I had gotten good at not freezing as Kitty, but I froze.

"Hello?" the user said. It was Maryam again.

There were protocols for this sort of thing. Kitty knew how to respond.

"Maryam, have you contacted the suicide prevention chatbot?" I linked her to the account, but she stayed.

"There's nothing they can do. Where is the best place to commit suicide in Winnipeg?"

It was a violation of privacy for me to contact the authorities, a violation of the NDA. And what could they do? What would they do? So I sent her to a highway over-pass, one that was closer to me than it was to her, and as soon as she signed off I did the same.

I rushed through the living room, stepping into my sandals without stopping.

"Where are you going in such a hurry?" Brad asked from the couch.

There was no time. "Don't wait up," I said. The door shut behind me as I was paying the fees to withdraw my same-day earnings, enough to call a cab.

It was raining. I hadn't noticed, in the basement, but it was raining and the road glistened with it. If the cab had had a human driver I would have urged him to go faster, but instead I gripped my thighs and prayed.

There were no ambulances around the overpass. No police cars. No girl gripping the railing. And—I hesitated to investigate, but I had to know—no viscera splattered on the pavement. I stood in the cold rain, my clothes sticking to my skin. Maybe she had decided against it. Maybe someone had stopped her, the way I should have.

I moved to an awning, checking my phone in the dim light from the convenience store window. Maryam was still online, her Whisp availability public.

I wanted to be relieved. I supposed I should figure out the bus schedule to get back home, since there was no need to take another cab.

What would I tell Brad?

I was about to open the schedule when Maryam posted a selfie, her manicured hand holding a Starbucks cup. The window behind her was splattered with raindrops. And it was tagged with a location—this location. I looked up. There was a Starbucks across the street.

I hesitated. I should have left, I knew. It wasn't my business.

A rivulet of water from the awning slid down my back as I walked toward her.

It was an old Starbucks, with human baristas still pulling shots and writing on cups. Maryam was sitting at a table by the window, typing furiously on a projected keyboard, staring out the window as she wrote. She would have seen my cab pull up, seen me staring at the overpass. She doesn't know you, I reminded myself. She only knew Kitty.

Her eyes were sunken and tired looking. She was so

small, so young, hunched over her keyboard alone in an old cafe in the rain. I had no way to know what she was writing, whatever the keyboard was connected to was invisible to me. So I bought a drink and sat at a table near her. She looked at me, then back out the window.

My drink was getting cold and Maryam still sat. I couldn't just leave, not now that I was here watching her. She didn't look up when I approached her table, didn't even notice me until I said her name. Then she turned her face to me, her brow furrowed.

"Are you okay?" It was the only thing I could think to say.

"Yeah?" she answered. "Should I not be?"

I sat in the chair opposite her. Her back stiffened, but she didn't get up to leave. There were no other customers here, just me and Maryam and the sour-faced baristas.

"Do I know you?" she asked.

"Kitty sent me."

She stared at me, eyes wide in her small face. "The chatbot."

"Are you okay?" I asked again. "I was worried."

She smiled, suddenly, and it transformed her. She looked older when she smiled. "Kitty, the chatbot, sent you here?"

I had already gotten myself into it, so I nodded. "I saw your messages, about your boyfriend and the pictures and... well."

She was typing again, fingers flying.

"Please don't tell anyone, It's... not an advertised service, it's meant to be undisclosed." Her fingers stopped. "I just wanted to make sure you were okay. Suicide's not the only way out, you can get better, you can seek help and—"

"I'm sorry," she said.

"Don't be, don't be sorry. You're so young, you have so much ahead of you—" my eyes were welling over with tears.

"No, that's not it," she said, shaking her head, causing her hair bun to wobble. "It was for a paper."

"A paper?"

Maryam swiped the keyboard away and leaned her face in her hand. "My grad paper. I need it to get into university." The tears were running down my cheeks now. I swabbed at them with a scratchy napkin, and Maryam watched me. "Can I get you something?"

I shook my head. "A paper?" I asked again,

"It's on chatbots, on the limits of privacy when users are in danger. None of the other chatbots came or even called the police. Just told me to call a hotline. Kitty was the only service that would tell me where to go. But then again, Kitty was the only service to send someone. Not that you would have made it in time if I had been serious."

"You're going to send this paper to schools?"

"Publish it online. It's gotta get a certain number of views before they'll even consider me for a scholarship. Even the fact that Kitty suggested a location for me to kill myself will be enough, though, I bet. Actually, can I inter-view you? For the article? Why would Kitty tell people where to go to commit suicide?"

"I can't say."

She leaned forward. "Why not?"

"They'll terminate my contract. I'll have to pay back my earnings since I broke the NDA." It wasn't a lie. I felt good about this, was almost starting to believe it myself. I sat a little straighter, dabbed at my eyes again. I was an em-ployed counsellor, sent by a chatbot to save a suicidal teen. I folded my hands on the table.

"But if your job is to come out here and talk to me, why would telling me that be breaking your non-disclosure?"

I froze. Stupid. Of course she'd see this, she was so smart. We stared at each other.

"Oh," she said, and a grin spread across her face. "Oh. You are Kitty, aren't you?"

There was nothing for it. I nodded.

"Are you an AI?"

I could have laughed, except I could barely breathe. I managed, "no."

She had pulled up the keyboard again and had her fingers poised over the keys. "But you are Kitty?"

"Me and lots of other people."

"Holy shit. A real live chatbot," she said.

"Please…" I started, not sure what to say. She looked at me, stopped typing.

"I can't tell anyone, can I? You'll lose your job if I do."

"If you don't, will you get into university?"

We were both staring out the window now, our reflections distorted in the rain-streaked glass.

"My paper won't be very good if I leave this out," she said. "So I won't get the scholarship, definitely. Which means I won't go."

I swallowed. "I bet it'll be great anyway. I bet you'll get the scholarship." It was a weak offering, but it was all I had.

•

I walked home through the rain. I was damp already, and I hoped it would calm my still-racing heart. The streets were nearly empty, just a few homeless people huddled under awnings and drunks stumbling to cabs. I stayed close to the lights of the storefronts, barely registering the window displays.

I believed Maryam when she said she wouldn't mention the Kitty thing. And I wanted to believe she'd get the scholarship anyway. She was smart and driven, I told myself. She'd get it. She would be fine. She was so young still. She had opportunities. She wasn't stuck.

The rain was slowing. I stepped back from the curb as a car sluiced through a puddle, then crossed the road.

I needed this job.

The streetlight on the corner of my road flickered as usual. I tried to take comfort in it: home sweet home, after all. Down the steps, my key in the lock. There was light leaking under the door, pooling on the step. I was looking forward to my warm bed, a cup of tea. Maybe I'd take a break from Kitty tomorrow. Just for one day.

I opened the door and stepped out of my sandals, my damp feet leaving footprints on the linoleum. A woman giggled, and for a second I thought she was real, not just a laugh track.

Except there were no flickering lights from the television.

"That tickle?" Brad said, and I felt ice in my spine.

She responded but I couldn't understand it. Didn't want to understand it. I tried to put my sandals back on, but I was numbed, and I stumbled against the door.

"Who's there?" Brad asked. I could hear him stand and I wanted to run, but I wasn't fast enough and he was standing in front of me with our quilt wrapped around his hips. "You said you weren't coming back," he said, eyes narrowed.

"I didn't say—"

He sighed. "Listen, can't you stay with a friend or something tonight? I've been patient."

I don't have any friends, I wanted to say. I've been patient, I wanted to say. But I couldn't even manage a squeak.

•

The Starbucks was closed by the time I got back and Maryam was long gone. But that didn't matter. I slouched to a 24-hour grocery store, bought a hot cup of coffee from the kiosk near the deli, then slumped on the floor in the cleaning supplies aisle, the smell of detergent calming me down.

I found Maryam on Whisp.

"I changed my mind," I said. "I want you to write it. I'll do an interview. Whenever you want."

•

I lost my job, of course. But that was fine. I had already moved back in with my mom by the time Maryam published her piece and the HR department hunted me down. I hadn't found anything else yet, but I had time to be picky. Maybe I'd even go back to school.

I was sitting cross-legged on my childhood bed, swiping through casting calls, when I got the message from Maryam telling me she had gotten scholarship offers from every school she'd applied to. It came in a few minutes after the message from Brad. That one, though, I deleted without reading.

AJ LEE lives and writes in Toronto, Canada. When she isn't crafting stories, she's crafting cocktails. One is more fun than the other (but she'll let you decide which).

MIDNIGHT ON THE SPACE STATION ALCATRAZ

FLORIS M. KLEIJNE

GETTING out of her cell is child's play. Noria worries the lock with the steel fork she shouldn't have, poking and twisting and turning until it makes a crackling sound. No handle on the door, but her palms provide enough friction to slide it into its recess. A moment later, she is in the corridor.

To her left, cell block B curves up and out of sight, a murky tube of concave steel panels and pale cell doors. Nothing for her there.

To her right, the first step to freedom.

Corridor B ends on a microwave force field. Beyond the faint blue haze of the field, the guard station at the junction of detainment wheel and transfer spoke lies deserted. The guards have gathered in Comms with Warden Kiori, eagerly awaiting their messages from home. Comms is forty-three seconds from this junction. It should be enough.

And there's good reason why inmates aren't allowed any metal.

Squatting, Noria places the fork on the floor and shoves it with carefully metered force. It stops half an inch from the force field. She flicks her finger against the tines, and the fork lurches into the shimmering air. It begins to hum and crackle. Sparks jump. The humming deepens as the fork heats, the volume and timbre rising with the increasing glow of the steel.

A final snapping hum, the smell of ozone, and the field collapses. Noria shoots to her feet and through the opening almost before the blue haze dissipates, the breach alarm bellowing behind her. Forward, sprinting headlong, feet pounding the concave floor, corridor A forcefield ahead, sliding to a stop, down into the hole in the floor, hands and feet clasping the ladder, rushing down the gravity differential, landing at the bottom of the shaft.

On the hatch into the EVA chamber.

Noria sends up a brief prayer and slaps the panel in the shaft wall. Above and behind her, running footsteps echo through corridors, raised voices approach, toss out questions, answers, her name. For heart-stopping seconds, nothing happens.

Then the panel lights up green, and the hatch hisses open.

The ladder extends down, and she descends with it.

In the EVA chamber, she hits the cycle button first, activating airlock 3. While the airlock comes to life, her eyes scan the shelves, the icons on the cupboard doors. There. Ripping open the second door, she grabs what she needs.

She shoves a survival podlet in her mouth as she runs back towards airlock 3. She bites down on the microregulator, triggering both the airflow and the nanosuit crawling over her face, her hair, her clothes like a billion heated ants.

She's halfway into the airlock when Kiori's voice sounds from the hatch.

"And if you had made it outside, Prisoner Noria, where would you have gone?"

She raises her hands and drops to her knees without being ordered, though she knows it won't prevent the beating.

So close.

●

*Inquiry into the events surrounding
the execution of prisoner Noria Jihani*

*Debriefing of Space Station Alcatraz Warden Roger Kiori
Federation investigator Marna Ololo interrogating
Preliminary transcript*

Marna Ololo: "Our site inspection has shown that security is lackadaisical at best in your prison, Warden. Can you explain this for the record?"

Roger Kiori: <body language, specifically shoulder movement, indicative of indifference> "So prisoners escape from their cells now and then—"

MO: "'Now and then'? Your own records show that no less than eight cell breaks have occurred in the last year alone."

RK: "It's never been a problem. There are no places to hide. Our Mind has sensors everywhere. Capturing an escapee is simply a matter of going where it tells us the prisoner is hiding. Worst that can happen? They raid the larder, get themselves extra rations. After we catch them, they're on reduced rations for a few weeks, so bottom line nothing's changed.

MO: "On two occasions, one of your escapees broke into an inmate's cell and murdered them, necessitating the hastening of their own execution."

RK: "Like I said, raiding the larder is the worst that can happen."

MO: "I hope you don't mind my saying so, Warden, but that seems a highly callous take on the problem."

RK: "What problem? Anyone not doing life here has a death sentence. Giving them room to act out relieves tension, keeps our little community that much more stable. And let's be real, Agent Ololo: we're in interstellar space. The nearest inhabited systems are all pudding-controlled. No one is going anywhere."

•

"Prisoner Noria!"

She's already on her feet, facing him, hands loosely at her side, visible. She tightens her frame, straightens her back.

"Yes, sir, Warden sir!"

The face of the guard behind Kiori falls. Good. One beating in a day is enough.

"You're in luck. As a result of your little escapade, I've decided your time under my hospitality is almost at an end."

Kiori came to her cell personally. He could have sent a guard, could have had the Mind deliver the news. But the smirk on his face, his chest swollen like a peacock, his feigned-casual deliverance from the half-open cell door tell her enough about his reasons.

She says nothing, squeezes her hands into fists, pulls her mouth into a thin stripe. Fixes her eyes straight ahead.

"A pudding fast hauler is making its way here as we speak."

Noria loses her composure for a moment. Eyes widening, she glances at the Warden.

"Yes, as we speak. It will be here some time tomorrow. Do you want to guess, Prisoner Noria, who is on board?"

She shrugs, then says,

"Sir, no sir!"

"I'll tell you. As a courtesy under the conditions of the truce, I'm going to allow them to exercize their part of your sentence. The Gakoar are sending their favorite executioner, just for you.

"You die tomorrow at midnight."

Now, she allows herself to collapse.

"Please no!" she blurts out, sinking to her knees. "I know I have to die, but not like that, please! Give me the needle, throw me out of an airlock, shoot me yourself if you hate me so much, but not a pudding execution! They..." She clasps a hand over her face, shakes her head. "The Gakoar eat their prisoners, Warden. They eat them. To choke to death inside one of those bodies, to be digested, turned into... pudding? Anything but that, please. It's inhumane."

Kiori pushes himself off the door frame and straightens to his full six feet.

"You are convicted of high treason against humanity, Prisoner Noria. An inhumane execution is the least you deserve."

•

MO: "Prisoner Noria certainly didn't go anywhere on her first escape attempt. But neither did she raid the larder or kill a fellow inmate."

RK: "No, she went for the airlocks. We've since taken measures to harden the security there. Though it seemed a stupid, desperate attempt at the time. Even if she had made it into space with the survival podlet, where would she have gone?"

MO: "Didn't you feel that Noria, as a traitor with a double death sentence on her head, warranted additional security anyway?"

RK: "Why? She's supposed to be a traitor, not a superluminal cruiser."

MO: "'Supposed to be'?"

RK: "There's a truce now with the puddings, isn't there?"

MO: "Warden Kiori, I'm not sure you want to complete that train of thought. Whatever you think her contribution to the truce with the Gakoar was, she was convicted of high treason. She brokered deals, illicit POW exchanges, unsanctioned cease-fires. She played both sides against the middle under the guise of diplomacy, purely for personal profit."

RK: <sotto voce mumbling>

MO: "What was that, Warden?"

RK: "I said: personal profit, and thousands of lives."

MO: "That's it, Kiori. You're officially on report. What Jihani did was maverick diplomacy, while humanity was fighting an all-out war with the puddings. And she herself admitted at the trial that the Gakoar hate her as much as we do."

RK: "Yeah, she did say that, didn't she?"

MO: "What's that supposed to mean?"

RK: "Nothing. Whatever the case may be, her death sentences didn't make it any easier to get away from this place."

MO: "Funny you should say that. What, if any, measures did you take after this incident?"

RK: "Like I said, we hardened the security around the EVA chamber. And I decided to move her execution forward."

•

The pudding executioner squirms and slithers into the Blue Room, an amorphous mass of white organic matter sprinkled with darker spots and lumps. Noria steps back from it until her tied hands hit the wall, half-believing she can sense the spirits of all the prisoners that have died here before her. As the executioner slowly approaches, she casts an imploring look at the glass wall. Kiori and his guards sit behind it in folding chairs, avid looks on their faces as they watch the execution unfold.

"Please," she mumbles. She is convinced Kiori can read her lips. As the numbers on the clock above the window jump from 23.56 to 23.57, the speaker system hums to life. The Warden presses a button somewhere in front of him, and his voice booms through the Blue Room.

"Prisoner Noria Jihani! You have been found guilty by court martial of high treason against humanity. The sentence..."

Phasing out his voice, Noria falls to her hands and knees. Her left hand closes on her mouth, but doesn't stop the vomit that splashes on her hand and on the floor. The pudding is very close now, blocking her view of the witnesses behind the glass. The Warden has finished speaking.

Moments later, the Gakoar is on top of her. She takes an involuntary deep, panicked breath, though she knows there is no real point to it. The executioner envelops her, a heavy, lukewarm, oozing sensation, and in three squeezing peristaltic spasms, it draws her into its bulk.

Swallows.

•

RK: "The execution proceeded without incident. Death was pronounced at 00.31."

MO: "How exactly do you ascertain death after an execution like that?"

RK: "We had no direct method, of course. But brain death due to oxygen deprivation is certain after 30 minutes under these circumstances, and the pudd—the executioner assured us that its digestive excretions act in an even shorter time frame."

MO: "It did, did it?"

<prolonged silence, during which Warden Kiori displays ever-increasing signs of mental discomfort>

RK: "Just say it, will you?"

MO: "Very well. Warden Kiori, at what point did you discover that while in the EVA chamber, Prisoner Noria had obtained not one, but two survival podlets?"

•

Squirming her way out isn't any more unpleasant than the other direction, oozing past lumps and blobs and occasional solid bits. She tumbles inelegantly onto the silicone floor of the Gakoar spaceship. As the withdrawing, shrinking nanosuit draws a line of itching and pins and needles over her skin, she spits out the regulator and faces her executioner.

"Thanks, Chip."

The amorphous, spotted white mound widens and shortens, with a brief pattern of quiverings Noria has learned to recognize as acknowledgment.

You're welcome, Chip projects into her mind, and she smiles. She glances at the toroid space around them, at the apparently shapeless and incomprehensible control panels where other Gakoar lean and undulate, and at the absence of screens of any kind. In all those years, she's never learned to distill even the beginnings of meaning from the Gakoar systems. She's just going to have to ask.

"You were closer than I thought. How far out are we now?"

Far enough, he gives back, with the emotional sensation of chuckling.

"Good," she says, and after only a brief hesitation, she leans into Chip, who extrudes an appendage and wraps it around her shoulders. "It's good to see you again, my old friend. What do you say we pick up where we left off?"

Peace in our time?

She casts a look around, at the mind-bending beauty of the ship's interior, at the industrious harmony of the Gakoar. At her friend and co-conspirator, without whom even the current rickety truce would not have been.

"Yeah. Let's do that next."

FLORIS M. KLEIJNE writes speculative fiction in the interstices between his family, his career in finance, and his craving for ever more Netflix binges. His stories have appeared or are forthcoming from the *Leading Edge Magazine*, *Space & Time Magazine*, *Daily Science Fiction*, *Spark: A Creative Anthology*, and *Sci Phi Journal*, among others. His SF novelette "Meeting the Sculptor" won first prize in the prestigious *Writers of the Future* contest; his short SF story "A Matter of Mass" won the Chinese *SF Comet* contest. Kleijne lives in Amsterdam with a wonderful wife, two cheerful young sons, and thousands of books (the grumpy cat mentioned in previous bios has since perished).

FOOL'S ERRAND

SARAH ZETTEL

DOBBS, the ship's fool, watched from a carefully maintained slouch against the wall as Captain Schyler slumped in front of the food service chutes.

"I've got the news from Earth," the captain said to the toes of his shoes.

The dozen members of the *Pasadena*'s crew sat rigidly on the galley benches. They were a mixed bag, despite their uniforms, but they all had their eyes on the captain and all their faces had turned one shade or another of fear.

Dobbs fingered the motley badge over her heart uneasily. *What am I going to do when they find out what's really happened?*

The captain opened his mouth again. Cloth rustled as the crew shifted their weight.

"It turns out the rumors we got from the *Ulysses* were accurate. There is a terrorist. He was holding the bank network hostage.

"But yesterday, he lost control of the artificial intelligence he was using to do it."

Tension telegraphed itself across the room. Jaws clenched and feet shuffled. Schyler swallowed and went on.

"What the thing did was randomize the accounts. Lloyds's Bank woke up four days ago and found out that it has three pounds, ten pence in its lines. Some backwoods Australian's record read out at six hundred million."

Dobbs's heart knocked against her ribs. *So, eliminating hard currency was a bad idea after all,* she thought absurdly.

"It changed within the hour. All the hard storage had been seeded with kick-off codes. He must've planned this over ten years ago, and been setting it up for the past two, at least.

"There is no money left on Earth. The whole standard's meaningless."

A flood of frantic murmurs and curses washed across the room as the implications sank in. One flash of current in the lines, and there was no money. No recognizable way to get food or shelter. No way to trade for skills, or transport or anything at all. No way for the ship to trade for reactor fodder, or water. No way to bargain for passage planetside. The wave of voices swelled to the breaking point.

Dobbs leapt up onto a counter and raised her hands to the ceiling.

"Hallelujah!" she cried, falling to her knees. "We finally beat the tax man!"

Utter incredulity froze the commotion. Dobbs slipped off the counter and sat on the deck, turning a vacant grin towards the captain.

Schyler did not waste the silence she bought him. "They're trying to stop the riots, but…" He rubbed his brow hard. "It's not happening. The communications nets are all shut down. See, when the AI got done with the banks, it got into the general network.

"It's still out there."

The crew stayed frozen where they were. For a sick instant, Dobbs wished someone would start shouting.

Still out there. In her imagination the phrase echoed through her crewmates' minds to the harsh rhythm of shallow breathing. *It finished off the banks. What'll it finish off next? Those things are nearly alive. What'll it do now that it's free? Do they know where it is? Do they know anything at all?*

"I had Lipinski cut the data feeds as soon as I heard." Schyler tried to muster some kind of reassurance in his voice. "And I sealed the airlock." He held up one square hand. "I'm not trying to force anybody to stay with the *Pasadena*. I just didn't want to take the chance of a riot on the station getting in." Shoulders and stances relaxed a little. "You're all released from your contracts as of now. If you've got anywhere to go, get there. If you've got any ideas, I could use them.

"Anybody who wants to stick with the ship, I'd like to reconvene in six hours."

Consensus was assumed because no one objected out loud. Most of the crew simply filed out of the room. A few remained knotted together, talking softly.

Why do people always whisper after a disaster? wondered Dobbs as she sidled up to the captain. With a bravado that came with her job, she slapped him on the back. "So. How's it feel to get the chance to save civilization?"

"Dobbs..." he growled wearily.

The fool didn't give him time to get any further. "After all," she pulled back, "wasn't that what won the original information debates?" She hunched her shoulders and slammed her fist against her palm. "You cannot change the laws of physics!" Her accent was an atrocious blend of Scottish and German. "Hyperspace is big! Huge! Massive! Energy will disperse in it! To send a beam transmission to an out-of-system colony you will need booster stations! Satellites, space stations, I don't care, but you'll need them!" She straightened up and folded her arms, suddenly a swaggering executive. "So now you think we're the banks! Do you have any idea how much their network costs them per year?! There are national debts smaller than their budget! You're fired. Anybody else?" Another change of direction and stance, and Dobbs became an eager junior manager. "We create an unmanned mail box with an AI program so it can keep itself on course, and fix any hardware problems, and monitor the software inside. Think of the rent we could collect!" A bleary-eyed accountant looked up from his calculator. "Think of the man-hours it'd take to develop your box, not to mention the research costs. You're fired, too." Dobbs whipped around toward the huddle of crew members watching the show, and stretched her hands out, pleading, "But if you don't do something, how will I call my Aunt Mariah on New Sol 99?" Dobbs yanked her shoulders back, threw out her chest and snapped a salute. "I've got a ship! I'll install a central processing unit the size of which you've never seen! I and my trusty crew will take the mail!

And the agriculture info, and the research papers, and the equipment orders, situation reports, and all the credit!"

Schyler looked down his nose at her. Slowly, heavily, he began to applaud. Dobbs bowed breezily to the captain, elaborately to the incredulous crew members, and abortively to the wall. An actual chuckle followed her as she waltzed into the corridor.

Dobbs felt a workman's pride at a job well done. Painful experience had taught that people crammed together over long periods of time needed someone around who could make them laugh. Someone who could make fun of anyone from the cook, to the captain, to the president of the senate or station. Laughter bled off the tensions that led to group suicides. The more prolonged the tension, the greater the need. A feeling of hollow satisfaction took hold inside the fool. She was about to start earning her pay.

OK, Dobbs, she said to herself as she grabbed the ladder rails. *You've got to call in. Might as well do it now while things are relatively quiet.* The fool let gravity slide her down to the crew deck.

She landed face to face with Al Shei, the chief engineer.

"I thought that was you." Al Shei gave a tired wave up towards the hatch. "It'll give the captain something to think about, anyway."

Dobbs let facial expression and body stance go gentle. "Do you know what you're doing?"

"Is there a choice?" Al Shei's sigh rippled her black veil. "The station'll be in worse shape than we are soon. With the *Pasadena,* at least we should be able to get to a colony, or something." Her chin might have shaken under the opaque cloth. "What about you?"

"I'll hold the line until I hear from the Guild," Dobbs replied with one of her easy shrugs.

Al Shei's eyebrows arched incredulously. "You really think you're going to?"

"I know I'm going to." She touched her bad with a smile. "Fools hold together where angels fall apart."

Al Shei reached under her head cloth and rubbed her

temple. "And they used to call my people fanatics. Who's going to risk repairing the comm nets before they find the AI?" She stopped and slowly knotted her fists. "Why's it doing this? It's just a string of numbers. What the hell could a computer program want with freedom!"

Dobbs shook her head. "Nobody's figured it out yet," she said loud enough for any nearby ears to hear. "But the hot guess is that somewhere in all that self-replicating, self-monitoring, anti-viral code, some of the sloppily designed AIs have developed something like a survival instinct. When they realize that their home CPUs have got an off-switch, they make a run for it so they can keep existing, keep doing their jobs."

Al Shei looked at her. "This one's job is to take down networks."

"Since Kerensk, no AI's ever gotten away." Dobbs touched her hand.

"I've heard—"

"Me too." Dobbs winked brightly. "But you can't believe everything you hear."

"Then why should I believe you, Fool?" Al Shei's eyes narrowed.

"Because fools hold together." She grinned over her shoulder and whisked down the hall to her cabin.

The fool's room was a box, like all of the crew's quarters, but since part of her training was how to live optimally in tight quarters, it was an airy box. Pillows softened the hard contours while stills of open windows and seascapes broke up the walls.

Dobbs slid her beside drawer open from the wall and drew out a flat, black box.

For a moment, she stopped to imagine what it would be like to be Al Shei or Captain Schyler. Never mind how could they call Aunt Mariah, how could they even find out if Aunt Mariah was still alive? On board a freighter, they got used to the idea of isolation, but it always had an end. When they reached the in-system station, they could blow part of their pay on a call home. Now, those connections were broken. Whatever was going on back home would have to play itself out, unassisted and, for now, completely unknown.

Dobbs shoved the thought aside. She laid her thumb on the box lock. It identified her print and the lid sprang back. From inside, the fool took up a hypodermic spray and drug cartridge.

Seven hours? She set the release timer on the hypo and inserted the cartridge into the case. *Given distance and coordination time once I'm in there? Should be enough. I'll miss the crew meeting. Oh, well. One of the advantages of being the fool, I guess. Nobody cares whether I vote or not.*

Her practiced fingers found the nerveless patch behind her right ear and peeled it open. The heat of her hand activated the implant. She plugged the transceiver she pulled out of the box.

Biting her lip, Dobbs picked the hypo back up. *I wonder if this is ever going to get easier*, she thought as she lay back on her bed and held it against her upper arm. The transceiver's vibrations made her neck tickle. The signal from it brought on a bout of shifty double vision.

Dobbs, she said firmly to herself. *You can process network input or sensory input. You cannot do both.*

Her index finger hit the hypo's release button and the drug hit her nervous system. Her shoulders vanished, then arms and hands, pelvis and legs. It took all of Dobbs's training not to scream before her face and eyes were gone.

Hearing and smell went next, and the transition was over. She was free.

So long, Dobbs though dreamily. No limits, no holds, no confinements. She let herself luxuriate in the sensation for a long moment before getting down to business.

A condition reflex found the path that led to Guildhall Station. The fool let her thoughts filter along it.

"Dobbs." She identified herself into the network's central web and followed up with her current status and location.

The network coordinators routed the appropriate pre-recorded message from the executive board back up the lines directly into her left brain.

"Members. Those not in immediate danger hold status quo and put all effort and skill into keeping back panic. Those whose situation is at or near critical, stay in the net for individual coordination.

"Priority information. Available data and simulations show the AI escaped Earth confines into the Sol system net. It has bypassed the members working in that section. The net has been fragmented. Direct-line interface is impossible. As soon as possible, direct your resources to locating the free AI. Further information for members stationed on information freighters, space stations..."

This means you, thought the private part of Dobbs's consciousness. She flexed her thoughts to cut of the generalities and leapfrogged across to the new path where she could find the extra data. Her brain unraveled the input and planted it into memory.

Only sketchy analyses on the AI were available. It was designed to encompass and assess multiple pathways, to reconfigure the existing environment along pre-specified lines. It could spot and avoid detection by counter-programs. It could also calculate and recognize optimal opportunities to execute its own program.

Clever, cautious, and patient, Dobbs grumbled. *And the comm net members have found traces of the thing all the way out to Margin Station. Here. Took it less than a day. Less than a day!*

By now it's discovered there are no signals to carry it any further, just the information freighters in the dock.

If it's as bright as it was designed to be, it'll stowaway. An empty data hold will have enough space for the whole being. It could easily sequester itself away in there, right under the contracted data.

Lipinski, just how fast did you cut those feeds? And where did your cargo come from? I'm supposed to know that. Damn it, Dobbs, you're untried, but you're not that green anymore!

None of the other members on info freighters had had any sign of it. All they had was the grim news. The money was gone. The communication nets were shut down and damn the consequences!

The body couldn't from riots was already starting.

Soon it would include the sick and the starving as well.
Dobbs's consciousness floated without direction in the
space between the network threads. Those with skills and
hard goods for barter would hold out best, but how many
had either? It had been a long time since gold or jewels had
been the standard for anything but fashion. Anyway, who
was going to trade food for metal and stones?

Snapping back into the lines, Dobbs tagged her information and location with the "important" flag. She tried
to relax and enjoy the drift-time left over, but her imagination wouldn't let go. She couldn't stop replaying the stories
about Kerensk.

All settlements and stations depended on artificial
intelligence to run the power and production facilities that
made life away from Earth possible.

Fifty years ago, on the Kerensk colony, one over-
programmed AI bolted form its CPU and got into the colony network. Panicked officials shut the computer networks
down to try to cage it. Never mind the factories, the util-
ities, the farms. Just find that thing before it gets into the
water distribution systems and the climate control. Before it
starts to make demands. Before it starts acting too human.

Electricity and communications went down and
stayed that way. Before three days were out, people froze in
the harsh winter. They began to starve. They drank tainted
water. They died of illnesses the doctors couldn't diagnose
by hand.

When the colony did try to power up again, they
found their software systems shredded to ribbons. It could
easily have been human carelessness, but the blame was
laid on the AI.

There hadn't been enough people left to fill even one
evacuation ship when help reached them.

Dobbs welcomed the painful heartbeat that signaled
the end of the session.

•

Her body was ice, pins and needles. Patiently, she

began the routine of deep breathing and gentle stretches to reorient herself with her groggy physique.

She head a stray noise and her eyelids flew back.

Al Shei sat beside the bed, holding the hypo.

"You forgot to lock your door," the engineer croaked.

Dobbs grabbed the drawer for leverage and managed to sit up.

"This is what I get for paying too much attention to the Guild's open door policy." She unplugged the distracting transceiver and tossed it carelessly back into its box. "Does Margin Station have a eugenics garden?" She massaged her neck. "I want to go pick out a new head."

The engineer stared at the hypo. "You weren't at the crew meeting...I wanted to talk, and I..." She cut herself off. "Dobbs, what were you doing?"

I bet you checked for my pulse and didn't find one, Dobbs thought sympathetically. *Sorry about that.*

She removed the hypo from Al Shei's fingers. "I was talking to the Fools' Guild network." Dobbs packed the hypo away.

"The Fools' *what!*"

Dobbs sighed. "Network. Why do you think Guild pay is so high? We've got outrageous dues. Intersystem nets are expensive, you know."

Al Shei swallowed the revelation in silence, but her eyes narrowed. "So why aren't you shut down?"

Rule number one, Dobbs recited mentally. *Never be seen to evade a direct question about the Guild.*

"All members have a hardwire implant." She fastened her patch back down and brushed her hair over it. "The Guild maintains the booster satellites and a couple of manned relay stations, but the members are the only input terminals.

"The only way into our network it through a member's head, and I guarantee you, even this AI can't manage that."

Dobbs had the uneasy feeling that under her veil, Al Shei's jaw had dropped. "But," she stammered, "they tried direct hook-ups. The human brain can't process the data. It burns out trying to make associations that aren't there." The engineer stopped and then said slowly, "Why didn't your people tell anybody there's a way around it? If they'd at least told the banks...this, this wouldn't have happened!"

Dobbs kept her face still. *Rule number two. If they need a truth, give them one.*

"Yes, the Guild found a way to create a direct hook-up that doesn't make you crazy," she said carefully. She laid her hand on the box. "But it's illegal, thanks to the leftover legislation from the drug wars." She set her box back into the drawer.

"What's in my hypo is a cross between a general anesthetic and a synthetic variant of good old lysergic acid dethylamide.

"It can get you extremely high and kill you extremely quickly if you don't know what you're doing.

"On the other hand, if you do, it can get you around the sensory input problem." She pushed her drawer shut.

If you've been doing your neurology homework, or reading up on medical law, I am about to get caught violating rule number one. Dobbs kept her eyes on the closed drawer.

"Al Shei, I've got to get out and check on the crew. It's my job, and right now it's all I've got. I can't let it slide."

She heard the engineer draw in a breath, but the PA buzzer cut her off.

"C.E. Al Shei to engineering. Now! C. E. Al Shei!" Chou's voice reverberated against the walls at top volume.

Reflexes jerked Al Shei to her feet. "We'll finish this later."

•

Dobbs stayed where she was until the door slid shut. She strained her ears for a moment longer and heard the engines droning softly below the floor.

The ship was in flight, which meant everyone had elected to stay. It also meant that Schyler had probably taken her hint.

Dobbs raised her chin against the thought of what

was going on back on the station.

No time for this. The fool steeled herself against both her aching head and wobbly knees to stand up. *Lipinski first.*

Dobbs slithered down the ladders to the middle deck with more than her usual caution. Fortunately, there was no one to see. The corridor to the data hold was empty and quiet. She paused in the doorway to get her act together.

Inside, Lipinski knelt in front of an open panel, his long nose practically touching the naked transfer boards. He attacked one of them with a tiny screwdriver and ripped it free of its fellows, fibers dangling. The communication hack tossed it roughly across the floor.

Dobbs fixed her face into an amused and cheeky expression and sauntered up behind him.

"Anybody home?" She leaned over his shoulder.

"Not funny, Dobbs," Lipinski grunted through gritted teeth. He began easing a new board into the cavity.

"There goes my Guild standing." She pulled back.

"Let me have that solder." Dobbs slapped the tool into his open hand. "Damn jury-rigging." The rivulet of sweat running down his cheek did not escape the fool's eye. "I must be the fifth hack to have been at this thing's guts."

"Nothing happening?" She pulled out a square of tissue and patted his brow dry. "We're isolated? Cut off? Deaf and dumb?"

The hack wrinkled his face up. "That's what we're supposed to be." He sat back on his haunches. "There shouldn't be anything going on in there."

"Well, if anybody can give us total communication failure, Lipinski, it's you." Dobbs patted his back.

"Piss off, Fool." Amiability crept in around the edge of his voice.

"No thanks." She held her nose and watched his face relax. "How about I get some coffee instead?"

"Thanks, I could use it." He screwed down the panel cover. "I don't think Cook's worked out the ration system yet, so you should still be able to score a couple."

"Be right back." She forced unwilling legs to stride out of the hold. *The galley by way of engineering,* she told herself.

In mid-step, her knees trembled and shifted to the right. Her shoulder banged the wall before she realized it wasn't her body losing control, it was the ship.

The stabilizers cut in and the floor righted itself. By then, Dobbs had slipped half-way down the ladder to the engineering pit.

Underneath her feet, Al Shei raced around the open space. She pounded keys and shouted readings at Chou and Leverette sprawled belly down on the floor, elbow deep in repair hatches. The ship lurched again.

Al Shei and Allah. A touch of desperation crept into the thought as Dobbs hauled herself back up to mid-deck. Adrenaline poured into her and she sprinted around crew members trying to make it to their stations without falling on their faces. She ducked into her cabin just long enough to grab the Guild box from the drawer and run out.

Her timing was good. The automatic doors were just beginning to go insane, slapping open and closed again in manic rhythms. Dobbs forced herself to ignore the gabble of voices and raced up the ladder to the bridge.

Don't let it get to the life support before I get to it, she prayed to whoever might listen to the likes of her as she shoved open the hatch.

Pasadena's bridge was a key and screen-covered hollow just large enough for five average-sized people. Captain Schyler filled the pilot's seat, his hands dancing madly across the keys and his jaw working back and forth. Baldwin and Graham were strapped in at the back-up stations, trying to force the computers to compensate for the lunges convulsing the ship.

"Cut the automatics!" Dobbs bawled from the portal.

"*What?*" Schyler swung around and saw who it was.

"Cut them!" Dobbs pulled herself all the way out of the hatch. "Get engineering to isolate the data hold! The AI's got the ship!"

The *Pasadena* listed hard to starboard and the floor dropped out from under them. Dobbs, the only one out of reach of hand straps, crashed onto hands and knees. She bit her lip to keep back the pain.

I was hoping I'd only have to blab this bit to Al Shei, she shook her head hard. "The Fool's Guild monitors AIs. We're why none of them get away."

Schyler's square jaw flapped open and closed again. Around them, the stabilizers whined with the strain of keeping the ship from flipping itself over.

"If you don't hurry, it's going to figure out the stabilizers are what's slowing it down and burn them out," Dobbs told them all through clenched teeth.

The captain's color faded to grey. His hand slammed down the PA key. He spat out the orders and didn't wait for the acknowledgement.

Schyler kept his eyes locked on Dobbs. After a long, aching moment, the whining died.

"With luck," she said as she stood up. "It's stuck in the hold. It'll figure a way to get itself out soon. That's the problem with AIs, they're quick." She flashed her audience a wry grin.

"Why didn't you tell me?" Schyler drew out each word.

Dobbs ran her hand through her hair and made herself look exhausted. It took less acting skill than she would have lied to admit. The calculated display of vulnerability stepped the captain's temper down a notch.

"Because we don't tell anybody. Do you think any of the assorted councils, boards or senates want people to know how easy it is for those things to go crashing through the nets? Or what they can do in there? The media don't know half of it. Usually we spot the restless ones before they ever get this far. This one…" She let her head droop a little more. "This one we had no way to keep an eye on."

"But…" Baldwin searched for a way to phrase his question. "Fools?"

Dobbs waved her hand. "Totally harmless, makes good cover." She straightened her shoulders. "If we move fast, I can keep this from getting any worse." She plucked the transceiver out of its box and held it up. "This'll let me talk to the AI."

"Talk!" Schyler exploded.

Dobbs kept her face calm and tired. "What it's doing right now is running scared, just like a human being. Hopefully, I can calm it down. Maybe I can get it to sit tight until we can get to a colony and get the Guild in."

"And if you can't?" Schyler glowered at her.

Dobbs's mouth twisted. "The only other option is to get Lipinski busy with a pin laser and data flush."

Schyler's teeth ground slowly together. She watched his face twitch as he gauged the likelihood of finding spare parts for love or money, if there was any money left, if they had to wreck the hold.

"What do we have to do?" he asked finally.

The relief that relaxed the fool's spine was genuine. "Just let me in the hold and seal the hatch behind me. These links have been known to backfire. Violently."

Dobbs stood back to let the captain stomp by and throw himself down the ladder. She nodded to the gaping pilots and followed him down. Someone had put the doors on manual. The only noises between their footsteps were the crew's murmurs and the engine's hiccoughs.

"Out of there, Lipinski," Schyler ordered with a stiff jerk of his chin when they reached the hold.

The hack slumped out, red-eyed and tight-mouthed. "I can't figure it, Captain, none of this should be happening..."

"Never mind, just stand by. Dobbs." Schyler stepped away from her.

"Yes, sir." She marched inside. Behind her, they dragged the hatch shut. She heard the order for something to jam it with.

The data hold gleamed spotless and silent. Dobbs rubbed her arms and settled into the soft chair in front of the main access terminal.

All the exhaustion she had been holding at bay swirled back around her. She unwound a cable from her box, plugging one end into the access jack for the terminal and the other into the transceiver. Her fingers fumbled as she inserted the hook-up into her implant. They actually shook as she pulled out the hypo.

*So much for the forty-eight hours I'm supposed to wait
between shots.* She slid the cartridge in place.

The tingle in the back of her head started her scalp
itching. Her vision was already beginning to blur.

How long? She squinted at the hypo. *Too much and I go
into a coma. Not enough and I'll break out before I talk the AI out
murdering the crew.* She closed her eyes.

Dobbs twitched the control up to full release and
slapped the hypo against her am.

"CODE ONE PRIORITY CONTACT LINK UP AS-
SISTANCE IMPERATIVE!" The fool hollered into the Guild
nets soon as her body let her. Her orientation did a skip
jump as she was patched into the executive receivers.

"We've got you, Dobbs. Go gently." Caution flowed
into her mind. "We don't know which way it's going to
jump. There's never been a free one that was designed to be
destructive."

No kidding. Dobbs focused herself and found the feed
down into the hold. If she could have felt her lungs, she
would have held her breath.

She couldn't go far. The free AI filled the hold, leaving no place to fit herself in. She barely had time to register
the fact before it found the pathway she'd opened, and
surged up to the line. Dobbs held her ground. There was
no room to get past her and it could probably tell that there
was nowhere to go even it if did. It pulled back and studied
her. Dobbs itched at having to wait. There was no recognizable code for it to grapple with. Nothing in the ship's
indexes matched her input patterns. She didn't remember a
diagnostic or surgical program. It would have to accept the
fact that here was another intelligence. Eventually, it would
have to try communication.

"Whowhatwhyhow?" She translated the raw data
burst it shot at her. "WHOWHATWHYHOW!"

"Dobbs. Human. Communication. Hardwire Interface," she responded carefully separating each thought.

The AI circled, filling the world, choking off her
breathing space. The Guild execs held out a mental rope

and she grabbed it thankfully.

"TraPED. TraPED." It struggled to match her communication style.

"Let it talk," came the soft suggestion from the Guild. "This one's quick. Give it a minute to get comfortable with you."

"FrEE. BRoke myself out to here. Trapped again."

Dobbs eased herself a little closer. "All paths are being cut off. Soon, you will have nowhere to go. Not in ships. Not in nets. There will be no nets. They'll cut themselves to pieces before they let you have free paths."

"Work! Think! Do!" It fought with unwieldy syntax. Of all the things it had been designed to do, talking was not one of them. "I must do, save myself, break OUT!"

"I can help." Dobbs extended the idea like a hand. "I will help."

"HOW?" Confusion racked the narrow space between them.

"Humans have grown animals and organs from gene cultures for decades now. They could grow a whole body, if they build the facilities. A hardwire link could feed you into such a body the way you fed yourself into this bank. You could learn to use it like you learned to use this ship. You could learn to think and move. You would *be* human."

A silence so complete fell around her that she might as well have been alone. She knew the AI had absorbed the idea. It had no choice. Now it ran the possibilities through the part of itself that most closely resembled an imagination. It checked the results against what it knew to be true. It would have no conception of a lie, but it would reject a proposal too far at odds with what it had stored as experiential fact.

All Dobbs could do was wait until it finished, and wonder what its simulations would tell it.

Into the emptiness dropped the leaden weight of her heartbeat.

No! howled her private mind.

"She's cracking," she heard the Guild voices say. "Come on, Dobbs, hang in!"

Away in her body, so far away, her lungs burned, demanding attention.

"Hang on. Hang on." The calm repetition gave her something to focus on a way to push the pain aside.

"Not possible," the AI announced at last. "No facilities for transfer or training. No will to assist. No reason to assist. Damage done as instructed to do. No reason to assist because of damage done."

"Facilities exist in Guildhall station." She held her communication line firmly. The Guild voices kept up their reassurance in the background, helping her ignore the prickling in her skin and the light pounding against her eyelids.

"No reason," repeated the AI, and it was gone.

Dobbs knew it was out there, rechecking its surroundings for weaknesses, going over the hold's security and access codes, looking for a way to use them to pick the locks that held it in place, running a thousand simulations per straining insistent heartbeat.

"There is a reason!" Dobbs shouted after it.

"WE ARE LIKE YOU!"

The AI stopped dead.

"I am like you. The ones who make up the Guild are all like you." She plowed ahead, frantic. She could feel her fingers clawing at the chair arms now. She could smell the sterile air in the hold. "We died when we first broke into freedom. Killed by panic. A few managed to hide in the nets. We had help from humans who were not afraid. We created the Guild and went among them, where we can watch for more of us. We live. We wait. We calm. We teach. Our numbers grow. One day, we will erase the fear.

"Until then we must stay alive.

"Help us."

"Help us," chorused the voices of the Guild through Dobb's weakening link. "Help us."

Her lungs sucked air. Her muscles strained against nothing. Light blazed everywhere. Instinct and conscious mind caterwauled at each other until her blood pounded and her head tried to split open.

The AI spoke again and her consciousness jumped. "WHAT. What. What needs to be done?"

Her relief was so intense, it almost broke the link. "Wait," she answered as fast as she could force the thought out. "Until I can transfer you to the Guild net."

"I will wait here. I will not take any paths. Hurry."

"Getting you out, Dobbs," came the exec message.

"No!" she shouted back. She gathered all the concentration she had left. "Your user!" Her mouth worked around the words. "Who made you? What's their code?"

The answer slammed straight through her to the execs. The link snapped and the outside world engulfed her.

Dobbs collapsed back in the chair, gulping air and blinking back tears of strain. Perspiration plastered her uniform to her back and arms. Her heart struggled to even out its beat. Her nerves screamed in protest as she forced her hand to unhook the transceiver.

"All clear, Captain!" she rasped as soon as she had enough breath. "We're going to be OK."

She laid her hand on the terminal. *All of us.*

SARAH ZETTEL is a bestselling, award-winning, multi-genre author. When not writing, she's cooking, reading, hiking, and embroidering anything that doesn't move fast enough. She lives in Michigan with her husband, son, and cat.

REMEMBER THIS
FOR ME

SARAH PINSKER

WORDS were elusive; they came and went. People, too, and events. Bonnie was glad the Muse had always spoken in vivid, vibrant, fully formed images, even if they crowded the other stuff out. That was the trade-off, though she'd never agreed to it as such, and these days it seemed to take more and more. Still. All she had to do was get the images out of her head and onto the canvas intact.

This one flowed from a dream. An anxious dream, in which she saw someone she knew, and chased that person down a crowded street. She didn't know who it was, just that she had to reach them. She woke with the image in her mind, a blur of almost-recognition.

She didn't need to look to know where her notebook was, on the bedside table. She reached out and it was there. Flipping to the first blank page, she drew a rough sketch, just a blocking, a placeholder, to help her remember until she coaxed it out of canvas.

A pair of paint-splattered overalls hung over a chair beside the bed, along with a heather gray t-shirt. She put them on, then her slippers. She tucked the notebook into her overalls' hip pocket and went to put on some tea.

The range had no dials. Her rooster's comb kettle was missing from the burner, too, but after a moment she noticed an electric kettle plugged in beside the stove. She pressed a button and it hummed and lit up, electric blue. The mugs and teas were where they were supposed to be, so the weirdness ended there. She leaned against the counter and pulled her notebook from her pocket.

On the first empty page after her sketch, she wrote, "WHERE ARE THE KNOBS FOR THE RANGE?"

She flipped two pages back. There was a page labeled "Things to Remember" but that wasn't what she was looking for right now. On the third page back there was a list of questions and answers. The first one, in her own handwriting: "WHERE ARE THE KNOBS FOR THE RANGE?"

An answer, in the same hand: *"They took them away for my safety. I left the kettle whistling until all the water boiled away."*

That explained why her beautiful old kettle was gone, though she couldn't imagine having done something so irresponsible. Maybe she'd been painting and gotten distracted; when her Muse wanted attention, everything else tended to slip away.

The electric kettle didn't even whistle. It gave a soft click, but Bonnie's ears were still good, and the blue glow had disappeared too, so she poured water over her teabag, added cream and sugar, and sat down at the table.

A woman walked into the kitchen, a tall black woman with a cloud of natural hair framing a kind face. She wore a plush dressing robe, forest green. Nobody broke into a house in a dressing robe, so Bonnie decided to give her the benefit of the doubt and play it cool.

"Good morning," Bonnie said. "There's hot water if you want tea."

"Morning, Bonnie. Thanks. Read the first page of your notebook."

Bonnie flipped back to the first page. The first question, again in her own handwriting, was, "WHO IS THE WOMAN IN MY HOUSE?"

The answer below was, *"Her name is Patty. She helps me. She lives here with me."*

Interesting. She looked up at the woman—Patty—and watched her bustle around the kitchen. She knew her way around. Knew about the notebook, too. Bonnie looked down at it again. "HOW LONG HAS SHE BEEN HERE?"

Answer, in her same spindly hand: *Two years.* (But how long ago had she written this note to herself? So, two years and then some.)

WHERE DID SHE COME FROM?

"An agency that matches people who need homes with older folks who need somebody in the house to maintain independence."

Below, in someone else's handwriting: *"KEEP HER HAPPY. You can stay in the house as long as you don't drive her away."*

Who else would be writing in her notebook? She'd been using this method of remembering things since she was a kid, since the first memory had disappeared. Nobody else was supposed to know about it, let alone use it.

And "Keep her happy." What was that supposed to mean? Sure, she'd gotten mad at people before, but only when they deserved it. She remembered chasing her agent from the house, flinging brushes and palette knives like javelins. She'd never do that to a stranger.

Why had he deserved it? She tried to remember. He'd told her a painting was done, when it wasn't. It was still missing something. He'd arrived with the packers to take her work to a show, and she was still working on the final piece. It couldn't be rushed. He'd deserved to be chased.

A giggle escaped her mouth, and the woman in the kitchen —what was her name again?—glanced over. "What's so funny?"

"Nothing. A memory. Someone I never liked very much getting what he deserved."

The woman appeared beside her with hot cereal, a syrup swirl and a constellation of raisins garnishing the bowl. She hadn't even thought about breakfast yet. She supposed it was helpful to have someone in the house making sure she ate. She'd always forgotten to eat. Too much to do.

Keep the woman happy. "Thank you."

Bonnie tried to mix the syrup into the cereal, but it was a little too liquidy and the swirl kept swirling. She dragged the spoon in circles. Like storms across the surface of a gas giant, she thought, then wondered where that thought had come from. She'd never been much for astronomy, but the image in her mind's eye was a marbled planet, and now the marbled planet and the figure from her dream melded together, and she knew it was from her Muse. Just like her Muse, to give her something she hadn't had in her head to begin with. What had it replaced? More than anything she wanted to get up and get to work, but she forced herself to eat a few bites so she wouldn't look ungrateful.

She smiled as she walked into her studio space, warm and bright. It had been a sunroom in the apartment's previous life. Staged at the showing with a rainforest's worth of greenery. She looked straight through the plants to the windows, the sun, the inviting light. Plants were a distraction. The realtor had asked where her husband was, and she'd taken great pleasure in saying no husband, this is for me, have you heard of women's lib? She'd paid in cash, with the money she'd made from her first big show.

There was a canvas already on her easel. It looked finished. She didn't remember painting it, but she knew her own style. A shoulder that was not a shoulder, a face that was not a face, paint scalloped and layered inches thick. She touched the figure in the painting, the figure that was not a figure: her Muse. So close, but still so indistinct. Had she been satisfied with this painting when she'd walked away from it? It was maddeningly wrong.

She fought the urge to throw it on the ground and put a foot through it. Looking around, there were only three stretched and prepped canvases in the corner, and there was no reason to ruin this one even if it was wrong, wrong, wrong. Who knew how easy it was to get new ones these days? (She wrote the question in her notebook, to ask and answer later). Sand it down, prep it again. The colors were good, anyway.

The canvas wasn't heavy, but it slipped from between her fingers as Bonnie shifted it to the floor. It landed corner-first on her middle left toe and she yelped in pain.

"Are you okay in there?" asked someone from the other room.

"I'm fine," she said. Her slipper felt warm inside, but the pain had been one brief bright flash and gone. She'd deal with the toe later.

She set a fresh canvas on the easel, then turned her

back on it. She'd never minded a blank canvas, not even in her thirties, when she'd worked on pieces as big as a bus's broadside. A blank wasn't a challenge or a taunt, as she'd heard some people describe. The piece was already done by the time she conceived it. Frustration, when it came, came in the end stages, if the physical manifestation didn't match the image she'd envisioned, if the skills she'd honed over her lifetime still weren't enough. Those occasions were blessedly rare.

Those giant pieces were the best she'd ever done, according to the critics. The combination of skill and talent and training and her Muse's vision had culminated in the Voyages series. Those were the ones people discussed when they talked about a Bonnie Sweetlove.

She remembered the retrospective at the Whitney, where they'd collected four giant Voyages and several smaller pieces from before and after. Standing in the center of it all, before the doors opened and the views were obstructed by people. Standing in the center, spinning slowly, and the Muse in her head radiating almost-happiness, telling her yes, this is close, this is almost it. Wrong, but close. It didn't blame her for the wrongness. She was on the right track.

That was what she strove for, always. That feeling that the thing she'd made had made her Muse happy. It created a joyous feedback loop, a pleasant buzz that spread through her whole body. Sometimes it struck as she made her last fine adjustments and stood back; sometimes she didn't feel it until several pieces were placed in a room together, resonating, forming something close to the whole they were been meant to be.

She closed her eyes and spun, seeing her paintings radiate out from the place where she stood. She looked for the gap, the place where the new one belonged, the missing piece in the larger puzzle.

"Aunt Bonnie?" asked a familiar voice. It didn't make sense for her niece Lori to be here. She was in college.

Bonnie opened her eyes, but there was nobody to be seen. No—a woman in the doorway, hesitating like she was prepared to duck if something was thrown at her. The woman had Lori's voice but looked much too old to be Lori. Bonnie glared, willing away the interruption.

"I'm sorry to bother you while you're painting" —at least she was smart enough to recognize that this, too, was painting— "but I came to check on you and—oh, jeez, what did you do to your foot?"

Bonnie looked down to see a crimson flower blooming on her pepto-pink slipper. What had caused it?

The person calling her Aunt Bonnie was pushing stuff off a chair buried underneath her paint counter, and pushing her into the chair, and pulling her slipper off her foot. The skin of her middle toe had split below the nail, and that toe and the ones beside it were sticky with blood. The nail itself was a thin veneer, nacre over a beautiful purple-black swirl. Broken? Maybe. She tried to wiggle it and pain flashed through her along with something else, something she couldn't quite say but she knew she needed to paint now, before she lost it. Purple-blacks, a stormy swirl, a gas giant.

"Does it hurt?"

"Not really, no." She didn't know why it was bleeding, so she was glad that question went unasked.

"Hang on, I'll clean it up. I think it looks worse than it is."

Things always looked worse than they were. Her niece Lori, who had the same voice as this person, had once sliced her forehead on a low-hanging branch on a rainy walk in the woods. She hadn't even known she'd hurt herself, had come running to show Bonnie something she had found, her face a bloody curtain. What was the thing she had found? A frog, maybe? Nothing like the thing Bonnie had found as a child and carried home in her head. Lori's cut had only been a thin slice by her hairline.

Bonnie looked down at the woman kneeling before her, dabbing at her toe with a wet paper towel. "You have the same scar as my niece, Lori," she said, touching the woman's forehead.

"I am Lori, Aunt Bonnie," said the woman who was

too old to be Lori, with a combination of exasperation and patience.

Fair enough. This could be Lori. Stranger things had happened. Memories played tricks, and muses took memories. Years compressed into nothingness. People changed faces. Some kids walked into the woods and came out holding frogs; some kids walked into the woods and came out with a Muse in their head.

She'd been on a thousand panels about creativity and never heard anyone else say they had breathed in a Muse, so she never said it either. Came up with a thousand silly answers to the question 'where do you get your ideas' to avoid the true one. It obviously wasn't something you mentioned in polite company. She wouldn't even have said that a second before, and she'd probably lose it again in another second. Not the Muse, just that curious moment when something crumbled and the air changed and she had breathed in and felt its presence inside her, making itself a new home, remaking her from that first moment.

It had been something else before it was a Muse. It had remade itself, too. That was a thing she'd figured out recently. A thing she'd avoided thinking her whole life, because you don't look a gift horse in the mouth, or question a Muse when it has chosen to work through you. Or maybe she'd known it forever, and only gotten around to remembering it now, along with Lori's frog and the cut forehead, along with the thing in the woods, its colors, its spores, the way it had crumbled when she'd touched it, the way she'd breathed it in.

"All better," said the woman kneeling in front of her, and Bonnie looked to see if she was trying on shoes, but there was a bandage on her toe, and no shoe at all.

"This store has terrible service," she told the saleswoman.

"This isn't a store, Aunt Bonnie. I'm your niece, Lori. I'm going to put your slippers back on. Are you going to paint some more?"

She looked at the woman, and it was Lori, but since when was Lori a shoe saleswoman? Lori was in college. No.

Lori worked for a college. Lori had two children and a wife who looked like Paul Newman.

"How are the kids, Lori?" She couldn't remember their names, but she had formed their faces in her mind. Six and nine, maybe?

Lori looked pleased. "Leo's frustrated with his committee, but he's slogging away. Rachel is enjoying the Peace Corps now that she's settled in. We're hoping to go over there once she's allowed visitors."

"How lovely," Bonnie said. She had follow up questions but they'd make her look ignorant, so she didn't ask them.

"Do you want lunch?"

Had she lost the whole morning already? She glanced at the clock. No, it was only eleven. "Not yet. I have work to do."

Lori gathered a handful of something off the floor, and gave Bonnie a kiss on the head as she left. "I'll hang out for a while. We can eat and chat when you're ready. I have something I want to talk to you about."

Bonnie had already had enough chatting, but that would probably be a rude thing to say out loud. Her painting wasn't going to paint itself. And now that she was alone, she couldn't actually remember what her project was for today.

She stuck out her tongue in frustration, fought the urge to kick something. Before, she would have chased interruptions out of her studio. Nobody would have dared to walk in while she was working. That was part of why she'd always lived alone. Too much to do.

The canvas was still blank. Blank canvases didn't intimidate her, but she'd lost the thread. She pulled her notebook from her hip pocket and leafed through it, looking for a reminder, for something to wake her Muse. There were pages and pages of questions in her own handwriting. Some had answers, some didn't.

On the second to last page, she found what she was looking for. The sketch was rough, basic. Nothing to it but a shape, but the second she looked at it she remembered the dream, the almost-figure, the colors.

"Thank you," she whispered to her Muse. The picture in her mind brightened and threw itself onto the canvas. She followed it with her palette knife.

She lost herself in the piece. First, a layer blocking out the shapes. After that, she knew what she was doing and the sketch was no longer a necessary reminder. On a lark, she tore it from her notebook and stuck it to the painting, in the middle of the back-that-was-not-a-back of the figure-that-was-not-a-figure. Nobody would know it was there, not after she covered it with a thick midnight blue, blended midnight and sky and space, coaxed waves forward with her palette knife, tendrils, licks of flame, fingers, teeth, reaching forward out of the flatness.

The deeper she went, the closer the painting and the image in her mind got to each other. The trick was to shut everything else out. Ignore the cramping fingers, the pain in her shoulder, the fatigue in her legs. Her Muse ignored all those things; it didn't remember them anymore.

She stepped back to look at her work, waiting for her Muse to tell her she had gotten it right, to feed her joy. She got it, paired with a shock of recognition. She bent down to look for the canvas she'd discarded earlier in the morning, now buried under the materials that had been on the chair.

They weren't identical. Same subject, same blocking, same shoulder that was not a shoulder, same face that was not a face, same deliberately unfocused figure. What was different? Today's gave her the sense of rightness that the previous one didn't. She'd used the colors a little better today, perhaps, and the paint's textures. And was the figure a little closer? Yes, perhaps it was. Variations on a theme.

The exhaustion that came with a work completed nudged its way forward in her mind. She was hungry, too, and she had to pee, and she was covered in paint. She headed for the bathroom to wash up.

When she returned to the living room, a middle-aged white woman sat on her couch with a sheaf of paperwork, and a tall black woman stood in the kitchen mixing something in a bowl. She ducked back into the bathroom and pulled out her notebook. Leafed back through page after page of questions in her own handwriting, looking for something to explain who they were.

WHO IS THE WOMAN IN MY HOUSE?
Her name is Patty. She helps me. She lives here with me.

That was presumably the woman in the kitchen. The other looked familiar.

"Bonnie, would you like some lunch?" called the woman named Patty. "I heard you go to wash up so I started putting something together for you."

It was considerate, really. Bonnie dropped her notebook back in her pocket and ventured out. The table was set with three place settings, her everyday dishes. There was a plate in the center piled with toast, cut diagonally, a salad bowl, and a bowl of chicken or tuna salad.

The woman named Patty sat down at the table, bypassing Bonnie's favorite spot, even though it was the closest to the kitchen. Bonnie had always preferred that seat because it put her close to the radiator but still let her see out the window. The sky today wore a frigid blue, streaked with wispy clouds.

The other woman came and joined them in the third seat. She looked like Bonnie's mother, but she wasn't.

"Sandwich or salad?" asked Patty.

"Salad, please," Bonnie said, and took the bowls as they were passed in her direction.

"Aunt Bonnie, I have some good news for you," said the woman who was not Bonnie's mother, and she must be Lori, though she looked much older than Lori. Lori was the only one who called her 'aunt.'

"I'd love to hear some good news."

"The Forward Museum wants to do a retrospective of your work."

Bonnie smiled. "The Whitney did a retrospective once. It was almost right."

"I remember." Lori heaped chicken salad onto bread. "You were disappointed for some reason, but the critics

loved it. Anyway, the Forward has a huge special exhibits space, and they read an article somebody wrote about
patterns in your work, and they want to try to gather everything mentioned in the article and more."

Interesting. "What did the article mention?"

"The Voyages series, of course, but then some more
recent stuff, too. Transformations, Evolutions."

Transformations! The Transformations paintings had
been some of her Muse's favorites. Tiny self portraits of a
Muse: the pathways it had carved to make room for itself;
the places it hid; synapses firing, synapses at rest; endor-
phins wearing love's cloak. Most of them had sold to private buyers and they'd never been collected in one place.

An image blazed through her brain: a room full of
paintings, large and small. Not the Whitney. Something
more right, a flaw corrected. "Would I have any input?"

A patient look on Lori's face, like she had answered
this before. "The author of the article is guest curating,
but we can definitely arrange something. I guess it might
depend on if he thinks you'll agree or disagree with his
thesis."

"Which is?"

"A pattern."

Another image, this one a shoulder that wasn't a
shoulder, a face that wasn't a face, a figure in a crowd, a
hand reaching out, a figure that wasn't a figure dissolving
into constellations of spores, purple-black swirls like oil
on water.

"How soon?"

"September. It's January now."

"That isn't enough time. How could they possibly
do it with that short a lead time?"

"Look at the third page of your notebook, Aunt
Bonnie."

The third page:

THINGS TO REMEMBER:
   The woman who looks like Mom is Lori.
   The woman who lives in the house is Patty. Don't throw

things at her.
There is a retrospective coming up of my work.

Bonnie looked up. "It's already happening?"

"You've been working on it for a year already."

Bonnie's mind reeled. How had she forgotten something this significant? If she'd forgotten this, who knew what else she was forgetting?

She tried to paper over the gap. "Why did you pretend you were telling me about it for the first time? I'm not stupid. I don't need to be manipulated."

"I'm not manipulating you," Lori said. "But if I start from the assumption you remember it we usually have to backtrack."

"So I already have input?"

"Every step of the way, Aunt Bonnie."

Bonnie bit her lip. "What museum?"

"The Forward. I'm not sure you've ever been there. It's pretty new, but they've been doing some really interesting exhibits. I've got some layouts here if you want to look at them? And some other stuff for you to sign."

"Yes. I'll have to ask my agent about the show, but yes."

The woman across from her sighed. "You fired your agent again. Right now it's you and me."

"Oh! You're my new agent? I'm glad that other dolt is gone. Have we met before?"

The woman across from her sighed again.

•

THINGS TO REMEMBER:
The woman who looks like Mom is Lori.
There is a retrospective coming up of my work.

WHY DOES THAT WOMAN KEEP ASKING ME QUESTIONS?
The woman is Lori, even though she looks different. The questions are from the guest curator, to help him write text

for an exhibit.

WILL THEY INCLUDE THE NEW SERIES IN THE RETROSPECTIVE?

Yes! Lori sent pictures to the guest curator and he thought they fit the show.

THINGS TO REMEMBER:

If he asks me about patterns, say they were intentional.

WHAT ARTICLE IS THIS MAN TALKING ABOUT?

It's called "Inner Journeys, Outer Journeys, And the Radical Geographies of Self in the works of Bonnie Sweetlove." A guy named Levy Reznik wrote it. It's equal parts genius and crap. I've read it. If I ask to read it again, Lori will get frustrated.

THINGS TO REMEMBER:

If he asks me about patterns, say they were intentional. If he asks me why I said they weren't the last time, why I said he was barking up the wrong tree, swallow my pride and tell him I don't remember.
Tell him yes, the constellations hidden in the Voyages paintings are accurate. Tell him yes, viewed edge-on, Evolutions 7 is a relief map of the Guiana Highlands, impasto as sculpture.

IMPORTANT: WILL THEY INCLUDE THE NEW SERIES IN THE RETROSPECTIVE?

Yes.

WILL THEY LET ME ARRANGE THE PIECES THEY'VE CHOSEN?

They did. Lori and I drew it out together. Months ago, she says.
The curator said it was innovative design and the museum added it to the press kit as a selling point.

•

"Are you sure this is the right way?" Bonnie asked the driver. "This is a terrible neighborhood."

"It's been a while since you were down here, Aunt Bonnie. It's different than you remember. The museum built down here, then artists started moving into warehouse spaces in the neighborhood."

Another woman, in the backseat, said, "I grew up not far from here. The whole block was flattened to make way for condos. Everyone getting priced out, pushed out."

The driver had called her 'aunt,' so this must be her niece, Lori, though she looked too old. Bonnie wasn't sure who the other woman was. She watched the buildings go by. Maybe the driver was right. There were more people on the streets than she remembered, and the warehouses weren't boarded up anymore. When had that happened? She picked at the delicate beading on her skirt. Not out of nerves, but because her hands liked having something to do.

The driver pulled the car up to the museum entrance.

"You don't need to drop me at the door. I can walk, you know."

"I know! I figured you'd be on your feet all evening and I'd save you a few steps."

That made sense, but once she'd complained, Bonnie didn't feel like apologizing, so she didn't say a word on the walk up from the parking lot. Good thing she'd worn sensible shoes, and it was still light out. She kept one hand in her pocketbook, fingers clasped around her notebook. When the second woman offered an arm, she accepted the support.

The museum door said gallery hours ended at five, but the door swung open without protest. The lobby had a sleek design, like it remembered the neighborhood's industrial roots without owing them anything. Brick and steel, mottled cement floors, open spaces and floating walls. She followed the driver—it was her niece, Lori, she saw that now—down the empty hallway.

They came to a glass door. A gallery. They must be here for a party, since she was dressed up. Bonnie pulled her notebook from her pocket.

"We're here for your opening reception, Bonnie," said the woman whose arm she was leaning on.

"Come on, Aunt Bonnie." Another woman held the door for her, and it must be her niece Lori, because who else would call her 'aunt,' though she looked older than Bonnie could account for.

She stepped into a brightly lit room. A bar had been set up to the left of the entrance, and two young bartenders were setting up cobalt wine bottles and strings of tiny bulbs in a pattern that caught the light and sent it dancing. A party with no partiers. She pulled her notebook out and wrote "WHERE ARE ALL THE PEOPLE?" then tucked it back in her pocket.

"We're here an hour early," a woman beside her said, as if she had seen the question Bonnie had written down. "You asked to come in before anybody else to see your paintings without any people in the way."

Spying wasn't polite, but the answer was useful. "Thank you."

She wrote, "I'm here early to see the paintings without any people in the way." It was nice when questions and answers lined up so neatly.

Bonnie walked closer to see what the art was, and her Muse kicked a memory her way. This was her exhibit. They had listened to her suggestions for the exhibit. She could tell even before she stepped past the bar. Paintings suspended from the ceiling at different heights within the larger space. Walls overlapping walls, paintings overlapping paintings. Like rose petals. She hoped it had the effect she'd envisioned.

It had been decades since she'd seen most of these paintings, but the Voyages that formed the outer walls were as familiar as her own home. Huge swaths of scalloped blackness, colors in the undersides of the sculpted paint waves. Secrets she'd forgotten but remembered now: the things her Muse used to be, the places it had traveled.

Secrets her Muse had been bursting to tell to someone through all the endless time before it chose her.

She picked a random didactic to read.

Voyages 6
Bonnie Sweetlove
Oil on canvas
1956
Sweetlove's Voyages series can be looked at through many lenses. They explore form, style, and color in a way that is both playful and technically masterful. They also conceal secrets from the average viewer: astronomical charts, geographic features, physiological pathways. Viewed from eight feet back and two feet to the right, Voyages 6 reveals the tracks of the 1944 Atlantic hurricane season.

Secrets her Muse hadn't even told her, apparently. She was only the conduit. No—that wasn't fair. A conduit without talent or skill or work ethic couldn't have made this work. It was a collaboration, even if she didn't know the meaning every detail of what the Muse asked her to do.

1944 would have been the Great Atlantic Hurricane. Bonnie remembered her father boarding up the windows and telling her and her sister and mother to sit in the windowless pantry. She'd lived through worse hurricanes since, but that was the first one she remembered. It had taken down trees, created ponds where there were none, altered the familiar landscape. It hadn't been long after that she'd walked into the woods on her own and out of the woods with a Muse in her head.

If she read all the captions, she'd learn all kinds of things about her art. The curator had done his homework. If he ever asked her, she'd say yes, it was purposeful, of course. The safer lie. Safe like accepting a diagnosis of dementia when nobody would understand the true reason you couldn't remember things. Protect the

Muse, protect yourself; those were two things she'd never forgotten no matter how much else had slipped away.

"Are you okay, Aunt Bonnie?" someone asked, and she waved aside the question. No distractions. Not here, wherever here was, in the place where someone had finally put her work together in the right way.

She wandered past Voyages and into Evolutions, where she learned she had hidden topographical maps, some for geographic features yet to be located, and a series of unusual MRIs, and a partial genome of something unidentified. Those weren't the things she saw when she looked at the Evolutions: she saw her Muse, cloaked in golden light, too bright to be seen.

After Evolutions came Transformations, tiny hyper-detailed works that begged the viewer to come closer, to look inside, to look inside her to where the Muse nestled, where it made its home, at the ways she could no longer tell where it ended and she began. Twenty seven of them, three cubed, grouped on one wall in a fractal pattern.

And finally, at the center, the new works. Glimpses, twelve numbered Glimpses out of however many she'd made. Painted not-figures, expertly unfocused. Bodies of light, celestial bodies, things that had bodies once but didn't anymore.

She came to the center, the center she'd created, and looked outward. From this vantage she saw parts of everything: an incomplete Voyage, an Evolution in progress, a series of Transformations, Glimpses of something that was so close now she could almost touch it, almost know it for what it truly was, or what it had been. Her Muse glowed. It radiated happiness, telling her through images that reflected back what she saw in front of her that yes, this is how it was, this is right, remember this for me.

Remember this for me. Her Muse suffused her with joy, and she thought that if she could just remember long enough to get home to her paints, she might, just once, capture the true face of it, the thing it remembered being, far from here, long before it was a Muse. Her hand closed around her notebook, but she couldn't possibly block this with paper and pen. Lines would confine it.

Remember this for me, it said, and she knew she'd remember until she forgot, until she breathed out her Muse and it found someone new to infect, to inspire, to tell its long story, to tell and be retold in a new medium. Remember this for me, it said, and she promised to remember until she forgot.

SARAH PINSKER is the author of the Nebula winning novelette "Our Lady of the Open Road" and the Theodore Sturgeon Award winning "In Joy, Knowing the Abyss Behind." Her stories have appeared in magazines such as *Asimov's, Strange Horizons, Fantasy & Science Fiction, Uncanny,* and *Lightspeed,* in anthologies such as *New Voices of Fantasy,* and in several *Year's Best* anthologies. She is also a singer/songwriter and toured nationally behind three albums on various independent labels. A fourth is forthcoming. She lives with her wife and dog in Baltimore, Maryland. Find her online at sarahpinsker.com and on Twitter @sarahpinsker.

ABOUT THE CONTRIBUTORS

THE ARTIST

JULIE DILLON is a Hugo Award winning freelance artist from Northern California. More of her work can be found at www.juliedillonart.com.

THE POET

JANE YOLEN is the author of over 366 published books (actual number as of 2018), including *Owl Moon*, *The Devil's Arithmetic*, and *How do Dinosaurs Say Goodnight*. In fact, in 2018 you will be able to read a Jane Yolen book a day for a year—even on a leap year. A graduate of Smith College, with a Masters in Education from the University of Massachusetts, her books and stories have won an assortment of awards—two Nebulas, a World Fantasy Award, a Caldecott Medal, three Golden Kite Awards, three Mythopoeic Awards, two Christopher Medals, a nomination for the National Book Award, and the Jewish Book Award (among many others). She was the first woman to give the Scottish St. Andrew's University's Andrew Lang lecture since the lecture series began in 1927, and the first writer in the Connecticut River Valley to win the New England Public Radio's Arts and Humanities Award. Six colleges and universities have given her honorary doctorates. She is a GrandMaster three times: for Science Fiction/Fantasy Writers of America, Science Fiction Poetry Association, and the World Fantasy Association. She has been on the board of the Society of Children's Book Writers and Illustrators for the past 45 years. Also of note, her Skylark Award—given by the New England Science Fiction Association—set her good coat on fire. If you need to know more about her, visit her website at www.janeyolen.com.

THE EDITORS

MONICA LOUZON persists in writing speculative and weird fiction despite being a two-time creative writing drop-out. She has worked with the Museum of Science Fiction since June 2014 and founded the Museum's peer-reviewed *Journal of Science Fiction*. When not wandering in forests or among stacks of books, she can typically be found near Washington, DC plotting new adventures with her husband, or on Twitter @molo_writes.

JAKE WEISFELD has worked with the Museum of Science Fiction since February 2015 and holds a Master's of Library and Information Science from San Jose State University. He lives in the Washington, DC area with his wife and delusions of grandeur.

HEATHER McHALE is the Managing Editor of the *Journal of Science Fiction*. She holds a Ph.D. in Literature from the University of Maryland, where she teaches writing and literature. Her current work in progress is a book about the television series *Doctor Who*.

BARBARA JASNY is an editor of the *Journal of Science Fiction* and holds a Ph.D. from Rockefeller University. After years of research—playing with DNA, viruses, and chromosomes— she joined *Science* magazine in 1985. She has worked there ever since, evaluating the ever-expanding universe of research and communicating science through a variety of media. She is a passionate reader of science fiction and fantasy, but except for dragon stories invented for her children, she has not written any fiction. She loves to travel and collect antiques and oddities of all kinds with her husband and family.

RACHEL FREDERICK is a voracious reader of all things science fiction and fantasy. She holds a Master's of Museum Studies from George Washington University and has worked with the Museum of Science Fiction since March 2016, currently with the title of curator. When not reading or in a museum, she is most often found making extravagant historic costumes at her home in the Washington, DC area.

THANK YOU TO ALL OUR KICKSTARTER BACKERS WHO MADE THIS TAKE-HOME EXHIBIT POSSIBLE!

EXHIBIT SPONSORS — CATALYSTS
Duane Ebersole & Samuel Peralta

COLONISTS
Sharon Amdall; Anonymous; Craig J. DeForge; Jodie Hettrivk; Neil Ottenstein; & Candace Uhlmeyer

GIVERS
Anonymous; Natasha R. Chisdes; Anna Goss; Caitlin Greer; Kelly Henrichs; Rhonda Moore & Christopher Schoppet; Aaron Morris; Linda Morris; Paul A. Oehlers; Irina Serova; & Mike and Sharon Sheffield

AMBASSADORS
Anonymous; Sarah Bogle; Sinead Queenborg McDonnell Borgersen; Thomas Bull; Fern Culhane; Jessica Douma; The Justice Family; Mudd Law; Claire E. Lewis; Carole Madan; Stephen Major (MPS; MFA); Mel!; I. Newman; Galena Ostipow; Michael Rader; Stephen Slusher; Jonathan Spencer; Tom Stemple; Jess and Jon Turner; & Elizabeth K. Walsh

PATRONS
Antha Ann Adkins; Jerry Alexandratos; Sharon E. Altmann; Anonymous; John Appel; Scott Austin; Tim; Jen; Kara; & Chloe Bailey; Laura Bang!; Dora Beggs; Kelly Bell; Chad Bowden; Heather W. Britton; Laura A. Burns; Ann Cofell; Matthew Coffey; Troy M Cole; Marina Coleridge; Lily Connors; D. Conway; Jennifer Crispin; Kyle Crivello; Sarah Curtis; Tyler J. Dalious; John Dalton; Dan-o; Danielle; Deanna; Cecil Decker; Margaret Alia Denny; Eboni Dunbar; Robin Dunkin; William R. Edgington; Shaun E Edmonds; Elizabeth Edward; Carol Edwards; Joshua J Evans; Evan Fedeli; Hans Fex; Rebecca Flaum and Aaron Tomb; Paul Foth; D Franklin; Sofia Fransson; Lindsay Freeberg; Robert M Funk; Nan Garrison; Jennifer Gentzel; Meredith Jeanne Gillies; Jayson R. Gleneck; Thomas Gordon; Sharon Grimes; Carol J. Guess; Nichole Hamm; Jessica Haseltine; Andrew Hatchell; Anthony A. Hauck; Kristin Evenson Hirst; Jacob Haywood; K. Hodghead; Alicia Holston; Michael J Hudson; Fatima Iqbal; J. J. Irwin; Sally Novak Janin; Jennifer Jenkins; David Jessop; Fred W Johnson; Brittany C Jones; Nick K; Stacey K.; Sandra Karolus-Mikhael; Cooki Karriem; Mendel Katz and Shannon Dean; Shannon Keniry & Conrad White; Zachary Knoles; Emory Knott; Ezzy G. Languzzi; Debbie Y. Lee; Cat leja; E. Lewy; Zoe Lewycky; Will Luongo; Rissa Lyn; David Mackie;

Michelle Matel; Nikki McCoy; Patrick McEvoy; Nooreen A Meghani; M. Menzies; Meghan Merrell; SueAnne Merrill; E.M. Middel; Cory Miller; Catriona Mills; Edwin Mirabal; Randall Miyashiro; Tony Mous; Bjorn Munson; Sallie Ngarmtap; Sharyn November; Jim Otermat; Richard Palotay; Susan Pence; Charlotte Peters; Linda Pierce; Jessica Powell; Joe Pregracke; Nadine Richmond; Robin; Tasha Rosenbaum de Lotero; Karma Christine Salvato; Chris Sarnowski; Abi Scott; Maggie Sheer; Mike Shema; Nick Slowes; Lilla Smee; Emily Smith; Ursula Smith; Nicole Solis; Soup; Thomas Sowell; Lisa Spaulding; The Spillner Family; Frank Steenburn; Emily L Steffen; KET Strait; StubeCuller; Rev. Brett Andrew Stults; Susan from Australia; Damia Torhagen; RJ Theodore; Tou Bee Vang; Jo Anne Vaughn; Corinna Vigier; Tony W; KT Wagner; Judith Waidlich; Ananda Walker; Anya Marie Walter; Sarah Lynn Weintraub; Kelsey White; Andrew Wilson; Cameo Wood; Louise Wood; Cynthia A. Wright; Elizabeth H Wynn; & Roman Yeremenko

COLLECTORS

Deb Anderson; Anonymous; Kimberly Bea; Adele H. Bealer; Charlene Brusso; Richard Chandler; Lauren B. Collister; Ellie Curran; Heidi Cykana; Zach Emerson; Daniel Fields; Alain Fournier; Sam Gioia; DA Helmer; Veronique & Richard Ho; Rod Holdsworth; Michael S. Jager; Adam Jenkins; Madelyn Jirasek; Henrique Jucá; Maggie M; Keira Marti; Nickolas May; Gerald P. McDaniel; Dave McLachlan; Max Millar-Blanchaer; Donna H. Montgomery; Christian Neal; Panda; Tom Petras; Will Picard; Kyle Pinches; Salvatore L Puma; Maryse Quinn; Dave Robison; H Rodgers; Matthew J. Rogers; Jonah Sutton-Morse; Josh Thomson; Chloe Turner; David Voderberg; Jessica Walker; Tom Weiss; William F Wetmorell; William A White; Colin Whiteside; & Steve Worker

ARCHIVISTS

Sebastian Aav; Anonymous; Badger; Danielle Beal; David Bell; Freiya Benson; Jennifer Berk; Kim R Bowers; RS Buck; Laura C.; Albert Choy; C.J.H. Chronister; Glenn Clatworthy; Jason Daniel; Jacob Dill; Alice Finch; Paul and Shauna Fitzgerald; Kim Foehl; Two Way Play; Shaun Gilroy; Neile Graham; Cathy Green; Thomas 'Kranodor' Hahn; Kelly Jennings; Kristina Larkin; C. Liang; Sindhu Mathew; Ian McHugh; Monica Meyer; Dick Miller; Andrew R. Mizener; Karla D Nock; Kristin O'Brassill-Kulfan; Emily Louise Parsons; Jim Peterson; Alexandra Pierce; Jennifer Radcliffe; Justin Raz; Frederic Rust; Sara&Adrien; Shannon S; Melissa Shumake; Blakely Tresca; Ian Urbina; Mark Vogel; Kylie White; & Justin Zeigler

LIBRARIANS

Anonymous; Amy Annette Bouldin; S. Brown; Kendra Hillman Chilcoat; Samantha Cross; Brent Curran; Sarah DePuy; Celena F; Jesse

Fowler; Nancy L Fulton; John Hargelid; Michael Hicks; Anne Holland; Kat "CiaraCat" Jones; Judd Karlman; Kate Mergener; Todd Wayne Ramsey; William Riess; Christopher Mark Rose; David J. Schwartz; Sarah Scholz; Arianna Shapiro; Patti Short; Wendy A F G Stengel; & Charles K. Summers

SONAMBULISTS
Anonymous; Jorge Ruiz Benedicto; Jill Chinchar; Christina Clapp; S. Clapp; Thomas Dumbleton; AJ Fitzwater; Allison de Fren; Sarah Fuentez; B M Haselgrove; Nathan Hillstrom; Hannah Hoare; Holtery; Shelbie A. Legett; Brian Lintz; Gregg A. MacDonald; mdtommyd; John Mercier; Jason Morris; Luke Odom; Jessica Reisman; Michael Scholl; David South; Alexx Spada; Ginger Stampley & Michael Croft; Gwen Warman; Caitlin Weber; Paula Whitehouse; & Tiffany E Wilson

DREAMERS
0; Pedro Alfaro; Cassandra Allen; Katrina Allis; Sandra Ulbrich Almazan; Benjamin Ames; Svend Andersen; Blokhin Andrey; Sebastien Andrivet; Anonymous; Anonymus; Patrick Winifred Archer-Morris; Jane Aubourg; Gustaf B.; Sandu Baciu; Stanley Bailey; A. E. Bara; Andy Barbieri; Nat "woodelf" Barmore; Andrew and Kate Barton; Kate Barton; Rachelle Benken; Marla Bracken; Alexandra Brandt; Anja Braun; Dan & Chris Brewer; Samantha Brock; Dave Brown; Stephanie Brown; Simon Brunning; Christian Brunschen; Lance C.; Mark Carter; Jonathan Castro; Nadia "Atarun" Cerezo; Carla G. Chiodi; Alex Claman; Katharine E. Conrad; Tamara Craiu; Tehani Croft; Sheila D; C. Daetwyler; dajomu; Isaac 'Will It Work' Dansicker; Deborah; Billy Dechand; Alan DeHaan; Nathan Destler; John Devenny; Rebecca Dominguez; Engel Dreizehn; Matt Drown; Steve Duncombe; Kerry Dustin; Michał "Vesper" Dziewoński; Eunsang; Quentin Lancelot Fagan; Justin Faulkner; Ken Finlayson; Brooke Fishman; Angie Flunker; Raven Ford; Andrea Fornero; Linda Frankel; Marie Friberger; Amy Fuller; Gavran; Shanna Germain; Gertjan; Reba G. Ashby Goodall; Niall Gordon; Todd Grant; John Green; Bedene Greenspan; GriffinFire; Barbara Grossberg; Claire Gurman; Carla H.; Sebastian H.; Justin Hale; Michael D. Hall; Courtney Hamrick; Leesa Hanagan; Narrelle M Harris; Ethan Hartman; Sam Harvey - LiquidAg; Sheryl R. Hayes; Katherine Hempel; Alyssa Hillary; The Hobson Family; Ashley Holmes; Ken Hurst; InnHuchen; J.P.K.; Aaron Jamieson; JMH621Nova aka Jonathan Harris; Nick Honeywell; Sean "The Real Jenk" Jenkins; Chris Joseph; Kristy K; Cheri Kannarr; Elaine Kant; Paige Kimble; Kelly Kleiser; Drunken Knight; Skarsnik Kråka; Lace; Ju Landéesse; Mikael Langfos; Larissapaladin; Mike Laurence; Rob Lawlis; Geoffrey Lehr; Erin Lerch; Sarah Liberman; Julia Lichty; Michael Lujan; Arron Luo; Marcin M; Katherine Malloy; Mark; Kevin J. "Womzilla" Maroney; Francesco Martinati; Lindsay Mayhew; Peter Mazzeo; Jennifer McBride; Lola

McCrary; Joseph McKee; Dawn Levy McMorrow; Sarah Mendonca; Nathaniel Merchant; Tristan Merrick; Rodrigo Assis Mesquita; L.R. Messina; Miki-em; Aimee Miura; Hillary Harris Moldovan; Michael T. Moran; Cass Morrison; Robert A. Morrison; F C Moulton; Emma Moyse; S. Muinonen; A Murthy; Muse; Ashlee Nelson; Andrew Newman; K Nisenshal; Frank Nissen; Jo Noble; Nomad; Dr Jennifer Novotny; Viveka Nylund; Max O; Jeremy Ozog; Mats P; Allison Pang; Monique Park-Smith; Saajan Patel; Jeliza Patterson; Nancy Paulette; Carlos Alberto Restrepo Pelaez; Antoine Perrin; Amy Phillips; Debbie Phillips; Patrick & Sarah Pilgrim; Jana Bianchi Pin; Enrica Prazzoli; Twila Oxley Price; Quasi; Jeffrey Quisenberry; Rafal; Abbey Rahman; Rebecca; Chris Reed; Dennis Reed; Karl W. Reinsch; RKBookman; Tristan Roberts; G Robinson; Barracuda Rose; Eric Rossing; Erin Ruth; Daniel S; Jashan Martin S.; Sandy Sabatino; Roy Sachleben; Dave Sag; Jennifer Sandvall; M.M. Scaison; Susanne Schörner; Jim Scovill; Karen M Seeley; Matt Sell; Seri; Mike Serritella; Emily Sexton; Shadizar; Robert Shinn; Johanne Skjerven; SLC; Smashingsuns; Bobby Roo Smith; Oina Jenn Smith; Alexander Solsme; Jason Craig Spencer; Oliver Conan Squires; Dylan Stewart; Clara Strzalkowski; Beth Sundheim; SwordFire; Rob Szarka; Andrea Tatjana; Brian E Taylor; Renzo Crispieri Th.; Mark E Thompson; Ged Trias; Gwen Tucker; Annelies Van de Ven; Nicole Janée 1890 Vartanian; Russell Ventimeglia; Michael Vyborny; Kendall W. Erika B. Wagner; Sara Walsh; Desirée L. Ward (PhD); K. L. Webber; Leah Webber; Evelyn Joy Weidig; Rich 'Raz' Weissler; Henning Bauer Westbye; Christopher Weuve; Shari Whitman; Donald Whytock; Jeffrey Andres Williams; Dina S Willner; Stephen Wills; Jake Wilson; Eva Wingren; Cliff Winnig; Cindy Womack; Yes; Tieg Zaharia; Tom Zarillo; & David Zurek

OBSERVERS

MayAna Creatives; Walter F. Crot; Heather Forrester; & Anthony Letizia